BY MARTIN WALKER

America Reborn
The President We Deserve
The Cold War
Martin Walker's Russia
The Waking Giant
Powers of the Press
The Eastern Question
The Money Soldiers
The Infiltrator
The National Front

The Caves
of Périgord

A Novel

MARTIN WALKER

Simon & Schuster

New York · London · Toronto · Sydney · Singapore

SIMON & SCHUSTER
Rockefeller Center
1230 Avenue of the Americas
New York, NY 10020

SIMON & SCHUSTER and colophon are registered trademarks
of Simon & Schuster, Inc.

Designed by Lauren Simonetti

Manufactured in the United States of America
10 9 8 7 6 5 4 3 2 1
Library of Congress Cataloging-in-Publication Data

ISBN 0-7432-2284-9

For information regarding special discounts for bulk purchases, please contact Simon & Schuster Special Sales at 1-800-456-6798 or business@simonandschuster.com

The Caves
of Périgord

CHAPTER 1

Time: The Present

E very interesting woman has a private smile, and Lydia Dean was startled by a brief, tantalizing glimpse of her own. Its reflection suddenly flashed on the glass covering a poster as she entered her cramped attic office, then it faded. She might almost have imagined it, and certainly there was no cause to smile. Determined not to show how much the interview with Justin had upset her, she closed the door firmly behind her and contemplated the imminent ruin of her empire. Yet for the first time that day, and despite the faint dismay at the prospect of unemployment, she felt her spirits lifting. It was a wry mood, inspired mainly by her sense of the ridiculous. Lydia never ceased to be amazed at the odd way her mind worked, the portentous phrases that suddenly popped into her thoughts. Empire? Ruin of Empire? She was simply ◆

facing the loss of a job that she did not much enjoy, although it allowed her to combine a career in art with a decent income.

It was a kind of empire, she mused, as she gazed at the map of the ancient world that hung on her wall. Her territory stretched from ancient Greece back to the dawn of time, from the plains of India to the Pillars of Hercules. From Hittites to Hammurabi, she had traveled it and researched it, and could read some of its dead languages. As a student she had dug into its archaeological sites, extracted shards of pottery from harsh earth, and even sacrificed her toothbrush to scrub them clean. And now, despite her new skill at fending off passes from politically connected Ministers of Culture who could barely spell the word, she was trying, and probably failing, to make a living from it.

Why on earth had she been so self-indulgent, so intellectually lazy when she first came back to England to go to graduate school? She chided herself, an internal and critical dialogue she was conducting more and more frequently. Art history was not a *real* subject, not like law or computing, or even business. Perhaps she should have concentrated on archaeology, she thought, until disagreeable memories surfaced of muddy campsites, a sore back, and amorous fellow-diggers who smelled rank. Certainly she should never have given up the research at the institute into the medieval art she really loved. Money was not everything. But the mortgage had to be paid each month. And today it had been made subtly clear that the auction house was unlikely to keep on paying her handsome salary as long as the market in her field remained so dismally, so unprofitably flat. Preclassical art meant everything before the Greeks and Romans. From Ancient Egypt to Babylon, Persepolis to the Holy Land, Lydia's empire covered continents and millennia, and yet never managed to bring in the sales and commissions that even the most obscure Impressionist painter could command.

"You—or rather your field—hmmm—not looking too promising, I'm afraid," the department head had mumbled over her modest list of proposals for the coming year. Like so many Englishmen, Justin spoke in irritating circumlocutions, as if grim news were best delivered impersonally. It wasn't just her field, she knew; her employers also blamed her. She had been hired not simply to trawl the market and scoop off the best for her auction house, but to find and charm the sellers with the best collections and to recruit rich customers. She understood, without any of her employers being crassly un-English enough to say so, that her youth and looks had secured her the job. But she was also expected to create the kind of buzz in her field that generated publicity and profits, and here she was failing miserably. She could offer only a few museum sales, which meant low prices, one private collection of Sumerian artifacts, and another of what could well have been looted from Scythian grave mounds, which would spell trouble.

"You are not living up to our hopes, Lydia," Justin had concluded, in that snooty way he had developed since she had declined his invitation to an intimate dinner. Justin, said the gossips in the ladies' room, was a predatory man. Lydia found him oily and distrusted his shirts, invariably blue checks or stripes, with white collars and cuffs. She was now careful to ask after the health of his wife and children.

It had been an unsettling meeting, leaving her with the distinct prospect of unemployment before the end of the year. Lydia walked across to her desk, and absentmindedly gave her usual pat to the head of the soapstone Egyptian cat that she had bought in Cairo, an evident but charming Fifth Dynasty fake, and told herself she had a right to feel miserable. Her career had stalled. Her window was speckled with a London drizzle and the mean, gray light belied the first hesitant buds of the daffodils she had seen in the park that morning. So, gloomily leafing through sale catalogs and trying not to recall that her thirtieth birthday was only months away, Lydia thought about changing her career. Evening classes, perhaps another degree through the Open University; she might consider economics or law. She couldn't afford to go back to law school in the States, even if she had wanted to. She wasn't ready to go home, nor back to mother, who was embarrassingly short of money since Lydia's father had died. And America had too many lawyers, anyway. The law here was different. Lawyers made money, and seemed always to be in demand. And David had been neither bored nor boring, and could even be quite amusing about his work as a patent lawyer. Firmly, she steered her mind away from that topic. Their relationship had been pleasant, but ultimately insufficient.

David was history. But then her career was facing a similar fate. So when reception rang to say they had a walk-in, she felt just the slightest flutter of hope. For her colleagues in paintings and furniture and jewelry, walk-ins were almost drudgery, constant interruptions to look at some battered family heirloom proffered by someone with a glint of avarice in the eye. Lydia hardly ever had walk-ins, and the handful she had seen were obvious fakes, offloaded on some gullible British soldier or sailor on leave in Cairo or Baghdad. The staff on the reception desk could usually tell at a glance but preferred to leave the official verdict to the experts like Lydia.

She walked down the stairs to the front hall—a tall, fit-looking man in a tweedy country suit and heavy brogues was being shown into the waiting room. His age seemed to be somewhat less than forty, but he dressed as if he were closer to sixty. The parcel he carried, carefully wrapped in brown paper and string, was obviously heavy but did not affect what Lydia suspected was a military stride. The tie was an anonymous heavy silk. His hair was short, his manner affable but brisk, and he smelled faintly of carbolic soap, a distinct improvement on Justin's musky cologne. He put the parcel on the table, gave her a smile with an amused twinkle in the eyes, held out his hand, and said, "How do you do? My name is Manners. I have just inherited this from my father and want to know if it's worth selling."

Lydia knew the country well enough to recognize from his speech and his dress a member of England's comfortable classes, old money and older schools. She shook his hand, introduced herself, and opened a drawer in the table to offer him a knife or a pair of scissors, but he was carefully unknotting the string. "I think it was an heirloom from the war," he said. "India, the Middle East, that sort of place. That's where my father served, mainly. He was a regular soldier, and retired to live quietly in Wiltshire for the past thirty years. This rock has been at home for as long as I can remember."

Lydia felt her face muscles tighten as the brown paper was unwrapped and the wooden case emerged, three or four times thicker than the usual picture frame to display something that shocked her. It was beautiful. There was no other word for it. Whenever and wherever this had been done, last week in some forger's garret or millennia ago, this assemblage of shape and color and texture punched her with a palpable force. Deliberately clamping down on the rush of wonder, she closed her eyes, freezing her excitement with a cold sense of professional duty. She must not jump to conclusions, but the usual checklist of culture, period, location, and style would not help her much here. One likely candidate leaped to mind, and she firmly repressed the thought. Remember the rules, Lydia; this had to be a logical process. The Hagar mountains of the Sahara might be a possibility, she was thinking, or part of a frieze from one of the rock churches of Cappadocia. She was trying to remember what little she knew of the rock art of Ethiopia and Zimbabwe, but Africa felt wrong. And it was certainly not from Australia. Possibly it was Yemeni, or perhaps India from the Deccan caves. But this beast was too fierce for any Hindu culture. The jaw was far too powerful, and the horns were curved like offensive, not defensive weapons. It was not just a kind of bull, she told herself as she opened her eyes again and focused on the power of that massive neck, the lethal swoop of horn. It was the essence of the beast. Fleetingly, an image surfaced from a holiday in Spain, the *corrida* of the feast of San Isidro in Madrid, prancing horses and a bull such as this, and blood in the ring.

But even as she tried to organize her thoughts, she felt a kind of outrage. It was a desecration of what had been a much larger painting, a chunk of rock just over a foot square and of uneven thickness, which had clearly been chiseled or levered with a crowbar from a rock face. Something marvelous had been defaced. This was the worst kind of loot, wrenched greedily from its setting, as if the looter had destroyed an ancient church to steal a single fresco. She looked up coldly at her customer. But Manners was oblivious to her reaction. He proudly displayed his heirloom, mounted on a dark velvet backcloth inside its thick wooden frame, and stood back, gazing hopefully at her as if expecting approval.

Lydia took a deep breath, wondering how to begin this conversation. She looked down again at the crude but somehow noble outline of an elongated horned animal in faded red and black, with some other scrawls on the edge of the rock, where the rest of the painting had been broken off and ruined when this slab of rock was wrenched free. She had to touch it, sure that some kind of illuminating force would flow from the rock into her fingers, explaining its origins and its power. Unsure of what it was or whence it came, all her instincts told her that this was the real thing. How could she ever have thought about changing her career? No lawyer ever felt like this. Perhaps doctors felt this sense of exultation when they saved a life, or perhaps teachers when a pupil suddenly surged into a new state of knowledge. She had not felt like this for a very long time.

"Do you have any more of this at home, or is this the only piece?" she asked.

"The only one," he replied. "My father had it in his study, standing on a bookcase. He never mentioned it, except to say it was a souvenir of the war—of the most dangerous part of his war. And that he had made the case himself. The only other thing he ever said was to my mother, and he told her that he knew it was at least seventeen thousand years old."

"Hardly," said Lydia politely. Her voice sounded almost normal, as her brain began to work again in its accustomed grooves. "If it is from North Africa, the Hagar paintings were still being done just a few hundred years ago. Cappadocian work might be seventeen hundred years old, but seventeen thousand years would predate whatever we now think of as the kind of civilization that could produce this kind of work. If it is genuine."

There were swiveling brass arms on the rear of the case. She pushed them sideways to remove the glass and with a brisk "Allow me," her visitor lifted the large and not quite flat chunk of stone free from the velvet. She took a magnifying glass from the drawer, and turned a spotlight onto the edge of the rock, studying what seemed to be a long scorch mark along the side of the rock. Perhaps the burning from some sort of thermal lance that had cut it free? Seventeen thousand years, she was thinking. There was one obvious candidate, too obvious to be possible.

"Did your father serve in France or Spain at all?" she asked quietly, her brain quickening but her stomach lurching at the thought of Lascaux or Altamira. Nobody could ever have done this to Lascaux. The French would bring back the guillotine for anyone who tried. So they should. She would even volunteer to sharpen the blade.

"Yes. As a matter of fact he was in France. Not for long. But in 1944, around the time of the invasion." She was suddenly aware of a sharper note in his voice, and a concentration as he looked at her.

"The Périgord, perhaps? The Dordogne region?" Through the magnifying glass, the lines of the bull looked coarse as well as decisive. Clay, she thought. Not finger-daubed, but a shaped point of tinted clay used as a kind of pencil. The muscles of the neck had been given force by a thinner layer of dappled color. How could that have been done? She curled her hand into a loose fist and put it to her mouth, remembering some long-ago lecture. Yes, this must be an example of the blowing technique. A wash of color in the artist's mouth, half-spat and half-sprayed through a half-closed fist would produce that effect. The rock had to be limestone. She was no expert on the oldest cave paintings of prehistoric man, but she knew that the bulls at Lascaux were ten, even twenty times larger than this. And she was certain that a painting such as this was never found outside its cave, and there was nothing of such size in any museum she knew. But if the rock were from the Lascaux culture, it would be priceless, and even historic. Unbidden, the thought came that this could be the very item to save her career. Properly handled, she told herself. It could also unleash the kind of scandal that could ruin her.

"Yes, I think he was in the Dordogne area," said Manners. "He was attached to Special Operations, with the French Resistance and all that. The summer of 1944, around the time of the D-Day invasion, I know he was in Périgord. He got a French decoration, the *Légion d'Honneur*. But this isn't French, is it?"

"I don't know," she said automatically, playing for time as the excitement surged through her again. "I'll have to check. If it comes from one of the French caves, then it could be seventeen thousand years old, or even older. But it would be about as illegal as any artifact could possibly be. We couldn't possibly sell it," she said, straightening to look gravely at the man. There was no twinkle in his eye now, indeed, no expression at all, which irritated her. "This is not portable art, in any event. It has been cut from the living rock, from a rather larger painting. In artistic terms, and probably legally, this is a crime."

He looked at her silently, his head cocked slightly to one side as if he were about to speak. His self-confidence made him quite an attractive man, she thought. She felt herself blushing, and he carefully took the string he had unwrapped from the parcel, wound it into a small skein, neatly tied the loose end, and tossed it onto the table. Then he carefully folded the brown paper, drew a very clean handkerchief from the cuff of his jacket and wiped his hands before picking up the magnifying glass and looking carefully at the rock's edges. He had very finely shaped hands.

"If you walk out with it now and take it home and put it back on the bookshelf, there is nothing that I or anybody else could do," she said, wondering if this were the right argument to make to this stranger. The last thing she wanted was for him to walk out with his rock. But if it stayed with her, she would have to contact the proper authorities. This conversation with a potential client had suddenly become very complicated. "I don't think you should do that. Not because you could make much money out of this, but because I don't think it would be right."

"Well, it's not my fault. I just inherited the damn thing," he said, squinting at the side of the rock. He straightened and then looked squarely at her. "I don't mean that. It's not a damn thing. I think it's marvelous. I always have, even as a boy. I used to go from looking at it in my father's study out to the fields to look at the cattle, wondering why this felt more like the real things than the Buttercups and Jennies I'd take to the milking shed." His voice trailed off, and he cleared his throat. "How can you tell if it is real? Carbon-dating?"

"Carbon-dating only works on organic material like cloth or vegetation. This is rock," she said, her voice crisp. "I would have to consult with an expert or two, send them photographs, see if any caves have been vandalized of paintings like this. But I can tell you there is no market in this kind of work, if I am right about its provenance. This is not a conventional item of preclassical art, this is prehistory from the very dawn of primitive man. Governments take this kind of thing very seriously." He was not reacting at all. Perhaps he did not understand her sense of outrage.

"Imagine if somebody tried to sell one of the stones from Stonehenge," she went on, thinking the English parallel might stir him. "If your father took this, even if the cave had collapsed and this had been plucked from a pile of rubble, then I think the French government would want to revoke whatever medal they gave him." He was nodding gravely, but without real comprehension. In fact, he was looking at her in that appraising, male way, that made this even more complicated. She would have to be blunt. "I understand you brought this here in good faith, hoping it might be worth money. But I have to warn you that it could land you in serious legal trouble if you tried to sell it. Not a windfall, sir, but quite possibly a prison sentence."

"So, none of this kind of thing is ever sold, nor ever appears at auction," he said. "There is no market, and so no value. I am left with a curious and highly unsavory family memento, and the thought that my father may have been a bit of a rogue."

"You are left with an obligation," Lydia said. "I think we ought to try to find out if this is real, and if so, where exactly it comes from. There may be a hole in a cave painting, although I don't know of one offhand. Anyway this probably belongs in a museum. Sometimes there can be a finder's fee, but in this case, which looks like the result of an act of vandalism, that might be difficult."

She looked at it again, noticing the way the curve of the jaw and of one of the horns followed carefully the folds and indentations in the rock, using the shape of the stone to give a sense of force and muscle in the beast. Where the jaw met the neck, the painter had suddenly blurred his line, as if to suggest movement. She had not seen the real Lascaux cave, only the copy that the French government had built when the breath of too many tourists threatened to damage the original. But she remembered this trick of the blurred line to suggest movement, and the way that artists would try to follow the shapes of rock on which they drew. If this were a fake, it was a remarkably fine one.

"What do you suggest I do? Take it home to Wiltshire and put it back on the bookcase?"

"No," said Lydia firmly. "I strongly suggest you leave it with me, and I shall give you a receipt, and ask one or two experts in the field where it might have come from. If your father found it in 1944, there were then very few painted caves. Lascaux was only found in 1940. If it comes from this region, or from the Spanish caves at Altamira, they'll identify it quickly enough. If not, we'll have to think again about its provenance. But the style says Lascaux, and so does your father's estimate about its age. But even if it comes from somewhere altogether different, I don't think you would be able to sell it, not publicly at least."

"How long would these consultations take?" he asked. "And how long would you want to keep the rock?"

"I'll photograph it digitally, and send that with an e-mail to two or three people. I should hear something within a day or two. Just to be sure, I'll send copies to an expert on the Hagar paintings, and check out one or two more possibles. I'm not an expert on Cro-Magnon man, but I know the people who are."

"Cro-Magnon, was he the one with the low, thick forehead, the missing link back to the apes?"

"No, absolutely not. Cro-Magnon man had a skull and brain cavity not unlike our own, and in creating these cave paintings he gave us the first recognizable human culture. He replaced—and we are not sure how—Neanderthal man, who did have a low, thick brow. But even his brain capacity was just as big as ours—even bigger, I seem to recall. I'm not even sure we know whether or not the two types could interbreed." Lydia was suddenly aware that Manners was watching one of her more irritating habits, twisting a lock of her hair around and around a single finger as she talked. She only did it when she was nervous. She dropped her arm to her side and spoke quickly. "Would you like me to give you a receipt for this, or do you want to take it away with you? I'd like to photograph it anyway, if I may."

He leaned back casually, perched on the table, and for the first time he smiled openly at her. It was a very agreeable smile, with no guile in it. "But if you can't sell it for me, why would you want to go to all this bother? Why not just refer me to a museum and save yourself the effort?"

"Perhaps I should," she said, and gave her coolest, most professional smile in return. "I suppose that having come across this, and suspecting what it might be, I feel rather responsible. If it has been wrenched away from a cave wall, I think we ought to try to get it back."

"Do you feel the same about statues from Egyptian temples and giving the Elgin marbles back to Greece?" His tone was curious, rather than aggressive.

"There are few hard and fast rules about this. The Elgin marbles were bought and exported under the legal rules of the time, and have been better cared for in the British Museum than they might have been in Athens in the past. And that is a case where political issues will probably outweigh any artistic argument. But if somebody in my profession knows something had been taken illegally from a tomb or a temple — or a cave — then we have a sort of ethical code that says we do not deal in it and alert the proper authorities. The laws against trafficking in stolen goods certainly apply to the art world, and there is also a moral consideration, particularly about something such as this." She gestured at the rock.

"Would all your colleagues here, or at other auction houses, take the same attitude? Or is this a particularly American ethic, to do with fear of lawsuits?"

"I certainly hope my colleagues would take the same view, on either side of the Atlantic. This is not about lawsuits, but about fair dealing," she said crisply, suddenly wondering whether the whole thing had been some kind of test arranged by her management. "Now, would you like that receipt?"

"Yes, please," he said. "And I have to be back in town on Friday. If I came in at about midday, perhaps I could take you to lunch?" He smiled again. "You have been helpful above and beyond the call of duty."

"I'm afraid we tend to be rather busy on Fridays," she said automatically, pulling a receipt form and a ballpoint pen from the drawer and starting to fill it in. "But I'll certainly see you here at noon. And if you leave a phone number, I can let you know if some firm information comes back to me before then."

Lydia took a dozen digital photographs of the rock, and weighed and measured it carefully before asking a janitor to take it up to her office. Then she sent e-mails and the digitalized photos to Professor Horst Vogelstern in Cologne and to the National Museum of Prehistory at les Eyzies in the Dordogne, in the heart of France's cave region. It had been founded by Denis Peyrony, the French scholar who had first identified the frieze of the horses in the Font-de-Gaume cave, and ever since had been the main center for the study of early man. She marked the museum e-mail for the attention of Clothilde Daunier, a curator renowned for her encyclopedic knowledge of Lascaux and the surrounding caves. Lydia knew her only by reputation. She had heard of Horst as one of the leading authorities on prehistoric art even before she met him at a reception after he had given a lecture at the Courtauld Institute when she had been studying there. As a courtesy, she sent another e-mail to her old professor at the Ashmolean in Oxford. It was not his field, but she thought he might be interested. At least he could confirm that it was not African. She pondered sending more e-mails to some of her classmates who were still working in the field. There was a boring Irishman, now teaching in Australia, who had been interested in cave painting, and that insufferable Californian who had gone into paleoarchaeology. No, she thought firmly. No need to reopen those old connections. She pulled out Ann Sieveking's *The Cave Artists* and André Leroi-Gourhan's *Dawn of European Art*, and increasingly fascinated, she read until the night watchman found her just before ten. She climbed the stairs again to her small office, just to look at it once more. The night watchman followed her, a rather dear exserviceman with a carefully tended long white mustache.

"Should I put that in the storeroom for you, miss?" he asked. Then he looked at it. "That's special, isn't it?"

"I think it is, Mr. Woodley. I think it could be very special." She smiled at him, feeling comfortable with the elderly man.

"Funny how you can always tell the real thing, the quality," he said, turning her desk lamp to illuminate it more clearly. "Very old, is it?"

"Probably seventeen thousand years old, if my guess is right."

"Crikey. Funny how you never think of art before the ancient Greeks. But it passes my test, miss."

"What's that, Mr. Woodley?"

"I get it now and again. First week I got this job, we had that Rembrandt in, and I got this shiver. I'll never forget it. I'd never thought much about art before. Never seen much, I suppose. But I got it then, and I got it with that El Greco we had last year, and I've got it now." He shook his head in solemn admiration. "Seventeen thousand years. Makes you think. I suppose that's what makes us human, making art, just for the beauty of it."

They looked at it together in silence, feeling the strength and nobility of a long-dead beast, and wondering about the mind and eyes and hands that had crafted it into something more potent than life. Those horns could kill, those haunches could breed, those legs could charge. Mr. Woodley was right to shiver, she thought. Less than two feet square, but it was an awesome beast. She felt a sense of sympathetic terror for whatever distant ancestors had gone up against it with spears and rocks and flint axes. In ennobling the bull, the artist had somehow ennobled the early men who had hunted it.

"You're quite right, Mr. Woodley," Lydia said quietly, thinking how foolish she had been that morning, to think of giving up a career that could give her moments such as this. "It's what makes us human."

"I'll take care of it for you, miss. Put it in the storeroom overnight. You'd better get on home."

She took the tube home to the small flat in Fulham, thinking about the great cave of Lascaux as she opened the door, and how much she would prefer a poster of those bulls of Lascaux on her wall to the insipid Monet print that now greeted her. She did not much like her apartment, given what it was costing her, but duty insisted that her living room and kitchen were always left tidy. Her morning coffee cup and juice glass were now dry on the draining board. She turned on the radio, tuned to the usual Classic FM, and put them away as she tried to identify the music, but it was some generic baroque chamber ensemble and she gave up. Her father would have been ashamed of her, after all the music he had played in her childhood. The small bedroom was as messy as the other rooms were neat, and she shoved tights and jeans and T-shirts and bedclothes into a great pile, and took them down to the communal washing machine in the basement of the converted old house. She had thirty-five minutes before she would have to load them into the dryer. Time to watch TV? To eat? The refrigerator held ketchup, one bottle of wine and two of fizzy water, some yogurt, and a wizened lemon. She would have to start planning her life better than this.

Lydia ate the yogurt, told herself she could put the clothes in the dryer tomorrow and went to bed. Ignoring her bedside copy of *The Hittites*, she was asleep almost at once. Her last thought was of the oddity of time. The oldest cave paintings, at the Grotte de Villars, had been dated by that legendary prehistorian Abbé Breuil to about thirty thousand years. The carbon dating of the charcoal they used in the Lascaux cave suggested the great paintings had been done seventeen thousand years ago. Which meant fifteen thousand years B.C., she thought. She could never teach herself to use that politically correct term B.C.E., Before the Common Era. So for fifteen thousand years before Lascaux, humans had lived around the valleys of the Vézère and Dordogne rivers, hunted and painted in caves, and carried on doing what their ancestors always had. And then came a the sudden explosion of talent and genius that created the stunning achievement of Lascaux. As the explosion faded, people embarked upon the next seventeen thousand-year march to the present day. The human race launched into agriculture and metals and towns and ships and politics; everything began to change as life seemed to shift into a higher gear. Like a video, thought Lydia, fast-forward. Instead of B.C. and A.D., you might call it B.L. and A.L. Before and After Lascaux. Before and after art.

The first response to Lydia's e-mails came the next morning as she was sipping coffee at her desk and taking detailed notes on the rock, perched on a chair at her side. Beyond its weight and dimensions, the colors and the shapes, there was not much to say. Not, at least, that could be put into plain words. The bull was in black and dark red, with muted shadings of red and yellow to give depth. There were some other lines, suggestions that the designs continued beyond the edge of the broken rock, but nothing she could begin to describe. And there was a line of three dots, and perhaps part of a fourth on the edge of the rock, equally spaced, in a reasonably straight line. Such patterns had also been found at Lascaux, but nowhere else, from her superficial researches of the previous evening. But there was no reference that she had found to any damage to the caves at Lascaux, no gaps in the drawings where the Manners rock might have been wrenched free.

She sat back, trying to assess whether she responded to the bull as a magnificent but crude drawing, or whether she simply felt awe at something so old, when the phone rang, and she recognized Horst's voice. He was speaking an English as precise and fluent as her own, with barely a trace of German accent, asking her warmly how she was and sounding much more friendly than one evening of pleasant chatter at a reception would explain. It was soon clear that he was excited by the photographs.

Yes, she still had the rock in her possession, she told him. It was on her desk. No, she had not yet heard from the museum at Les Eyzies, but she felt it possible that it was from Lascaux, even though it was so small. No, her auction house did not intend to put the piece on public sale, but simply to establish whether it was real and where it might have come from.

"I know where it's from," said Horst. "It is from Lascaux, the style and detail are unmistakable. But this is different. It is a miniature, by far the smallest of any bull that I have seen and it is not from any cave I know of. This could mean that somebody has found a new cave, with Lascaux-style art. But why would they be so foolish as to approach an auction house if they want to make some money from this? They must have known you wouldn't put it on open sale. Who is this person who brought it to you, do you know anything about him?"

She described Manners, told Horst of his father and the inheritance, and the possible connection to the Périgord region in 1944, and added, "I don't think he knows the first thing about cave paintings. He was happy enough to leave the piece in my care, and for me to make inquiries to trace it. He seemed genuine and rather innocent. I don't think he's the type to trade in looted goods. And if he were, he would hardly have come to us. But I can quiz him some more when I see him—he's coming in again on Friday to see what I have found out."

"If I came over, would you introduce him to me?" Horst asked. There was a sound of rustling down the phone as he leafed through a calendar. "I can change a lecture, put off a student or two, and fly over on Thursday in time to take you to dinner. By then, we should have confirmation from les Eyzies that this comes from an unknown cave."

"I haven't got my diary to hand—I'm not sure I'm free on Thursday," she said quickly. "Perhaps we'd better wait until we do hear from les Eyzies."

"I'm not giving up the opportunity to see this piece, and Friday morning may be my last chance, if your mystery man decides to take it away with him again. I'll call you again after I hear from Clothilde at les Eyzies."

Within the hour, the Frenchwoman was on the line, more formal and much more cautious than Horst. No, she could not be sure from the photographs she had seen that this was Lascaux work, but it certainly looked interesting. And no, it did not come from any known site. A lot of caves were damaged in places, or eroded, but she knew of no rock scar from which Lydia's exhibit might come. Then she wanted to know if Lydia or her company had informed anyone else.

"Only Horst Vogelstern, in Cologne, and Professor Willoughby at Oxford," said Lydia. "Horst phoned me this morning to suggest that it might come from a new cave, not yet discovered or known about. He seems very excited. He wants to come and see the rock, before the owner comes back on Friday."

"Horst and his theories," sniffed Clothilde. "He is so ambitious to make a big coup and become famous. You know he is trying to persuade people to finance a TV series on prehistoric art. Some theory about an undiscovered cave is the kind of thing he could put into the newspapers and magazines, and then he could make his TV show and write a best-seller and get rich. Horst was a very good researcher, but he gets carried away by his dreams."

"It sounds as though you know him well," Lydia ventured, intrigued by these personal dynamics between scholars.

"Too well," snapped Clothilde, and then went on, almost apologetically, as if Lydia were owed some explanation. "He worked with me here at les Eyzies for two years, and we were very good friends. We were very happy. Then it ended. You know how these things are."

Lydia supposed she did. Or had once, but not for quite some time. David had been almost a year ago.

"I'm sorry," she said. "I had no idea. Look, if this is embarrassing for you I can tell Horst I have put the entire thing in the hands of your museum."

"No, not at all. It was all some time ago, and Horst and I are good friends and colleagues. But I do know how much he is driven to succeed, to make the splash. So I have my doubts when he jumps at conclusions about new caves. We have not fully investigated all the old ones. Remember it took many years even in the well-known caves for the right people with the right lighting to see that there were paintings and carvings. The caves are very big, Lydia. The one at Rouffignac has it own railway line inside, you know, and it was only forty years ago that people first realized that there were cave paintings under the walls and ceiling where the tourists used to carve graffiti." She paused. "But, Lydia, there is something much more important now," she said. "You cannot let the owner take this away. We may never see it or hear of it again. This is French national *patrimoine*, you know, national heritage, like your Crown Jewels in the Tower of London."

"Not my Crown Jewels. I'm American."

"All right, like your Constitution, or George Washington's house. It is the oldest thing that makes us what we are. This belongs to France. We shall have to get some legal document over to you to stake a claim, I suppose."

"You seem pretty sure it's genuine, and French," Lydia said, startled. "I think all that is premature. The owner seems quite happy to leave it in my hands, even when I said that it was my duty to get this item back where it belongs."

"Well, he may say that now, but he could change his mind. We have to put this on a proper footing. I want to come to London this week to make a visual identification, and file a statement for our Embassy legal officer. We are checking with the Ministry of Culture in Paris and with the Foreign Ministry. Nobody here at the museum knows the procedure."

"I think you all ought to calm down," Lydia said. "Legal procedure and all that sounds as if you suspect a crime, but the current owner has obviously been acting in good faith. And if it cannot be shown to be stolen property, I'm not sure if the law comes into it. But I'd better check with our own legal department and see what they say. Why don't we talk again later today or tomorrow, when we both know what the legal position is?"

"For me, that is fine," said Clothilde. "I think it is getting beyond just me and you. Lawyers and government officials and diplomats are already starting to get involved in this. And then the politicians cannot be far behind. Our President comes from this part of France and takes a personal interest in Lascaux. But you are right, let us wait and see what these officials want to do. In the meantime, I want to come to London tomorrow to see the piece. I can hardly give anyone a serious opinion from just your photos. I can get an early flight from Périgueux to Paris and be at your office before lunch. Will that be O.K.?"

It was, of course. But then Lydia had to think about explaining this sudden international incident that she had unleashed to her department head, to the legal department, and probably to a director or two. And all of them would be glumly aware that none of this fuss and bother would have the least financial benefit to the auction house. Ten minutes with the legal department left her convinced that this could become an expensive mess for the company. There was no sale in view, only embarrassment.

She rose, and then checked herself. That would never do. She would have to think positively. What was Clothilde saying about Horst suspecting that an undiscovered cave could be just the break he needed? Perhaps the break could benefit her and the auction house. After all, she had been the one who first identified the rock as a possible example of Lascaux art. The publicity department could certainly do something with it. She picked up the phone to call them, but checked herself again. She should at least call Manners. It was his rock. She looked at the card he had left her, with a country phone number that gave no reply. The London address was the Cavalry Club, and when she rang she learned that he was Major Manners, and he was summoned from the bar. He sounded pleased to hear from her.

"It looks like the real thing," she told him. "Two of the top experts in Europe are coming in this week to look at it on the basis of the photos I sent them. They both think it is from the Lascaux time and period. One suspects that it comes from an undiscovered cave. The other thinks it comes from part of a known cave that has not yet been fully explored. But I think you'll find the French authorities very determined to recover it, since they are convinced it comes from one of their caves."

"You have been working fast, Miss Dean. I'm very grateful to you, and think I owe you that lunch I offered. But when you said the French are very determined, you sounded a touch ominous."

"Well, Mr. Manners, the French museum experts naturally told the Ministry of Culture, who are considering their legal position. They would have to show that your rock came from France, and while most experts would probably agree that it does, there must be some doubt about that so long as they cannot point to the cave from which it is supposed to have come. Then they have to show that it was removed from France at a time when it would have been against the law to do so. And if your father obtained it in 1944, there was then no such law in France. And as the Dordogne region was then territory under German military control, different courts might find that your father's souvenir is legitimate war booty, or legally the property of the British Army. Our own legal department says it's a bit confused. It is clearly in your hands, and you are equally clearly blameless. This is a case where possession is a large part of the law."

"Do I need a lawyer?"

"I think you might want some legal advice. If you want to hang on to the painting, you'd find that fighting this kind of case could be expensive. But you may want a lawyer who can negotiate a settlement, or our auction house can act for you. If the French calculate the costs, they will find an uncertain legal action far more expensive than paying you a finder's fee or an honorarium."

"What sort of sum might that be?"

"Negotiable. But if the French are convinced that it is real and they want it, they may be persuaded to offer ten thousand pounds or so. Perhaps rather more."

"If you were to act for me, your commission would be what?"

"The standard rate is twenty percent. But that would be the firm's commission. It's the firm's expertise you would be hiring."

"What if I were to hire someone privately to act for me?"

"Still twenty percent. I can give you the names of some good independent agents."

"I've got one. The deal is done. You are appointed my agent. I'm quite happy for it to go back to the Frogs, but the more they can be induced to pay, the better. And now you really must let me buy you lunch."

"Thank you, but probably not this week, which promises to be rather hectic. And I couldn't just take off my company hat and act for you privately. It doesn't work like that. Now, how do you feel about publicity? I think it might help. Sensational find, British war hero, that kind of thing. Since we both know that we want the painting to go back to France, what we want to do now is jack the price up, which is where publicity comes in."

"Fine by me. It's in your charming hands, Miss Dean. But take care of the dear old rock for me, and get the best price you can. And I'll see you on Friday at twelve, and possibly your European experts too."

She rang down for a janitor to take the rock to the strong room, filled in the deposit slip, and where it asked for an estimated value, she boldly scrawled "ten thousand pounds." She saw it removed and signed for, and then feeling far more confident than she had for some weeks, walked into Justin's office without knocking to inform him that she might just have the publicity coup he had been looking for. Finally, after a busy half hour with Justin, a lawyer, the publicity manager, and two interested directors, she left them telling the janitor that they wanted the rock brought back up so they could all look at it, while Lydia went off to ring the Arts correspondent of *The Times*.

Clothilde Daunier stood five feet tall, with an extra three inches for a splendid skein of auburn hair piled atop her head so carelessly that the cut must have been expensive, and she was dressed to match. She had a bustling manner, a wide grin, and despite some envy at her clothes, Lydia liked her at once.

"I expected you to bring the French ambassador, the Foreign Legion, and half the lawyers in Paris," she began, pouring coffee. Lydia's tone was friendly and confident after the compliments she had heard from her colleagues that morning. One of the directors had come up to Lydia's attic to congratulate her on the excellent publicity, so she was feeling highly confident about her job.

"I am sure they will come if required," laughed Clothilde, and rummaged into a deep Hermès bag to bring out a bottle and a small glass jar, sealed with rubber. "For you, some foie gras from Périgord, and a bottle of Monbazillac to drink with it. Forget your English rules about leaving sweet wines till the end of your meal and drink it slightly chilled with the foie gras."

She sat down, brought a thin file of photos and photocopies from the bag, lit a Marlboro before Lydia could explain about the No Smoking rule, and said, "You know I worked with Monique Peytral, the artist who reconstructed all the paintings at Lascaux?" Lydia shook her head. She knew the precise and life-size copy of the original cave, built to protect the original from the damaging microbes and carbon dioxide brought in and breathed out by an endless trail of visitors.

"I was the technical adviser on the project, re-creating the Hall of the Bulls and the Axial Gallery. We did a good job, and half the tourists who come have no idea that they are seeing a very clever copy. But what this really means is that everything at Lascaux is engraved onto my brain. I know it very well, and your bull is a Lascaux bull. Your row of dots are Lascaux dots, from a common Lascaux design. This rock is probably from Lascaux artists. I would almost swear to it—except that the bull is so small. I have no idea where it is from. We surveyed that cave fully. There are no unexplored parts to it, and I know your rock does not come from the Lascaux cave. So it may be a copy, just like the ones Monique made, or Horst may be right and it comes from a cave we do not know about. That would be revolutionary. Or it comes from one of several caves nearby, which would be very interesting to a few scholars, but a lot less dramatic. Unless, of course, your rock was surrounded by similar paintings and we have a whole new cave gallery we never knew about. All these things are possible, but first I must see it."

Lydia rang down to the janitors' department, asked for the painting to be brought up, and in the meantime handed to Clothilde a copy of that day's *Times*. There was a small paragraph on the front page, and then a much larger story on page 3, alongside one of Lydia's photographs of the bull, and a headline that read MYSTERY OF FRENCH CAVE MASTERPIECE IN BRITAIN. Tucked into the middle of the story was an extremely flattering photo of Lydia, taken by the publicity department. Clothilde looked at the story, at the photographs, looked back more closely at Lydia and grinned, and then the janitor rang to say they didn't have the rock. It had never been sent down again to the strong room after the directors called for it to be brought to them in the boardroom the previous evening.

"Who signed for it?" Lydia asked, irritated.

"Mr. Justin did, miss," came the reply. "He just kept it up there, and it was never checked in here again last night. It must still be with him."

She rang off and called Justin, whose line was busy. She went down the corridor to his office, suddenly aware that she was walking into some kind of crisis, and his usually impeccably dressed secretary was looking disheveled as she tried to speak on two phones at once. Lydia looked into the office. No Justin. She went back and stood squarely in front of the secretary, who mouthed at her "boardroom."

She took the stairs and found two uniformed policemen standing in the corridor. The boardroom doors were wide open, and she heard the sound of raised and angry voices. It was crowded with several people she did not recognize, two of the auction house directors, and messy with a great deal of paper on the floor. There were champagne glasses on a Regency table, a couple of empty bottles on the priceless carpet, and the smell of a party nobody had bothered to clear up. So there had been a celebration here last night to which she had not been invited.

Typical Justin, she thought grimly. Then she saw the firm's security officer standing over Justin, who was sitting at a disarrayed Georgian desk with his head in his hands. He looked up as she stood hesitantly at the door.

"It's your damned rock, Lydia," he said over the hubbub. "It's gone. Disappeared overnight. We've been burgled."

"What do you mean, burgled?" she demanded in the sudden silence. "Why wasn't the rock put back in the strong room?"

"The boardroom was locked, somebody forced the door. Your bloody rock is the only thing that has gone," Justin said.

"That's not the half of it. The police are here, with more coming," said the publicity director. "And we have half of Fleet Street and the BBC on the phone, all wanting to do their own versions on this"—he looked down at a copy of *The Times*—"this place that you call the Sistine Chapel of prehistoric art."

"I didn't call it that," Lydia snapped. "That was the phrase used to describe Lascaux by the great French historian the Abbé Breuil. He was a churchman. I suppose we would have called him an abbott."

"I don't give a toss about abbots. I do give a toss about the fact that *The Times* Arts correspondent is rather cheesed off that he was given only half a story. He only found out this morning that the late Colonel Manners who was the original owner of this chunk of rock was so highly thought of in Paris that the current President of the Republic came over two weeks ago for a private visit, simply to attend his funeral. This is going to be an even bigger story tomorrow. Thanks to you, we've got a very nasty scandal on our hands."

"In more ways than one," Lydia snapped back, furious at this attempt to shift blame toward her. "I have a French expert from their national museum sitting in my office waiting to see this piece of prehistoric art. And I have an eminent German expert about to fly in to see what I believe to be the most important and unique work of art that this department has found in living memory. From the signs of celebration in this room, you seem to agree with me. And in the midst of guzzling your champagne, you gentlemen seem to have lost it."

"Not lost it," groaned Justin, his nervous hands smoothing out the storeroom receipt that carried his signature and made him responsible. "Burgled."

CHAPTER 2

The Vézère Valley,

approximately

15,000 b.c.

There was always mist in the mornings, hanging damply above the fast-flowing stream and spilling across to the limestone cliffs and the humped hills that shaped the river's course. But even when the sun of early spring had burned off the mist, a fog of another kind still lingered in the valley and remained throughout the day, thickening as the sun sank each evening and the fires were heaped higher to keep the night chill at bay. This more stubborn mist was marked by a scent that kept the game away and forced the hunters to start each day with a long trek to reach the places where the reindeer herds might be found. The animals had always known that smoke meant fire and fire meant danger in the forest. Now they were also learning that the smell of smoke signaled the presence of man, and that this valley was wreathed constantly with his presence.

The trees near the river had gone, cut down laboriously with flint tools to feed the fires. The river took strange courses, where stones had been heaped along the shallower stretches to make fords where man could cross. There was the smoke, and above all, there was the noise of man. He was the least silent of all living things. His young chattered and laughed and screamed in their play. His womenfolk called out constantly to their children and to one another, and chanted strange rhythmic dirges as they came down to the riverbank three times each day for water, and then slogged back up the slopes with their burdens. The men themselves roared in their triumph as they came back to the valley carrying the butchered reindeer, slung by their own sinews to poles borne on the hunters' shoulders. And behind it all was the constant toc-toc-toc, like the sound of a vast flock of woodpeckers, as men chipped and chipped away at the flint stones to make their tools. Noise and smoke and the destruction of trees and the constant, hanging scent of their fires in the valley they had despoiled. That was the essence of man.

Gazing down the river, watching the smoke from more fires than he could count spiral and linger down the valley as far as he could see, the Keeper of the Bulls knew that there was more to his people than the sounds and signs of their presence. More than speech, more than communication, more than the skill at working in groups that kept the meat coming to the caves, there was the work that was worship. It glared and

pranced and brooded on the walls of the cave behind him. The Keeper
of the Bulls looked down at his hands, spread out the fingers, looking at
the red and yellow clays that filled his nails and stained his skin. He
lifted a hand to his mouth. He could smell the colors. Idly, he sucked,
wondering for the hundredth time whether he could taste any difference between them. He fancied that he could, when he took the soft
moss to paint the blackness of the bulls, smelling their power, tasting
their darkness. He felt the familiar tug of the beasts' presence, and took
a deep breath to begin the chant that would prepare him for a new day
of work, the song that he made to the bulls.

As he sang, he knelt before the small fire glowing at his feet. To his
left hand lay the feather, the most perfect and precise of his painting
tools. To his right hand lay the moss, the most crude of them. Beyond
the fire lay the small piece of dung from the holiest of animals. He had
rolled it himself, mixed it, moist and warm and fresh, with the colors
that he would use. Blowing on the fire as he chanted, he waited for the
precise words to place at the fire's heart first the feather, then the moss.
He smelled the acrid burning of the feather, waited for the billow of
smoke from the damp moss, and then he reverently placed one red and
one yellow ball of dung into the flames. He stood, stretching his arms
wide, ending the chant as the sun burned through the mists and sent
glints of sparkling yellow fire along the river. Closing his eyes and bow-
ing his head, he thought of the great haunches that he would paint this
day, of their power and their solidity, feeling in his head the swelling
shapes that he would use to portray their force. Awake, and purified, he
dreamed of the bulls. But then came the voice.

"Father, you must come." The voice was high and piping, almost
squeaky with nervousness. Or perhaps fear. The Keeper of the Bulls
tried to think clearly through his shock, his anger that the boy would be
foolish and disrespectful enough even to come to this place, which he
had no right to see. At least the child had waited until the chant was
complete. He understood that much of the ritual, although he could

not take his place among the workers in the cave until he had grown to manhood and killed his beast. He was a good boy, the Keeper of the Bulls thought proudly, always scratching shapes and drawings in the mud with a stick, born to the work. "The women . . ." the boy squeaked on. "It's Mother."

"Go," shouted the Keeper of the Bulls, his anger suddenly overcoming his concern that the birth was going badly. "I cannot come now. I am purified. I must do my work. I will come after."

He heard a scurrying down in the rocks, and suddenly saw the boy's back as he ran downhill toward the fire close to the river where the women gathered. Childbirth so often went ill. This was his second wife, who had given him two sons since his first wife died in childbirth. Now perhaps he might be able to take another. He turned and marched solemnly to the cave, ducking under the low roof of the entrance, and then standing motionless while his eyes became accustomed to the darkness. There were too many poles supporting the scaffolding to risk blundering ahead until his eyes adjusted to the light of the small lamps with their wicks of juniper. He heard the scuffling above him of other painters, crouched on the scaffolding as they worked, and the first sight that came to him clearly was the Keeper of the Horses, the other priest whose work he most admired after his own. The Keeper of the Horses had a young daughter, who would soon be old enough to wed. A girl, young and fresh, and awed by his status as the Keeper of the Bulls. He smiled to himself as his sight improved and the head of the greatest of the bulls began to emerge in the dim light of the lamps.

This was his work, the commemoration of the bulls. And he studied as if for the first time his greatest achievement—the way he had caught movement and a sense of distance by varying the shape of the horns. The farther horn was always a simple curve. The nearer horn began the same way, but then toward the tip he changed the line of the curve, almost reversing it, so that the head appeared suddenly to be moving, to be portrayed not simply in profile like the deer and horses always were but as great beasts that might almost be charging out into the cave itself. He sighed in satisfaction, and nodded gravely as he looked down to the last work he had done, on the chest of the bull when it sank to the forelegs.

Yes, it had worked. Just as the different shape of the horns had seemed to turn the bull's head toward him, so the separation of the forelegs maintained the effect. The rear foreleg thrust out forward, at a down-sloping angle to show that the bull was moving. Then before he began sketching the front foreleg he had drawn thickly the deep sagging muscle of the lower chest. Then the foreleg itself, marked off from the chest and belly by pure white space, to make the leg stand out and seem almost to move. It was perfect. Every trick that he had learned here, in the months and years in the semidarkness of the cave, they were all coming to fruition with this bull. It moved, and its movement was not simply forward but at an angle.

"This is the greatest of your work," said the Keeper of the Horses. He was standing easily on the scaffolding, each foot braced on a different pole, as he worked in the curve where the cave wall sank to become the wall. He was close to the head of the great bull, sketching lightly in the place between the two horns. "I shall pay tribute to your work with my own."

The Keeper of the Bulls squinted to see the faint shape of a horse's head emerging from between the horns. He picked up one of the lamps and moved closer, climbing easily up the scaffolding poles to stand behind his fellow priest.

"You see, my work will be here, the finest I have ever drawn, a noble creature who will be imprisoned by the horns, but staring down to honor what you have done," said the Keeper of the Horses. He was a slim, wiry man, with thinning gray hair bound back from his face with a leather ring. Smaller than the Keeper of the Bulls, and quick in his ways as befitted a Keeper of the Horses, he had the finest teeth in the valley. They were white and even, and had not a single gap. The Keeper of the Bulls tried to remember the face of the man's daughter. He thought perhaps her teeth were as perfect as her father's. He enjoyed the thought.

"He will have a mane of black, a skin of chestnut, a head that is neat and alert, his ears pricked forward as he shows his respect to the greatness that confronts him," the Keeper of the Horses went on. "Is this well, my friend?"

The Keeper of the Bulls squeezed his friend's shoulder and grunted approval. He climbed down, making way for the young apprentice who was waiting to clamber up with two small wooden bowls of freshly mixed red and black clay. The Keeper of the Horses had completed his sketch with charcoal, and with feathers and smoothed blunt sticks in his belt, was ready to begin the real work. His own apprentice was sitting, cross-legged and patient, the colors already mixed on flat stones before him and with a lump of almost black clay soaking in a bowl under a heap of damp moss. There were two lamps ready to illuminate his work. This was good, and the Keeper of the Bulls nodded approval. The youth looked relieved. The Keeper of the Bulls had a strong arm and beat the apprentices who displeased him, or even exiled them from the work.

"Bring me water to drink," he told the youth, and turned to consider the day's work as the apprentice moved swiftly to the cave entrance, carefully avoiding the scaffolding. The previous week, the most senior apprentice had been banished from the cave for knocking away the supports of the higher platform in the narrow cave beyond where the Keeper of the Bison was at work. He had been a talented young man, who mixed a splendid auburn red and whose sketches had won admiration. But for the carelessness and disrespect, he had been sent off to work for the women. Even the hunters would not have him.

The Keeper of the Bulls pondered how to proceed. He wanted to depict those haunches, that weight and power that had come to him as he chanted over the holy fire. Holding the lamp close to his ear, he looked closely at the rock where the haunches would be painted. There was a jaggedness, a faint thrusting of a yellower rock coming through the thin chalk skin that made the cave such a perfect surface for the work. He passed his fingers lightly over the line of the yellow rock, thinking he could use that line to add bulk to the haunch, to hint at the swell of muscle. The line of the back was already complete as far as the tail, a fine sweeping curve that established the power of the shoulder and then rose for the swell of the haunch. He would leave a space for the root of the tail, knowing that the absence of line could be more telling than the most perfectly drawn one, before starting the curve of the haunch. He would separate the rear legs again, just as he had done with the forelegs, to maintain that illusion of a half-turn. But how to distinguish between the legs, where there was no hanging muscle of chest. Suddenly, he smiled to himself. A beast as noble as this would have mighty genitals. He put his left hand to his own loins, cupping them gently, as his right hand began to sketch with charcoal. And as the thought of the daughter of the Keeper of the Horses came into his mind, he felt himself stirring under his hand. He had not thought of his woman, or of the birth, at all.

At the fire by the river, the banished apprentice sat tiredly in a brief moment of rest before the women ordered him to feed the fire again, or to get more wood or to bring more water. The screams of the woman lying on the great mat of sewn-together reindeer hides had faded to moans. He could see nothing of the birth. The other women huddled around her, some still holding down her shoulders and legs. Suddenly one turned to him, speaking coldly, and told him to run to the flint makers and bring back the sharpest piece they had.

"It must have a good gripping stone. Just a chip of flint won't be enough. We'll have to hold it firmly," she said, and turned away to shout more instructions to a young girl.

He rose and began running along the river and then up the hill to the quarry where the flint men worked, the sound of their constant tapping even louder than his labored breaths. He paused as he approached, catching his breath and looking carefully on the ground ahead. Even the most callused feet could still be sliced by the shards of flint that littered the earth. The flint men themselves wore leather moccasins with wooden soles bound to them. They were men he hardly knew, who kept to themselves almost as much as the Keepers who worked in the cave, and were just as strict in their hierarchy. The head of the flint men, whose main work was to teach the craft to the young apprentices, ignored the youth's approach for a few moments before looking up. The youth explained what the women needed.

"For a bad childbirth?" the flint man asked. He was old and white-haired, with strips of hide tied around his hands to protect them from the stones. "I'll have to make something."

He rose and went to the pile of stones the youngest apprentices constantly brought down from the quarry. Sifting carefully though them, he picked out a smooth rock that was almost a perfect globe, only one end jagged and split. He came back to the circle of watching apprentices, picked up his knapper, held the globular stone firmly against the flat rock that served as his anvil, and explained what he intended to do, and where his first strikes would be. He lifted his right hand, and brought the knapper down sharply onto the stone, hitting at an angle and just above the first break in the smooth globe. A large sliver of stone broke off. He turned the globe and repeated his strike, and then handed it to an apprentice and told him to do the same. Within the time it took for the banished apprentice's breathing to return to normal, a sharp flint knife, with a perfectly smooth and round haft to fit the hand, had been produced. The flint man tested the edge against the hair on his own arm, and nodded approval. He tossed it to the waiting youth, who turned and ran back to the women at the fire.

As he reached them the young girl who had been dispatched came running back, breathing easily, with two handfuls of fresh moss from the riverbank. As they handed over their items, the young man caught the scent of fresh blood. There were no more moans coming from the woman lying on the reindeer hide, and the other women had ceased to hold down her legs and shoulders.

"Is she dead?" the girl asked. A tired woman, bloodstained to the elbow, nodded grimly and sighed. "The child still lives within her."

The two young people squatted near the fire, and watched as the oldest woman took the sharp flint and drew it firmly down the swollen belly of the dead mother into her groin. The girl gasped and turned her head aside. The youth watched intently as the blood welled, trickling slowly down the woman's sides to the hide. The old woman repeated her stroke, muttering softly to herself, and then two more women began to peel the parted skin aside. The old woman began working with the flint knife inside the belly as yet another woman squatted over the dead one's head, and began mopping up blood with the moss so that the old one could see to work. The young girl turned her head back to watch as the old one threw the flint aside, and reached deep within to draw out a small, still baby, a multicolored cord hanging from its belly and glistening in the sunlight. She looked at it carefully, poked her finger into its mouth to clear it, and then bent down to blow into its nostrils. She did this three times, squeezing the baby's tiny chest each time, and then she slapped its rump quite hard, and the baby's arms waved and it began to cry. It was a girl. The old one held the baby as another woman knotted the cord with a strip of leather, and then cut it. They wiped the baby clean with more of the moss, wrapped it in a reindeer skin, and then laid it by the fire.

"We helped to save it, then," the young girl said. He noticed that she wore that plain leather neck cord of the not-yet-betrothed, and her hair was rich and glossy. She turned and smiled at him, and he saw that her teeth were white and perfect. Her eyes seemed very large to him. "But the mother died. Did you know who she was?"

"Yes, she was the woman of the Keeper of the Bulls. She had borne him sons," he said. "Did you know her?"

"Of course. My father is the Keeper of the Horses. And you are the bad apprentice who was sent away from the cave, the young man who now has no craft and no name." She looked at his naked neck. No bone on a thong to show he was a hunter, no stone to show that he made flints, no piece of bark to show that he was wood gatherer and guardian of fire. Above all, there was no feather to mark him as an apprentice to the Keepers in the cave. They must have wrenched it from his neck when he was banished. "What will you do now?"

"Wait," he said curtly. "They will punish me for a season by making me work with the women, and then they will take me back. That is what your father told me when he came to visit me with some food after I had been beaten and sent away. He is a kind man." He looked at the girl, suddenly intent on the way her cheekbones framed her face and at the soft down on her cheeks. "He is a good man, and his work is very fine. He said that I had talent and the Keepers would not let such a gift go unused. It would do no honor to the beasts of the cave."

"He is kind. When I am sick, he goes into the woods to bring me honey, even when the bees sting him," she said. "But since you have no name, what shall I call you?"

"Deer-runner was my boyhood name. Keeper of the Deer will be my name when they take me back to the work in the cave. Call me Deer," he said, very conscious of the soft swelling of her young breasts. This was no child, but a woman soon to be betrothed. He wondered what her father's plans for her might be. "And what do I call you?"

"My family calls me Little Moon. My father says the moon was very small when I was born."

"He has not sought to betroth you yet?" he asked.

She laughed, almost childishly. She was still very young. "No, he says we must wait until Little Moon is more of a full moon. But my new mother thinks it soon will be time."

He looked at her silently, enjoying her face but somehow alarmed by his own pleasure in her. He would not be eligible for betrothal until his apprenticeship was complete. Another season of banishment from the cave would take him into the summer, then at least two more seasons of apprenticeship meant that it would be midwinter before he became a Keeper. If her mother thought it was time, this girl would be betrothed before the summer was over. She could be carrying her first child by the time he became a Keeper and was entitled to take a woman. The thought put a hollowness into his belly, a feeling he had never known before. Little Moon. She was looking shyly at him from under her lashes.

The cackle of the old woman cut into his reverie. He had to bring firewood to build the pyre for the dead woman, the pyre that her man would light at dusk as the women stood around and sang the death song of motherhood. He rose to go, and hardly knowing what he was doing, stopped and said, "Little Moon, I shall be a Keeper this winter. Wait for that."

She looked at him, expressionless, as he turned to go. She had never seen before any young man without the mark of his craft around his neck. The bareness of his chest rose unchecked to his neck and head. When he turned, she was suddenly aware of the intentness with which she studied the slimness of his waist and the way it swelled out to the muscles beneath his shoulders, and the way his fair hair fell and splayed in curls upon them. She watched him run, Deer-runner. She could call him Deer, he had told her so. Her hand came up to touch her own bare thong, the mark of the virgin.

The Keeper of the Bulls thrust his torch into the stack of wood, and stepped backward as the fire began to crackle beneath the body of his woman. They had told him it was a girl child. His sisters could take care of it. The woman had brought him two sons. She had kept a decent home. His water was always warmed at the fire for his morning drink. Her thighs had always opened dutifully to his desire, and there had been moments when she clasped him with warmth. He thought back to the earliest days, when she had been young and lithe and at first frightened beneath him, and then languorous and eager. That time had passed with the first son, passed along with the sleepy talk and the laughter, passed along with his growing obsession with the work and the cave. With the bulls. He could name them in the privacy of his own mind. But not to others, and never to those outside the chosen circle of the Keepers. For those others, it was only to be named the work, or the beasts.

He looked around at the gathering people, flickering in the firelight that held the dusk at bay. Grease on their faces after the feast. A long, low moan coming from the women at the far side of the fire, rising into the chant of mourning. Then the men of her kin came forward. A hunter, to lay a bone upon the pyre, and a waterman, with a wriggling crayfish, his splayed thumb and fingers squeezing its head into stillness as he laid it on the fire. The Keeper of the Bulls waited, until all had done, and then stepped forward to lay his own feather upon the flames that would consume the mother of his sons.

It was the cave that had brought so many others here, to pay respect at the pyre of his woman. The leader of the flint men, the chief woodman, and all the men who led the hunt. The leaders of the fleet young men who chased the game and of the spearmen and slingers who killed it. The trackers and even the limping old head of the small group of crippled and older men who set the traps and placed the nets for the birds and fishes. And it was the cave that had brought the headmen of the other communities along the river, for while they had their own priests and artists and their own holy caves, none of them had had his vision to fill a whole cave with the holy beasts.

Still, there were men here whose skills he envied, not for himself, but for the greater power of the cave itself. His Keeper of the Bison — only to himself did he ever think of his colleagues as "his" men — was old, half-blind, and barely adequate. The bull he had worked on today had almost openly showed his contempt, painting over a crude red bison that he thought of as little more than a stain on the wall. He hadn't even bothered to consult its Keeper about painting over it. He caught himself. He must not do that. There was an etiquette in the cave, as the Keeper of the Horses had come to him in the morning to consult about the placing of his horse between the horns of the bull. That was the proper way, showing respect. That was how it must be done, he cautioned himself. But it was hard. It was his vision, his cave, not to be demeaned by the daubs of second-raters. In their hearts, his colleagues must know this, which made it all the more important that he be seen to show them proper deference.

He would miss this woman, lying dead before him, about to go into the flame. Not just her body or her care, but her counsel. She had understood his vision from the moment that the hunters had first entered the miraculous cave and summoned him to see the great white space of the walls, the perfect round of the ceiling where it narrowed. He remembered the sense of lust as he had first seen it, probing into the belly of the earth as he had later probed into the belly of his woman. She had understood that this could be the holiest cave of them all, and it was her counsel that made him raise the idea so carefully. She had told him to sound out the oldest Keepers first, to make it sound like their idea, while she had subtly worked on their women. He would miss that, miss her gentle reminders of the need to pay respect to their other Keepers, to praise the crude work of that fool, the Keeper of the Bison. He had only himself now to keep voicing the warnings, to bite down on the urgency that seized him when he saw how the cave should be, and to keep silent when his heart cried out in pain at the sad daubings others made as they carried out his vision.

The flames were catching hold now, and he smelled the first warm, cooking smell of his woman's dead flesh. Like boar. He bit back the sudden rush of saliva in his moth. The smell would turn sour soon enough, as sour as the loneliness of his own hearth with no woman to clutch for warmth in the nights. He must take a new woman before the winter came, a young one, ready to make more sons. As soon as the ashes of the funeral pyre had cooled and been scattered by the wind and rain, he would talk to the Keeper of the Horses. Most of all, he must keep talking to himself, reminding himself, imposing that discipline upon his own imperious spirit, which might otherwise tear asunder the Keepers in division and rivalry. They must be guided, not commanded, gently steered rather than driven. Perhaps this was his woman's last farewell to him, her last gift in death. The wisdom of her counsel, not the girl child he had yet to see, was how he would remember her.

He watched as the flames died, waiting until the ashes were just a glow, and turned to his colleagues on either side. The Keeper of the Horses and the Keeper of the Deer both nodded, and as he led the way uphill they marshaled into line the others who would be granted the honor of the cave. First the leaders of his own people, the flint man and the hunter, the waterman and the woodman. Then in courtesy, the Keepers of the other clans, almost humble at the knowledge that they were about to enter into a place far greater than their own caves. Then from each clan, a chosen leader. He looked back. Perhaps forty men, none of them young, were climbing the hill behind him, their way lighted by his apprentices carrying torches that had been kindled at the pyre.

When he reached the cave, the oldest apprentice scurried forward, using his torch to light each of the small stone lamps that the elders would carry. When they were ready, he stepped into the mouth of the cave and began his chant to the beasts, the song of supplication that sought their permission to enter and display their pride and strength to the men who would enter to worship. Once, as a young apprentice at another, lesser cave, he had stood with the torch as another Keeper made this same song, and a great bolt of lightning had crashed down from a clear night sky to strike and break a tree nearby. They had all fled the wrath of the beasts. That moment had always stayed with him.

Even though he came to this cave each day, although he worked here and had made this place and the great bulls had grown under his own hand, he was reminded that this was their place even more than his. A power had been engendered here that had reached and grown far beyond his art and beyond his skill. And as he led the way into the darkness, and saw the first flickerings of the lamps begin to invest his bulls with life and power, he felt awe.

Deer, his arms folded across his hairless chest, watched grimly as the line of men disappeared into the cave, and the other apprentices, with whom he should have stood and held the torches, spread out into a line of sentries in front of the entrance. They could not see him, but he could not be part of the ceremony, could take no pride in the paints that he had mixed, the colors that he had applied, the first beginnings of what he knew would be his life's work. He would be lucky if he were allowed back into the fold before the next festival. It would be midsummer, he calculated, the feast of the longest day. It would be up to the beasts themselves, he thought automatically. And then he examined that instinctive thought. Up to the beasts? No. Up to the old men who spoke and ruled in their name. His fate rested with the Keepers. With men.

He edged back deeper into the trees, and squatted, aware that his head was reeling with this strange, invasive idea. He had always been told that the beasts themselves were the governors of the cave and all the hierarchy and structure that flowed from it. His people were the people of the cave, the servants of the beasts, the blessed folk who had been chosen by their skill to breathe life and holiness into the bare rock and darkness. Did not all the clans along the river come this night to pay homage to the beasts of the cave that the Keepers had conjured from the skill? Surely they had.

But he shared that skill in abundance. He was touched by the beasts, infused by them with the skill that made him the most gifted of the apprentices. He knew that his colors were the purest, his work with the moss the most sure and precise, his touch the most assured of all those young men who stood now with their guttering torches outside the cave. And he was not among them because an old man had slipped and fallen from his scaffolding and blamed him for the tumble. The beasts had been silent. The old man's petulance had shifted his life, forced him from the cave to work for the women, until such time as the Keepers judged his sin atoned, and summoned him back to the work.

How dare they block his skill in this way, these stubborn old men? Some of them had less skill than he, despite their life's work. The bison in the cave were a disgrace. The deer were a strange fancy, antlers tangled like brambles—like the thoughts of their elderly Keeper who drank too much of the soured honey that sent men reeling. They had no place in the cave. They breathed no spirit into the rock. His own deer were better.

He closed his eyes, remembering the cave. The Keeper of the Horses was a worthy custodian of his beasts, a Keeper who could judge colors and form, from whose every line Deer knew he was learning some addition to the skill. And the Keeper of the Bulls was an artist touched by the very beasts he conjured, of a gift so rich and true that Deer marveled at the perfection of the memories in his mind. They were the very essence of bull.

And yet, and yet. They were all the same. Gigantic. Dominating by their very size. Each using the same tricks, the white space between limb and body, the different twists of the horns to hint of a turning, the outflung kick of the legs—he saw them all in his memory, recognized their worth as devices. But they were all the same. There was no balance, no variation of scale. There was simply the worship of dominance, expressing the greatness of bulls by sheer size. He squeezed his eyes tighter, remembering not just the bulls but the beasts around them, the context in which their vastness dominated. Were it not for the delicacy of the horses around them . . .

The Keeper of the Horses made them large and small, made them toss and browse, understood the horses he made as a herd and as separate, distinct beasts. Deer told himself that he must be honest here in his judgment, must even be cruel. There was no single horse that came close to the bulls as a single work. But it was in the numbers, in the use of them as balance and as artistic forms that lightened the great brooding weight of the bulls, that Deer felt he recognized the touch of a master. The bulls were power, the horses were grace. But the power of the bulls would be ungainly, even crude, without that lightness of the Horses. The Keeper of the Bulls was painting for himself, Deer suddenly thought, but the Keeper of the Horses was painting for the cave. As the thought formed, he expelled a great gust of air, without ever knowing that he had been holding his breath. He felt lightheaded.

Then, so unexpected that his skin seemed to jump, there came a touch on his arm. "My father said that I would find you here," whispered Little Moon. He could barely see her, just the play of shadows from the torches outside the cave and the gleam of her eyes. "He wants you to wait here until morning, when they come out. He will come to see you then."

"Why does he want to see me? Did he say?"

"Just that you should wait for him." She made no move to go, kneeling quietly at his side, her eyes on the cave.

"Does he know that we talked, you and I, Little Moon?"

"I did not tell him," she said. "I think perhaps my mother did. She asked me, after you had gone, what we had said. And she said that I should know you were disgraced, banished from the cave to work for the women."

"Does your mother know that you are here now?"

He felt, rather than saw, the quick shake of her head. "It doesn't matter. I am here on my father's bidding. But I must go back soon."

43

"Not yet," he said, and ran his hand along the smoothness of her arm. She flinched back, and then relaxed.

"Do you remember what I told you, that you should wait until I am made a Keeper?"

"Yes, I remember," she whispered. "But this is for my father to decide."

"He is a good man, Little Moon, and a great worker in the cave, Perhaps the greatest. His beasts love him, and stir with life at his touch."

"You should not talk of this with me. The cave is not for women."

"Every other cave of every other clan is for women," he said. "There are women in other clans who do the work of the cave. I have seen them. It is only us who have this law, and only in this cave."

"I should like to see it, someday," she said. "My father says it is a place of marvels."

"Then you shall, when I am Keeper. I shall show you. I want to show you my work."

"But you are only an apprentice. They have not let you begin yet."

"I had passed the last test of the apprentice. I had done my first work, not in the great cave, but far deeper in, where the passage narrows and the floor falls away. That is where the apprentices who are about to be made Keepers do the work that the other Keepers judge. That was where I made my work, my swimming beasts. There is a line of rock within the rock of the cave, a dark and curving line like a river that is in flood. And that was where I plunged my beasts, into this flood as you have seen them swim in the river after winter when the waters rush. They are part of the water, and the water is a part of the rock. They flow together—" His voice broke off. "They are good work, Little Moon, and I would show them to you, my swimming deer."

She gasped in shock, her hand leaping to her mouth. "You named them! You must not—you named the beasts."

"Only to you, Little Moon, and you will see them. You will see them and know what they are, and inside your head you will think that these

44

are indeed swimming deer and this is indeed a river. And then you will think like me that naming them in your head is the same as naming them in your mouth, and wonder why we have this strange rule that says we only call them beasts or the work."

"My father says . . ." she began, but he interrupted. "This is me speaking now, not your father. This is me, thinking that I do not like this rule that says the cave is not for women, and I do not like this rule of never saying the names of the beasts. And I do not understand the rule that says the work can show bulls and horses and deer and bison and bear, but we never work on the one beast that sustains the people. The reindeer that feed us, that clothe us, that give us their horns for the flint men to work with and the needles for the women to sew with and the hides that make our tents and keep us from the wind and rain, they are not honored in the cave. And this is strange. So many rules are strange."

She rocked back on her heels, bewildered by his words, which challenged so many of the rules that she had grown up accepting as if they were as much a part of the laws of life as the heat of fire, the wet of rain. And then hearing the names of the beasts, and him telling her more of the cave than she had ever heard, and then saying he would show her. And the touch of his hand on her arm.

"I must go back now," she said. But did not move.

"I say them only to you, Little Moon. Until this night, I have not even said them to myself." He let go of her arm. "I will wait here for your father. And I will wait even longer for you."

She rose, a sudden shiver on her skin although she felt warm, and looked down on him for a long moment before slipping silently back through the trees, and then darting back downhill to the tents of her family.

They came out of the cave at dawn, drawn and silent from the long night watch, to find the women waiting with water and cold meat. As they drank, the spell was broken. Men strolled off to the trees to piss, hawked the cave's damp from their throats, cleared their noses and broke wind. The Keeper of the Horses paused on the patch of level ground before the cave, looking quickly to left and right, drifting across to the edge of the trees and standing so that he might be seen.

"I await you, Keeper," came the soft voice. Good, the boy was being careful, still behind the tree. Little Moon must have been clever to have found him. He sidled around to join the youth, led him deeper into the trees.

"Have you learned your lesson now, apprentice?" he asked.

"The lesson of banishment for the fall of an old man that I did not cause? What is there to learn from this?"

"No, the lesson of discipline. The lesson of respect for your elders. The lesson that we must sometimes suffer things without a cause, but accept that suffering for a greater purpose. You have the gift, Deer-runner. Your place is in the cave, with the work, among us."

"I have respect for my elders, for my teachers, for the workers such as you, or the Keeper of the Bulls. I have much to learn from you."

"Listen, I want to bring you back into the cave," he said, gripping Deer by the upper arm, shaking him slightly. "You should be a Keeper by now. You know that. Anyone who has seen your swimming beasts knows that. But I must be able to tell the other Keepers that you have learned the lesson of humility. That you respect the judgment of your elders. Do you hear me, Deer-runner?"

"I hear you, Keeper." To himself, he said: I hear you, father of Little Moon.

"It is not just a company of workers that you join, a group of skills and talents. It is a group of men, with their own weaknesses and pride. And one thing to remember is that old men whose limbs are no longer sure as they climb the poles can be too proud to say that, and lash out at

46

a young or nimbler person nearby. Men hate to blame themselves for their feebleness and faults, just as I see you not wanting to take the blame for your own impetuous pride. Do you hear this?"

"I hear you, Keeper. And I thank you for the lesson."

"You will be humble before the Keepers. You will admit your fault to the old man. You will take the blame upon yourself. You will keep your head down and your voice silent, and if you trust in me and are guided by me, you will be a Keeper before the festival of the longest day."

"Why do you do me this kindness, Keeper?" he asked, hoping that the man would say it was because Little Moon had asked him.

"Because of your swimming beasts," said the Keeper, turning Deer toward him, gripping him by both shoulders to stare him in the face. "And perhaps because one day when I have gone and you see a young fool who has the gift but seems doomed to waste it, perhaps you can do the same for him." He grinned at the youth, liking him for his clear gaze and the respect he showed. "Just as someone did for me, a long time ago."

CHAPTER 3

Arisaig, Scotland, 1943

Captain Jack Manners was exhausted; sweating so much in the chill Highland rain that he thought the desert fever had come back. His pack was full of rocks. The absurd little Sten gun with its narrow strap was cutting into the side of his neck, and his feet were sopping wet inside the heavy boots. At least in North Africa they had worn comfortable desert boots of light suede. It never ceased to amaze him—the only part of the British Army actually fighting the Germans dressed like a bunch of holidaymakers, in beards and shorts and corduroy slacks, cravats around their necks to keep the dust out. Some chaps even swore by their silk shirts, cool in the heat of the sun, warm as the chill of the desert night made the hard ground as cold as the stern metal of their tanks. Yet back here in Britain they were playing at soldiers, demanding glossy boots and pressed uniforms and close shaves even though there were never any razor blades. And they weren't even fighting! When the reinforcements came out to Egypt from England, it took them weeks to get ready to fight Jerry. Still, he thought with a fairness that had been bred into him so hard it had become instinctive, it had taken him and his Hussars at least a year, and some decent tanks and a decent general, to learn how to fight Jerry. And given the right ground and enough time to dig in against our air power, Jerry could still dish it out.

"You need some hate in a war such as this, Jacques," panted the man beside him. "When the body fades, and the will fades, then must come the hate."

Jack Manners did not respond. He slogged on to the top of the hill, bracing against the wind that whipped off the Irish Sea like a volley of cold knives, and plodded grimly down the next slope until the loom of a rock promised some relief from the weather. He nudged the Frenchman beside him, edging him across to the rock. Then Jack took out his compass, and checked the bearing again.

"Remember what they told us," he said, speaking in French. "Five minutes rest every hour." He knelt down, shuffled off his pack, and began kneading the calves and thighs of his partner, who had ducked his head inside his parka to light a cigarette. Jack had long ago given up trying to stop François from smoking on duty. Last thing at night, he stubbed one out, half-smoked, and woke in the morning to relight it. The Frenchman's legs were trembling with the strain of the climb.

"I have never understood your English masochism. In all the war I have seen, in all the battles I have endured, I never once had to march. I took aircraft and stole cars, borrowed motorbikes and even a bicycle. But never marched," said François. "You only make us do this to keep us busy, like you make your conscripts paint the coal white in the barracks and pick up all the matches from the parade ground."

"Remember what we learned from Rommel—train hard, and fight

easy," said the Englishman, slapping François's calf to signal the brief massage was over. "Your turn."

François knelt and began rubbing warmth into the Englishman's legs. It felt blissful, feeling his blood flow again. He wanted to close his eyes and savor it, but this was an exercise. He had to keep his eyes open. Christ knows when an instructor would jump out from behind a rock, stage a mock ambush, haul them in for another of the mock interrogations.

"Don't talk to me about your bloody Rommel," said François. "That's the trouble with you English. You admire your enemies. The more they beat you, the more you worship them as honorary English gentlemen."

"We beat Rommel," Jack said calmly. "We beat the living daylights out of Rommel and his panzers. You know that, François, you were there. But first we had to learn his lesson."

"I know. Train hard, fight easy. Train together, never fight apart. I learned it, too, even before you. We had Rommel and his 7th Division coming at us and through us in 1940." The last words were torn out of his mouth by the wind's rising howl. François stood up, slapping his hands together, spitting out his cigarette, shouldering the pack, and preparing to move off. "And we held him off for a week at Bir Hakeim, even with those silly little antitank guns you gave us."

"You're forgetting something," said the Englishman. François shrugged and knelt to pick up the glowing ember of the cigarette, squeezing out the glow with his hardened fingers, then shredding the tobacco into the wind, screwing up the tiny shred of paper and stuffing it into a pocket. No traces. They marched on down the hill toward the loch, the ground getting steadily wetter, both men scanning the shore and the dead ground for signs of ambush. There would be one, somewhere before the end of the exercise.

Jack Manners needed no reminding. That was when they had met, in that dreadful summer of 1942 when Rommel's Afrika Korps had broken through the British lines south of Tobruk, and destroyed the Free French at Bir Hakeim with day after day of tank and Stuka bombardment. Jerry had picked off the undergunned and underarmored British tanks in his usual style and rolled them all the way back to El Alamein. Jack, on leave in Cairo, had suddenly been called in as a French-speaker to help organize a reception for the pitiful remnants of General Koenig's Free French garrison. François had got out on a German motorbike, a BMW he had taken from a dispatch rider in an ambush, and ridden north to join the British and keep on fighting. That was the meeting, Jack supposed, that made this partnership and this posting and this blisteringly bloody training course in Argylle inevitable. But if he were honest with himself, he'd have volunteered for SOE anyway.

Special Operations Executive, fulfilling Churchill's orders to "set Europe ablaze," was how the lecturers told it. They hadn't done much in the past three years. A few escape lines to get downed RAF pilots out of Occupied France and into Spain, a few sabotage operations, some intelligence tapped out on wireless by frightened operators waiting for the German direction-finding trucks to track them down. He would never have volunteered for that. But this new operation of the Jedburgh teams was going to be different. Training the French Resistance, bringing in the arms that could let them fight, and then leading them into battle behind the German lines to destroy the bridges and the communications that would otherwise bring the panzer divisions that would throw the Allied invasion force into the sea. No spying, no skulking about the French countryside in some shabby civilian clothes. He would wear his uniform and fight as a soldier. That was a mission worth training for. Suddenly he felt François's hand close tightly on his arm.

"Over there, opposite the island," the Frenchman breathed. Jack peered into the darkness. The man had eyes like a cat. Maybe there was something, a bulky shape, perhaps some movement. It looked like a lorry. It was hard to tell. "We go round behind them," François said. "We ambush them."

"Careful," said Jack, his tiredness and his fever quite gone. "It is a favorite trick they use. The tethered goat. They show us a target that looks easy, tempting us to ambush them, when they have the real ambush set up to catch the ambushers. You go right. I go left. We meet on the loch shore. If we see no signs of ambush, then we hit the lorry from the back. If one of us sees an ambush, take it out with a burst from the Sten, and the other rushes the truck. If one of us gets caught, he sets off a Thunderflash to warn the other. See a Thunderflash, then get out of here and back to camp. Hear a Sten, rush the truck."

They separated, moving swiftly down the hill, almost instinctively avoiding the loose shale that would betray the sound of their footsteps, skirting rocks that were light enough for a silhouette to stand out. The three-week course had taught them a lot. Jack felt the ground start to flatten beneath his feet, and knelt to stretch out his hand, feeling for a trip wire before the inevitable track that follows the loch shore. Nothing, but he felt the sudden absence of heather, and ridged mud and flint beneath his fingers. This was the track.

He paused, listened, and then crawled across. No trip wire on the far side. He could see the lorry more clearly now against the water, about fifty yards to his left. No sign of movement. If he were setting up the ambush, it would be straight ahead, one man facing the truck to see any sign of movement against the water, another facing this way to watch the track. The wind was still strong enough down here to cover the sounds of his movement. He leopard-crawled along the slight ditch by the track, aiming to get thirty yards to the flank. Grenade-throwing distance. Cautiously, he parted the thin grass to peer through. A minute passed before he saw the movement, a fleeting blur that could have been a man's head.

He slipped the Sten from his shoulder, pulling the bolt back as he rose, and then sprayed the ambush point with a short burst of blanks as he charged it. He changed direction to his left and fired another burst, dropped and rolled to the right, and fired again. Rose and half-darted, half-staggered the last few yards to the ambush and jumped into the depression, to see an outraged sheep scamper complainingly away. A blaze of lights from the truck caught François, charging upon it from the loch side, as two Commando sergeants brought their hands together in slow, ironic applause.

"Not bad at all, laddie," came a cheerful Scots voice from his rear. "If Jerry starts putting sheep on duty, you'll have them cold. But he's not that short of men, yet."

The instructors slept in comfortable rooms in the grim, granite country house. At least, Jack assumed they were comfortable from his own billet in the Nissen hut, a semicircle of corrugated iron that ran with water on warm days and grew a sheen of ice on cold ones. The tiny iron stove in the center of the hut could toast one side of anyone standing over it, while his back froze. His clothes were always damp. There was room to hang only socks above the stove. He and François had been the first of the Jedburgh teams to arrive, and had grabbed the lower bunks closest the stove, and put their kit on a third, to reserve it for the American officer who was supposed to join them.

"The Americans are always late," said François. He was lying on his bunk, smoking, as Jack tried to secure his socks so that they would not drop onto the stove and burn. "Three years late in 1914, two years late this time. So they are improving. Maybe our American will turn up next week, bringing us tinned peaches and Lucky Strikes."

"At least they brought us some decent tanks in the desert," Jack said. The socks looked secure. He'd already lost one irreplaceable woolen sock to that damn stove, and even his mother's dedicated knitting could hardly keep on unraveling old cricket pullovers to make him new ones. Maybe if the Americans could bring as many socks as their troops were distributing stockings to the English girls . . . He damped down the uncharitable thought.

"Ah yes," mocked François. "One wonders how we foolish Europeans ever managed our wars without them. Marlborough, Napoleon, Bismarck—if only they had had American tanks."

"Bismarck was no general. He was a politician," said Jack, reasonably.

"So he did more damage, perhaps. The politicians are the enemy, Jack. The ones who tell us what we are supposed to be fighting for, beyond the obvious logic of defending our countries and our women. Beware the politicians. They lost France, nearly lost England, and will probably lose Europe even if we do win this damn war. You are right, my friend, about the Americans and their wealth. They have ensured that we will win this war with their bombers and their tanks and their factories. But I do not think they have understood that the most important war will be the one that comes next, the one against the Communists."

Jack shrugged; François was always talking about Communists. There was no point to telling him that Uncle Joe Stalin and the Red Army were holding down two hundred German divisions on the Eastern Front when the British had been fighting just four of the bastards in Africa. One war at a time was Jack's motto, and he'd count himself lucky if he got through this one.

"You will see, my friend, when we get to France," said François, lighting yet another Players from the stub of the one he had been smoking. "Today it looks as if the Communists are the main part of the Resistance. But the moment we start rallying men to ambush the German columns and blow up the bridges, the Communists will disappear with their weapons. They will disappear and watch us Gaullists die with our patriots, and then they will creep back out from their cellars and use the guns we fly in to take over what is left of France. They will do the same in Italy, in Belgium, and Holland. The next war has started already, my dear innocent Englishman. And the Americans will be late for that one too."

The door of the Nissen hut opened, and a gale blew in. It was followed by a large green kit bag, a curse, and a very wet young man in an almost white belted raincoat and a small pointed forage cap, which seemed designed to steer the rain straight down his face and neck. A big round metal helmet hung from the strap of the gas mask haversack that was slung over one shoulder, and bumped rhythmically against the rifle that hung from the other. He was also burdened by a pistol holster, a map case, an electric torch, and another haversack on his back.

"Do you always carry all that?" inquired François politely, in his precise English.

"Only when I'm traveling light. You ought to see me drop in by parachute," said the American, dumping his burdens one by one and spraying water over the bunks as he flung open his raincoat to approach the stove. Jack stretched out a hand to save one of his socks from falling onto the top of the stove. The other had been spattered with the rain that the American was shaking from his oddly cut dark hair. His head was shaved, except for a wide strip that ran proudly from front to back.

"Captain James Tecumseh McPhee, U.S. Rangers, at your service, gentlemen. Don't ask about the Tecumseh, I get touchy. And I'm so hungry and so wet that I'm touchy enough. Just let me hug this stove and get some warmth into these godforsaken bones, and if one of you guys wants to look inside that big haversack he'll find a bottle of Johnnie Walker's finest, which my ancestors invented specially in order to survive this fucking climate." He put his hands within a millimeter of the glowing stove lid and sighed deeply. Suddenly he broke into French. "We all need one drink, and I need three, and I'm sorry about knocking down the sock."

"They stopped serving dinner about two hours ago, I'm afraid," said Jack. "But I'm sure the cookhouse can do you a SPAM sandwich."

"SPAM," grunted the American. "As my great-grandfather's old commander once said, war is hell." He turned from the stove to the haversack, pulled out a bottle of scotch, a large can of ham, three oranges, a bottle of Martell brandy, and a smaller can that he tossed at the recumbent Frenchman.

"Foie gras," said François, in tones of worship. "I have not seen foie gras since 1940."

"It's my last can. The reason I volunteered for this crazy assignment was that I reckoned it was about the only chance I'd get to find some more." He pulled out another can of ham, and then took a complicated knife from his pocket, prized out a can opener, carved his way efficiently around the rim, and brought out some oatmeal biscuits. He tossed the can opener to François and opened the scotch.

"When my great-grandfather heard General Sherman make his celebrated remark, he thought to himself that war could be made pretty tolerable so long as one kept lots of good friends in the commissariat, a pearl of wisdom that he passed down through the family. I have made bosom buddies of the modern equivalent, the ferry pilots who bring the B-17s over here. A doting mother, a moderately considerate father who was too bad at making money in the twenties to lose any in the Wall Street crash, combines with regular transatlantic flights and a decent scotch ration to permit me to test great-grandpa's theories to the limit. And once we get to France, I guess we live off the land for as long as our livers can take it. Gentlemen, here's to war," and he passed around the scotch.

"You wouldn't happen to have a Sherman tank hidden in that magnificent haversack, old boy?" inquired Jack as he took the bottle. The American's eyebrows lifted, and he smiled sunnily, waiting for Jack to continue. "If we're going to live off the land, as you say, we might find one comes in rather useful."

"The land," intoned François, inhaling the scent of the foie gras on his biscuit, "is not what it was, since the Boches have been at it. But we shall conduct ourselves in the spirit of your admirable great-grandfather, and no doubt we shall get by. And if starvation threatens, we can always count on our intrepid English colleague to catch himself another sheep.

After our last exercise, I can tell you that he is very good at hunting sheep."

"Better than foxes, I guess," said the big American around a mouthful of canned ham. "At least you can eat them."

In the three weeks remaining of their fieldcraft training at Arisaig and Loch Ailort, the American showed that he had little to learn. Fit and fast, and fresh from parachute training and Rangers school in the States, he won grudging praise from the instructors and the affection and respect of the English cavalryman. François, who had already accepted Manners as a comrade of the desert war, was more guarded with the American. It began when McPhee said casually that he had read François's book about the war in Spain, and asked if he had ever some across a college friend who had volunteered for the Lincoln Brigade. Manners had no idea what they were talking about, and had never heard of the book. Nor had he known that François had written one.

"You didn't know our little partner here was a glittering light of the French intelligentsia? College girls back home would buy his book and moon over that sexy photo in the frontispiece even if they couldn't understand a word of it," he explained. "François is the European civilization we're all fighting for, Jack. We're just the rude mechanics, you and me."

"Your Lincoln Brigade were all Communists," said François. "They did what Moscow wanted, not much for Spain."

"Well, I guess some of them probably were," McPhee said lazily. "But the guy I knew, he just wanted to stop fascism. He got back, too. He's in the Marines now, in the Pacific theater. But a lot of British guys went to that International Brigade, Jack. Maybe even some guys you knew."

"Barely knew there was a war on, old boy. I was in Palestine at the time, putting down an Arab rising, and then India, playing polo at

Quetta." Jack laughed. "Great training for tank warfare, polo. The old regiment hung on to the horses as long as they could, then they put us into armored cars. Never could understand why the wretched things didn't go when I tried to feed them oats. The only chap who seemed happy with the conversion was the farrier. He said there wasn't much difference between horseshoes and tank treads."

"You have just been introduced to the subtlety of English humor," François explained. "Jack here fought his way back and forth across Africa two—or was it three?—times. Against the Italians, all the way to Benghazi until Rommel's panzers pushed them back to Egypt. And then back again to Benghazi until Rommel pushed them back to Egypt again."

"See, I told you." Jack laughed again. "Just like polo. We called it the Benghazi handicap."

"A simple soul, our Jack," said François. "No politics in the desert. Just war as a kind of cricket."

"Why aren't you flying, François?" the American wanted to know. "You flew in Spain, shot down a few fascists as I recall."

"The Allies are not short of pilots in this war," François replied. "But there are not enough Frenchmen ready to go back and work with the Resistance. The war in the air is simple. The war on the ground in France will be complicated, at least for me if not for you two. You are just fighting a war. Like all Frenchmen, I have the peace to think about."

When they were posted south to Stevenage for the demolition course, just as the Allies took Sicily and the Italians pulled out of the war, McPhee had the more to learn. He seemed confused between the use of plastic explosives in cutting charges to take out pylons and railway lines, and the ammonal for the lifting charges to destroy bridges. Manners came up with the memory trick that seemed to help him. P for plastic and for precision; A for ammonal and to annihilate. But when they moved on to Huntingford for the course in industrial demolition, the American seemed to get confused again.

"Not too good on destroying things, fellas," as the doctored lubricant grease with the grit that would grind away at industrial bearings smeared itself onto his clothes and face. "I guess it goes against the grain."

They lived in one another's pockets, always training together, given weekend leave passes at the same time. Once, they went back to the Manners family home in Wiltshire, a small country house with one wing that had been rebuilt after the Parliamentarians had destroyed it in the English Civil War. "You would always be a Royalist, Jack," François had laughed, as McPhee shook his head in disbelief at the age of the place and the deferential pleasure of an elderly serving man and the even older cook at the return of the young master. His father, the general, was somewhere in India. His mother appeared for meals, but was otherwise in her garden.

"I guess we know what you're fighting for, Jack." McPhee grinned as they took the train back to London, ready to start the black propaganda course at Watford. "For the King-Emperor and the old landed estate."

"Did you not know, McPhee?" François interrupted. "This was a farewell visit. The house has been requisitioned to become a brigade HQ for American troops. Her ladyship will be moving out into the lodge, from which redoubt she will try to protect her garden against your gallant countrymen."

"I didn't know Mummy had told you about that," said Jack. "But it won't be for long. We get the old place back, once the invasion goes in and the war is over."

"I sure hope the guys take care of it," said McPhee, embarrassed. "Maybe I'll know somebody in the brigade, tell them to look after it."

"A pity you do not know somebody among the Germans who have been occupying my house since 1940," said François.

In the silence that followed, as François smoked and McPhee stared out of the train window, Jack realized that a pattern had been established. The Frenchman needled the American, even when he did not mean to. There was a constant irony in everything that François said, and a bitterness that he did not bother to conceal. Jack took it equably. He had come across far odder types in the desert, and had learned to tolerate eccentricities in the regiment.

They were comrades in arms, bound together by duty and by a common mission, and he admired the Frenchman's brains and grit even if he didn't follow the chap's obsession with politics. But the American seemed in his own way as clever and as well read as François, just as attuned to the political minefield they were heading into, but somehow less nimble than François in discussing it.

"I never asked you, Jack," François broke in. "How do you speak French so well?"

"A governess I had before I went away to school. She was French. And then skiing at Chamonix in the winter, Cap d'Antibes in the summer, I kept in practice. Just seemed to have an ear for it. And never much liked lying on the beach, so I'd go and talk to the fishermen and the waiters," Jack replied. "Then, the interpreter's course was something to do while I was in Quetta. Couldn't play polo all the time. So I was assigned to liaison duties during the phony war, based in a corps HQ at Longwy on your Maginot line. I suppose that's how we first met, when they were looking through the files in Cairo for any odd bod whose docket said he spoke French when you came back with General Koenig's boys, after Bir Hakeim."

François nodded. "And you, McPhee. Your French is good, too."

"Usual way, François. A sleeping dictionary, a *petite amie*. I was in France in 1939, best year of my life. Springtime in Paris, a girl, a crazy idea that maybe I could be a writer. Can't figure whether I fell in love with her or with France, and while I was working it out, I ended up speaking a language I never could handle at school, although they tried hard enough. Hell, you learn a lot in bed."

"Perhaps we should try to find you a pretty teacher of demolitions," laughed Jack. "Then you'd sort out your fuses and your ammonal fast enough."

"Explosions in bed," grinned François. "There's an idea."

"Don't worry about me, you guys. We have the best part of another year of training before we get sent in. Figure it out. We in the Jedburgh teams are meant to drop into France just before the invasion to help coordinate the Resistance. There'll be no invasion this year, not with the American troops still coming in, and the new front in Italy. Besides, the summer's just about over and we can't cross the Channel with the storms coming on. We'd never be able to ensure supplies to the beach-head. So the invasion will be next year, May or June, '44. So we'll drop into France in May. That gives us nine, maybe ten more months. More training. Winter in Scotland, underwater demolitions training in those freezing lochs. I have all the time in the world."

"You are right, of course," François said. "Except for one thing."

"What's that"?

"The Germans. More precisely, the Abwehr and the SD, the Sicher-heitsdienst, and the Gestapo. They are not idle. They roll up the Resis-tance cells with a dismaying regularity. If the clever chaps in Baker Street who devised this whole operation think that there are too few networks on the ground for us to work with when we drop in, they may send some of us in early, to have the time to build up our own teams. At least, that is what my Free French masters think in Duke Street. And since Jean Moulin managed to forge the various Resistance factions into a single structure, the Gaullists probably know the situation better than the Englishmen in SOE."

"But Jean Moulin has gone, disappeared, arrested," said McPhee. "Night and fog, that good old German way."

"It is a dangerous game, Resistance, and a lot of people disappear. It will be dangerous in Europe for a long time I think. After the Germans, we might be playing it against the Russians," said François. "And I think we three will be playing it long before next May, McPhee."

CHAPTER 4

Time: The Present

Lydia had expected to find Clothilde difficult. She would have been entitled to be furious at a wasted trip. Instead, she found the Frenchwoman a comfort, as she helped satisfy the demands of the police for an authoritative opinion on what the stolen rock was and what it might be worth. She was quite splendid with the man who came from the insurance company, informing him that he might count himself fortunate that Lydia had listed the value at a mere ten thousand pounds.

"For once, we can use the word priceless and mean it," she had snapped, eyes ablaze with professional righteousness. Lydia found her admirable. And Clothilde was even useful with the hapless Justin, who was obviously terrified of her. And she bullied the directors into matching the ten thousand pounds she decided her museum could offer as a reward. So after the paperwork and the meetings with directors and the police and insurance affairs had all been dealt with, it was evening, and when Clothilde asked Lydia if she could recommend a quiet hotel, she insisted that the Frenchwoman come and stay with her. It was, she felt, the least she could do. Clothilde wanted to go to Chinatown for dinner, saying it was the one food she missed in Périgord. She devoured most of the Peking duck she insisted they eat, attacked a vast plate of Szechuan beef, chattered amusingly about a holiday she had taken in China, drank three beers, and tried to pay the bill. Lydia, who had seldom enjoyed an evening more, firmly refused.

"I accept only if your auction house is paying," said Clothilde. "And if they are not trying to blame you for all this mess."

"Why do you say that?"

"Because they will want to blame somebody, and you are a woman. That is how male-dominated organizations tend to work. And that was the impression I had at your office."

"I'm afraid you might be right. They were dropping some pretty strong hints about my desk failing to bring in enough money even before this happened."

"Not enough product, or not enough rich clients?" Clothilde grinned. "I know something about your auction houses."

"Not enough of either, not for my preclassical area. I don't seem to be very good at rounding up rich collectors."

"A friend of mine in one of the Paris auction houses, an Egyptologist, had a similar problem," said Clothilde. "So she got the list of all the people who had come to the last few sales of Napoleon's materials—and that is a very big thing in France—made a deal with a travel agency, and offered to guide historical tours of Napoleon's Egyptian expedition. She took them to the site of the battle of the Pyramids, told them about the Rosetta Stone, and then took them down the Nile in a luxurious boat. By the end of the trip, she had a whole new list of clients and made a lot of money. You could do the same."

"That's a splendid idea," said Lydia, trying not to think about the lack of Napoleonic enthusiasts in Britain, or the reluctance of wealthy collectors to visit those remoter parts of Iraq and Central Asia that produced the bulk of her treasures. Quickly, she signed the bill she had charged to her credit card. "That advice is certainly worth a good dinner, even if my company were not paying. Which they are," she lied. But she let Clothilde pay for the taxi.

"You are being very reasonable about this theft," Lydia said when they were back at her apartment, sipping the malt scotch that had sat untouched in the cupboard since the end of the affair with David. "In your place, I would have been outraged."

"Oh, I can be outraged if there is a point to it. But there isn't," said Clothilde. "I am fatalist about thefts, ever since I was burgled as a student. They are a fact of life. And if the police find the rock, then all will be well. But I doubt that they will, so we are left with an even deeper mystery. But then we had a mystery to begin with. Where did it come from, where is the cave of its origin, and why this bull, which is almost certainly by the hands of Lascaux, should be the only miniature we know of? That is three big mysteries that already confront us, and now we have a fourth. Who took it and why?"

"That makes five. Add a sixth—where is it now?"

"I assume an art thief who knew what he was doing somehow heard about the find and broke in. If so, he will try to sell it, and we may hear of it that way. Or when he realizes there is no market for these things, he will find a way to accept the reward we have offered. And then we are back where we started, examining the rock for any clues to its provenance. But I shall start on that next week. We have a national laboratory that does computer enhancement, and I already sent them your digital photos. I am almost certain already that this is no modern copy, but that should make sure. And since you photographed the backs and the sides of the rock, we have a chance to narrow down the geology."

"I wish I shared your confidence. I keep thinking the thief could simply destroy it. Or we might never hear of it again. Remember that this rock has sat in an Englishman's home for fifty years, and nobody had the slightest idea that it existed. So presuming it does come from an unknown cave, its secret has been well kept."

"That is the part of the mystery that intrigues me. It even excites me," said Clothilde. "This Englishman worked with the Resistance in Périgord. So there are records. We can track down the people he worked with, ask the old men who still survive from those days. There are some friends of my father where I can make a start."

"Was your father in the Resistance there?"

"Yes. He was shot by the Germans, but some of his old comrades are still alive."

"I'm sorry, I had no idea."

Clothilde shrugged and reached into her bag for another cigarette. "I never knew him. He was shot during the Liberation, a few months before I was born. And then my mother married again, after the war, so I had another father, a good man. A teacher, still alive. He and my mother still live in the district, and he writes about local history. He wrote a book that was quite controversial, about the Resistance. These things still matter, in France, to the old men and some of the politicians."

"It must have made things complicated, when you and Horst were together. His being a German."

"Not for me. I was born after the Liberation. So was he. These were things other people had done, not us. My adoptive father felt the same way. He liked Horst. But for my mother, it was difficult. And Horst is not very German, if you understand me. He is more like an American, in some ways. He studied in America, you know. He drove a French car, spoke French well—almost as well as he speaks English."

"I rang him today with the bad news, told him not to bother to come to London because there was nothing to see. He was much more furious than you," Lydia said. "He said he'd probably come over anyway, to talk to the owner, see if he could find out any more about where the rock came from."

"That's Horst," Clothilde smiled, rather fondly. "Once he gets his teeth into something, he doesn't give up easily. Maybe that's the German in him. Or the scholar. And he's right, what's more. The Englishman who first had the rock is the key to this. We assume that he brought it back from the war as a trophy, from the Périgord. So either he found it, or somebody gave it or sold it to him. Your Englishman was no scholar, and his son thinks he was no expert on the caves and the paintings and never showed any more interest in the matter. So it seems logical that he did not find it himself. Somebody local must have helped him or shown him, and then had some very strong reason to keep quiet. And who did he know locally?"

"The Resistance," said Lydia.

"Exactly. So that is where I shall start. But perhaps you could help, Lydia. There must be records here about his military career, where he served, where he was. Could you find that for me, and the names of any networks that he worked with, any reports that he wrote?"

"Yes, I'd like to do that. There must be records in France, too."

"There are the *Compagnons de la Résistance*. They are like a club of the old comrades, and they must have archives and memoirs. I can ask them, as the daughter of a Resistance man. Maybe the Communists will have something. My father was with them from before the war. I think he might even have been a party member. A lot of them were, in the Resistance. I will ask my mother, although my stepfather might know more. He will certainly know all about the local records and archives. Then there is a place in Bordeaux, the *Centre Jean Moulin*, which is named after one of the Resistance heroes, the one who was caught and tortured by Klaus Barbie of the Gestapo. You remember the Barbie trial?"

"Vaguely," said Lydia. "I never had much reason to be interested before. But I think I might be seeing the son again. He asked me to lunch, and I owe him an explanation about the theft. I can ask him what he knows about his father in the war." Lydia refilled their glasses, and grinned at Clothilde. "He's not bad-looking, if you like the military type. Officer and gentleman. No longer young."

"The military does that to them, after a certain rank. They age years with each promotion. Catch them young, and they can be very exciting. But then they get accustomed to commanding things and become tiresome, unless you want to make the effort. And having taken one look at military wives, I never wanted to join them. Garrison towns and being polite to the general's wife. Not for me," she grimaced. "Do you like soldiers?"

"I never came across one before."

"There is no sign of a man in your apartment," Clothilde said directly.

"No razors in the bathroom, you mean?" Lydia laughed as she felt herself blushing. "The last time there was a man in my life, he was far too discreet to leave anything like that. He always carried a portable electric razor and a clean shirt."

"I would not trust that type," Clothilde sniffed. "Always ready for adventure. And that, in my view, is a woman's prerogative."

At the Savoy Grill, which Major Manners said was the only place he really knew for lunch in London apart from his club, Lydia solemnly handed him a company check for ten thousand pounds with her apologies for the loss of his possession.

"That is the value I placed on it. That is what our insurance therefore pays out, or will if they know what's good for them, even though the rock was not placed in our storeroom," she said, and sipped her champagne.

"I therefore owe you two thousand pounds," he said, smiling.

"Under the terms of our agreement." He was wearing a town suit today, a good one in dark blue, a striped shirt, a tie that looked regimental. His handkerchief was still in his cuff. She could detect no aftershave, which pleased her. There was an awful lot of male cologne in the art world, and she did not care for it.

"No," she said firmly. "That was contingent on my doing some work that resulted in the sale of your rock, or at least its amicable disposal in a way that left you with no further obligations to France or anyone else. That is hardly the case now," she said, thinking of the band of journalists and TV cameras thronging the street outside the salesrooms. "But there is one thing that troubles me. You barely mentioned your father's service in wartime France when we spoke. Now I find that the President of France makes a private visit to his funeral. You must have known France was very important to him."

"Naturally I did, but not from my father," Manners said easily. The question did not seem to embarrass him in the least. "His reminiscences were all about the Middle East and North Africa, a bit of India. He hardly spoke of France at all. Nor did we visit it much when I was growing up. It was always Austria or Switzerland for the skiing, and summers in Scotland. He took me fishing, taught me to shoot. That kind of thing. Never much of a one for beaches or casinos. The south of France was never his style."

"Did he never go back to Périgord?"

"Not that I know. But I can't say I followed his movements closely," he said. She did not know him well enough even to guess whether this straightforward, rather bluff manner of the plain-speaking officer and gentleman was real, or just a surface skin he wore, like a uniform. She had never known any soldiers. Perhaps they were all this way; what you saw was what you got. But Manners had a quick mind, possibly even a subtle one. She suspected there was more to him than he wanted to display—at least, she cautioned herself, display to *her*.

"What about Paris?" she asked him. "Catching up with his friend

François Malrand, the rising political star. Did he keep up with his old comrade-in-arms, de Gaulle's protégé?"

"Maybe he went when I was at school or when he was serving in NATO. I think he was stationed there in some staff job when the HQ was still at Fontainebleau. before de Gaulle kicked them out to Brussels in the 1960s." He shrugged and fell silent as the waiter came with their smoked salmon. "He went off to the races at Longchamps from time to time, I seem to recall. He won a lot of money once."

Remember his father, she told herself. There was obviously a lot more to old Colonel Manners than he had ever allowed to meet the eye. Working underground with the French Resistance, staying on the run from the Germans. That must have meant something to do with Intelligence, a skill at keeping secrets. Perhaps his son was the same way, hidden depths.

"Fathers can have a lot of privacy in our kind of family," he went on. "I was away at school, and he'd retired before I went to Sandhurst. Maybe they sometimes met in London. I wouldn't know. But that friendship didn't seem to play a big part in his life. He said nothing when Malrand won the election. I found no letters among his things, and I was as surprised as anyone else when the French ambassador rang to say that the President planned to come to the funeral. I'm slightly surprised you knew. It was kept very quiet."

"Until the newspapers got hold of it, you mean."

"Yes, until then." He ate neatly, she noticed, without paying much attention to the food. Lydia was getting rather tired of foodies; men who made exaggerated talk of sauces and dishes and treated fashionable restaurants as if they were something to do with art.

"Did Malrand come to your house after the funeral?" she asked, making the question casual. She felt uncomfortable, turning the conversation into an interrogation.

"Of course, took a drink, said some gracious things. Stayed about ten minutes. He'd said a few words at the grave, about my father being a great friend of France. That sort of thing. Spoke very good English."

"Did he look around the house, go to your father's study? I'm wondering whether he may have seen the rock—I presume it was on display in your father's room."

"No, I don't recall him being anywhere but the hall and the main drawing room. He strolled around the garden with me a bit, saying he remembered it from the war. Apparently he'd been to stay with my father. He spoke about my grandmother and her garden, made me walk him up the drive to the lodge, where she lived when the Americans took over the house." He put down his knife and fork, finished his champagne.

"But I see what you mean. If my father had picked it up in France, that was the time they were working together in Périgord. He may have known something about it. But if my father was up to no good and pinching bits of France's glorious heritage, then the President of France would hardly have gone out of his way to honor the memory of someone he suspected as a thief. As for the old man's study, it was a bit of a mess. Books and maps everywhere. He always had some thought of writing his memoirs. Never did, or at least nothing I ever saw or found beyond some notes. There were maps of the Western Desert all over the place, spread on tables and window ledges. The rock was behind one of them, on a bookcase. But it wasn't in plain sight, even if Malrand had looked in. He did ask me, though, if my father had ever finished his memoirs. They knew one another well enough for that. The only other sign of his time in France was his copies of Malrand's books; each signed by the author. I started one of his novels, but couldn't finish it. Not my kind of thing. But I liked his book about the war in Spain back in the 1930s.

"You seem jolly interested in all this," he went on, picking at the salad the waiter had brought them. He didn't seem very pleased with it. But he had not been much interested in the food, simply ordering what she had already chosen. "It must be your American curiosity."

"Nothing American about it," she said, suddenly conscious of her accent. "Anyway, my mother's Scottish."

"But you are American, or Canadian. And not just by your speech. It's your manner—you are very direct, very determined, going straight to the point. Look at the way you put me to the question all through lunch. And your interest in the origins of this rock of mine is a lot more than I'd have expected."

"Why do you say that? That 'rock of yours' was entrusted to our care. We lost it. And the police do not seem at all hopeful of getting it back. They said it was a very professional job, by someone who knew what he was looking for and exactly where to find it."

"That must narrow down the list of suspects," he said.

"Well, it narrows it down to those people who had seen a copy of the next day's *Times*, and the first edition was on sale in London by eleven P.M. on the night of the theft. And then it was on the paper's Internet site before midnight and on the BBC Radio news at the same time. A million people could have seen or heard it, noticed the reference to the auction house and me. There are some very alert thieves in the art world."

"But you are not responsible for its loss. It was stolen. There's a difference," he protested.

"I still feel responsible, and not only to you. There's a responsibility to the thing itself, as a piece of history or a work of art. We still don't know if it's genuine. We still don't know its provenance. There may be a marvelous cave out there somewhere. That's what my German expert says, and he seems pretty keen on tracking it down."

"What about that French woman from the museum?"

"Clothilde—she was quite ready to pay you an honorarium for the piece. And she has arranged for the museum to offer a reward for its return, which may be the best chance of getting it back. She wanted it, just from seeing the photographs. But she said they are always looking for new caves, some long-term project with an echo sounder or something. It was all a bit technical for me. She seemed pretty confident they'd find it eventually, if it is there to be found. But what do you do now, cash the check and forget it?"

He sat back and looked her squarely in the eye. "Cash the check, certainly. Send you your commission. But then—well, I'm between postings and have some leave. I was in Bosnia for eighteen months, and then I start a staff college course in September. I thought I might spend some of this windfall on a trip to Périgord, look around my father's old stamping ground. Visit a few of these caves and see what all the fuss is about."

"You'll probably run into this German chap, Horst, and into Clothilde, whom you would find amusing," said Lydia, suddenly wondering if Manners was the French woman's type. She smiled to herself. She wouldn't give him much chance of escaping Clothilde's clutches if the Frenchwoman decided on a summer fling with a dashing English officer. Dashing, there was a word she had never used before in connection with a man. She rather liked the sound of it.

"Will you take your family?" she asked, suddenly curious.

"The family isn't really mine anymore. That is, I was married, but it didn't survive a couple of long tours in Northern Ireland. I was divorced six years ago. My son and daughter are away at school and I only get to see them on the holidays. My ex-wife lets me take them skiing and sailing, and to pantomimes. I brought them back to my father's place last summer and taught them to ride. We went to a Club Med the year before that, the kind of place that keeps them busy." He looked suddenly rather sad, Lydia thought. He forced his face into a slightly twisted grin. "As you can tell, I miss them. But what about you? You said your mother was Scottish. And your father?"

"American, from Minnesota, with lots of Norwegian ancestors."

"How did your parents meet?"

"He did his military service in the Air Force, based in Scotland, in the education branch. He told me he spent his free time helping out at some experimental theater in Edinburgh, and that's where they met. She was a teacher. They married, went back to Minnesota, and went slowly broke running a bookstore, so he ended up teaching in the local school." She was going to stop there, but Manners's silence was sympathetic. She didn't want to tell him about the cross-country skiing trips and her father's ramshackle bookshelves and the piles of paperbacks in the bathroom and the magic of his bedtime stories. Time to change the subject. She drank some water, put the glass down decisively. "Ten thousand pounds will finance quite a luxurious jaunt around Périgord for you." She smiled to herself, thinking that Clothilde would certainly help him to spend it.

"Eight thousand pounds. You keep forgetting your cut," he objected. "I mean it, Lydia. We had a deal, and what's more you gave me good and honest advice. You persuaded me that this damn rock deserves to be back in its place, rather than in my father's old dusty study, or adorning the wall of some overpriced penthouse. And you were the one who spotted what it was, or what it might be. You gave me the courtesy of your expertise. You earned the money."

"I told you, I couldn't accept it." She had been in England long enough to feel faintly embarrassed at talk of money. At least, of her money. And she wished he would not press her. It was out of his character, somehow.

"Well, I have an alternative proposal," he suggested, tentatively. "Please don't misunderstand this, but why don't you come too? If you won't accept the money, let me put it to good use by financing your trip. You are interested, and you know a damn sight more about these caves and the art than I do. I'm sure you'd like to see the caves, and you have the contacts in place, people like your Clothilde and your German chap. You say you feel responsible to the piece as a work of art, and here's your chance to do something about it. Do come. Separate rooms, naturally."

She looked at him, startled. What an extraordinary suggestion. She hardly knew the man. "What do you mean, a chance to do something about it? If there's one place the rock won't be, it's back in its home ground in Périgord?"

"How do you know? But if there is a black market trade in the stuff, rich and secretive collectors, that's going to be the center of it. I take your point about a million people potentially knowing that the rock was in your building on the night it was stolen. But only one in a thousand would know its value, and only one in a thousand of them would be in a position to do something about it. Burglaries aren't set up at a moment's notice, at least not this kind."

"I'm no detective," she protested. "This is something for the police."

"And do the police know the art world as well as you do? Do the police have the slightest idea of the kind of work this is, what it comes from and what it means. Do they know its context? It will probably all fizzle out, but it will give a purpose to our trip. I'm all for learning my way around the caves and the prehistoric paintings and all that, but I always like to have some point to my holidays. I'm not one just to potter round open-jawed with a guidebook like some casual tourist."

"Anyway, I couldn't possibly accept your kind offer. I don't like people paying my way, and this is just another way for you to bestow money on me that I don't deserve," she said. "Nor could I get away. I have two sales here in England next week and another one in Milan."

"Splendid, I'll need another week to wrap up my father's affairs with the lawyer, and you can meet me in Les Eyzies on the way back from Milan."

"Major Manners . . ." She imagined her mother at her elbow, prodding her to accept, just as she had always accepted invitations on Lydia's behalf throughout her childhood.

"Lydia, please, call me Philip."

"Major Manners, I fear this is not a good idea." So there, Mother. But then, even more forcefully than the thought of her mother came the thought of what Clothilde would say.

"Well, let me put it another way. I'm out of practice at this, Lydia, but I'm also asking you because I enjoy your company and I want to get to know you better. If I am going to fulfill my own responsibility to this piece of rock that my father owned, then I have to know more about it. So in your own terms, and you are the one who made me think this way, then I need your professional services, quite apart from the fact that I also find your company congenial. So please come."

"Let me think about it," she temporized, suddenly reminded of Clothilde's plan to recruit clients by organizing historical tours. The caves of Périgord, good food and wine, an undemanding lecture from Clothilde, it could be an agreeable jaunt for wealthy art lovers with a vague interest in prehistory. And it would be a very useful idea to float at the auction house. A preliminary reconnaissance would certainly be required. She looked at Manners thoughtfully. "In the meantime, if you are serious about doing something about this rock of yours, there is something you could do. The place to start would be your father's war record, what he did, with whom he worked in France, any clues to the people that he may have met, someone who might have given him the rock or showed him where to find it. As his son, presumably you could get those easily. At least it would be somewhere to start."

"There's a good idea," he said. "But then in a way, I suppose I already started. I wrote off to Malrand when you first told me about the theft, asking if he could shed any light on my father's time in Périgord. I told him about the rock, and apologized for what seemed to be a pretty shabby bit of souvenir hunting. After all, as President of France, it's almost his property."

CHAPTER 5

The Vézère Valley, 15,000 B.C.

D eer knelt on the grassy slope before the cave, his head bowed in submission, as the shapes emerged through the morning mist. The apprentices, after a surprised glance, ignored him. The Keeper of the Bulls came to stand over him, saying nothing for a long moment, and then moved on into the cave. Then came the old man he had been waiting for, the Keeper of the Bison. To his relief, Deer saw that the Keeper of the Horses was with him, the one man he knew who would speak for him.

"I seek your pardon for my clumsiness and anger," Deer said as the

Keeper of the Bison stood before him. The old man leaned on his stick, studying the youth as his breathing eased. Then he hawked and spat to one side. Deer kept down the blaze of anger. The old fool must know that he had simply slipped and fallen, that Deer had not jolted him from his perch. Maybe by now he had convinced himself it really was Deer's fault. He kept his eyes downcast.

"I collected these, to ease your bruises," Deer went on, proffering the three kinds of herbs on the flat stone. The old woman had told him what kind to gather, and he had been in the woods before dawn broke to seek them.

Seeing the old man remain immobile, the Keeper of the Horses bent and took the flat stone. "The boy has some sense, after all. These are the same that I was given, when I fell from the honey tree," he said. "It seems he means it, his apology."

"Perhaps," said the old man, studying Deer. "How good do you think he is?"

"At the work? I don't have to tell you. I'll show you," and the two Keepers walked uphill into the cave. Deer remained on his knees, waiting, knowing that the old man was being taken far into the cave, down the cluster of rocks at the end, and around the narrow twist into the next chamber to see the deer he had painted, swimming in the river of rock. He hoped the old man kept his feet. Deer's knees hurt him, although he had thought to bring handfuls of soft leaves to kneel on. As he waited, he fingered his bare neck, wondering whether this would be enough to let him wear the feather of the apprentice painter again.

They kept him waiting all through the day, as the sun rose high in the sky to clear the mist. He could see the fishers haul the long, curving fence of woven reeds and twigs deep into the water, as the older children were sent upstream to splash and throw stones and drive the fish into the calm water where the fishers waited, their spears poised. As the excited children came closer, shrieking and tossing great fans of water droplets into the air to catch the sunlight, Deer saw the boiling on the surface of the water as the fish darted for cover. The spears of the fishers rose and fell, like herons' beaks. The boiling suddenly became intense inside the lagoon made by the reed fence, and the men in midstream began pushing the end of the fence back to the shore, turning it back upon itself to capture the fish within. The women clambered into the river, pushing their reed baskets beneath the surface and then hauling them out, gleaming flashes of silver as the fish jerked and tossed as they were carried back to the bank.

The distraction took his mind from the numbing pain in his knees and the heat of the sun upon his sweating body. There were two bright fires inside each of his knees, burning deep into the bone. If he sank back to rest his weight on his haunches, his feet blazed with agony from the tiny pebbles on the ground. If he rose to ease his feet, his thighs groaned achingly. He dared not lean forward to rest his weight upon his hands. Twice, he heard a shuffling sound from the mouth of the cave, as if someone had come out to watch him. Once, he saw a flash of eyes in the woods to his left. He kept his gaze firmly forward, wondering if the children might start throwing stones to torment him, hoping that the fishing would keep them down by the river all day.

He was still there at dusk, when the Keepers came out of the cave, and the fires down by the river were beginning to flare in the long twilight of summer. The other apprentices were told to go home, and three Keepers suddenly loomed over him.

"I am getting old, and need young bones to fetch my water and take the ache from my shoulders after a day in the cave," said the Keeper of the Bison. "You seem to have some knowledge of the healing plants. You will come with me and do my bidding, but you are too clumsy to work with me in the cave."

His head still bowed in contrition, Deer fought to understand. He was no longer to serve the women, but to be nursemaid to an old man. That wasn't what he wanted. He wanted to get back to the work of the cave. His face twisted, and he began to shake his head.

"You will be apprenticed to me in the cave," said Keeper of the

Horses, quickly, warningly. "I have much work to do, and need the extra hands."

"Here," said the Keeper of the Bulls, holding out a leather thong with a small feather attached. "Go with the Keeper of the Bison, and give him your young arm to clamber back up the hill tomorrow. Then make colors, and when they are done, join your new master. He spoke for you. And remember this time of your banishment from the cave. One more mistake, and out you go, forever."

As they walked off, Deer collapsed onto his side, trying to roll onto his back, but his legs would not obey him. His knees would not straighten. He groaned aloud as he tried to shuffle on his hands down the hill after the Keepers, dragging his useless, fiery legs behind him. Suddenly there were feet beside him, the shocking coolness of water splashed onto his back, a great handful of dripping moss wiped across his face and he sucked greedily at the moisture as firm hands began to slap and grip his thighs. He felt a great softness as someone sat on his legs, trying to straighten his locked knees. His joints blazed with a final pain, and then eased, and Little Moon helped him stagger to his feet and down the hill to the river.

At his sister's fire, the Keeper of the Bulls sat watching his newborn daughter gurgle in her sleep. He had taken her to his chest, listened to her heart, acknowledging that she was his, wondering if in some years to come she would grow to resemble her mother, and benefit some future man with her advice as her mother had helped him. The baby stirred, and his sister casually put the infant to her breast.

"Where will you sleep now?" she asked.

"Here," he grunted. Near his new daughter. He owed his wife that much. If she cried, he could always move. All fires were open to the Keeper of the Bulls. He took a twig, peeled it, and began probing at his teeth where some of the fish was stuck. He should have saved one of the fish bones from his meal. That was the kind of thing wives remembered to do.

"You need another woman now," his sister said. She gestured at the baby. "Her mother would have been the first to say so."

"I know." He looked into the fire. "I will speak to the Keeper of the Horses. He has a daughter, I hear."

"She is young. But comely."

"Too young?"

"Girls are never too young, at least to warm your bed and tend your fire and your meals," she said lightly, passing her hand softly over the beating pulse in the head of the baby at her breast. "But you want more than that. You want company, like you always talked to this child's mother, talking and murmuring into the night. You never talked much with the other men, even when you were a boy. You always liked talking with women. And Little Moon is too young for that. She has everything you need except wisdom."

"All the better. I can teach her wisdom myself, my wisdom."

"You could, but then you'd never know if you were hearing her wisdom or just your own. You want more than that," she said.

He considered her, his youngest sister, whose eyes were as cool a gray as his own. She had always been close to him, since he was a youth and she was an infant, accustomed to crawling into his lap and settling there to sleep. He had taken great care over her marriage, entrusting her to the bravest of the young hunters, the one who would lead the hunting pack someday. That had not worked out too well, since her man had come back with a leg mangled after fighting some hungry wolves away from a new-killed deer. He walked with a limp, still the most cunning of the hunters, but he would never lead the pack. He shrugged; men could not order the ways of the beasts.

"You remember Leaping Hare, my husband's friend," she said, almost carelessly. That meant she had something important to say.

"He died, fighting the wolves. He saved your man," said the Keeper. He remembered the sad trail of dejected hunters, carrying the corpse, the wounded man, and the reindeer they had saved from the wolves. They were exhausted as they staggered back to the river. He remembered the keening from the woman, the way his sister had run to meet the forlorn little band, her hand to her throat, and remembered the woman with her, who had sunk to her knees and cried the death song over her man in a high, shrieking voice. Not a voice he would want to hear at his fire each night.

"He left a woman—Silver Eel," his sister went on. "She has no children. She is a daughter to the fisher clan, and my friend. Still young, but wise. She will be a healer, some day."

"This Silver Eel, she has passed her time of mourning?"

"Long since. And she needs a man." She paused, considering whether to say anything else. He waited as she pondered. Finally his sister said, "She helped me all day with your baby."

"You said she was barren."

"No, I said she had no children. Not by Leaping Hare. But Leaping Hare sired no young. Whatever you say, we women know it is not always the woman who is barren."

"Summon her here to your fire tomorrow, before I go to the cave," he said, his eyes on his new daughter. He trusted his sister's judgment, but he remembered that high voice. "Say nothing to her. I would first see and talk with this comely young daughter of the Keeper of the Horses. I am in no hurry."

Farther down the riverbank, at a fire where the guts of fish still sizzled in the embers, the Keeper of the Horses studied his youngest daughter, his favorite. She had been a pretty child, and now she was as lovely as her mother had been. He loved to watch her, each movement graceful, even now as she turned to pick another bough, and placed it carefully on the fire. He had seen her help Deer down to the riverbank, before darting back here to his hearth. Deer and Little Moon, that would be an interesting match. Not a good match, for Deer had neither father nor mother still living, and no brothers. Deer would bring only himself to the family of the woman he took, no influence or honor, except what he could build for himself as the most talented of the apprentices.

Thoughtfully, he probed his teeth with a fish bone. Deer was a gifted youth, and a clever one, clever enough to take his advice, and to display the right contrition. Deer could go far. He would be a Keeper soon, the youngest of them. That would be honor enough. Little Moon liked him, that was clear.

But Deer was a wayward lad, too proud, too sure of himself. Too young to understand the ways of the Keepers, to accept that they had to show a proper respect for one another, even when their powers were fading. Or even when they had never had much talent in the first place, like the Keeper of the Bison. Deer as a Keeper would upset the delicate balance of respect inside the cave, unless Deer would consent to be guided by his wisdom. Deer's talent, cautioned and schooled by the Keeper of the Horses' advice to keep his pride and his temper under control. That could work. Deer had no father; he would listen to the father of his woman.

Across the fire, Little Moon put a testing finger into the clay-lined hole in the ground where the water was warmed by hot stones. She took a clump of moss, dipped it into the warm water, and began to cleanse her face and neck before she slept. Always neat and clean, his Little Moon, with breath that smelled like honey.

But could his advice and counsel be enough to control Deer from another clash in the cave? The Keeper of the Bulls was his friend, he supposed, certainly the most valued of his colleagues. But there was an ambition there, a sense of power. He virtually dominated the cave already. If not for me, he thought, the Keeper of the Bulls would decide everything, from the design of the cave to the colors they used to the choice of apprentices. There would be a clash, someday, between the Keeper of the Bulls and Deer. Keeper of the Deer, he corrected himself. A clash like that between aging father and growing son, between an old bull and the young one. Keeper of the Bulls would not content himself with this cave. He would want other caves, greater grandeur for his work, more honor to his bulls, more Keepers and apprentices to dominate. He already was the loudest voice in council, using the authority of the cave to push his views against the leaders of the fisher clan and the hunters and the flint men. He was hungry for power in a worrying way.

"You went up the hill to the cave, my daughter, and came back with a limping man," he said softly.

"Deer could not walk, my father, after kneeling all day. I took him damp moss, and gave him my arm to come back to the village."

"While the rest of us were eating, you left with some fish rolled into bark."

"He had not eaten. We had plenty."

"You like Deer, my daughter?"

"It was hard, to make him serve the women; and to take away his necklace so that he had no place among us."

"That is over now." She was good at not answering questions, this daughter of his.

"Deer will be a Keeper soon, a man with an honored place. And soon you will be of an age to take a man."

Silence from his daughter, a silence so dense he could almost touch it.

"Your mother has talked to you of this, of taking a man, tending his hearth," he went on.

"Of course I have," his woman snapped, her voice muffled from the skins she was wrapped in. He had wondered if she were really asleep. "If we had to wait for men to start telling their daughters about the life that awaits them, we'd wait forever. And what I have told her is to stay away from the bold young boys. But she's your daughter—she never listens. Now you had better make sure she listens to you."

"You will listen to me, Little Moon," he said. "You will not go to Deer again without my permission. You must not even think of him as a man until he becomes a Keeper. You will not go with any of the young men, but will stay by your mother all day and do her bidding. Do you hear me?"

"Yes, Father. But it was staying by my mother that I met Deer, when you punished him by sending him to work with the women. So that must have had your approval," she said boldly.

No fool, his daughter. As quick of tongue as she was quick of foot. He smiled to himself; she'd be a handful for any man, just like her mother.

"You know what I mean, Little Moon," he said, leaning forward to dip the moss into the warm water and swab his face before he pushed the big log deep into the fire and crawled into the skins alongside his woman. "And there are many other men in the tribe beside Deer."

"But he is the best painter of all the apprentices. You said so yourself," Little Moon said softly, almost to herself. "And he respects you most of all."

He gave no reply, easing himself alongside the curving, familiar warmth of his woman.

"Now see what you've done, you old fool," his woman murmured fondly, taking his hand to fold it to her breast. "Always meddling, that's you."

CHAPTER 6

The Audrix Plateau, Périgord, 1944

The elderly Lockheed Hudson ground through the night, the engines hammering so loudly that Jack thought every German in France must hear them. He was cold and he knew he was frightened, and wondered if he looked half as calm as François and McPhee had done as they pulled themselves easily into the plane ahead of him. McPhee was still cursing good-humoredly at the waste of all his parachute training. Expecting to drop into France, they learned at the briefing that they would land on a makeshift grass strip, then the aircraft would load up with a return group of passengers to fly back to RAF

Tempsford. It felt too ordinary, Jack thought, to mark his first foray onto enemy-held soil. Well, the first in Europe, at least. He had been behind Jerry lines often enough in the desert, if anybody was ever really sure where the lines were.

"Three minutes." The curtain behind the cockpit was flicked back and a head came out to shout the warning. They had been flying for nearly four hours, as calmly and as quietly as if it had been one of those prewar flights from London to Paris. No sudden maneuvers, no hard turns or dives, and not a trace of flak. It seemed almost too easy. Slowly the plane tipped over onto one wing. That meant they were circling, looking for the lights of the landing zone. They had devices these days, he knew. S-phones that let the copilot talk to the reception team on the ground, and Eureka sets that brought the aircraft in precisely to a ground beacon. They were carrying two more Eureka sets on this trip, for delivery to the French, part of the cargo that was strapped down behind him. Guns and radio sets, ammo and grenades and plastic explosives. He knew the stuff was safe enough without a detonator, even in a crash. At least he knew that in theory, but his flesh still crawled at the thought of the potential explosion piled up behind him. Silly, really. In a crash, the cargo would crush him into a pulp long before any explosion. The plane leveled out and then turned again on to the opposite wing. The pilot must have seen the three landing lights, got the right recognition signal showing it was the Digger network waiting down there and not the Germans. The engine note fell back as they lost height and he felt the flaps go down, heard the grinding of the undercarriage as they prepared to land.

"Jean-Marie, the dog has had three black puppies." Jack bet that was theirs. Among all the usual lists of family messages and snatches of poetry that came with the news bulletins on the BBC French services, he suspected that was the one to prepare the reception committee for this night's landing. He had felt some unconscious echo of recognition for Jean-Marie's puppies. It was almost a tradition before the teams flew out, listening to the previous night's radio messages and wondering which was theirs. He imagined the Germans listening in frustration as they heard these public broadcasts beaming out from the powerful British transmitters, knowing they were hearing coded orders and alerts and confirming drop zones for the secret war in France, and not having the slightest idea what they meant.

The engines were throttled back sharply. A thump, a bounce, and they were down, careering jerkily along some French plateau. And if they were lucky, not a German within miles. Don't speak too soon, he told himself. A German ambush never opened up when the aircraft was landing, only when it was down and they could bag the lot.

The landing went on, it seemed forever, as the aircraft lurched like a tractor over a plowed field. He tried to look at François, give him a thumb's-up, but he could see nothing in the darkness of the plane's hold. Then he felt a friendly slap on his knee as the plane slowed, and began its turn. McPhee. He leaned forward, gave a thump on the broad back in return. The engines revved again. The pilot would taxi back all the way to his landing point, ready to take off into the wind with the minimum of time on the ground.

This was the most uncomfortable ride he had ever had in his life, worse than a tank going over ditches. His mouth already dry with tension, he made himself gulp and breathe deeply. The flight hadn't bothered him at all; it would be too shaming to get travel sickness while taxiing, or to throw up at his first sight of France. Finally, they stopped, the engines just ticking over. The copilot came out to open the hatch and guide them out. The two radio operators went first, each reaching up for the suitcases that held their sets. Then François, McPhee, and then him. François was already embracing somebody on the ground. Shapes dashed past him, reaching up into the belly of the plane to take out the cargo. Another figure loomed at his side, slapped him on the shoulder, and hustled him away, muttering words of welcome amid gusts of garlic.

He tripped over something metallic and noisy, hurting his leg, Barbed wire! No, bicycles. Then came a whiff of warm engine oil and he saw the shape of a farm tractor. At the far side of the bicycles, a group of people in coats began walking toward the Hudson for the long flight back. One of them was a woman. Perhaps he should warn her not to bother taking back French perfume. The girls back at Tempsford and in Baker Street got so much that they used it in their cigarette lighters.

Apart from the pitch darkness, the field was like a busy station platform when the express was about to leave. There seemed to be people everywhere, a whole village turned out for the event. He heard children's laughter. Men rushed about with trolleys, calling to one another. The tractor started up. He was pushed aside as women picked up bicycles. The plane's engines built into a roar. Another push on his shoulder, and then he saw the glow of the cigarette and recognized François. McPhee was with him and a man with his arm around François's shoulder led them away from the bicycles, through a gap in a hedge into a field that was heady with the rich stench of manure, and where there was a small truck. They were all piled into the back, banging into milk churns and trying to untangle their legs as the truck moved off, gears grinding. He no longer heard the plane, but it must be off by now. England was a long way back, and his nausea had passed, although his stomach was tight. And suddenly, as if on a signal, they all began to laugh, great gusts of it as they pounded each other's shoulders and backs. The Jedburgh team was down safely and racketing along some country lane. Somewhere in France in a truck that stank of sour milk and dark French tobacco. All according to plan.

The barn was dry but cold, the straw banked against the walls, their rucksacks leaning against them. The man who had led them to the truck reached behind one of the straw bales and pulled out a bottle of cognac and a small, thick glass. François drank it first, and then the Frenchman, and they embraced again.

"My brother Christophe," said François, introducing them. "We call him Berger, the shepherd."

Berger stood back, looked at his brother in khaki, his hand stretching out to finger the Cross of Lorraine on one sleeve, and then looked at Jack in his English battledress, at McPhee in his olive drab. He was dressed like a farmer, in a flat cap and moleskin trousers, a patched old overcoat that was held together with string. His hands were dirty, but Jack noticed that the nails were well cut. And when he spoke, it was the French of an educated man.

"My God, what are we to do with three men in uniform?" he asked. Jack thought it was a fair question. But that was policy for the Jedburgh teams. They were not spies, to skulk around pretending to be Frenchmen. They were not meant to go near towns, but to stay out in the countryside with the Maquis. Their uniforms were deliberate, to boost the morale of the cold and hungry French boys who had taken to the hills and woods rather than be conscripted to go and work in German factories, to remind them that they were soldiers. It should also mean, with any luck, that if Jack or McPhee were captured they would not be shot as spies.

"You put us to work, Christophe," said François kindly. "You take us to every group of Maquis you know from here to Limoges and down to Cahors, and we call in the arms drops and we show them what to do."

"So the invasion is that close?" his brother asked eagerly.

"I doubt it, not this early in the year. But we need time to teach them, time to organize, time to rebuild. The Gestapo has been busy. Apart from you and Hilaire, there are not many networks left."

"You know Hilaire is coming up to see you?"

"And you know these suspicious Allies of ours," Francois grinned. "The gentlemen of Baker Street want to make sure their star agent keeps a close eye on dangerous Gaullists like you and me. The same with our two Anglo-Saxon friends here. Baker Street needs you and me to set up the network, Christophe, but they send these two Francophones along to watch us." François winked, to take the sting out of the remark, but Jack didn't think he was joking. Nor, from the level way he looked at Jack and McPhee, did Christophe.

"But equally you can keep an eye on us, François," said the Englishman. "Make sure we don't call in any arms drops for those Communists you're always grumbling about."

"You see, Christophe? You must be careful of this man," smiled François. "You might think he looks and sounds like just another stupid English cavalry officer. Don't be fooled. They sent us a brainy one."

"Jesus, now I know why the Krauts have been winning this war," said McPhee wearily. "They just had to walk in while you French were sniping at each other and spending the rest of your time watching the British. Let's stop this shit and get on with killing Germans, like we're supposed to. Let's start with you, Christophe. Is this barn meant to be our base? Because if it is, it's too damn near the landing ground. And what happened to our radio operator?"

Christophe was older than François, in his early thirties, and he looked like a civilian. Whatever military service he might have done was a long time ago. Thicker-built than his brother, with the same dark complexion and oddly light, gray eyes, he took his time before answering the American. He turned to his brother first. "Another cavalryman, François?" he asked.

"Parachutist," said his brother.

"You have my sympathies, Monsieur," Christophe said to McPhee. "Your great skill is to drop in from the skies, and we poor squabbling Frenchmen have somehow managed to organize ourselves well enough that we can hold an airstrip so you just fly in and walk out of the plane. We have not spent all our time fighting each other and being suspicious of the English. But then we have known the English for a long time around here. All this land used to belong to them, though it has been ours now for five hundred years. And I don't think the Germans will last here nearly as long as the English did."

"If you know the land that well, I sure hope you have found us a better base than this," said McPhee.

"We have indeed. But this is where we stay until we are sure the Germans are not sending out patrols to look for you. Sometimes they do, sometimes they don't. But they always hear the planes, and they always mark the area where it came down. So we never use the same field twice, and we never use the same barn twice. You have learned security in a schoolroom, my dear American ally. We have learned it in a harder school. So never think of me as Christophe again. I am known as Berger."

Jack found himself nodding in understanding as Christophe spoke. He had heard that tone of bitter, undisguised resentment before, when the British spoke of the American troops and airmen flooding into their country. Overpaid, oversexed, and over here. That was the phrase. And the British still had all the pride that came from never have been invaded, from never having given up. For a Frenchman, living with the defeat of 1940 and the shame and guilt of surrender, and seeing German troops occupying their land, it must be a thousand times worse.

"McPhee," he interrupted. "Calm down. Remember what these chaps have been through, what they put up with day after day. To have survived this long, they know what they're doing."

Christophe didn't even glance at the Englishman, nor did he seem to notice McPhee's half-apologetic shrug. He just carried on talking with cold control, like a teacher handing out punishments to a schoolboy.

"From here, you will be taken to a house where there is the meeting with your man Hilaire. Then you will go east, into the hills of the Massif, to meet your first Maquis. Your radio operator is already on his way there, as you would have been except I was ordered at the last moment to arrange security and facilities for your meeting. This has not been easy. I have not slept for three nights because of this. And if you think I am suspicious, wait until you meet those frightened young scarecrows who have just wanted to escape this war. I don't think many of them are going to be too eager to use those weapons of yours, at least not until the invasion comes and they can see that you mean it. What you will find is a handful of men that I trust, and who will listen to you and train with you because I tell them to and they trust me. Most of them have known our family and me all our lives. Most of them are old soldiers, some from the Great War and a few from 1940. They know the country and they know how to fight. They need you only to bring them weapons and explosives, and to show them how to use them. As far as they are concerned, and as far as I am concerned, this is a French battle, with French leaders, French blood, and French objectives. You may think we are all on the same side. In my view, we simply happen to share a common enemy."

"Lest an impure blood pollute our thresholds," mocked McPhee, half-singing the line from the "Marseillaise."

"Shut up, McPhee, and grow up. Please," Jack interrupted. He was feeling sick again. He also felt that all McPhee's protests had missed the most important single feature of the night's events. The flurry of activity and unloading as they had landed had left all the guns and all the explosives in the hands of Christophe's men. And he knew that they would stay under Christophe's control, with carefully rationed items made briefly available for educational purposes only. Any shooting or demolition that would take place would be at Christophe's behest. So what?—so long as they killed Germans. And he was going to have to learn to call the man Berger. The American was looking at him aggressively. Jack reached across for the brandy bottle. "This war's going to last a long time."

They knew that Hilaire's network was a legend, one of the biggest of the SOE's networks in France and one of the most productive. They had been told no more by Baker Street, for what they did not know they could not betray. But there was always gossip at the training camps, where someone had said that the agent known as Hilaire had been promoted again, to lieutenant colonel, the highest rank of any SOE officer in France. And there was more loose talk from the RAF boys at Tempsford, who told them of two RAF aircrew from a downed bomber walking in uniform into a certain bar in Toulouse and asking a stunned waiter in schoolboy French for help. The waiter dropped the tray in astonishment on top of a table occupied by plainclothes Gestapo, and Hilaire himself had spirited them out and away in the confusion, and got them over the Pyrenees. It was one of the RAF pilots who had dropped the name Starr. And it had been François who had said casually one evening that Monsieur le Maire had originally landed by boat in southern France, and got to Lyon just as the circuit known as Spruce was being broken up by the Gestapo, and decided to move to Gascony.

"Monsieur le Maire?" Jack had asked.

"Starr's cover is so good that that he has been made deputy mayor of some little commune," François had said, shrugging as if everyone knew that. Jack had shivered at the looseness of SOE's security.

Just after dawn, they had left the barn and driven south in the small truck over a country road, crossed a larger road when the coast was clear, and darted across a small bridge and railway line into a thick apple orchard. They left the truck hidden, and walked half a mile through wooded country until they reached what had once been a formal garden, laid out with gravel paths, with a small château at the end of the drive. The shutters on the narrow turret windows were all open, which Berger said meant all was well. They went into a side door, which led to the cellars smelling of oak and long-spilled wine, where a middle-aged man with a mustache and Sten gun nodded deferentially to Berger, and gave a vast grin when he saw François. He gestured at a table where a bottle of wine and some water stood beside a big loaf of country bread, some apples, dry sausage, and a large cheese.

"Strange bread," said Jack, swallowing a mouthful of the yellow-brown dough.

"Made from chestnuts, which is the flour the peasants used around here for centuries," said François. "Now there is a shortage of wheat again because the Germans take it. So people have gone back to the old ways. Try the sausage. It's *sanglier,* wild boar."

Another door opened and a woman came in quickly, tall and gaunt with gray hair and a distracted look. François leaped to his feet and hurried across the room to embrace her. She began to cry quietly as she looked at him, patted his cheek, rubbed the rough British serge of his uniform. Berger joined them and kissed her on both cheeks. Jack suddenly realized that this château was François's family home, a frightening risk to take however little time Berger had been given to set up the meeting.

"My mother," François introduced her. Jack stood, somehow constrained to bow. But then a short, squat man with a round head and a dimple in his chin followed her into the cellar, moving fast but lightly on the toes of his feet like a boxer. His hair was short and neat, his gray trousers pressed, and his shoes polished. But for the open collar, he looked like a prosperous lawyer. Behind him, another man came in wearing a dark suit and carrying a revolver. He closed the door and leaned against it.

"Hilaire," said the short man, putting out his hand to the woman. "Madame, I thank you for the hospitality." His French was good, but with an accent that Jack could not place. Very northern, perhaps Belgian. He moved to the table, took an apple, and sat down.

"You ought to know I was against your coming so soon," he said to Jack and McPhee, his eyes swiveling to take in François. "But since you're here, we have to make you useful." He turned to the man leaning against the door and beckoned him over.

"Call this man Yves. He's a foreman at an aircraft propeller factory in Figeac. They turn out three hundred variable-pitch propellers each week for the Luftwaffe. It's a small plant, so the RAF haven't much of a hope of hitting it. Yves reckons he can do the job with some small explosive charges on a couple of key machine tools they brought in from Germany, but sometimes they are searched going in and coming out. I want you to give him some plastic, some detonators, and show him how to use them. Today, just as soon as we are done."

He finished his apple, sipped at some water, and took out a clean white handkerchief to pat his lips. "I suppose I should have said welcome to France. And thank you for bringing me in another radio operator. My own is getting tired and I'm worried about her security," he went on. "Then I want you out of those uniforms today. We can't have you wandering around dressed like that. It's insane, whatever London might say." He gestured at Christophe. "Berger here—and I want you to call him nothing but Berger from now on, because that's how I know him and London knows him—is taking you on first. He'll get the uniforms back to you when you start training his boys. Then you'll be shipped back down to my area to do the same. Again, you must travel in civilian clothes."

"In the meantime, we'll be sending people to you for special explosives training. We're going to cut every railway line and every telephone line between Toulouse and Paris in the course of this spring, and keep them closed until the invasion. Berger has the list of targets, and the sooner you hit them the better. I want the first two taken out within the next twenty four hours. The Germans get edgy if a plane lands and nothing happens—they like to think there's logic to things. Blow something up and they'll feel they know what's going on.

"We are going to demolish as many bridges as we can to stop the Germans sending reinforcements from the south. We have a whole German army based down here, including one SS panzer division, and that's where we want to keep it. And that's where you chaps come in.

Blowing bridges will slow them down, but armored divisions carry their own bridging equipment. So you'll be training the boys with the bazookas and the mortars who will be ambushing those tanks and their soft-skinned transport every time they move. An armored division covers forty miles of road when it moves, so there'll be no shortage of targets. Under normal circumstances, they could use road and rail and get those tanks from here to the bridges over the Loire in a day, maybe a day and a half. I don't think we can stop them, but I think we can keep them stuck down here for a week or more. An SS unit is half as big and strong again as a conventional panzer division. If we slow them down, it could make the difference between the invasion succeeding or getting thrown back into the sea."

He stopped, looked up at the woman, and then rose courteously to ask her to leave. He gestured Yves to follow her and the man with the Sten gun, until just the five of them were left.

"Right, end of pep talk," he said. "Two things I want to raise. First with you, Berger. These three chaps are a team and I want them to stick together. I know your brother can be useful in your network and I know you have jobs lined up for him. Don't do it. I know your men and mine want to see British and American soldiers on the ground here working with them, but most of all they want to see the Free French in uniform. He may be a brother to you, but for my chaps he's a symbol of de Gaulle and a French army. You lose him on some freelance operation and I'll never forgive you.

"Second, for you two. Consider me now to be putting my military hat and badges on, and I outrank you so this is not advice. This is an order. You will accept all orders from Berger as coming directly from me. Is that clearly understood?"

"Yes, sir," said Jack at once. McPhee followed a moment later.

"And you will make no remark to anyone at all about French politics. You will doubtless hear about politics, even be asked about it. You will meet and train Communists, socialists, Catholic militants, and even people who until recently were Vichy sympathizers, and you will treat them all alike. You will realize that there can be a certain tension between them. You should know the difference between the FTP, the *Franc-Tireurs et Partisans,* as the Communists call themselves, and the Gaullists. They are FFI, the *Forces Françaises de l'Interieur.* This is none of your business, and whenever the matter comes up you will say so and that is all you will say. SOE has no political ax to grind here in France, and if the French ever thought we did, our usefulness here would end at once. If I hear that you have broken this order, I will send you back if I can. If I must, I will have you shot here in France. Is that understood?"

"Yes, sir," they chorused.

"Right, good luck, and I'll probably see you down south in a month or so. Berger will let you know. Now off you go and show Yves how to blow up his factory." He took another apple from the table, and dismissed the three of them, remaining behind with Berger in the cellar, the door firmly closed.

"Looks like we finally ran up against the grown-ups," said McPhee.

CHAPTER 7

Time: The Present

The temple to the Resistance known as the *Centre Jean Moulin* inhabits a classically French urban palace of four stories, two wings, and three grand windows on each side of the entrance, and dominates the Place Jean Moulin in the old center of Bordeaux. It stands opposite the Cathedral of St-André, where Eleanor of Aquitaine married the King of France in the twelfth century, before proceeding to remarry herself and her lands to King Henry of England and perpetuate for three centuries the English occupation of the city and its region. Lydia had learned all this, strolled around the cathedral and reread the entries about Jean Moulin in Foot's official history, *The SOE in France*, before she heard a merry toot on a horn. She turned to see Major Manners grinning at her from the seat of an open-topped elderly Jaguar, his hair in disarray and looking boyish.

"Am I late, Lydia?" he called.

"No. I was early," she said, stuffing Foot's fat tome into her usefully large bag, a lesson she had learned from Clothilde, and walking briskly to the car. It looked red and mean and luxurious and she savored it, as Manners clambered out and walked around the beast to open the passenger door and escort her in. She felt relieved that she had chosen to wear slacks, and had a silk scarf in her bag. Convertibles were hell on hair.

"Lunch," he said, and drove off with a luscious mechanical growl. They went around the cathedral square, down two streets, and reversed into an embarrassingly narrow alley. He led her into a small but decently furnished restaurant called the Wolf-something, which had an impressive number of points in the extract from the Gault Millaud guide pasted proudly beside the door. A young woman with dark bags under her eyes greeted him effusively, stared coldly at Lydia, and showed them to a table by the window.

"They say we should eat the seafood ravioli and the fish in beurre blanc," he began. "You are looking breathtakingly lovely. Milan must suit you. Or perhaps it is Bordeaux."

"Or perhaps the educational value of Eleanor of Aquitaine's cathedral balanced by Jean Moulin's memorial," she said coolly. "Two great French people who each in their way chose the English. A happy augury for our task, I trust. And thank you for the compliment." She looked at his tousled hair, the odd smut from the road on his reddened face, and surveyed the denim shirt and antiquated tweed jacket. They suited him. And for the first time since she had met him, he looked younger than his age, which she had ascertained from a quick check of Debrett's to be thirty-eight. And he was indeed divorced. "Your choice of food sounds excellent. Might I begin with a Campari and soda, please?"

"No. When I booked the table, I asked them to prepare some champagne. I want to celebrate your arrival, and drink to the success of our venture. And thank you for coming, Lydia."

"Thank you for meeting me. Now, where are we? Do you have your father's war records?"

"Yes. And better still, I have a reply from Malrand, from the Élysée Palace itself, on the thickest notepaper you ever saw. And an invitation to have lunch with him later this week at the family place near Le Buisson. An invitation to us both."

"I haven't got a thing to wear that is suitable for lunch with a head of state, let alone the President of France," she said, as a flute of champagne was placed before her. "In fact, I'm not sure I even own anything suitable."

"I don't think the ancestral jewels are called for. He called it a very informal family lunch, and suggested that I not bother to wear a tie."

"Worse still, Manners. Any girl can dress decently for a formal lunch. Informal ones are the very devil."

"The last time I was called Manners was at school. Please go on using it," he grinned. He was looking more boyish by the minute. Boyish and merry. And still dashing. She grinned back, liking this version of him on holiday, and getting a sketchy sense of how he must have looked as a schoolboy. Emboldened, he went on. "Manners sounds much better than mister or major, and I was never all that fond of Philip."

Two plates of giant ravioli arrived. There were three on Lydia's plate, two white and one black, with some overflow calimari nestling against some shredded tomatoes with white slivers of garlic peeking above, like snowfields on summer mountains. It smelled divine.

"*Bon appétit*," she said, and took a bite. Delicious. "The war records?"

"Thin. He was in a Jedburgh team, one of three. Most of the Jedburgh teams were set up in the same way. One Brit, one Yank, and one

Free Frenchman, who in my father's case appears to have been Malrand," he said, and took a forkful of his food. Silence. Evident appreciation. He had not been this attentive to his food at the Savoy Grill.

"Jolly good grub," he said, as Lydia continued to eat. He put down his fork and carried on talking.

"They trained together in 1943, and dropped into France together early in 1944. The record is unclear about the date, but in French accounts Malrand is given credit for some sabotage operation against a propeller factory in February. Most of the Jedburgh teams arrived much later, with the invasion in June. But one or two of the earliest trainees were reassigned to SOE and were sent in early, where there was a particular problem of local organization. My father's team was the earliest of them all. They were assigned to a network called Digger, and did a lot of demolition work before the invasion. My father got a DSO and a Croix de Guerre for operations against an SS panzer division. He then got his *Légion d'Honneur* for helping to liberate Toulouse in July, which is a long way south of Périgord. By October 1944, he was back in England and assigned to the team setting up the military government in Germany. That was the end of his French adventure. So whatever he did here took place between January and October of 1944. Nine months. People can have a baby in that time."

"Well, that all fits with what I found out," said Lydia, who had eaten as much as she dared, with a fish in beurre blanc to follow, no fitness center in sight, and a presidential informal lunch looming menacingly on the horizon. "Your ravioli are getting cold. You eat, my turn to talk."

"The Digger network was run by Malrand's brother, Christophe," she said, "as a kind of subsidiary of a much bigger network called Wheelwright that was one of the great triumphs of SOE, the British effort to help the Resistance. Wheelwright was run by a man called Starr, one of the top agents of the war. He used the cover of a Belgian mining engineer who retired with his loot from the Belgian Congo. He settled into France so well that he was elected deputy mayor of a tiny place called Castelnau-sous-l'Auvignon, which gave him the right to issue all sorts of genuine identity papers and ration cards and petrol coupons. For the Resistance, this was like a bank robber having the keys to the Bank of England. Starr was, in fact, a star. He held the highest rank of any SOE man in France, and was one of the very few who was able to combine Communists and Gaullists into a single network without friction. At least until de Gaulle showed up, well after the liberation, and had a huge row with Starr. De Gaulle insisted that he be evicted from French soil within twenty-four hours. But of course by then, the French civil war with the Communists was well under way.

"Starr was the uncrowned king of southwestern France," she went on. "He got more arms and supply drops than anyone else, over two thousand of them, and lost hardly a one. He built a private army of nearly ten thousand Maquis guerrillas, which your father helped train, and together they liberated the city of Toulouse. You'll see why that's important in a moment. But what I hadn't realized was what an extraordinary job they did. I made a note of one German report I came across. It was from Field Marshal Von Runstedt, the German Supreme Commander in the West." She pulled out a notebook and began to read aloud, "'The HQ of Army Group G near Toulouse was at times cut off' — he's talking about late 1943 and early 1944, six months and more before D-Day," she interjected. "'It was only with a strong armed escort or by aircraft that they could get their orders through to the various armies under their command. The main telephone lines and power stations were frequently out of order for many days.' How about that?"

"Very impressive indeed — I had no idea the Resistance was that effective before the invasion."

"Anyway, back to the smaller Digger network. It was based around the city of Bergerac and the Périgord, and operated all the way to the remote uplands of the Massif Central. Malrand himself was part of it, until he was wounded and captured in a German ambush not long after the invasion. Led by your father, Resistance fighters from brother Christophe's network rescued Malrand from the prison in Toulouse, as the Germans were pulling out to the north. Your father saved the life of the current President of France, which is presumably why he came to the funeral."

"That's amazing, Lydia. You *have* done well."

"No. It's all in the published record, in the official history and Malrand's irritatingly oblique memoirs. And the bad news is that it is only context, more than the kind of detail we need. Apart from the names of Starr, Malrand, and his brother Christophe, and a few radio operators who are all dead, I have found absolutely nothing that will tell us more about your father's time in Périgord. The American member of their Jedburgh team is a dead end. His name was McPhee, but he didn't survive the war."

The fish in beurre blanc arrived and with it a bottle of Château de la Jaubertie, of which Lydia had never heard, but which was so glorious that she asked Manners how he had known to order it.

"I didn't," he confessed. "I just asked the people here to serve what they thought best. They said it was a dry Bergerac, where they come from, which also happens to be the area we are heading toward, so it seemed the right thing. Seems to go with the fish all right."

Lydia cocked a skeptical eye at him. She was learning that Manners was seldom so deviously formidable as when he pretended to be just a bluff English simpleton. This was Bordeaux, heart of the proudest wine region of France. A decent restaurant in this city would no more offer a wine from a little-known appellation like Bergerac than they would recommend Coca-Cola.

She opened her mouth to say: "Bullshit, Manners—you ordered this and you knew what you were doing." But she paused and wondered what Clothilde might have done in such a situation. She would have accepted what he said and stored up the useful knowledge for the future, and appreciated a man who had obviously taken some care to provide her with a memorable lunch. Thank you, Clothilde. Now all I have to do is ask you what on earth I wear to lunch with your President.

"You did choose well, Manners, coming to this restaurant," she said, calculating that he must have reconnoitered the place, and the street, and discussed the meal and planned his parking in advance. Very flattering that he was going to such pains.

"Picked it out of the guidebook," he mumbled. "Lucky, really."

Manners gasped with pleasure as they climbed the steps into the Jean Moulin building, and found a small exhibition spread before them. He pounced at once upon a tiny motorcycle that looked like a child's toy. The label said that it was a type developed to be dropped by parachute to help the Resistance leaders get around.

"I learned to drive on one of those," he said fondly. "My father brought one back from the war. It's still in one of the outbuildings somewhere. Made a fearful racket, and pumped out tons of gray smoke." He squatted down to peer more closely, occasionally glancing up at her with enthusiastic delight. Lydia found herself smiling back in what felt like genuine affection. Friendliness, perhaps, she told herself. He was very appealing in this boyish mood.

"The old man never said it was a Resistance bike," he said, rising. "I remember when the tires rotted, and I tried to fit an old set of scooter tires. No good—too fat."

Lydia steered him toward the reception desk before some other military antique drew his attention. She had made an appointment with the curator of the museum library, an elderly man with a small red ribbon in his lapel. He came down to greet them, casting an appreciative glance at her before clasping Manners's hand in both of his. Once in his small office upstairs he poured three small glasses of a golden wine, insisting that they drink to the honor of the late *capitaine*.

"He was always the *capitaine* to us," said the old Frenchman, speaking serviceable English. "Whatever rank he reached later. We all liked him, because he was always cheerful, and could make us laugh. He was a very good leader, the kind who led without your noticing that he was in charge. He taught me how to strip a Sten gun. That was in Toulouse, when we liberated the city."

"I had no idea you knew my father," said Manners. "That makes our job a lot easier. He never spoke much about the war, so I'm really trying to find out more about what he did, the people he knew, and whether any of them could still be found. I'm very pleased indeed to meet an old comrade-in-arms—and hope to meet some more."

"We are very few, those who remain," said the old man. He looked at Manners neutrally, then at Lydia—the look of someone who had learned caution in a hard school. "Not everyone wants to remember. The war was a long time ago. So long, we even get Germans coming here now. There was a time we would have kicked them out, but you cannot blame the young ones. And half of the people in Wehrmacht uniform weren't Germans at all. There were Russians, Ukrainians, Latvians, Poles—all hauled into the German Army. Some of them even joined us. And some of our worst enemies were other Frenchmen."

"You mean the Milice?" asked Lydia, thinking he might need some gentle prodding. She had read about the pro-Nazi militia who supported the Vichy regime.

"Not just them. But they were bad. They and the Gestapo were the worst. We had political problems too, in those weeks around the Liberation. The Communists, mainly, and some black market people. A long time ago." He shrugged and pushed across the desk toward them a small pile of books in French, and a folder containing some microfiche.

"I prepared this for you, after Mademoiselle telephoned me," he went on. "I knew your father from late June of 1944, when he came south to help train us in the Maquis and take us into Toulouse. But he was in Périgord and the Massif for months before that, so I have put some books and memoirs together about the Périgord networks, not just the Berger network that he worked with, but *le Réseau Soleil* as well, a separate network. And then in the microfiche, there are transcripts. We did a lot of oral interviews with old Resistance members, making sure we have their memories before they died. We have them on cassette, and these are the transcripts. There are three who knew your father, including Berger himself, God rest his soul. I still don't have on tape the one I want most, but it takes a lot of time, being President of France." He grinned. "Malrand has promised to do an oral interview once he retires after the next election. But you'll find a copy of Malrand's final report to the FFI in the folder."

"Excuse me," interrupted Lydia. "You mentioned *le Réseau Soleil*— were they attached to the Berger group? I thought Soleil was more of an independent."

"Some might call him a gangster, or a black Marketeer, mademoiselle," shrugged the old man. "I think of Soleil as a good *résistant* because he killed Germans, and he fought for France. You are right to call him independent. He didn't take many orders, neither from us in the FFI nor from the Reds in FTP, nor from London. But gangster— not really, except that we were all gangsters part of the time. I did a few armed robberies, but only of the *bureaux de tabac*. You can imagine how desperate we were for tobacco and cigarettes in the Maquis. It was always tightly rationed, and London never sent us enough, so we used to raid the shops. Except that time when Malrand and your father stole the German cigarette ration from the stores at Brive. We had a lot of smokes then."

He poured another glass for each of them, took out one of the old-fashioned Gauloises packs, a flash of bright blue, lit it, coughed, and sat down. "At my age, you need a little vice," he wheezed. "Those books— I kept them for you, although there are people here who want them. You'll find one of them in the library. An American, I think, but speaks good French. He's looking at Périgord, as well, at what we have on the Jedburgh teams. I told him the material was reserved for a special project, and he'd have to wait. You'll find the microfiche reader in the library—I presume you know how to work it, mademoiselle? I know your French is more than good enough to read the instructions."

"Lydia," said Manners. "I wonder if we could do two things at once. If you tackle the microfiche in the library, I can carry on talking to our friend here about his memories of my father and pick his brains about other old comrades. We'd get on twice as fast." His tone was as friendly as ever, but there was just a touch of briskness about it, of someone accustomed to delegating matters, that Lydia realized she had not heard before. But the suggestion made sense. She nodded coolly.

"At what time does the library close, monsieur?" she asked.

"Officially, at five P.M. In fact, as long as I'm here, you may stay. But not the other members of the public, of course. But then, we keep special hours for old comrades, and the son of Capitaine Manners . . ." He gestured grandly.

As Lydia left with her pile of books and files, she noticed that Manners had taken one of the old Frenchman's cigarettes, and they were pouring yet another glass of the sweet golden wine. Officer's privileges, she grinned to herself. If they drank the afternoon away, then Manners would have to let her drive the Jaguar on to Les Eyzies. She was still smiling when she entered the library to find Horst perched on a desk and glowering at her.

"So you are the special project for whom the Périgord materials are reserved," he said coldly. "There must be more money at stake than I thought in this cave painting if an auction house is investing its time like this."

"I'm on vacation," she began, then brought herself up short. She owed him no explanations. "And you must be convinced that this rock of mine comes from Lascaux, or you wouldn't be here, pretending to be an American."

"Not your rock, Miss Dean. The Manners rock, or, should I say, France's rock? But yes, I think it's real. I told you that. And the only place we are likely to find out where it comes from is to look into the wartime exploits of Mr. Manners. It was not difficult to find that he was in the Jedburgh teams in Périgord, and this is probably the best library on the Resistance in Périgord, so this is the place to start." He pushed himself off the desk, a lithe movement, and gave a friendly smile that reminded Lydia that this man had been Clothilde's lover for some time, and she was not a woman to waste her time on uninteresting men.

"May I look at the books that you aren't using?" he asked, courteously enough. "I quite understand that a beautiful young woman will always take precedence in France, even leaving aside the fact that this is a Resistance shrine and I am a German."

"Don't be silly, Professor," Lydia said. "Of course you can look at the books while I'm using the microfiche. And the librarian thinks you're an American. I won't give away the little secret of your nationality—if you think it still matters."

"Among these old Resistance types, it certainly matters. And so it should. My countrymen behaved monstrously around here. I understand their attitude, and have to live with it. But let's be practical. Have you heard anything more from the London police about the theft?" he asked. "It seems very suspicious, the rock disappearing almost on the very night that it is brought in."

"It *is* suspicious, even though it was the next night. And all the police have told us so far was to give us the authorization to make the insurance claim. The whole art world and auction community know about the theft, so I doubt that it will surface in the salesrooms. We hope that the reward offer will persuade the thief to make a discreet approach in the usual way."

"But you have heard nothing as yet?" he asked, leaning forward to leaf through the books she had brought.

"Not when I left London. I have been in Italy, but if there had been an approach, I would have known. I'm surprised—I'd have thought a thief would have worked out by now that twenty thousand pounds is about the best he's going to get."

"Perhaps the French will offer more." He was riffling through the index of a book about Soleil, put it down and picked up Malrand's memoirs.

"I doubt it—half of the reward money comes from the museum at Les Eyzies. The French won't bid against themselves."

"If the President of the Republic takes a personal interest, you might be surprised at what the French can do, Miss Dean. The Périgord is Malrand's home region. This was his war. Manners was his comrade, and now it looks as if Manners was looting France's heritage when he was meant to be fighting Germans. Did Malrand not know what his British friend was doing? Did he not care? Malrand's war record as a Resistance hero was the key to his political career, and now this comes along to cast a shadow over the presidential past."

"That seems a bit fanciful, Professor. You may be convinced that this rock is Lascaux work, but I'm not half so certain, and I have seen it. You have only seen the photos."

"So why, my dear Miss Dean, are you wasting your holiday in the Resistance library?"

"Because I feel responsible," she burst out. Calm, Lydia, calm. The man was only scoring points, infuriating and perceptive points. And surely that was a mocking smile on his face, the self-satisfied beast! Whatever had Clothilde seen in this fellow? She went on evenly. "What may have been an extraordinary piece of cave art was entrusted to us, and we lost it, and we have a duty to try and put that right. At least, I think we do. But I don't see that presidential politics comes into it. And I came here because this was where my plane landed. I'm off to the Périgord region to look at lots of caves because I now think I don't know nearly as much about them as I should."

He looked at her quizzically and smiled easily, the practiced grin of someone who had often been told that his smile was charming. "Perhaps you are right, Miss Dean. Your motives do you credit. My motives are scholarly, but I'm sure we can agree that were we to find where this rock of yours came from, it would enhance both our reputations. I think we have much in common. Perhaps we can work together, share the burden. Who knows—perhaps even share the glory, if we are lucky?"

He slid into the chair at the desk before her, opening a laptop computer and pushing the button that whirred the thing into life. "Let me tell you my thoughts," he went on distractedly, as he waited for the screen to settle. "I thought I would make a timeline of the locations we know that Manners visited, plot them against known sites, interview any former Resistance people he worked with, and see if that leads anywhere. What about you?"

"Nothing so organized, I'm afraid. I imagine he was all over the Vézère and Dordogne valleys, where most of the known caves are to be found. But I had thought of asking his old comrades, although if they knew anything definite about undiscovered caves, I presume they would have been discovered by now."

She found herself looking at the books by Horst's elbow. There was one she recognized, *Das Reich*, the account of the Resistance battle to slow down the march of the German SS panzer division from Toulouse north to Normandy. Some photocopies of a dense German text peeped from beneath the book. She made out the initial Kr and the letters B-U-C-H. *Kriegesbuch*—the war diary of a German unit. He had been busy.

"Can I buy you dinner this evening, Miss Dean?" He casually scooped his books and papers into a neat pile.

"I'm sorry, Professor, but no. I have an engagement." Obviously Horst didn't know Manners was in the next room. No reason why he should, but equally, no reason to let him know that Lydia's quest was serious enough to be accompanied by the rock's current owner.

"Well, perhaps another time. And you must call me Horst," he smiled. "I'm sure we will meet again on our treasure hunt. You said you were off to Périgord soon—doubtless we'll run into each other in Les Eyzies. I'm staying at the Cro-Magnon Hotel. How about you?"

"I don't know yet," she said lamely. "Excuse me, Professor, but I really ought to start looking through this stuff—the sooner I'm done, the sooner you can have it."

"Horst, please. Not Professor," he said, turning back to his laptop. "But good hunting. To both of us."

As she sat at the microfiche and inserted the first of the miniaturized films into the reader, Lydia began thinking about how soon she could pretend to go to the ladies' room, and warn Manners not to come into the library. Secrets and intrigue already, Lydia. How silly, as if the Germans were the enemy again. She turned to the spare prose of Malrand's military report, so different from the florid style of his memoirs.

"My theory is that we save money on hotels and spend it on food and drink. I never saw the point in paying for an expensive hotel room when all you do is sleep in it," said Manners. Which is just the sort of thing a chap would say to lull a girl's suspicions, thought Lydia, as he led her into the dining room of the Centenaire. Two Michelin rosettes; she was looking forward to this.

They had left Bordeaux and the kindly old curator at six-thirty, Horst having long before been shown to the door as just another member of the public to whom closing hours applied. Claiming to have drunk no more wine, Manners had taken the wheel and the Jaguar had raced past mile after mile of vines: Lydia had seen the signs for St-Emilion and Lalinde de Pomerol and her mouth was watering already. At one crossroads, delving into the glove compartment to find a map, she found a small leather pouch, which she recognized as a traveling chess set. Well, well, she thought to herself, he *does* have hidden depths. After consulting the map, they had driven to a tiny hamlet, not much more than a bend in the road, a small river, and a pretty miniature château. Their Hotel du Château was just across the park, and she had a view of the turrets from her room. It might not be expensive, but it was well chosen. Manners allowed her precisely ten minutes to wash and change and they raced the three miles into Les Eyzies, parked, and walked into the restaurant with a few minutes to spare before 9 P.M. He was wearing a rather jolly pink tie with his blue suit. Given no time to iron her clothes, Lydia was playing safe in black cashmere and her expensive gray flannels. The restaurant was full, and moderately noisy, the clientele too discreet or self-absorbed to break off their conversation to study the latest arrivals. Shown to a large table by the wall, they ordered two glasses of Kir Royale and began to study their menus in silence.

"The menu for me. The foie gras, the *sandre*, and the duck," he said as the somber gentleman approached with the wine list under his arm and his badge of office, the small silver tastevin, gleaming on his chest. Lydia ordered the foie gras and the fish, chose lamb instead of duck, and in serviceable French Manners asked the sommelier which wine he would recommend. Did Monsieur know the wines of the region, unpretentious but charming? Only the Jaubertie and Pécharmant, said Manners. A thoughtful nod, a courteous inquiry whether Monsieur had considered a Pomerol, and business was concluded with a glass of Monbazillac for the foie gras, some Badoit water with the fish, and a Château Nénin. It had been competently done, thought Lydia, looking appraisingly at her companion. An extremely grand restaurant, and he had surmounted the hurdle of ordering the wine without showing off, and with a courteous consideration for the sommelier's expertise. She approved.

"Well, our adventure is shaping up according to all the proper conventions," said Manners, as the two glasses of champagne arrived, touched with rose by the cassis. Another waiter brought some *amuse-gueuls*, a morsel of salmon, some black pudding, and a small sphere of foie gras topped with a black flake of truffle. "We have a Holy Grail to look for, a château to stay in, an extremely fair maiden, and an enemy."

"I think the most you can say of Horst is that he is a possible rival." She smiled at him, enjoying the thought of herself as a fair maiden. She had related the encounter with Horst as they raced through the flatlands of Gascony.

"Point taken. No dragon. Still, he's German, which is the next best thing." He grinned. Lydia had a feeling that nobody had ever told Manners he had a good smile, or if they had, he hadn't paid attention. Looking at the healthy way he was polishing off the tiny snacks, he'd probably been too busy eating.

"Old Morillon, the chap in the library, has given me three leads," he went on, after a swig of his Kir. "Three old men. One is from the Berger network who lives near a tiny village called Audrix. There's an old railway man from the Communist FTP in le Buisson who worked with them. I have their addresses. And then there's Soleil himself, still alive, but his memory is not what it was. But at least we have his memoirs, which do not mention my father. Apparently he used to be some kind of Communist, but broke with the party after the war. I have his phone number, but he was always very cautious about who he sees, so Morillon is going to call him on our behalf, and see if the old chap still has enough of his marbles to be worth seeing. That's about it. Morillon himself was never north of Cahors, and only knew my father during the Toulouse operation. But he did say one thing about the Berger network that I found interesting. They sometimes hid the guns and ammo from the parachute drops in the remote caves along the Vézère valley. Caves were good because they protected the stuff from the damp, and he said my father was always on the lookout for a good cave."

"That seems obvious, but it's a useful connection," she mused, tearing her attention away from the elusive taste of the truffle. "He could well have found a cave with paintings—except how has the cave remained unknown ever since? There must have been some local Resistance people in on the secret, if only to carry the weapons."

"I asked Morillon if the caves weren't too dangerous. They make terrible traps if the Germans were on their heels. And then probably some of the German troops would have been stomping around the better-known caves for their own interest. A lot of them apparently went to look at Lascaux itself, which was only discovered in 1940."

"That reminds me. Among the microfiche I went through was something called the order of battle for Army Group G, under General Von Blaskowitz, in charge of defending southern France. It assigned him three armored divisions, one motorized and thirteen infantry divisions. How many troops would that be, Manners."

"We normally reckon about ten thousand to a division, but armored divisions tend be larger and an SS panzer division would have twice that number. Then there are the troops attached to corps and army HQ. At least two hundred fifty thousand troops, but that was to hold down the whole of southern France, which contained something close to twenty million people. Not all of the troops were Germans, as Morillon said this afternoon. And a lot of the German infantry units were composed of old men or convalescents from the military hospitals. They had entire battalions of ulcer sufferers—it made it easier to organize their diet. Even the SS panzer division was being filled up with Volksdeutsch, the ethnic Germans from Czechoslovakia and Hungary and Alsace-Lorraine. Some of them didn't even speak much German. And the troops were spread out, guarding the Atlantic and Mediterranean coasts, controlling the big cities like Lyon and Marseilles, the industrial centers like Clermont-Ferrand, patrolling the railways. Bear in mind that Périgord was not terribly important to the Germans, except for the rail and transport links. Not much industry, no great population centers, just a handful of important factories. They had the Vichy police and paramilitaries to do most of the patrols—and the dirty work."

Their foie gras arrived, just long enough in the pan to toast the outside and warm the flesh within, with a steaming portion of onion confiture on one side of the plate, and a tender bed of baby leeks on the other. She took some liver. It had the taste of luxury. She sipped her Monbazillac. Sweet gold.

"I think just one restaurant meal a day from now on, Manners," Lydia said. "I don't mind putting on weight in a good cause, but this is too princely."

"Grand, I call it. What's the point of coming to the home of the best food in France if we don't enjoy it?"

They finished their liver, sat back and cleansed their palates with the mineral water, and then leaned forward to address themselves to the lightly grilled fish. Hearing a burst of laughter, Lydia looked casually around the room. There was a loud and jolly English family talking of plonk and fizz, some serious French tables concentrating on their food, a table of three businessmen talking in low voices, and a rather fetching pair of young lovers, their heads close together and eyes sharing secrets. The laughter had come from the English family. From behind her came a murmur of what might have been German, except for the constant sound of throat clearing. Must be Dutch. I wonder what they all make of me and Manners, she mused. Not lovers, certainly, but not married either. Friends, then, which is what she supposed they were becoming. Or allies, which is what they were. Or possibly, she smiled to herself, adventurers. What kind of adventure would be up to her.

And that, she told herself with a thoughtful glance at the rather appealing and likeable Manners as he tasted the Pomerol and pronounced it sound, was how it should be!

CHAPTER 8

The Vézère Valley, 15,000 B.C.

The great hunt was always the day after the sun and moon had appeared together in the sky the previous evening, in the time when the river waters were at their highest and the bears lumbered sleepily from their caves and the first flowers came on the trees that would give the sweet and tiny fruit. In the days of the ancestors, it had always been a hungry time, when all the men and boys of the tribe and all the younger women would take to the hunt at once. But now that the reindeer flocked so thickly on the hills and valley to the north and the fish danced in the rivers, there had been only three hungers that the

Keeper of the Horses could remember. He had never had to leave any of his own children out for the wolves, although he remembered that as a youth he had lost two sisters that way.

But he liked this time, the feeling that they were doing as their fathers and ancestors had always done, taking all the men of the tribe on the great hunt that would leave them all gorged with meat. He liked watching the boys taking their first turn in the long line of beaters, and the way they would all work together, the flint men and the fishers and the woodmen, shaping the stakes and bringing the stones that would force the reindeer to the cliff where they would tumble and fall onto the rocks below. Above all, he liked to watch the boys who were to become men dart down into those rocks and learn to kill, to mark the beast marks on their chest with the blood they spilled. He liked to watch the prouder, taller way they walked, even under the burdens of the long boughs with the reindeer slung upon them, as they marched back into the village as men. He felt like part of a river that always flowed. His father had done the same, and then taken him to the hunt to teach him the ways of it, and now his own father had flowed on down to the great sea. He would flow down too, one day. But now he was still part of the river of his people, flowing endlessly, the old going before, the young coming on behind.

They always began with the sacrifice at dawn before the cave. And because the Keeper of the Bulls made his sacrifice each day, it had become the custom that he led the sacrifice for this day of the hunt. It had not been that way when he was younger, thought the Keeper of the Horses. They had all done it together then. And now he felt a snatch of disappointment, as he stood in line before the cave with the other Keepers, while the Keeper of the Bulls took the sacrifice alone, and the chief hunter knelt before him, and the leaders of the flint and fisher and wood men knelt to the side.

Did it matter, the way the Keeper of the Bulls always pushed himself forward, always took the lead? Did it matter that he somehow took the credit for the good hunting and the plentiful reindeer? Even for the fish. It did not matter much to him. He liked to stand to one side, looking at all the men of the village gathered together just for this rare occasion, all feeling part of a great family. But he found himself noticing for the first time the deference with which the chief hunter bowed to the Keeper of the Bulls, the look of awe and respect on the faces of the young men, the way the boys trembled as if something was being done that was far beyond their imagining.

The Keeper of the Bulls gave them something to be awed by, sure enough. He carried off the ceremony with a great and ponderous dignity. He took the wood chips from the woodman, the ax from the flint man, the long bone of the longest fish that the fishermen had caught and piled them before the great bull's skull that loomed over the sacrifice fire. The chief hunter, still kneeling, his head still bowed, proffered a reindeer hoof in his two outstretched hands.

"That the game may not run from our spears, we burn this hoof to you, Great Bull," chanted the Keeper of the Bulls, in a voice that carried far beyond the gathered men and the women at a respectful distance below. He took the hoof, and placed it on the fire. The chief hunter leaned forward and bowed his forehead to the ground before the bull's skull. That had never happened before. As the stink of burning fur drifted among them, the Keeper of the Bulls placed his hand on the skull, between the two outstretched horns, and chanted, "The sacrifice is accepted."

A great murmur of approval came from the gathered men. The Keeper of the Horses glanced sideways to see if any of the other Keepers were as startled as he. No. Their eyes were fixed on the ceremony, and they too were nodding in agreement and respect.

The chief hunter took a scrap of reindeer hide, bowed again, and proffered it to the bull's skull. The Keeper of the Bulls took it, placed it on the fire. "That the hide of the game shall not keep out our weapons, we burn this flesh to you, Great Bull," he chanted. Again the sacrifice

121

was accepted. Again the low roar of approval, louder this time. Then the chief hunter took from behind him a reindeer's skull, the antlers still attached, and placed it on the top of his head. Shuffling forward on his knees, he bowed again to the bull's skull, as if the reindeer were saluting the lord of beasts, as if some new hierarchy had suddenly been presented to the men of the village. And from their roars of approval, it had clearly been accepted.

Another man came forward, the former chief hunter who was now the leader of the fishers. Too old and slow to keep up with the hunt, he had applied his great skill with the spear to the art of spearing the biggest fish that were too strong and wily to be caught by the fences of woven willows. He had learned the cunning way of the water, which always bent the spear as it broke the surface to send it foolishly past the fish that were the lords of the river. But the chief fisher had learned to use the river's magic against its fish, and his thrust with the great barbed spear seldom missed. Now on his knees, a great pike in his outstretched arms, he shuffled forward to lay his offering before the skull.

The Keeper of the Bulls leaned down and took from behind the skull a great headdress, raised it to the skies and drew it over his head, settled it on his brow. Men and women alike drew in their breath with wonder at the monstrous shape. The long brown eagle feathers trailed down to his shoulders, and the smaller white feathers affixed in their scores to the curving wooden eagle's beak thrust forward beyond the Keeper's face. A man with the head of an eagle.

"The lord of the air salutes the lord of beasts," he chanted from beneath the great beak as he bent his knee before the bull's skull. "The beings of water and land and air salute the lord bull."

The silence was absolute as the bull's skull seemed almost to tremble in the still air. The Keeper of the Bulls, suddenly in his mask become half-bird and half-man, rose and turned toward them, his arms outstretched like mighty wings. He looked up, and the eyes of the crowd followed. And from the rock outcrop on the hill above came a beating of real wings and a great eagle rose into the sky, cawing as it flapped and began to spiral upward above the assembled people.

"The sacrifice is accepted," called the birdman.

Who had devised this unprecedented ritual? The chief hunter and fisher and the Keeper of the Bulls must have arranged it, even rehearsed it, among them. The Keeper of the Horses dragged his eyes back to the rock outcrop whence the eagle had appeared and saw a flash of movement. Human, he was sure. It would be simple enough to catch an eagle by digging a man-sized hole, covering it with brushwood, and placing a lure on top. A dead rabbit or bird would do. And then as the eagle stooped, the hunter in his hole could quickly draw tight the looped thong that would imprison the eagle's talons. He had seen it done. And it was no great trick to release the bird at a certain, well-timed moment. A trick, but a clever one, he thought.

But what was its purpose, this carefully planned ritual? It had been as dramatic as it was curious, even moving in its way, he thought. But it made him uncomfortable, as though the river of the tribe's life in which he took such comfort had suddenly been diverted into a different path, its flow broken and disturbed by the plunging splash of a great stone. He shivered. Still, it must be over now and the hunt could begin.

All around him, the men were stamping their feet and cheering. The boys were dancing with excitement, strutting and thrusting their feeble spears forward as if facing a real enemy. He glanced again at his fellow Keepers, caught the watery old eye of the Keeper of the Bison, who shook his head slightly, leaned forward and spat. At least not everyone was caught up in the madness. He looked again at the cheering men, all their eyes aflame, and turned to the Keeper of the Bulls, who stood with his arms outstretched above the fire, his eagle's head almost ghostly in the smoke.

"Let the great hunt commence," he chanted.

They came upon the herd while the sun was still climbing in the sky. The band of men was stretched out now, the two best hunters scouting far off ahead and out of sight. The older men were trailing badly, the boys all clumped together at the front of the line but with sense enough to be silent. The sign the scouts had left was a forked stick, thrust into the ground, with three twigs placed in the shape of an arrow to point the way. The chief hunter picked up his pace from the steady lope he had maintained since they left the village, sprinting uphill to the next ridge, and then dropping to squirm forward and keep his body from suddenly appearing on the skyline. He came back to the main body, and in another unusual feature of this strange day, went up to the Keeper of the Bulls, as if telling him alone where the herd was placed and where the beaters should go. The Keeper of the Bulls nodded his approval.

The Keeper of the Horses knew this place. He had hunted here before as a young man. There was a river valley ahead of them, and some distance to the left a steep drop to the water. He watched the hunters take the boys off to the right to form the line of beaters. The hunters would anchor each flank of the line, and then race forward to make the line into a curve, using their bows against the reindeer on the sides of the herd, less to try for a kill than to drive the herd in the desired direction.

With the rest of the grown men, the Keeper of the Horses began loping toward the riverbank, to set the jaws of the trap that would force the game over the drop. This was the real test of the chief hunter's skill, less to find the herd than to coordinate the movements of so many boys and men so that they would all be in the right place at the best time. Chief hunters who closed the tribe upon an empty trap did not last long. There were always keen young hunters eager to take over. The Keeper of the Horses found himself hoping that the trap might be empty this time. The tribe would miss a feast, might even go hungry awhile, but another chief hunter might not be so ready to fall in with the strange new rituals of the bull's skull.

There was still no sign of the herd when the men reached the cliff above the drop to the river. This was a good place. On this nearer side where they approached, thick trees gave way to a jumble of rocks before the cliff edge. The herd would avoid the trees and the rocks could be held by just a handful of men. The rest of them ran swiftly along the cliff edge, looking for the place to set their fence. Every man carried three poles, each one almost as tall as a man and lashed together at one end with sinew. They spread out the other end of the poles to form a tripod, and then placed each tripod perhaps ten yards apart, from the cliff edge up toward the direction from which the herd would come. They lashed skins to each tripod, to make it look like a solid shape, a small teepee, flimsy but appearing solid enough to dupe the reindeer. Each man then sat behind his tripod, waiting for the time. Some of them tossed blades of grass into the air, testing that the breeze still came toward them. The Keeper of the Horses ambled across to the cliff edge and looked into the drop. It was the height of three or four men. It would serve.

"So we are now all worshipers of the bull," grunted a voice behind him. He turned. It was the Keeper of the Bison, looking ancient and leathery. He had done well to keep up with the pace of the hunt.

"Worship?" he replied. "I respect all men, and pay due tribute to each man's skill. I honor all beasts, those we hunt and eat and those we watch with caution from afar and those we no longer see in these lands. I bow to the sun for its warmth, to snow for its cold, and to the river for its water. And to the Mother for the gift of life that lies in a woman's belly. Just as our people have always done."

"And I fear lightning and the great sounds of battle in the skies before a storm," said the old man. "I have lived too long to devote myself to a single beast, or to bow before a single man."

"Our Keeper of the Bulls seems to have persuaded many of our people otherwise. The chief hunter first among them."

"Chief hunters don't last long," the old man spat. "But what does our Keeper of the Bulls want?"

The Keeper of the Horses shrugged, and looked back away from the river. The herd should be coming soon, although he could as yet hear no drumming of hooves, no high-pitched cries from the beaters.

"You must stop him," said the old man patiently. "Already, we are changing as a people. We are becoming worshipers of the bull, led by the Keeper of the Bulls. Do you see what he is doing?"

As the Keeper of the Horses nodded, he heard the first piping cry from the far-off beaters, and then the tremor beneath his feet. The herd was coming. "We will talk of this again, old friend," he said. "Back to our posts."

Deer felt exultant, the thrill of the hunt upon him, until he reached the great cloud of dust that was all that he could now see. The hunters had led them at a fast run for as long as it took the sun to move a hand's width across the sky. One of the advance scouts was waiting for them, leaning on a rock just below the skyline, and he trotted quickly to meet them. The hunters conferred and then fanned out to either flank, and begun the slow walk toward the herd. The scout led the boys, using his bow as a guide to slow them so that the hunters could move ahead and become the points of the great curve that was advancing on the herd. He led them up to just below the ridge, halted them as he looked over again, and then waved the two points of the horn forward. His arms outstretched above his head, the bow clutched between them, he held the impatient boys for as long as a man could hold his breath, and then turned with a great cry and led the rush over the ridge and down toward the startled herd.

There were more than a man could count, a great gray mass that turned as one to stare at the sudden shock of shrieking boys, and then raced away. As the movement began, the great mass broke up; Deer saw individual reindeer trotting back and forth along the rear of the herd, as if steering them on. He saw bigger reindeer edge out to the side of the herd, as if taking guard on the vulnerable flanks. But still the mass moved, gathering speed, not panicked yet, but moving just slightly faster than the running boys.

It had seemed easy to yell and shriek as he ran, as if his lungs contained all the breath in the world, until they reached the dust the herd had left behind them. Dust in his eyes and mouth, fresh dung beneath his feet. Suddenly Deer could see nothing, choked as he tried to shout, stumbled as his foot slipped in some moist mess. Disoriented, he kept running, glancing to either side to see if he was still in line, and found two smaller boys edging toward him, as if for company. As long as he was in the dust, he must be behind the herd, running in the right track. He hawked the dust from his throat, and whooped feebly, hardly a sound at all to match the drumming of the hooves. He choked again, bent and picked a pebble to suck to get some moisture to his tongue, and carried on running, the boys at his side now.

Suddenly a crazed reindeer with an arrow in its belly appeared before him, panicked into running the wrong way. He pointed his spear, but ran to one side. It darted past him, blood splashing into the dust. Some always broke free. On again. How much farther? He had seen the cliff and the distant hills beyond the river when they rose above the ridge. No distance at all. They must be almost at the funnel the men would have formed.

Another beast came at him, an arrow in its eye. It was almost upon him. He darted to the side, bowling over one of the boys, but the rough flank of the reindeer slammed his chest, sending him spinning into the dust. A sudden cry of human pain, and he saw the other boy tumbling beneath the beast's hooves, as it stamped and trampled to free itself from this sudden obstruction.

Deer picked himself up, helped to his feet the boy he had knocked over, cuffed him away from the sight of the trampled youth, and ran on. It was the firmest rule. The line of the beaters must always drive on. It must never flag, never turn aside to help a wounded friend, and never allow gaps to appear through which the herd might escape. Deer ran on, the dust thicker, the haunches of the herd suddenly looming close as the narrowing funnel slowed them. Now he could hear the cries of the men on both sides. Now was the crucial moment. Leaping forward, he jabbed his spear into the haunches ahead of him, great gray bulk after brownish mass, jabbing to keep them moving, to keep up the momentum and panic that would finally take the beasts over the cliff to their deaths.

This was the most dangerous time. Crowded together, their pace slowing as the pressure of beasts increased, this was the moment when the reindeer would be forced against the flimsy barriers of men and the skin-covered tripods. Some of them would find this was little enough barrier and burst through the line. Others would flee to the rear. This was when men and boys started to die, as the hunted took revenge on the hunters. This was the moment when safety lay only in the relentless jabbing of the spear, and the trust that the boy beside you would be jabbing too, holding the line with the discipline that was the mark of man against the beast.

His chest aching from the slamming of the escaped reindeer, his throat dry and his vision blurred, Deer knew that his breath was coming in raw and grating sobs. But he could smell the sudden taint of blood amid the dung, and staggered as his foot almost tripped over the fallen body of a young beast. If they were trampling their young, the panic was complete. Jab again, and again.

Suddenly they broke. The herd found space and ran forward. Enough of their leaders had fallen down the cliff to make a ramp of their own dead and broken bodies. Slipping and sliding, skidding and scampering, the rest of the herd rolled and heaved and fought their way across the still-warm corpses. He saw rumps pause and tauten, as the remaining beasts nerved themselves for the only escape. And then he was at the cliff edge, bellows of pain and exhaustion coming from below him, as what seemed like a living, crawling mat of beasts squirmed down to the river. Some were already swimming across.

Deer sank to his knees, exhausted, his chest sucking great gulps of dusty air as he coughed and bent, dimly aware of other boys doing the same beside him. His breath easing, he looked along the line of beaters, seeing gaps here and there in the line of tripods. There would be dead men after this hunt, and one stricken boy that he knew of. Clutching his spear, he began to haul himself to his feet. And failed. The shaft was slick with blood. It ran thickly down his arm. It was splashed all up his legs. His chest and belly were a thick paste of blood and sweat.

He felt a great push in his back. The hunters were driving the boys down into the still heaving mass below. He lost his balance at the cliff edge, and half-stumbled over, trying to turn so that he could keep his trunk on the cliff rim. But the hundreds of reindeer had kicked away whatever edge there might have been, and Deer slid on his stomach down the slope for only the briefest drop, before his leg slipped into the writhing warmth between two beasts. Terrified of his leg being crushed, he squirmed and hauled himself onto a heaving back and realized that his spear had broken. He still had the flint point, so he drove it like a dagger into the space between the shoulders, just below the hump at the base of the neck. A great tremor came from beneath him, but the beast stayed upright. He leaned forward, grabbed an antler with one hand, and rose to his knees on the back of his kill. Now he had leverage and struck down, now to a neck to his right, now to his left, now into the haunch of a beast that was trying to kick and push itself out of the mass. His own beast was still at last and suddenly seemed to lurch down. He dove across to another, grabbed an antler as it tried to buck him off, and drove his weapon down into the neck. Again.

He dove for the plunging back ahead, colliding with another boy who was trying to mount the same beast, and they both rolled off to the side, and suddenly there were no more backs to cling to, only a shallow, lumpy, living slope down which he sprawled and fell, an antler scoring its way along his side. And then he splashed into the water of the river, the coldness a shock until he got his head into the air and realized that it was a soup thick with blood. As helpless as the reindeer that cannoned into him, sending him back beneath the surface, he felt an intense communion with the beasts. They were him and he was them. Deer. Reindeer. Morsels in a soup of death.

He was floating. Too tired to swim. His eyes full of water and tears. He bumped gently against a dead beast, looked and saw the killing ground upstream. He pushed off from the reindeer's haunch and struck out for the shore one-handed. His broken spear was still fixed in his hand. Stones underfoot. The shallows. He staggered out to the shore. No cliff here. Just a shallow climb up a rolling stretch of grass and shrubs to the men milling at the cliff edge. One foot before the other. And again. His head bowed, he suddenly focused on his legs. Clean of blood and dung. The river had cleansed him. His chest was bruised, and there was a long scrape down his side, with pinpricks of blood just welling.

The Keeper of the Horses emerged from the crowd of men and stood before him. His hand and arm dripping with blood, he placed it flat on Deer's chest, and then traced two bloody circles around Deer's nipples. With his other hand he scraped blood from his arm, and daubed a waving line on Deer's belly. So, he was acknowledged as a man now. It felt as if it were happening to someone else.

"We should call you Deer Rider," he said. "You did well."

Deer looked at him without comprehension. Now he would have to go back to the river to wash himself clean again. He did not want Moon to see him like this.

"The old man died," said the Keeper of the Horses. "Some beasts broke through and crushed him."

Deer looked down. A crumpled body, pitifully small, one thin white leg twisted askew at the knee. A skin had been placed over the crushed skull. His nursemaiding days were over. Too spent to say anything, he bowed his head. He'd miss the old man.

"We will need another Keeper," said Moon's father. "Think of that."

Deer lifted his head, and then shook off the man's hand. He lurched toward what was left of the Keeper of the Bison, and lifted the skin. The eyes were open. Gently, Deer smoothed the eyelids down, and then straightened again. He looked back along the sloping stretch of ground that the beaters had covered through the dust. Grimly, he set his teeth and plodded back through the bloodied earth and between trampled young deer to find the broken brown body of the boy who had run beside him. The chest was crushed and the youth had no face. Now Deer's tears flowed thickly. When he felt Moon's father's hand on his shoulder, he turned and half fell against the man's chest, sobbing like a child as two strong and reeking arms came around him. And he felt the sticky blood on his breast and belly bind the two of them together, more closely than he had ever hoped to lie with this man's daughter.

CHAPTER 9

Périgord, 1944

A thin frost was forming as McPhee and Manners crept along the riverbank. There were four young Frenchmen in a ragged line between them, coming along for the experience. Manners had a filthy headache, after handling the crude "808" British version of the plastic explosive. It stank and gave off pungent fumes when he had soaked it in warm water to make it malleable. But it was powerful. Less than a pound would be enough to blow the railway points apart. He had a dozen charges in his rucksack, each sewn crudely into a cloth bag.

At the rail junctions of le Buisson the east-west line to Bordeaux crossed the north-south line from Agen to Périgueux and up to Limoges and Paris. It was a small station, with a German patrol coming around four times each night to check on the small permanent guard of three of the Vichy paramilitary, the Milice. Just to establish that had taken three nights of surveillance, to the frustration of the French, who had thought the simple arrival of the Jedburgh team would trigger an instant orgy of demolitions and mayhem. They had to be taught that nine-tenths of guerrilla war was patience and observation. McPhee had two hand grenades for the Milice hut, and the Frenchmen had Stens. François was with another small squad about three miles back at a sharp bend in the road to Belvès, the route the patrolling German lorry would take.

The night was bright with stars, but no moon. McPhee insisted on wearing his uniform, just as he insisted each day on shaving the sides of his scalp with ever-blunter razor blades. The skin above his ears was nicked with tiny cuts, but his bizarre Mohican tuft survived. Manners had taken Hilaire's advice and was wearing dark blue French overalls and an old leather jacket. He was freezing and he was hungry, and the spring water up in the hills had given him the runs, and his head throbbed. He was about as miserable as he could ever remember being, but it was not the cold that made his hands tremble until he tucked them under the straps of his rucksack. He stepped through a thin sheen of ice and into a puddle. At least his boots were almost new.

Berger's vaunted team of Maquis had turned out to be one tough old sergeant from the colonial army, an even older veteran of the Great War, a wiry corporal from the Alpine troops, and fourteen hungry and dispirited youths, who had taken to the hills rather than be conscripted for forced labor in German factories. Apart from one Marine deserter, only three of them had any kind of military training, and one had been a mechanic in the Air Force. They could fire a rifle, but had never fired or stripped a submachine gun, and there was no point in wasting ammunition by giving them revolvers. Berger had wanted to boost their morale with a gigantic explosion, something big like a bridge. Gently, François and Manners had dissuaded him. There was a limit to their stocks of explosive, and the bridges that mattered were well guarded.

Better to start small, to give the best of the young Maquis a taste of action against a relatively soft target. And the *coeurs d'aigulles*, the points that allowed a train to switch from one line to another, were complex pieces of casting. A single destroyed stretch of rail could be repaired within a day. A network of points could take a week to replace, plus another few days to repair the signals.

Ahead of Manners, the line had stopped. McPhee signaled him to come up to the front. At least there were no hedges in this country to be pushed through or skirted. He slogged forward, ignoring the distant growling of a heavy engine. Too far away to worry about.

"That was the German patrol truck, heading back to Belvès. That gives us a couple of hours before they are due back," said McPhee. "We're about two hundred yards from the station. You can see the railway line there on the right. I'm going to stake out the Milice hut with the sergeant. You take the boys and start laying the charges. I'll give you thirty minutes, then I'll put the grenades in."

Manners waved the Frenchmen on, as McPhee and the squat little sergeant from the colonial wars began a running crouch toward the station. Manners put Frisé in the lead; the one they called Curly. He at least had seen some action in 1940, in the Corps Francs, which took patrols out from the Maginot line, and felt very proud of being promoted to corporal. He had also seemed to be the fastest at grasping the basics of demolition when François and Manners had shown the group how the detonators worked. It was a straightforward fuse, and they all had lighters. Just so long as they remembered to stuff the charges into the V of the points.

It was a very small town, and the station was almost on the outskirts. Frisé took them quickly past darkened houses, over a narrow road, and past a squat war memorial from 1914–18 until they reached the level crossing. The rails and their crucial points spread out in the starlight like a great fan. Manners opened his rucksack, gave each of the Frenchmen two charges, and pushed them toward the rails. Just as he began placing his fourth charge deep into the points, there came the sound of distant gunfire. Automatic bursts, then single shots. It wasn't McPhee—the wrong direction. The German patrol! But they were still miles away.

"Finish your work," he snapped at Jean-Claude, who had stood up and was staring around wildly, a charge still in his hand. The Frenchman bent again to his task. Manners had two charges still to place, and then came a flash of red light at the station fifty yards down the line, and the crack of a grenade, then the burst of a Sten as McPhee hit the Milice hut.

"Finished," called Frisé, shepherding the other young Frenchmen back to the level crossing. Manners scampered across the rails, taking out his shielded red torch to check on each charge. He had placed his own by touch alone. There was more firing from the station. Then from far up the road, the unmistakable ripping sound of a belt-fed MG-34, a German machine gun. François was in trouble. A distant, flat boom. François was using his Gammon grenades, homemade bombs that eked out their pitiful arsenal.

"O.K." He waved them back to the rails. "Ignition now." He had given each of them a "Tommy" lighter, more reliable than matches in wind—as long as they could get the petrol. His own sparked and flared. He had six to light, the Frenchmen only two each. He didn't have enough fuses to link them all together to a single firing point. The fuses caught. They now had just over a minute to get clear. McPhee was on his own. François was on his own. The rule was that they each had to make their own withdrawal to the agreed rendezvous. Back at the level crossing, he slapped the chattering Frenchmen on the back, more to be sure they were all there than from any sense of congratulation. One, two, three.

"Now, move." He led them back past the war memorial, skirting the main street where they held the market each Friday. No point in cautious creeping. They were running now. He heard windows being opened and furious French whisperings, and the explosions came in sharp, metallic cracks as he pushed the boys up toward the hills that rose above the river. He counted them—ten, eleven—no number twelve. No more firing from the station. McPhee was either dead or escaped. Another explosion. Twelve. All the charges had worked. The French boys had done well. No more sounds from the Belvès road. As he pounded up the frosty hillside, his rucksack felt curiously light.

McPhee and the colonial sergeant were already waiting for them at the rendezvous, a sagging ancient barn in the hills behind the hilltop village of Limeuil. The sergeant was cleaning his Sten carefully. McPhee had taken watch outside, and once he and Manners had exchanged passwords, the American solemnly shook each of the young Frenchmen by the hand.

"I heard all the explosions," he said. "Well done."

"Any trouble with the Milice?" Manners asked.

"Piece of cake. I think they were asleep, but then the firing started and as one of them opened the door, I tossed a grenade in. One of them survived long enough to start firing a rifle through the window, but the old guy got him with a Sten burst. We went in, got two Lebel rifles and their ammo, and an old revolver, and ran for it as your charges went off."

Manners congratulated the old sergeant, and moved to the back of the barn. On an earlier visit, they had found some rusty lengths of corrugated iron, put them together as a low lean-to, to make a place shadowed enough to light a tiny folding Tommy cooker without the light showing. He put some water on to boil and poured in the jar of concentrated soup he carried. It was bitterly cold, and now that the boys had stopped moving and their adrenaline surge had passed, they would need hot food. Without being asked, Frisé took a loaf of the yellowish chestnut bread from his pack and began sawing thick slices. The colonial sergeant took the guard duty outside.

"You heard the machine gun?" Manners asked McPhee as they crouched over the little pebble of solid fuel, its chemical fumes stronger than the smell of the soup.

"I don't think our French buddy's going to make it," McPhee grunted.

"Don't write him off that easily. He has a way of getting out of tight spots."

"The truck was going away. So they wouldn't have ambushed it, there'd have been no point. The Krauts must have spotted them first. François was the only one among them who'd ever been in action. If the Krauts were any good, it would have been like potting rabbits."

"He had a couple of men who knew what they were doing, the chap who was in the French Marines and the Great War veteran. And they had a lot of cover."

"Yeah, but they didn't have a Spandau. That thing rips out bullets like I never heard."

They dipped their enamel mugs into the soup, and Manners took one out to the sergeant. Nothing, he said. No explosions, no firing, no sound of trucks yet. The Germans would probably wait for daylight before sending out a damage assessment squad with a strong patrol. Manners sent him back inside to drink his soup and took the watch. Inside the barn, the sounds of excited conversation died away as the boys settled down to sleep in the straw. The stars were brighter than ever, almost as bright as they had been in the desert. He traced the handful of constellations he knew, Orion's belt and the plow, which led him up to the Pole Star. It was a good night for parachute drops, and he wondered how many more tiny knots of frightened, excited men were out in this cold French countryside, how many stripped-down bombers were lumbering back to England after dropping the arms and supplies they used as pinpricks against the million-man army the Germans kept in France. Seventy divisions, Von Runstedt was supposed to have. Seventy divisions, and two thousand tanks. And Rommel had kept a British army on the run in North Africa with just two divisions and less than four hundred tanks. The invasion was going to be a nightmare. But if he and the Maquis could keep Army Group G tied down here in the south, that was almost a third of the German forces who would not be driving the Allies off the beaches.

It was nearly dawn before the survivors came. Manners heard them coming through the woods long before he heard the whispered password "Laval." No Vichy or German troops would ever dream that the Maquis would use the name of the Vichy political boss as a password. Nor the reply, "Pétain," although the Frenchmen liked to make it sound like *"putain"* —whore.

They were shivering with cold in shirtsleeves and pullovers. They had taken off their jackets to make an improvised stretcher for the Great War veteran who had taken two bullets in his thigh. There was a whiff of French tobacco in their air, and François arrived, nonchalantly bringing up the rear with a Spandau over one shoulder. The men putting down the stretcher clinked from the belt bandoliers around their shoulders.

"You got the gun," Manners marveled.

"Got the gun, the ammo, the truck, and eight Boches. And two Schmeissers. A successful night. We heard your explosions."

"So how did it start? Did they spot you"?

"It started by accident. We had a tree all ready to roll onto the road in case the patrol came back, but we lost control of the thing in the dark and it rolled out on its own, just as we heard the truck coming from le Buisson." He lit another cigarette from the stump of the one he had been smoking, his hand trembling. "Get my boys some food, can you? And take a look at that leg. He could walk a bit, but the tourniquet needs loosening. He'll need a friendly doctor."

Back in the barn, as McPhee made more soup and the colonial sergeant began loosening the tourniquet in the light of Manners's red torch, François continued with his tale.

"There was no time to move it, so we had to ambush the truck right there, as soon as it stopped for the log. It didn't look suspicious, still half on the bank, and only blocking about half the road. So the truck stopped, and we opened up. One of them got off a burst with the machine gun from the roof of the cab, but luckily he was firing the wrong way and the Marine threw a Gammon bomb, and that was it. We shot two of them trying to scuttle down the road. We lost one dead, and the old man was hit."

"Was the truck a write-off?"

"We pushed it off the road and burned it, took the guns and came back this way. It was easier than I thought, except for burying poor little Jeannot. I don't think he even fired a shot." He lit another cigarette. "The boys behaved well. They trust their guns now, and the Gammon bombs. And us. They'll be even better next time."

"Next time won't be so easy. The Germans aren't idiots. There'll be no more single-truck patrols, and they'll start trying to ambush us."

"I know. But I have an idea." The Frenchman went across to fill his tin cup, puffing on his cigarette between swigs of soup. "What is the most vulnerable but essential part of our operation?"

"The radio, no question."

"Correct, and the big danger is their direction-finding trucks, right?"

"Right."

"How many do they have, for this part of France?"

"I don't know, but they'll be a special unit, corps troops, probably assigned to the Gestapo. No more than a company for this region. Say eight or ten trucks at the most."

"And they always hunt in threes?"

"They have to, to triangulate the bearings on the transmitter."

"So with three successful ambushes, we close them down."

"You mean we use the radio as bait? Can we afford to take that risk?"

"We take that risk every time we transmit. Might as well take advantage of it. The thing about the trucks, they are stuck to moving on roads and decent tracks. So we pick our spot, somewhere near a road the trucks must use. And we hit them. It's not just the specialized trucks; it's the personnel. Those guys take a lot of training."

"Let's be smart about this. We have to set the trap somewhere outside the area we normally use, because after an attack like that the Gestapo will scream blue murder until the army sends in reinforcements to hunt us down."

"Fine, we'll go east, into the Massif, somewhere the far side of Brive. It's nearly empty country, not like round here. But we'll need some more parachute drops, both here and over in the Massif. That will mean one of us going across there to scout out drop zones, probably me, because we'll have to liaise with the local Maquis. My brother knows the FFI types in Brive, but most of the guys over there are Communists."

"So perhaps you aren't the best chap for the job."

"They don't like British imperialists either. Maybe McPhee is the one to send. We must discuss this with my brother. But there'll be plenty of work here. Tonight's work will bring new recruits to train. And a lot of angry Germans to make us keep moving."

"I want to keep hitting their railways, taking out the points network. That's their Achilles' heel," Manners insisted. "Take out the points on the east-west line and they can only run one train a day. Take them out on the north-south lines and we close down half of southwestern France. Now the boys know what to do, I think we can use them to set off the charges as a train is coming, so we get the derailment as well as the track."

"They are local boys. They won't do that to passenger trains."

"I'd rather derail freight trains. They are tougher to move. They have to bring a mobile crane in to clear it, and there can't be too many of those on the French rail system."

Late in the morning, a sweating Berger came into view with a young woman, gray-eyed and with wind-blown blond hair, whose arrival made the men fall silent and pick up their already clean guns to tend them again. The two of them were wearing trousers and anoraks and carrying rucksacks, as if out for a hike. Their rucksacks were full of wine and food and Caporal cigarettes. The woman went straight to the old man, asleep and pale on his stretcher.

"She's a doctor," said Berger, straightening his back. "Well, almost as good. She's a vet. I thought you might need one. How is he?"

"In shock, lost a lot of blood. I don't think the bone was hit but there are two entry wounds and only one exit. One bullet's still in there," said McPhee. "I dusted the wounds with sulfa powder—it's the best we've got."

"What's the news from le Buisson?" asked François, through a mouthful of bread.

"Good, very good," Berger said as the Maquis gathered around him for the news. "It was a great job, boys. All the tracks and points are gone. One of the railway men told me it will take two weeks to repair, even if they can get the new points. With the Allied bombing in the north, they can't cast new points fast enough. The Boches took all the French stocks last year, because of the bombing of their rail network. The bad news is that two companies of Boches have arrived and commandeered a house beside the station. It looks like they will put a permanent guard there."

"Are they taking reprisals?" asked Frisé. "I have family in le Buisson. So does Lespinasse."

"Nothing yet, but they beat up a few people when they did their search. A new squad of Milice is on the way with some Gestapo, according to the railway men, and apparently they are bastards. Le

Buisson is in for a rough time. The priest told me that ten guys have taken off for the hills already."

"Do we know where they are?"

"Up somewhere in those woods above the Gouffre, the big cave. There are some remote farms up there, sheep and cattle. They'll be all right. One of our emergency camps is nearby, where we have a small arms dump. Frisé, you'll know some of them. If you go across the river tonight, find the guys, and we'll meet you at that camp near Audrix tomorrow evening."

"Did the railway men know where the rail repair train would come from?" asked Manners. Back in England they had been told that the French railroad workers, traditionally left wing and with a strong trade union, would be their most useful informants.

"Due from Bergerac tomorrow. Why?"

"That means it will come through le Bugue?"

"Of course, but why?"

"I'd rather derail one of those than almost anything else. Are there any good ambush points?"

"There's the bridge over the Vézère, but that will be guarded," said Berger. "Then the track runs along the road by the river, with a steep wooded hill on one side. There would be places there, but it's close to le Buisson, and the Boches would be there within ten minutes, unless they are already patrolling the line."

"We have not told you of our new secret weapon," said François. He lifted the tarpaulin off the Spandau. "The Germans are in soft-topped trucks. So we ambush the repair train, and when the Boches come along the road to the rescue, we ambush them from the far side of the river. This gun is accurate up to a kilometer. We'll do a lot of damage."

"Do we have time to set all this up?" interjected McPhee.

"I have to go back to the dump to get some more explosives, which means crossing the river. And I'll need the electric detonator," said

Manners. "And then find an ambush point. We have to move now, and find a good firing point for the Spandau, then pick a rendezvous point. We also need to be sure that the Spandau is firing accurately from the moment it opens up—so has anybody ever used one, apart from me?"

"Of course," said François. "We used them whenever we could capture one in the desert—much better than those little Bren guns you British gave us." He looked down at the coiled bandoliers. "I have more than enough ammo, but I'll need two men to carry it. I'll take the Marine and the sergeant. They can both use a rifle."

"We rendezvous at the Gouffre—it's about two miles through the hills from that stretch of rail track," said Berger. "François, you had better go with Manners to agree about your firing point and his ambush point. Manners, you'll need some men to give you covering fire after you blow the train. McPhee, you go back with the rest of the men to the Audrix camp."

"What about him?" McPhee jerked his thumb at the wounded veteran, who was swigging wine from the bottle Berger had brought. The vet patiently took the bottle from him, and finished bandaging the leg.

"Sybille?" called Berger. "*Comment va-t-il?* How is he?"

"He'll have to stay here, unless there is a warm place nearby where he can go. I'll have to take the bullet out today, and I'll need boiling water," she said.

"O.K. There is old Boridot's farm in the next valley. He's a taciturn old buzzard, but he fought in the Great War. He'll help, but I will have to come along to talk to him. McPhee, you and your men come with me and the vet to carry him, and then you head off for Audrix. All agreed? Any questions? Right, leave that food here for another time, pack up those guns, and let's get moving."

There were no points along the stretch of single-track line, only culverts. It took five pounds of plastic to blow a culvert, and Manners couldn't spare them. So he used the culvert as cover and decided on a simple charge to blow the track. He only had fifty meters of detonator cord and one detonator box. He tested the box, leaning down hard on the handle, and the little clockwork dynamo produced a spark. That would do. He took a handful of icy mud from the bottom of the culvert, and smeared it over his charge. The fumes of the 808 explosive had started his headache again.

He felt terribly exposed. The railway ran alongside the road, and three times he had to duck into the culvert when traffic came by. There was a priest on a bicycle, then a German truck preceding a staff car, and then a gasogene, one of the civilian cars converted to run on gas generated by charcoal because of the petrol shortages. The gas bag was draped over the roof, and the things were so underpowered that they had to be pushed up steep hills. But for wartime France, it was often the only civilian transport on offer.

He checked his watch. Almost four, and the sun was going down. He put his ear against the rail—no sound of a train yet. He peeked over the rails at the road. It was clear in both directions. He looked back up the hill and waved to where the three boys were installed, ready to give him covering fire if he needed it. His detonation point was as well concealed as he could make it, behind a big tree and a fallen log. He took the metal mirror from his shirt pocket and flashed it over toward the copse where François waited with the Spandau. He got an answering flash, and then sent the quick burst of Morse to say that he was ready. God knows what they would do for signals when there was no sun.

His head was almost bursting with pain. He darted across to the road on top of the riverbank, and clambered down to dunk his head into the icy water. He held it below the surface, counted to ten, and came out gasping. That was better. The road was still clear. One last quick check of his charge, and he tidied the site, smoothing out the hollow in the gravel where he had knelt. So much easier to work in daylight. He put his ear to the rail again. Still nothing. No, perhaps a faint vibration somewhere deep in his head. He lifted his head, shook it to clear the water from his ears, and lowered it again. Yes, definitely a vibration. He clambered back up the hill to his detonating point and squatted behind the old log, smoothing his wet hair back with his hands. That was a foolish indulgence. He'd probably catch a cold, and he had nothing to use to dry his hair. He took off his leather jacket and used its woolen lining to soak up the worst of the water. That was better, and the warmth of his body would soon dry out the lining. Now he could hear the train.

It took a very long time in coming along the level track, but the sound of the laboring steam engine was bounced back from the slope of the hillside. Certainly a freight, and heavily loaded. It must be the repair train, and if it weren't, it would still block the line until they could get a crane in.

He saw the smoke first, and then something came into sight. Not a locomotive, but a flatcar, piled high with sandbags protecting a machine gun post. Then the locomotive, and the gantry behind it for the big winch and pulleys. That was the repair train, and the poor undertrained fools were so unaccustomed to ambush that they didn't know that they had played into his hands. Thank God they weren't veterans from the Eastern Front battles against the partisans. The timing was always tricky when trying to derail a train with a single charge. But now he could detonate it beneath the flatcar, and the sandbags would contain part of the force of the explosion to rip an even bigger gap in the rail. And take care of the machine gunners. But what if they had another machine gun car at the rear? Oh Christ, he hadn't thought of that. But no time for that now, and he pressed down on the detonator handle just as the flatcar reached his charge, and ducked his face deep into the leaves.

The explosion was a hugely satisfying thud that sent the fallen log trembling, but when he raised his head to look, he couldn't see a thing. Sand everywhere, falling into his damp hair, getting into his eyes, drifting down through the savagely shorn trees. It formed a great dust cloud made thicker by deep gouts of black smoke from the stricken locomotive and the sharp hiss of escaping steam mixed with the terrible scream of grinding metal as the rest of the train derailed.

Slowly his vision cleared, as he heard his Maquis shrieking with joy from above. There was no sign of the machine gun or the soldiers, and the flatcar was folded almost in two where the locomotive had pushed it against the trees as it slumped from the gapped rail and toppled sideways to plow along the hillside. The repair train itself had jerked the other way, off the rails and across the road, and the gantry with the pulleys and the flatcars with their spare rails and the freight cars with their precious spare points had all toppled down the bank of the river where he had bathed his head only minutes beforehand. Down the track, two more freight cars lay on their side, but the last one was still on the rails. No sign of more Germans. Movement below him, where the driver was clambering out of the side of his wrecked train and bending to help haul something out. The fireman . . . Christ.

"There may be some Germans left. Keep a watch here and at the far end of the train," he called up the hill to his men, and he slid and staggered down and around the front of the train to help the engine driver. The steam was coming out so fast that he felt sure the boiler wouldn't burst, but the smoke was everywhere, and the side of the engine was too hot to touch. His pulled his hand inside his leather sleeve, used that to get a purchase, and then he could put his hand under the fireman's armpit and haul. They got him out and onto the road. The driver was too dazed to do anything but fall to his knees and vomit copiously. Manners went back to the crushed flatcar. No sign of the machine gun, and only the naked trunk of a single German soldier, his helmet still on his head but his legs gone. Then he saw another German, a bundle of clothing that had been blown into the cutting. Almost unconsciously, he tugged at the buttons on the blouse, pulled out a pay book and a wallet. It should tell him what units the Germans were using, he thought, stuffing them into his blouse.

He clambered up the hill toward his men, the mud easier now with the fine layer of sand to give his boots a grip. The boys were standing in full view, their weapons hanging loosely by their sides, enthralled by the sight of the wrecked train. One threw his arms wide open to embrace Manners and the others began spontaneously to applaud. But there was no time for that. Manners bundled them up the hill, away from what was now an ambush site for François. They had to be well clear before the German patrols arrived from le Buisson. Christ, they'd be angry. This line would be out for days, and a whole freight car of replacement points had fallen into the river. Maybe they could do something to make sure they could not be salvaged. Perhaps if he booby-trapped the door . . .

Lungs heaving, their hands and faces scratched from the climb through the woods, they got to the ridge in time to see the German trucks coming along the road from le Buisson. God, they were badly trained. They should have been spaced at least two hundred yards apart in this country, and there should have been an armored car to lead them or at least a couple of motorcyclists. Had they no fear of an ambush?

François waited until the trucks slowed to take a sharp bend in the road where it crossed the railway line, still almost a mile from the train crash. And then as the lead truck turned and rumbled across the crossing and down the slope, François had a perfect head-on shot with no deflection and he held his aim as the first short burst hit the road just ahead and the truck rolled into it. A sustained burst and the truck slowed as if it had hit a wall, and careered off the road and into a ditch. The second truck drove into the same burst of fire, drove through it and failed to make the bend and rolled into the river. François paused, switched his aim, and raked the last truck, now stopped just before the level crossing. The two trucks stuck in the middle were trying frantically to turn, soldiers leaping out into the trees. The last truck exploded as the petrol tank blew up and ammunition began to cook off. Long raking bursts into the trees, and then the sound of single shots as the rifles began firing at the soldiers. François would have to change the machine gun barrel soon. Another two bursts into the two middle trucks. More single shots. Now the Germans were firing back, but firing anywhere, François's position still unspotted. Time to go. His Frenchmen were capering with joy behind him, the fools. They'd attract bullets. He pushed them down the slope beyond the ridge toward Audrix. His headache had quite disappeared.

Boridot's farm looked deserted and ramshackle and the small vineyard was thick with weeds. But the vegetable garden was well kept and blooming with early radishes and some of the fattest cabbages Manners had ever seen. There were some chickens pecking in the yard, and two dogs chained to rings in the stone wall. They came barking at Manners until their chains yanked them back as he pushed Berger's bicycle through the sagging gate. It was held closed by a piece of old rope that looked as if it had come from the same batch that now served Boridot as a belt. The old farmer wore a faded red handkerchief on his head, the four corners tied into tiny knots to keep it in place, and wooden sabots instead of shoes. And his teeth gripped the aged pipe between his teeth with the same determination as his hands kept the gleaming shotgun pointed at Manners's chest.

"I have come to see the wounded man, the one who was shot in the thigh," said Manners, suddenly conscious that he did not know the wounded man's name, that he sounded foreign, and that a German might be asking the same sort of question. The barrel of the shotgun looked very big indeed. He scoured his mind for something reassuring to say. Had not Berger said that old Boridot too was a veteran? "You will remember from the Great War that it is the rule in the British Army that an officer must see to the comfort of his wounded men."

"It is all right, *Grand-père*. This is the English officer," said a woman's voice, and the vet he had seen the previous day appeared in the doorway wiping her hands on a towel. She was wearing a full gray skirt and a white blouse, buttoned neatly to the neck, with her fair hair tied up in a large knot. Even wearing the same sturdy boots, she looked far more fetching than she had dressed in baggy pants as a hiker. "I know him. Berger introduced us."

"Is he really your grandfather?" Manners asked her as the shotgun was lowered and the craggy old man came forward to shake his hand.

"No, I just call him that. I've known him all my life," she said, coming forward to be kissed on both cheeks. It was a French greeting Manners always enjoyed, although it made him slightly uncomfortable, and he did it clumsily with an abrupt jerk of his head. She carried a scent of faded lavender, like the bowl his mother kept in her sewing room. He remembered her name was Sybille, and there was amusement in her eyes as he stepped back.

"How is your patient?"

"I've known worse, but not since the last pregnant cow whose calf was turned in the womb," she said. "I'm glad to see you, because you must tell London to start sending medical supplies in the parachutes. Not just those field dressings, which will get us all arrested and shot if the Germans find them. We are short of everything, even aspirin. But the new sulfa drugs, can you get London to send some? And plain white bandages? And scalpels and gut for sewing wounds?"

"I'll try, Sybille. But I think they are more concerned with inflicting wounds than treating them."

"Well, come and see the old goat. Perhaps you can order him to stop trying to put his hand up my skirt."

"Shows he's better," grunted Boridot. "A little *apéro*, to take the heat from the day?" He led the way inside, which smelled as gamy as a badger's den. There was a huge cheese made from ewe's milk on the table, and an earthenware dish containing a fat pâté beside it. On an old couch, whose broken fourth leg had been replaced by a large stone, lay a middle-aged man with a clean bandage on his thigh and a half-filled glass in his hand.

"My own *pineau*," gestured Boridot proudly, and took his handkerchief off his head to wipe it around a cloudy glass. He filled it with a reddish-brown liquid from a liter bottle, and handed it to Manners. He poured himself another glass, and Sybille picked up the drink she had been sipping before she came to the door. The ration of four liters a month did not seem to be affecting this farm.

"How goes it?" Manners asked the recumbent man. He looked half-drunk, and sounded even drunker when he said he felt well enough to fight some Germans again. Manners reached into his blouse to give him a packet of English cigarettes. Alongside the Players, he found the dead German's pay book. *Feldgendarmerie,* Military Police—that told him nothing. He opened the leather wallet and found, to his surprise, a traveling chess set, with flat pieces that fit neatly into slits in the leather. No name or identification on it, so it might be useful to help the boys pass the time. He closed it, slipped it into his breast pocket, and then handed the cigarettes to the wounded man.

"Do you want to get us all killed?" Sybille asked dryly. "The Germans find those, and we're all dead."

"The Germans find a wounded man with a bullet hole in his thigh and we're all dead anyway," he replied neutrally. "Besides, old Boridot would blow them away."

She looked at him, just a bare hint of a smile on her face. No makeup hiding that fine skin, good eyes, he thought, the catalog forming in his mind by reflex. But somehow she seemed to want to make herself look plain. Tiredness, perhaps, too many years of war and occupation. With enemy soldiers around, he could understand an attractive woman wanting to look drab.

"I want to thank you for taking care of him," he told her formally. "I understand the risks you must be taking."

"I'm the one taking the risk, with that glamorous horse doctor," belched the man on the couch. He lit a Players, looked at it suspiciously, and then handed the packet around.

"It's the best care you're going to get, so treat her with respect. Otherwise, she might saw your leg off next time," Manners said firmly, lighting Sybille's cigarette. "May I pay your fee, madame? We are well supplied with currency."

"This cigarette will more than repay me. Besides, I've known this dirty old man since he used to watch us coming out of school to run home to our lunch. There's not much to buy, anyway. Now if you had some coupons for clothes, or some of that parachute silk. . . . My husband sometimes smoked these, before the war. We went to London for our honeymoon," said Sybille, and held up the glowing cigarette to watch the way the smoke curled. "God, I've almost forgotten what it tasted like."

"Buckingham Palace, Tower of London, Houses of Parliament," chanted the drunk on the couch. "Not very romantic."

"We've all forgotten a lot of things from peacetime," Manners said. He wondered where her husband was now.

"Is your husband a vet as well, madame?" he asked.

"He was a vet. He was killed in 1940, somewhere near Calais with an artillery regiment which was wiped out holding the town to let the English escape from Dunkirk. Horse-drawn artillery, against panzers."

"The Germans have horse-drawn artillery too," he said quietly. "And nearly a hundred thousand Frenchman got out with us at Dunkirk."

"I'm not blaming the English, monsieur. I blame the Germans, and that rotten government we had, and the whole foul, political mess of the prewar days. Communists, fascists, royalists, socialists, radicals—I spit on all of them." She smoked her Players. "I think these things are very bad for the health. But not as bad as war."

"Well, I blame Hitler," said Manners.

"If not him, the Germans would have thrown up some other arsehole. They always do. Hitler, the Kaiser, Bismarck," said Boridot. "We should have finished the job back in 1918. If we'd marched on to Berlin, Jacquot, and stayed there? That would have done it."

"We were both glad to get home, and you know it," said Jacquot. "I thought I'd had my share of German bullets, last time."

"You're just going to have to remember how to dodge them, Jacquot," said Manners, relieved to have a name for the man. "I rely on the old soldiers like you to teach the young ones how to do it." He put his empty glass on the table, thanked Boridot, and turned to go. Sybille rose too, and in automatic courtesy, he asked if he could escort her anywhere.

"You seem determined to get me arrested, monsieur," she laughed, as he helped her don a thick jacket of black wool. "Yes, I'd be pleased if you rode with me. But if we see any Germans, you have to promise to jump over the hedge."

"No bloody Germans round here," called Jacquot as they left. "We killed the bastards."

They rode in single file up the cart track, her bicycle even older than his, but well cared for, the chain oiled and no rust on the wheel rims. He rode behind her, looking at the neat ankles that disappeared into her boots, the well-shaped rump above the basket that was tied above the rear wheel, filled with the straw to protect the eggs Boridot had given her.

"I can't give you any parachute silk," he said as they reached the wider track and he could pedal along beside her. "It's a firm rule. Security, you understand." She snorted. "But I promise to buy you a set of the finest silk lingerie in Paris when this war is over."

"Very well, monsieur, I will accept that as my fee for treating Jacquot and all the others I fear you will be sending me. You must buy them from Lanvin, if you please. And how many Frenchwomen have you promised such a gift?"

"Just you. I'm not sure I could afford the amount of silk that some of these farmers' wives might need. A lot of them seem to take very large sizes."

"That's an insult to French womanhood," she replied, and he couldn't tell if she were joking. She spoke again. "I won't ask where you are heading, but you'd better wait before we reach the road to le Bugue, and then follow me. There may be a Milice patrol. I presume you have papers—you had better tell me the name on them."

"I think I should turn off before le Bugue, rather than ride through it," he said. "The name on my papers is Alain Guyon, but I'd like you to know my real name—Manners, Jack Manners."

"Jacques. But to be known as Alain," she said. "Well, Jacques, if you don't follow me you'd miss the chance of a perfect omelet, and I'd miss the chance of another of your cigarettes." She grinned at him, and suddenly she did not look plain at all. "I can imagine the kind of food you boys make for yourselves. Come back and eat. Go through the town and past the church to the square where the men play *boules*. Just across the street you'll see the sign for the vet. Use the surgery entrance. I'll put up the 'closed' sign if there's any sign of trouble."

"Now you wait here until I'm out of sight," she added. "And one more thing, Monsieur Jacques."

"Yes," he said, nervously, not sure of himself now that she had suddenly taken charge.

"You might want to hide your gun before you cycle into the town."

CHAPTER 10

Time: The Present

The Château Malrand looked imposing as they first drove up the long gravel drive from the road, but then it seemed curiously to get smaller the closer they approached. It was not at all as grandiose as Lydia had expected of the country residence of the President of France. Her sense of proportion was jolted again as she suddenly realized that the drive was taking them past the formal garden and what she had not realized was the rear of the building, and around the side to deposit them abruptly into the entrance yard. What from the rear had been a reasonably proportioned seventeenth-century building with three stories and a turret with a pointed spire became from the front something shrunken. There was a narrow, almost mean little door on the ground floor into the base of the turret. And then a stone staircase began by being as wide as their car and then shrank to the width of a single person as it reached the main entrance on the first floor. It was topped incongruously by a small glass portico, an afterthought to keep off the rain while waiting for the door to be answered.

As Manners parked the Jaguar, Lydia looked behind her and realized that the real entrance drive had come that way, from the river and what must once have been the road along the river's bank. The glint of the Vézère lay perhaps a quarter mile down a handsome avenue of trees, which were flanked on one side by vines and on the other by an orchard of neatly pruned apple and pear trees. Before the trees began, an outbuilding in bright new stone overwhelmed the old stables. They had already passed one guard post as they had left the road. This was clearly another, with three big, black Citroëns parked alongside it, and three tough-looking young men leaning too casually against them. In the doorway of the new building, a big bald man with a thick stripe of mustache cupped his hand to his ear, listened attentively, and then nodded at them. As Lydia looked again at the front of the château, realizing that this had once been a small medieval fortress before the Renaissance window had been knocked into its facade, and before some seventeenth-century Malrand had rebuilt the rear, the front door seemed to open by itself. The effect was almost eerie, until a maid appeared, tucking her hair into a white starched bonnet, to guide them in.

Malrand awaited them in a large and rather cold room that ran the entire width of the house. He stood smoking a yellow cigarette before his Renaissance window, dressed as if going for a stroll, in sturdy brogues, corduroy slacks, and a tweed jacket, his checked shirt open at the neck. His clothes were somehow familiar. Lydia suddenly recalled a rather grand shop on one of the Paris boulevards just by the Madeleine called Old England, and her curiosity was satisfied. He looked just like one of the window displays. His hair was thick and white, his face strikingly pale apart from the sharp redness of his cheeks; his thin nose and lips gave him a hawkish look. He appeared far more intense and less tranquil than his photographs in the newspapers, as if still full of a youthful nervous energy.

"Welcome to my home, Major Manners. It is over fifty years since your father first stood where you are now," he said genially in excellent English, his voice like gravel after a lifetime of smoking, as he advanced upon them with hand outstretched. "I knew that you were accompanied, but had not known that we were to be honored by the presence of such a lovely woman." He took Lydia's hand, bowed slightly, and raised it to within an inch of his lips. "Mademoiselle, a perfect English rose."

"American, Monsieur le Président, and honored to meet you."

"American? Then this is almost like old times. A Malrand, a Manners, and an American, here in the old château, just as we were when we first landed back in 1944. It would be too much of a coincidence, mademoiselle, for your name to be McPhee?"

"Too much indeed, Monsieur le Président. My name is Dean," she said, a little irritated. His security men would not only know her name and nationality but he had probably checked out her ancestry, her education, and her tastes in everything from food to music.

"Mademoiselle Dean," he said. "An Anglo-Saxon rose. Have a glass of champagne, and come and admire my new vineyard. We now have some decent wine again, for the first time in over a hundred years. You know about the phylloxera, the disease that wiped out so many of our vineyards in the time of Napoleon the Third? In Bordeaux and Burgundy, they were wise enough to replant with good American vines from California, which resisted the disease. In these parts, they decided there was more money in tobacco. A great mistake. So the only wine we grew here was our own *pinard*, the rough stuff that used to be given to the soldiers when they got two liters a day as part of the rations. We drank it ourselves, too. More fool us."

He was putting himself out to be charming, with considerable success. Lydia, who had been fretting about the suitability of her ivory silk dress with a red scarf and shoes, felt herself relaxing quickly. Not too quickly, Lydia, she warned herself.

"Mademoiselle Dean, or if I may call you Lydia, you are far too beautiful to keep calling me Monsieur le Président. It makes me feel even older than I am. If you must call me anything, call me François, since we are all off duty and at our ease and you are my most welcome guests. I have to suffer far too many formal occasions, so indulge me in a happily private one." There was a distinctly jolly twinkle in his eye, and Lydia recalled reading one or two scurrilous accounts of his romantic reputation. It had probably done him no harm with the voters.

"I'm afraid, sir, that a very thorough look through my father's papers found no draft of his memoirs, just a few jotted notes and chapter headings," said Manners. "They were mainly about North Africa, rather than his time in France. There were a couple of letters to my grandmother, one which mentioned meeting you in the summer of 1942, after the Gazala battles and Bir Hakeim, and another about the visit you paid to our home. Apparently Granny rather took to you."

"Probably because I told her that I thought your house was a great deal more comfortable than my own. More attractive, too." He turned to Lydia. "Don't you find this house a terrible muddle? Not knowing whether it is an old fortress or a comfortable château—quite apart from the place being back to front."

"It is rather distinctive, monsieur—I mean, François."

"Thank you, Lydia. You say my name charmingly. Well, it would have been good to have had the memoirs of such a distinguished old soldier and great friend of France," said Malrand. "I want to hear all about this rock painting of his that you found, and whether the police are going to get it back, but that had better wait until our final guest arrives. I asked her to come a little later, to give us time to chat, and Lydia, you know about these things. What do you think of my fireplace?"

"Renaissance, Italian-style, quite early. Good marble, pity about the damage to the caryatids," she said automatically.

"German bullets. Used it for target practice after I was arrested," Malrand said. "Anything else?"

"Yes, the plaque," she said, bending to peer at the great irregular iron plate attached to the rear of the fireplace, to bounce its heat back into the room. "It's marvelous. Are those your family arms?"

"No," he said with a wink at her and a wicked grin at Manners. "The English did not win all their wars, whatever they like to think. They are the arms of the Talbots, a great English family, and my ancestors looted it from their château down the river after we kicked the last of the En glish out five centuries ago. Not long afterward, that Malrand's great-grandson invaded Italy with Francis the First in 1515."

"The invasion that brought the Renaissance back to France," Lydia said.

"Yes, and the fireplace." Malrand turned to Manners. "We did our best to pass the Renaissance on to you English a few years later, at the Field of the Cloth of Gold. But your King Henry the Eighth was more interested in women, I think. Understandable, of course."

"Why do you French and English tease each other so?" she asked, smiling to take any offense from the question.

"Joan of Arc, Trafalgar, and Waterloo," said Manners. "I suppose the French think we have a lot to answer for."

"There were battles that went the other way—Hastings, Calais, La Rochelle, Fontenoy," Malrand snapped. Then he caught himself. "No, it's not that. That's not what I want to say. After all, during the Revolution, it was Frenchmen who made my palace into a public dance hall, Frenchmen who turned Notre Dame de Paris into a temple of reason, and held a mock mass with a prostitute on the main altar. Ah, the English, what can I say about the English? They who gave me refuge and guns and hope and helped me come back to liberate my poor France." He gazed off into some private space.

"It's an intimacy, like an unending Catholic marriage in a family too poor to own more than one bed," he went on. "We have fought, invaded each other, loved each other's women, fought alongside each other for a thousand years. There are no two peoples on earth who have shared so much, and stayed so different, and yet retain this profound, almost frightening attraction for one another. You drink our wines, we drink your scotch. You English holiday here, fall in love with old France and buy houses. Our young French people fall in love with your music and your tax laws and open businesses in Kent. I have a young great-nephew who tells me he will be a millionaire when he launches his computer company later this year. He went to Brighton to learn English, fell in love, started a company, and now his children are English."

Malrand paused, his mood too intense to be interrupted, sipped some champagne, and took out a cigarette. Instead of lighting it, he walked across to Manners, and put his hand on the Englishman's shoulder. "Sometimes I think we are twins, you and I, separated at birth. Sometimes I think of that old Greek legend of the man and the woman constantly trying to reunite into the original whole. Your father, you know, was as close to me as my brother."

"That reminds me, sir," said Manners. "I thought you might appreciate some memento of my father, and when he first gave me this, he said it came from the war, from France." He reached into his jacket pocket and brought out the leather chess set Lydia had seen in the car.

Malrand took it, opened the flap, and looked at the tiny chips of ivory with black and red chess symbols painted onto the rounded ends. The thinner ends slotted into tiny slits cut into the checkerboard of light and dark squares on the leather. "I remember him with this, playing chess with McPhee," the President said softly. "It came from a dead German." He passed his hand gently over the leather. "I am very glad to have this. Thank you. But it must come back to you someday."

From the courtyard below came the racing blip of an engine, a squeal of brakes, and the almost tidal roar of the gravel being plowed up by a car being driven too fast and stopped too quickly. Lydia looked out of the window to see dust rising from behind a small Japanese convertible, with Clothilde merrily flashing her legs at the security men as she took off her high heels to skip through the gravel to the entrance stairs.

The President's white wine had been extremely good, Lydia thought, dry enough to counter the richness of the crayfish salad, and yet with enough fruit and flowers to hold up well on its own. She nibbled a little bread, and sipped it again. In London, she'd paid over ten quid a bottle for a Chablis that was a lot less appealing than this.

What she really wanted to know was whether Clothilde had already enjoyed the presidential favors, or was she simply trying rather hard to do so. She was not quite flirting, but nor was she being the cool, professional Clothilde of her meetings with Lydia's bosses and the police and the insurance men back in London. She was being witty, gay, and just a little irreverent about the changing fashions in interpreting the cave paintings. Lydia knew the Abbé Breuil had seen them as a hunting ritual, portraying the beasts that the tribes needed to catch and eat. That had always seemed quite reasonable to Lydia as a hypothesis, although she remembered reading that the bones left in the middens of their campsites seldom came from the bison and horses that were most frequently depicted. They mainly ate reindeer, as she recalled, which were not that common in the cave art.

"Then came the 1960s, and the revolutions," said Clothilde. "We had the political revolution in Paris that got rid of de Gaulle, then the sexual revolution, the intellectual revolution."

"The what?" asked Manners.

"Structuralism. France's great contribution to the age. Everything had to be reinterpreted. There were no authors, only texts, and your reading of it was as valid as mine, worth no more and no less than the considered opinion of the most learned professor."

"Intellectual revolutions must always begin by discrediting the existing professors," Malrand. said with a smile. "How else can they be pushed aside to make room for promotions for the brilliant young revolutionaries? The phenomenon is not unknown in politics." He turned to Clothilde. "So, structuralism invades the caves?"

"Indeed, Monsieur le Président. Only in this case, the attack came from my teacher, André Leroi-Gourhan. He made a statistical and rigorously structural analysis of the cave paintings and found them divided between male and female symbols. There were quite enough phallic symbols and vulvas to justify this approach, but it must be said that this fit with the spirit of the times."

"There was neither phallus nor vulva before the 1960s?" mocked Manners. Precisely the question she was thinking, thought Lydia, but did not presume to ask.

"Oh, every generation has to think it discovered sex for itself," said Malrand. "My grandfather talked of *la belle époque* before 1914. My father waxed lyrical about the delights of the Jazz Age. And of course, we had the war. But continue, madame. The poor celibate priest, the Abbé Breuil, is confounded by the assault of the sexual organs."

"He was not much of a priest," Clothilde said. "He spent all his time in caves. But Breuil had trouble with sexual organs. There's a famous cave painting in Africa, which he identified as the White Lady or the White Goddess, which is what everybody called it until somebody noticed that she sported an impressively erect penis. I'm surprised that even a priest could have missed it."

Manners was now blushing, Lydia noticed, and much as she was enjoying Clothilde's performance, she rather approved of his reaction. To her sudden dismay, she felt the President's foot brush against her own, and stay there. Heavens, what on earth was the protocol of rejecting a presidential pass at his own luncheon table?

"The whole point of structuralism was that it was supposed to be an all-embracing system, a theory of knowledge that could explain and account for everything," Clothilde went on. Malrand was clearly fascinated. "So after the phallic symbols, Leroi-Gourhan had to bring all the rest of the cave art into this male-female dualism."

"Male and female animals, I suppose. A bit like Noah's ark," suggested Manners.

"Not at all, Major Manners. Leroi-Gourhan suggested that that was a grand plan behind the cave art, and he found enough sexual symbolism to conclude it was used for initiation ceremonies into sexual adulthood. The problem was that with some obvious exceptions like the bulls or the pregnant horses, it was often not easy to tell which was male and which was female among the animals. So Leroi-Gourhan decided that all the bison were female symbols and all the horses were male."

"I thought you said some of the bison were visibly male and some of the horses were pregnant?" objected Manners.

"I did. But when did a French intellectual ever permit some tedious little fact to stand in the way of a sublime theory?"

"Magnificent, madame," laughed Malrand. "You make this Leroi-Gourhan sound like some politicians I know. But even if this ingenious theory is now exploded by the wisdom of the present day, you have established the predominant role of France and French scholarship in this field of prehistoric art. The good Abbé Breuil, the inventive Leroi-Gourhan, and now our new experts such as yourself." He bowed courteously to Clothilde. The fun and games were over. Time for the President's business. Lydia noticed, with only a slightly spiteful glow of pleasure, that Malrand had not asked Clothilde to call him François. "So, madame, you are persuaded that this tragically vanished example of cave art comes from the hands that gave us Lascaux?" Malrand asked.

"Hands in the generic sense, Monsieur le Président. Not a single pair of hands. A group, a culture, a tradition that created Lascaux. Yes, of that I think I am convinced."

"So, French without question."

"I would stake my reputation on that, with the smallest caveat that this could just possibly have come from the Altamira culture of Spain. I doubt it most strongly, since the stylistic traditions are markedly different. But I must warn you that Spain would certainly feel entitled to make a claim. We shall have to move quickly to secure this treasure for France."

"Which is to say that my ownership of the item would seem to leave me a choice of buyers," smiled Manners.

"Possibly—if you can show that your father was ever in Spain," flashed Clothilde. "We know he was here in the Dordogne."

"Indeed so, but you seem to suggest that an auction between Paris and Madrid might be in prospect."

"It is to avoid such an outcome that we have offered the reward," she retorted briskly, before looking across the table to the young woman opposite. "Lydia, you must see the justice of our case."

Lydia, feeling distracted by the pressure of Malrand's shoe upon her own and hoping it would not mark the silk, muttered something about its being Manners's decision, and all a bit academic unless they got the thing back.

"What I don't see," said Manners, with labored reasonableness, "is why this single painting is so precious to you. You have one big cave full of the things, dozens of other caves with other works. What's so special about this one?"

"Perhaps I, as one who knows a little of public opinion, might try to explain," said Malrand, silencing Clothilde's eager reaction by simply talking over her.

"Madame's estimable museum at Les Eyzies, thanks to a generous state grant that I authorized, is being rebuilt, greatly extended, and modernized," he began, sitting up in his chair. Lydia suddenly had a vision of him at a public meeting, and took advantage of his movement to slide her shoe gently from beneath his. She crossed her legs, putting her feet out of temptation's way.

"It will become an even greater attraction for the tourist trade, on which this region depends for much of its prosperity, if it were to include, as the highlight of the collection, a genuine example of the finest example of prehistoric art in the world. Since we do not know where it comes from, we can hardly put it back. We are therefore free to display it, as the new museum's prime exhibit, the Mona Lisa of the Louvre of prehistory." He bowed graciously to Clothilde, who turned bright red.

"The publicity alone will bring crowds," he went on sonorously, as the maid brought some plates of a temptingly pink lamb. Scents of rosemary and garlic arose. He poured some of his red wine for Lydia, Clothilde, and Manners, half-filled his own glass, and raised it to the table.

"Eventually, no doubt, the search for the lost cave will catch the attention of scholars, the imagination of the public, and the curiosity of schoolchildren. The good citizens of Les Eyzies and the Dordogne in general, with their hotels and restaurants and shops, will reap the advantage. And France will benefit from the advance of knowledge and the wider dissemination of her unique place as the custodian of the art of humanity's ancestors." The President paused, and looked around the table. "I think I can guarantee you that there will be no difficulty in finding state funds to ensure this happy outcome, whether for a greater reward, or indeed, Major Manners, as compensation for your loss. Your family deserves well of France, and we are a generous people."

You cunning old devil, Lydia thought in admiration. You're rehearsing this and using us as your test audience. She could see him now rehearsing a public statement, perhaps on television, announcing some lavish reward for the return of France's property. National pride, high culture, lots of profits for the merchants of his home region so that the reward would look like a clever investment rather than a cost. And a generous gesture to the son of a war hero of France's Liberation—*that* would get approving headlines in Britain. How clever these politicians could be. Lydia, thinking hard, saw no downside in the gesture Malrand was preparing, except possibly some waspish articles in the Spanish press. Across the table, her eyes bright with the prospect of becoming queen of this new Louvre of prehistory, Clothilde looked ready to die for her President.

"That seems a most statesmanlike plan, sir," Lydia said, suddenly thinking it unwise to call him François in front of Clothilde. "I am sure my auction house would be happy to fall in with your wishes."

"Ah yes," said Malrand. "Your auction house. That reminds me. They are campaigning very hard with my friends in the British government to keep a tax-free rate for the London art market. Is that not so?"

"Indeed, sir." All the London auction houses were forecasting gloom and bankruptcy if the new European tax plan went through, although it probably meant they would just shift the most lucrative sales to New York and Switzerland.

"I often think there are far too many taxes," said Malrand. "Perhaps France should reconsider this tax scheme. I'm sure our friends in the Paris salons would agree."

Lydia felt the room sway slightly. Sipping champagne and admiring Renaissance windows and feeling her toes squeezed, she had rather lost track of what it meant to be lunching with the President of a country. An unimaginably powerful man, who could change national policies at will, who could drop or propose taxes that could affect the livelihoods of thousands of people. A new wave of prosperity for the merchants of the Dordogne, continued fat profits for the art houses of London, just casually tossed onto the luncheon table. Suddenly she thought of the phone call she could make back to London with the happy news. No, this deserved more than a phone call. This could wait until her triumphant return. Better treat it rather casually. Perhaps over a drink with one of the partners. Just had lunch with Malrand at his country place—I think I've half-persuaded him to drop this silly European tax plan on art sales. That should be worth a raise. A raise? Ye gods. It should be worth a partnership. A little game of footsie under the table was a picayune price to pay.

"And now a toast," said Malrand. "That this lost part of our great national heritage will soon be home, where it belongs." They all drank and began to eat their lamb.

"We will sadly not have time to linger too long over our coffee," Malrand said casually. "I have arranged for us all to visit Lascaux this afternoon. The real one, that is. We might as well remind ourselves of the heritage we are all trying to safeguard."

They had driven up the road that ran along the Vézère, past their hotel at la Campagne and through Les Eyzies itself, past the high limestone cliffs that contained cave after cave. Layer after layer of continuous history. Lydia worked it out. Say twenty-five years to a generation, four to a century, forty to a millennium. Seventeen thousand years since Lascaux. Seventeen times forty. Six hundred and eighty generations. And there were still people living in these caves into the twentieth century, some perhaps even descended from the originals who had carved and drawn upon the cave walls the first evidence of a distinctive human sensibility. Who could tell what genes had drifted down from the people of Lascaux to this placid loveliness of modern France? So all but the last two or three generations had been born and bred and died in these gray cliffs, looking at this river, at these blue skies. Probably never dreaming that one day tourists would stand in line to come and tread along the stones where they lived, and pay money to see the carvings they had left.

"Have you visited any of these caves?" Lydia asked Lespinasse, the bald-headed security man with the mustache who had seemed to be in charge of the security staff back at Malrand's house. He was driving them in one of the big Citroën limousines. To her relief, Malrand had whisked off Clothilde in another car. She remembered one of her mother's phrases about some men being NSIT, not safe in taxis. Malrand would probably have qualified. Lespinasse had shown her and Manners into this one, and a dark blue Renault Espace followed them with some of the tough young security men.

"Of course, mademoiselle. I was born and raised in le Bugue and used to play in Bara-Bahau, our local cave. My father was with President Malrand in the war." He did not turn his eyes from the road but directed his voice to Manners. "He knew your father, too. They blew up railway lines together. My father's dead now, like yours. I met yours when he came out to the funeral. He always came to funerals, your father. He signed the book at Papon's, the funeral parlor, when he came to pay his respects. Came to the church in le Bugue and to the grave."

"Really," said Manners. "I never knew."

"Must have come four or five times. Always stayed at Malrand's place. I picked him up a couple of times at the station at Périgueux and drove him here. They always sat up half the night talking, the two of them. It's normal. I have some old comrades from the time we were in Lebanon. I like to see them, drink a pot or two. You're a soldier too, I hear."

"Yes, but there's not much about Northern Ireland that I like to remember. Which unit were you in?"

"Paras. I served my time, finished as a sous-off, and then applied for the security detail. Malrand was already President. He and my father fixed it up." Lespinasse leaned forward, punched the cigarette lighter, and fired up a Gauloise. They were cruising quite fast along the open road.

"Are you always based here in Périgord?" Lydia asked.

"No, mademoiselle. I'm deputy chief now, so I always travel with the President, in France and abroad. I met them all with Malrand, your Thatcher, and Gorbachev, and Yeltsin, Reagan, and Kohl. Japanese whose names I can't remember. I got to know some of your English security people, the ones from Scotland Yard. We went on some courses together. They came and used our special driving school at Nantes, and we spent two weeks with your SAS at Hereford. Tough guys. You did the SAS course, didn't you?"

"A long time ago," said Manners. "I'm back with my regiment now." Lydia raised her eyebrows—that came as a surprise. But then French security would have checked out his career. Manners seemed eager to change the subject. "Were you in Lebanon when the bombs went off? The one that killed a lot of your chaps and then the Americans."

"Yes, but I wasn't in the barracks at the time. I was off with the UN in the Bekáa Valley. A bad time. But you know what Napoleon said about the quality he wanted most in his generals?"

"Yes, that they should be lucky," said Manners.

She glanced at him. Some sort of communication had taken place between the two men that Lydia could not begin to decode. A month ago, she might have jumped into the conversation to make some joke about men joining armies to recapture the boys' clubs of their youth. Lydia smiled inwardly. It would have been the direct, the American thing to do, forcing the two men to turn their attention back to her. Clothilde would never have done it, being far too subtle in her wiles to stoop to the obvious, and perhaps that explained to Lydia the unconscious decision she had made not to interrupt the two men and the contact they had established. She was learning a lot from Clothilde. That elaborate flirtation with Malrand over the sexual symbols of cave art had been fascinating to watch, a most accomplished and discreet seduction of Malrand through his passion for ideas. It did not seem to have made much impression on the pragmatic Manners. But then the English were supposed to be suspicious of ideas. What, she wondered idly, would be the technique that would affect Manners in a similar way? Clothilde, she suspected, would know by instinct, and would probably employ the right technique out of sheer habit. Lydia was far from sure that she would. By agreeing to join him on this jaunt in Périgord, Lydia told herself, she had made no commitment, although she had not ruled out the prospect of a pleasant romantic dalliance should the mood take her. Manners, she suddenly thought, might not be thinking in the same way at all. What mysteries men were.

They turned off at Montignac, crossed the river, and then ignored the signs that steered the tourists toward the mock cave that had been built for them, taking a side road that wound up the hill and through a thin screen of trees. Looking down, Lydia saw a long slope falling to a stretch of flatter land by the river, then the ground rising from the small town of Montignac beyond. Screen out the town, she thought, and this is the view the artists of seventeen thousand years ago saw as they left the cave each evening.

The Vézère Valley, 15,000 B.C.

D eer was sketching, as he always did. Down by the riverbank, sitting cross-legged by the water, a small stretch of moist clay smoothed flat by his hand, and a twig drawing lines that seemed to flow unbidden from his fingers. Somehow it was never beasts that sprang from the clay at times like this. What was emerging now was that fallen tree on the far bank of the river, the sad way one branch leaned into the water, while the heavy trunk just squatted on the shore. The water built up around the obstruction of the branch, making a fat lip that flowed into two arms that raced along either side of the bough and set the leaves dancing into the sudden turbulence of the river. Heavy lines for the tree, lighter lines for the flow of water, but how could he capture the way the leaves danced? Quickly, he scratched three tiny shapes alongside each other. One leaf that was curling up, another that curled down, another bent into a suggestion of movement and merged into the one of the lines of the water. That was almost right.

"It's the tree," said a surprised voice. "The tree in the river." Little Moon put down the skin in which she was fetching water, and bent over the sketch in the clay.

"Those are the leaves in the water, and that is the river," she said eagerly, while Deer's eyes fixed on the dappled lights that flowed over her face from the sunlight reflected on the water. She turned, looking at the fallen tree. "I didn't think you could draw trees. I mean, I didn't think you could just draw what you see. What is just there."

"How can we draw anything unless we see it?"

"But I thought only the beasts were drawn." Her voice was low with an automatic respect.

"In the caves, yes. Only beasts. But if you want to draw beasts, you must be able to draw other things. At least, I do. What I learn when I draw a tree, I can use when I draw a beast. Look, you see this water?" He pointed at the clay. "How do you draw water? I cannot. So I draw movement, and the shape in the movement. You see how the river flows around the tree, piling up behind the branch. That is what I try to draw. If I can find the movement in the water, I can put movement into the beasts."

She looked again at the stretch of clay, and then at him.

"I am not to talk with you, my father says." Quick as a bird, she flicked her head to look up toward the village. "I just happened to come to this stretch of bank for the water. We are smoking the meat you brought back from the hunt."

"It is the easiest way down to the river," he said reasonably. Along with the other apprentices from the cave, he had spent the previous day cutting saplings and fixing the frames that the women would use to scrape and dry the reindeer skins. Then they had dug the fire pits and erected the teepees above them where the reindeer meat would be smoked.

"What else do you draw?" she asked.

"Flowers, and those hills over there, and the moon at night, and the ways caves appear in the curves of rock like a smile appears on a face."

"A face? You cannot draw faces. You cannot draw people. That is forbidden."

"Does your father say that?"

"When I was younger, I used to make shapes in the clay. Like you, only not as good. I did little figures once, like sticks. Big thin ones for men and round ones for women and little ones for children and my father was angry and rubbed them out. Drawings capture the spirit, he told me, which is why they paint the beasts in the caves. It is forbidden to draw people."

"It is not forbidden to draw trees or water."

"I don't know."

Suddenly he leaned forward to put a hand into the river, splashed water on the clay, and smoothed out his tree. "Show me what you draw," he instructed, and put the twig into her hand.

"I cannot," she said, darting her eyes up toward the village again. "I must take the water to soak the skins and dampen the fires for the smoking."

"Do it without me looking. I'll get your water." He rose, a fluid movement, picked up the skin and its carrying stick and splashed through the shallows to the deeper water where the current flowed fast and looked back to see Little Moon kneeling over the clay, the twig darting quickly across it. He threaded the stick through the holes that had been carefully sewn in the edges of the skin, filled it with water, and used the little thongs to secure it. He came back with deliberate slowness, watching the village and the small humped tent where the old Keeper of the Bison used to sleep. It was his now. The village was stirring busily, smoke already rising from the narrow holes at the top of each of the teepees where the meat already hung, sliced by flintknives. The sun was already a hand's breadth above the hill. His eyes turned back to Little Moon, and he felt that strange sensation when he was not just looking, but seeing. There was the curve of Moon's back, the fall of her hair, and then the flat plane of the clay, and the river dancing below it. The shapes fitted together in a way that he could almost feel, a balance of curve and flatness and movement. She looked up and broke the pattern, but in a way that pleased him. Her eyes danced, just like the water. Her limbs were smoother than the clay.

He splashed toward her, holding out the dripping log with its sagging skin full of water. She rose and took it, their hands touching, and then she turned and left, as quickly as she could under the heavy burden, staggering once as she changed her step to avoid stepping in her sketch in the clay.

He stayed in the shallows, reluctant to step forward and see what she had done. He looked across once more to the village and at the bustle beyond where smoke rose and the sound of the Flint men knapping their stones brought the accustomed rhythm to the day. Way up the hill, a thin trail of smoke twirled by the entrance to the cave. The Keeper of the Bulls had made his morning sacrifice. The other apprentices would be trudging up the slope to mix colors and build more scaffolding. The Keeper of the Horses might need his help today. Deer had already learned the way the Keeper of the Horses made the manes, blowing the colors from his mouth through the different shapes he could make with his thumb and finger.

Finally, unable to put off the moment any longer, he moved slowly forward through the water, as if it were as thick as mud, to look at Little Moon's sketch. And caught his breath with surprise.

It was a man's shape, thighs emerging from the river, the waist curved and the weight of the chest and shoulders taut to take the weight

of the log and the skin, filling in the river. The head was just a suggestion of shape, and a few swift curls of hair. There was no face, no identity, but it was him, as he had been just a few moments ago. Him in the
river, as caught by her. Caught. No, that was not the word she had used,
the word she had learned from her father. Captured. She had captured
his spirit. Indeed she had. He admired her work, the curve of thigh and
back, the suggestion of hair. The water was just three quick lines,
scored deeper where they began and then becoming shallower, in a
way that suggested both movement and direction. There was a curl of
wave by his forward thigh that he liked. A man in the river. Him.

Guiltily, he looked up at the village, and then splashed water over
her sketch with his foot and smoothed the clay clean again. As he went
to his work, he thought that his spirit did not feel caught, but that he
would like to be captured by Moon. She had seen something in him
and been moved by it, and had depicted it. But then, the sketch had
already disappeared, taken by the river. Would it be so easy to capture
her? A few hasty lines in clay? It could not be so easy, or everyone
would do it. But that way she had balanced the curve of his thigh
against the curl of the water, that was good. He could use that. She had
the talent, Little Moon. She should be working in the cave, but women
never did. He had never asked himself why not before. But then he had
never seen a woman draw before. He had never seen a drawing of himself before. Looking up to the cave and feeling eager to begin, Deer felt
as if the world had suddenly been reinvented and he was bursting with
possibilities.

The Keeper of the Horses was becoming angry. All the other Keepers
were agreed save the Keeper of the Bulls. There was a gap amid the
ranks after the old man's death. They needed a new Keeper, and Deer
had done his part in the hunt and was now a man. He was the obvious

choice, the most talented of the apprentices, and had been chosen by the old man himself. Had he not told the Keeper of the Horses that the boy should have his own lamp after his death?

"Why do you object?" he repeated, angrier still by the way the Keeper of the Bulls had perched himself on this rock above the other Keepers, looking down upon them rather than sitting with them in the circle, as was the custom. The Keepers were all equal. The man was becoming insufferable, as if he were trying to become leader. They were a brotherhood, bonded by the great work of the cave. There were no leaders or followers among them, only Keepers and apprentices. And the cave itself was ritual enough, without this new business of skulls and eagles and great ceremonies that rested on clever tricks. He had taken the other Keepers up the hill to show them the pit and the brushwood where the eagle had been caught and then released.

"The boy is still young," objected the Keeper of the Bulls.

"He is a man. He killed his beasts," said the Keeper of the Ibex, who had been more offended than any of them when he saw the eagle's pit, aware that he had been fooled. "We all saw him kill them well, leaping from back to back like a mountain goat. Deer is no boy any longer."

"We nearly banished him from the cave," came the next objection. "We only just decided to let him back in. Perhaps that was a mistake."

"You know as well as I do that the old man stumbled on his own. He felt very bad about blaming Deer. That was why he took the boy under his wing, made him his special apprentice, taught him all that he could, left Deer his lamp," said the Keeper of the Horses, striving to keep his voice reasonable.

"The old man made his choice," said the Keeper of the Ibex. "He made Deer his heir. He passed on his lamp. You know what that means. We cannot go against a Keeper's final wish."

"The old man was wandering in his own head. He was not what he had been," said the Keeper of the Bulls, his voice sullen at not getting his own way. "He even left his work unfinished."

"Deer is finishing the coloring of the two bison. He has a master's touch that boy, and the old man knew it and welcomed Deer's completion of the work."

"So let him finish that work. The boy has shown a certain talent with his deer, but as apprentice he must complete his dead master's work. The two beasts on which the old man worked are but half-done."

"They are done, save for the last of the coloring. And Deer has improved on what he was left," said the Keeper of the Horses. "The old man told me of his pleasure at Deer's idea to depict one of them shedding its winter coat. It is no apprentice's common task that Deer has done. It is a master's work. The old man knew that, and treasured the boy for his talent."

"I need to think more of this," said the sullen voice. "There is no rush to decide, and the work awaits us." He rose to go.

"The work requires a full brotherhood of Keepers," said the Keeper of the Bears. A squat, dark man who lived apart, he seldom spoke, and remained stubbornly seated on the ground. Nobody else rose. The council was still in session, whatever their high and mighty colleague might want. Odd, thought the Keeper of the Horses, how much resentment had built up toward the Keeper of the Bulls. As if that ritual he had staged before the hunt had offended the other Keepers, just as much as the trick he had played. It had certainly offended him, something new in the world that threatened changes he could not foresee.

The Keeper of the Bulls studied his colleagues thoughtfully, and instead of walking back to the cave, slid down the face of the rock to join them in the circle. He was shaking his head almost sorrowfully.

"Perhaps I am being harsh on the boy," he said, his voice different, almost ingratiating. "Forgive me, my friends, if I am still dark and low in my spirits after the death of my woman. I still think of her, and my bed is cold and lonely."

Silence as the rest of them considered that. Certainly he had been acting strangely since her death.

"This is not about your bed. It is about filling the brotherhood of Keepers," said the Keeper of the Bears, in the stubborn way of a man who has seized on a single point and will not let it go.

"You are right," said the ingratiating voice. "But we are all men here. We know that a man needs his bed filled and his heart lightened by a woman."

"Nothing to stop you taking one," said the Keeper of the Ibex. "The mating time is soon."

"My colleague of the horses, you have an unwed daughter," came the voice, confident now rather than ingratiating. "Come, let us settle everything at once. Give me your blessing and the hand of your daughter and we shall bring Deer into our number."

By the manes of my horses, the man is as crafty as he is brazen, thought Little Moon's father. He is making a bargain over this. He has no right to block Deer's advancement, but seeks to win something for himself in return. In his irritation, the Keeper of the Horses was about to dismiss the idea out of hand, but forced himself to control his tongue. He could have no credible objection to the match. Most of his colleagues would think it a wise move. It would bring honor to Little Moon, to be the woman of such an influential man, and useful to him, to be linked by kinship as well as the craft of the cave. But not like this. And not at all, he suddenly thought, as he studied the big man leaning back easily against his rock, in the circle but still somehow separate from it. This was a man who would do anything to get his own way, use the trickery of the eagle, and seduce the hunters and the fishers to him. Looking at the man's eyes, shadowed but cruel and somehow contemptuous of fellows in the brotherhood, he knew that the Keeper of the Bulls was a dangerous man, a man too touched by his sense of the power of the bulls that obsessed him. Some of their angry, stubborn spirit had invaded his, just as the Keeper of the Horses felt touched by the grace and lightness of movement in the beasts that he drew.

"This is not a matter for our council," objected the Keeper of the

Ibex. "This thing of the daughter is between the two of you. Deer has nothing to do with it. The matter of Deer is for us to decide, and speaking for myself, we have decided. The youth is the new Keeper."

"I must speak to my woman. She will want a say in the future of our daughter," said the Keeper of the Horses, suddenly seeing how best to seize this moment and get the decision on Deer settled. He wanted to think more about this sense of danger he felt from the Keeper of the Bulls. The man would not be crossed, but he could be guided, and perhaps outmaneuvered. Even as he began to speak, the Keeper of the Horses felt he might pay a heavy price for this day's work. "But I am glad that you have changed your view and seen the wisdom of your colleagues. We can now tell Deer that we are as one, all agreed, and with the shade of our departed colleague guiding us to the right decision. The Keeper of the Bison will rest happily, now that Deer has taken his place. Let us go and greet our new brother, our new Keeper." He rose, saw the other Keepers rise with him, and leaving the Keeper of the Bulls alone, walked back into the cave.

Deer filled his mouth with the bitter ocher, and putting his cupped hand to his lips began to blow the reddish-brown color onto the calcite. He had mixed it with care, not too brown, for that would look like the background wall of this narrow part of the cave, far around the corner from the great hall of the bulls. The air was bad here, and the lamp flickered feebly, smoking and making his eyes weep. It was a bad place to work, but the old Keeper had chosen this spot for his great work, and Deer must complete the bison. It was the least he could do for the old man, who had shown him such kindness after his early coldness, as if making up for having Deer banished from the cave. But it was also such a pleasure, taking the outline sketch of the two great beasts, back to back, which the old man had left for him to complete.

He had skill, that old one, thought Deer as he stood back, bracing himself to fill his mouth again with the thick liquid he had brewed. The beast to the front was poised to charge, its horns raised and its massive shoulders tense. The old man had used a flint in the wall to give a different color and texture to the front hoof, a flash of lightness that suggested the ground was about to be pawed. And the other beast to the rear, caught in mid-charge, its mouth gaping open as it sucked air and its horns high and vicious, leaped away. Such movement in both directions, but the whole kept tensely together by that point of stillness where their haunches joined and overlapped. Deer felt ashamed that he had ever doubted the old man's talent, and humble, for not having seen before the real force of this work he was now completing. Earlier, he had looked at the two beasts separately, and neither one had seemed to him well done. Now that he was working on them himself, he understood that they were not two separate beasts but one mass of force and color held in a balance so tense that he could feel it.

Deer had traced a great double curve with a carefully shaved charcoal twig to guide him, and filled in the bulk of the bison with a paste of charcoal and the two kinds of hard, dark earth that seemed almost to flow when they were placed in a hot fire. That gave the great looming blackness that had appeared to Deer to be too overwhelming, until he had suddenly thought of making the forward beast appear to be in molt. In one of their last conversations, he had excitedly put the idea to the old man, that a great curving band of reddish brown would lighten the composition, and the curve could be used to balance the power of the other beast's charging motion. And that was how the beasts looked in spring, when they began fighting for mates. The thick dark winter coat gave way to the reddish brown of summer. The old man had nodded and pondered the proposal. That night, he had plucked a handful of the dark winter hair of the bison from the skin on which he slept, and studied it by the firelight before telling Deer that he was right. They would use the red-brown color to show a molting beast.

"You are almost done," said the voice of Little Moon's father beside him. "But there is still one trick for you to learn." The Keeper of the Horses leaned forward and cupped his hand along the charcoal line, and called back for one of the apprentices to join them to watch what he did.

"You can use a hand to guide the blowing of the color, to make a line over which the color will not pass. Otherwise, you will have to paint over it again. See, the line of the hand can follow your charcoal trace. Now you, young apprentice, watch how I put my hand, for you must learn how this is done. Come, Deer, blow your color, just a small amount, so as not to overlap my hand."

Deer did as he was told, saw how the line of color stopped. The apprentice stepped forward and replaced the Keeper's hand with his own. Deer filled his mouth once more and blew again.

"Your color is good and thick," said the Keeper of the Horses. "Now, watch how I use my two hands together down here, where your tracings meet in the pointed curve. You see, my hands are not quite enough, they gape where the two palms meet. So we take a scrap of deerskin from our pouch like this, and you, youngster, fold it small to fill that gap between my hands and cover up to the traced line. Like that, yes. Now, blow again, and the curve will be properly filled with color."

They all stood back, and admired the way the colors now met without blurring. And then, without need for a word, all gathered around the haunch of the bison to repeat the trick where the traces formed another point as the red-brown color dwindled away at the root of the beast's tail. Again the two hands, again the folded scrap of deerskin, again the gentle blowing, as they panted in the bad and smoke-filled air. Then it was done, and they all staggered back down the narrow passage, clambered up and around the bend in the rock, and out through the great cave into the open air to fill their lungs and clear their blurring eyes.

"It is done," said the Keeper of the Horses when their breath had eased. "You are the new Keeper, a full member of the brotherhood. It was decided this day."

"All were agreed?" asked Deer.

"All were agreed, eventually. All admire your talent. And all will be impressed by the way you completed the old man's work. They are probably clustered around now to look, while we take our air."

"Then when will the ceremony take place?"

"It is not decided, Perhaps the night before the time of mating. That might interest you. A man now, and a Keeper, you will be able to take a woman of your own."

Deer studied him cautiously. Little Moon's father must know that Deer had already made his choice. Would he even have raised the topic if he had not been prepared for the question Deer must now put? Would he have backed Deer so strongly to become a Keeper if he did not think Deer worthy of his daughter's hand?

"There is only one maid whom I would take at the mating," he said, more boldly than he thought he could.

The man was silent, studying him carefully, a half-smile on his face. He looked down at his hands, still stained with the ocher that Deer had blown in the cave. He rubbed the sides of his palms together, and watched the grains crumble and fall, some of them sparkling in the sunlight. The color bonded him to Deer in a certain way, he thought, Deer's breath and the liquid from Deer's mouth, where they had worked together.

"I seek your Little Moon," Deer plowed on.

"You are not alone in that," said the Keeper placidly. "The Keeper of the Bulls also seeks my Moon." The shortened name was what they called her in the privacy of the family. The Keeper caught himself; he was treating Deer as if they were already kin.

"But he is old and. . . ." Deer's voice trailed off. "Little Moon herself would not take him."

"What my Little Moon wants is not the most important thing in this.

I have to take the decision, with my woman, and think what is best for us, for the brotherhood of Keepers, for the village. And he is a very powerful man, renowned among the villages up and down the river. It is a great honor for Moon."

"She would be a great honor for me," said Deer simply, hanging his head. Now he knew why her father had done it this way, raising him up with the news that he would be a Keeper, and then casting him down with this warning that Moon would be given to another. A thought came to him.

"Do you know she has the talent, your daughter?" he said.

"I know. So does her mother, but women are women. There is no place for them in the cave. The brotherhood would never allow it."

"The brotherhood seems suddenly to be allowing a lot of strange new things," Deer retorted. "Did the brotherhood know of this new thing of the eagle's head and the bull's skull? Did the other Keepers support the Keeper of the Bulls in this?"

"No, and many are troubled by this."

"And yet this is the man to whom you would entrust Little Moon?"

"I have not decided. But one of the new things that you must consider is that I may not have much choice. The Keepers may be disturbed, but the hunters and the fishermen and the flint men—all seem to welcome the new ways, and to welcome the power of the man who brought them."

"But you are her father. Nobody would go against your decision in this."

"No, but these are strange times. Fathers can fall sick or have accidents. Young suitors can meet with mysterious deaths. These are dangerous times, Deer."

CHAPTER 12

Périgord, 1944

They had walked all night loaded down with the remaining explosives. The new recruits carried the ammunition in sacks, staggering over the heavy ground along the hills that flanked the north bank of
the river Vézère. Now they were shivering in a shallow cave, unable to
light a fire, and not nearly as far north of Les Eyzies as Manners had
wished. He was more tired than he could remember being, and more
dispirited than he had ever been in the desert, even fleeing from Rommel's tanks amid the wreckage of a broken army. At least then there had
been a sense of refuge, a strong base on the Nile where his unit could
regroup and refit, the promise of a bath and a square meal.

It was the meal that was making him guilty, an omelet of fresh eggs and a glass of wine and a handsome woman sitting across the table, with Jean Sablon singing "*Vous, qui passez sans me voir*" on the windup gramophone that needed a new needle. He had not heard the song since his schooldays, on holidays with his parents at Cap d'Antibes. The waiters would sing it late at night as they stacked the chairs on the tables. He had told Sybille about that, falling in with her own mood of nostalgia for another time, before the war.

He should never have gone with her. She could be shot just for sheltering him in her home. And an officer should not eat until he had taken care of his men, far less relax in a comfortable room with curtains at the front window and the sight of a small garden through the French windows at the rear. He could taste the omelet now, the garlic and the butter, and hear Sybille's casual comment, "A vet never goes hungry—the farmers see to that." He had stayed no longer than it had taken him to eat and smoke a cigarette, but he had felt the lure of peacetime stealing over him, a reluctance to rise and go.

Sybille had been matter of fact, in a way that intrigued him. He thought of self-confident girls back in England before the war, and the nervous ones who came out to Palestine and India looking for husbands. The fishing fleet, they called them. And he thought of the nurses and secretaries and coding clerks he had seen on the arms of staff officers when he was back in Cairo on leave from the front. Sybille was like none of them, with their instant gaiety and relentless energy for tennis and horses and dances. And she wasn't like the women of wartime London with their brittle hunger for fun and parties, and the haunting way they sobbed in cinemas. Sybille had simply cooked, and ate, and asked him about his family and put another record on the gramophone. It was Charles Trenet, singing "*Je Chante,*" which he remembered from Haifa before the war.

"When I can, I live in the times before the war," she had said when he was leaving. "But I seldom can. Under Vichy it was not too bad, but now that the Germans are here, they won't let us live in the past. And their presence has brought the Resistance and people like you and now the war is everywhere. I just want it to go away."

It was that damned sense of nostalgia that was getting him down, that taste of a little normality that had made it so hard to ride back and creep around a darkened countryside and sleep in caves with his head on a pack that stank of plastic explosive. He was a professional soldier, dammit, not a guerrilla. Every time he set an ambush he found himself thinking how he would guard against it, how he would react and bring his men through if he were wearing a German uniform. He checked himself. That was the desert war, when there had been no civilians, and the Germans had fought clean. Like all of the Eighth Army, he respected the Germans of the Afrika Korps, and like a lot of them, felt he had more in common with Rommel's chaps than he did with some of the so-called Allies. No, that was unfair. McPhee was first-rate. He couldn't hope to fight this damned guerrilla war with a better comrade-in-arms.

It was the bloody anarchic nature of this war that was dismaying him, he realized, the lack of familiar rules, of that comforting routine of batmen and tea and a pressed uniform and even parades. It was the reversal of the knowledge that had been so natural to them all in the desert, that the Afrika Korps abided by the same kind of rules. Prisoners would be taken and treated decently. The wounded could be left in the knowledge that the other side would look after them, if possible. He missed the sense of organization that came with being part of a battalion, a brigade, a division, an army. And he fretted under the knowledge that he was utterly responsible for the safety and food and supplies for the almost demoralized pack of French boys around him who had not the slightest sense of a discipline he could rely on. And he was also responsible for the reprisals the Germans would take, the burnings of farms that fed them, the shooting of men and women who helped him.

He had known about this, even been trained for it. But what Manners never expected was that the sense of a modest victory over the German train networks and their patrols should now strike him as so hollow, a success that would unleash upon him only the new pressure of reprisals and German reinforcements. The better he did, the worse it would get. And there would be no Afrika Korps rules here, no prisoners taken, and no wounded could be left for the Gestapo to torture. He didn't even feel much confidence in the other trained members of the team, despite the way François had staged the ambush. François had been late to the rendezvous, and was now snoring beside him, one arm flopping casually on the captured German machine gun. He should wake him. There was much to do. They had to meet Berger today, contact the radio operator, arrange another parachute drop, organize some food for the men, and then march again all night to hit the railway line that connected Brive and Périgueux. A good twenty miles north of the last attack, it would serve to spread the German search.

"We should have been ten miles north of here by now," said McPhee, sitting up and shaking his head from his brief sleep. "The Germans will be all over these roads tomorrow."

"Today, you mean," said Manners. He shrugged. "Untrained troops, a night march. You can't expect too much. The boys are cold and hungry and frightened."

"They're not the only ones," grunted the American. "How much plastic we got left?"

"About twenty pounds. Enough for one good attack on a junction or a lot of little rail breaks."

They watched the first glow of dawn through the cave mouth, the sudden gleam of a lazy curve in the river, the silvering frost on the grass. Behind them, the click of a petrol lighter, a sudden soft glow, and the whiff of tobacco. François had woken.

"You'll kill us all, with those smokes of yours," grumbled McPhee, standing up to stamp his feet and rub some warmth back into his arms. "You just lit up the whole cave. Half the German army just pinpointed us."

"I lit it under my jacket," François said reasonably. "And there are no Germans here."

"No food either."

"But breakfast is just over the hill—a farm I know well." François went outside to piss, standing with his back to them, his arms braced on his hips, puffing plumes of smoke into the lightening sky as he released a long stream to salute the dawn. Manners shivered, as some thought suddenly ran through his head that he had seen this sight before, that men had stood at the mouths of caves and pissed into the dawn light since the days when they had first come down from the trees and learned to stand. It was eerie, as if someone had walked on his grave. These caves were spooky places.

"We can't all go to your farm. There are twenty of us now," objected McPhee. "Too many of us to feed."

"You don't know the Périgord," François grunted over his shoulder, and turned, buttoning his trousers. "They'll feed us all, warm milk straight from the cow, some chestnut bread and goat cheese. But we don't all go at once. We three go first with Frisé, then Manners and I go on to meet my brother and the radio operator. McPhee, you and Frisé then take back some milk, and bring the boys to the farm, no more than four at a time. Then we all meet tonight at the big Rouffignac cave. I know that area. There are good plateaus for parachute drops, a lot of woodland to train the boys in the Barade forest, and not enough roads for the Germans."

"What about food?" Manners asked.

"A lot of small farms. We'll be fine," said François. "Now let me have one more cigarette and then let's get that milk."

"What are the chances that someone among those small farms will tell the Germans, or the Milice?" McPhee broke in. "Just because you know the area, François, that doesn't mean you can trust everybody."

François looked at the two men for a long moment, than came and squatted in front of them. "A year ago, I would not even have taken the risk of coming back here, to my own château, my own district, where I was brought up with half the boys and was taken fishing with their fathers, and fed tartines by their mothers."

"But that was last year," he went on. "Before the RAF started sending a thousand bombers every night against Hamburg and the Ruhr. Before the Germans were beaten at Stalingrad, before we threw them out of North Africa, before we knocked Mussolini out of the war and put our armies back into Italy. And when that happened, Hitler dropped this pretense of southern France being run by Vichy and sent his armies down here too. So now we see the Boche trucks and soldiers, and watch them take our food and chase our women and arrest our young men to send them to Germany to work in their factories. Now we are occupied, and so the only people who might betray us are those too committed to Vichy to change their coats."

"That's still a lot of Frenchmen," said McPhee grimly.

"True. A year ago, to be honest, I'd have said most Frenchmen either supported Vichy or weren't prepared to do anything against it. Most people want a quiet life, and so long as there were no German troops down here, people could fool themselves that the war didn't much concern them. But now only a fool thinks the Germans have a chance of winning, and anybody with any sense wants to make sure they are on the right side when this war is over." He stopped to duck his head under his jacket and light another cigarette, and emerged to blow a thick plume of smoke into the cave. "Your war may be decided. Ours isn't. I keep telling you the big question is whether the right side will be the Communists or the Gaullists."

"Where the hell do you get all the smokes?" McPhee said. "They're supposed to be rationed."

"They are. It's a system they call the *decade*. Every ten days, an adult is entitled to two packets of twenty, or some rolling tobacco. But every adult includes a lot of nonsmokers. My brother has a friend who's a gardener in a nunnery. Eighty nuns and none of them smoke. So the gardener gets their ration, and gives most of them to my brother for his boys. And then this is the Périgord. The best tobacco in France is grown here. Come on; let's get moving."

The B Mark II transmitter was a feeble but cumbersome beast. It was two feet long, weighted thirty pounds, required an aerial seventy feet long, and could transmit its dots and dashes of Morse at no more than twenty watts. Berger had already lost one radio operator in Bérgerac when the Germans started using the trick of turning off the power in one subsection of the city after another to see when the signal died. Now he refused to use main current at all and had rigged up a small dynamo that could be powered by a bicycle, maintaining that the risk of shifting the transmitter from place to place around the woods of Périgord was less than that of detection.

François and Manners drafted their message, and Berger took the back wheel from one of the bikes to rig the dynamo, and the radio operator pulled off the top silk sheet from his one-time pad and began to encode. Manners checked the coding, and they left him alone to transmit; another of Berger's security rules. They had cycled about an hour down the woodland tracks and came to the brink of a steep hill where the track wound down to a road. The embankment of a railway loomed up behind it, and the stately arches of a viaduct bridging a steep valley on the far side of the road. Just before the viaduct a small building stood beside the rail track, the raised red-and-white bar of a level crossing beside it, ready to seal off the small road that disappeared steeply into the valley. A red signal flag was tied to the base of the bar.

"Miremont-Mauzens," said Berger. "It's a railway halt. That's where we meet them. The flag means it's safe." He turned to his brother. "François, you stay here with the bikes. They know where you're from. You'd just annoy each other, get into an argument."

François shrugged and lit a cigarette. "Don't worry, my dear brother. I am getting quite good at staying out of arguments. Just ask our English friend how polite I am being to our grumbling American, difficult as it is."

"McPhee's all right," Manners said. "He was just cold and tired and irritable this morning. So was I."

"That I understand," said François. "Let's hope that is all it is. But I get the feeling that he likes needling me."

"So do I," grinned Manners, to take the sting out of the remark. "So would anybody who knows you. You're rich, a famous writer, handsome, and a war hero. Don't be surprised if the rest of us mere mortals try to take you down a peg or two, François. If you were as dumb and ugly as me and Berger here, you'd have no trouble."

"You see why I like this cunning Englishman?" François smiled at his brother. "Even when he disciplines me, he flatters me."

"He didn't flatter me," said Berger flatly.

"Well, you haven't seen him fight yet. I did, in North Africa. He has our French *élan*, and their German thoroughness. We're lucky to have him on our side."

"We had good teachers," said Manners, making a joke of it. "We've been fighting you bloody Frenchmen since 1066."

Berger and Manners walked down the path to the road and crossed the rails to use the cover of the trees to reach the building. They had fifty yards to go when Berger stopped and turned and looked grimly at the Englishman.

"He calls himself Marat, and I don't trust him very far," said Berger quietly. "He used to be a railway man, but went off to fight in Spain with the Communists. He came back to France in 1939, and then disappeared. If you ask me, I think he went to Moscow. He came back in late 1941, after Hitler invaded Russia. He claims to have men everywhere, in Brive and Périgueux and Limoges, even Bordeaux. I think what he has mostly is his old friends on the railways and in the rail unions. And a lot of Spaniards, refugees from Franco who fled here when the fascists won. His information has been good on the rail system and convoys. He wants arms, but there's no sign of their using them against the Germans. On the other hand Hilaire said I had to take you to him and arrange supplies. So I follow orders. I won't speak much."

"He and François are old enemies?"

"He and François have never met. They just hate each other on principle. If they met, they'd start to argue. François calls himself a socialist—they hate the Reds more than anybody. They'd probably try to kill each other."

"Does this Marat have access to a radio?"

Berger shrugged. "Not one of ours. He always dealt with your F Section, that special French section of SOE you used to deny having, the one that deals with Communists and others who oppose de Gaulle. I presume he got supplied by one of their networks in the north. You probably know more of this than I do."

"So why does he want to meet me?"

"Because he wants more arms and explosives, to stockpile for his precious revolution. And you heard Hilaire back at the château. London wants the Communists supplied. But they are not using my drop zones nor my people. Anything you want to set up for them, you have to do it alone."

"So why have you set up this meeting? If you wanted to keep me away from him, you just had to say the meeting place was unsafe."

Berger eyed him steadily. "You don't know much about the secret world, do you?"

"I suppose not." Manners felt very small and rather lost, as if the war he had been fighting had taken place in some altogether different dimension. But he put his question again. "Why are you helping me to meet him?"

"First, Hilaire told me to do it, and I trust Hilaire. Second, if any arms are going to the Communists, at least I'll know when, where, and who has them. Third, even if this Marat won't use his supplies against the Germans, more and more of his people will know he has them and will want him to use them. Some of them are French first, Communists second."

"This is a vipers' nest you people have built for yourselves."

"True, but we had some help from Hitler. And from Stalin." Berger closed his eyes and grimaced. When he opened them his eyes were clear but curiously empty. "It's time you met Stalin's representative in this part of France."

Marat was of average height, thin and balding, wearing round spectacles and smoking black tobacco in an old and much-charred wooden pipe. A beret and scarf and cloth shopping bag were on the battered table at which he sat reading a book as if he were just another local waiting for a train. He looked up as Berger steered Manners inside, and peered at the Englishman.

"Are you the one that helped pull the fireman from that train you blew up?" he began. Manners nodded.

Marat rose and shook him by the hand. A surprisingly strong grip. "Then I thank you for that in the name of the railway men's union. And I congratulate you on a busy start. Le Buisson will be out of action for weeks. Your Winston Churchill should be pleased." From the shopping bag, he pulled a dark bottle and three glasses.

Berger interrupted. "I'll go outside and watch. You don't need me for this conversation."

"I think, for reasons of mutual confidence, it might be better if you stayed," said Marat. He had an attractive voice, and spoke a precise, formal French. He might have been a railway worker, thought Manners, but he was a well-educated one. "I know we have some problems between our two organizations, but we only have one enemy. And the fact of these new arrivals from London means that we are getting ready for the invasion at last. Then we can start fighting Germans together, my dear Berger."

"You haven't done much about fighting them yet," Berger said flatly. "And I don't feel comfortable without someone on watch."

"That's already taken care of. My sentry has been watching you since you came down the hill." He turned and rapped twice on the window. As Manners watched, a young and dark-haired woman in a shapeless gray overcoat slipped into view from the trees, with her hand inside the shoulder bag that hung at her side. Marat went to the door, and spoke to her briefly. She nodded and merged back into the trees.

"I have some information for you," Marat said, coming back to the table to open the bottle and pour out some drink. "But first, some Calvados, liberated from the supplies the Germans ship back to their fat wives." He pushed the glasses toward them, ignoring the way Berger's hands remained firmly clenched by his sides. "They are bringing a second repair train from Bordeaux, but this one will be well guarded. They are also bringing in a special unit, the Brehmer Division, to scour the area for the new nest of terrorists. They have armored cars, their own radio-direction teams, and they work very closely with the Gestapo. So, I drink to your good health and also to your good luck. You'll need it." He drained his glass, and grinned at Manners, who found himself rather liking this Marat.

"We know this, because they are bringing the armored cars by train from Metz, where they have been active in the Lorraine, and we see their transport orders," Marat went on. He sat down again, and pushed out a chair for Manners, ignoring Berger. Manners sat and caught a glimpse of the book Marat had been reading. Michelet's *History of France*. Manners had never read it.

"Be warned, this Brehmer unit learned its business fighting Russian partisans. They are ruthless and good, and you should be ready to leave this area within a week, or even less. They will be based at Périgueux, and they have to choose whether to start with you or to tackle Colonel Georges and his Maquis in the forests near Limoges. In your place, I'd head south for Cahors or east to the hills. But don't stick around for them to catch you. I can give you a couple of days warning of their arrival at Périgueux."

"So, there are my cards on the table before you. What I need from you is guns for my boys. Guns and grenades and something to use against tanks. Don't send those British PIATs of yours. They're useless. We want the American rocket launchers, the bazooka. And Sten guns and Bren guns and ammunition. And those silenced pistols so we can assassinate German sentries and those Gestapo bastards. And we need a drop this week, before this Brehmer Division gets here. I have two drop zones for you to approve, both in the forest of Lanmary north of Périgueux."

"Why ask me?" said Manners. "You have already been getting supplies, and you have access to a radio."

"Yes, the Stationer network." Marat smiled at Manners's surprise. "It is a good network, but careless. They have been using the same drop zones too long. That is not a risk I want to take. I need to secure my line of communications, as the generals say."

"You won't get bazookas. London wants you alive as guerrillas, hitting and running, keeping the Germans on the move and off balance. They won't give you weapons that fool you into thinking you can stand and fight. Not against tanks."

"With bazookas we can ambush tanks as they pass though the narrow streets of our towns and villages," Marat bridled.

"You can do that with Molotov cocktails. Have you ever seen a bazooka fire? It shoots out a great tail of flame and smoke. Every German in sight opens up. Bazooka men don't last long. They can't even kill tanks with a frontal shot, the armor is too thick. They can immobilize them by knocking out a wheel or a track, or penetrate the engine compartment at the rear. That's if they are lucky. You can do better with a Molotov. But my advice is when you see a tank, hide your guns and run. Believe me, I've fought German tanks. I had artillery and fighter bombers and antitank guns and our own tanks to fight with, and they could still beat us. With just guns and grenades and bazookas, you'll just end up dead."

Marat nodded coolly. "Well, at least you aren't making promises you can't keep. But you will get us the guns and ammunition?"

"I cannot guarantee anything," said Manners. "I send requests to London, not orders."

"A request will do. One more thing. I need as much abrasive paste as you can deliver, the stuff we can put on wheel bearings that makes them seize up and lock solid. It's a lot less dangerous than explosives and more effective in the long run. Tell London that the real weakness of the Boches is that they need low flatcars to move their tanks. The usual flatcars are too high for the tanks to pass through our tunnels. If we can sabotage the low flatcars—and there aren't many of them— then not a single German tank will get through France by train."

"What do you want the guns for?" Berger interjected. "You say your Colonel Georges has six hundred men up in the Limousin, and he hasn't done much with them so far."

"To assassinate your precious de Gaulle, of course. To kill priests and capitalists." Marat laughed, showing bad teeth. "That's what you think, no? Preparing for the great day when the Red Army marches in to liberate the groaning French proletariat. You are a fool, Berger, dreaming up your own nightmares and then choosing to live in them. Even if I wanted to turn my guns on to Frenchmen, how many of my boys do you think would be prepared to follow me? It's hard enough to get them to kill Milice."

"I thought the party prided itself on iron discipline." Berger mocked.

"Maybe in Russia, where the workers already run the state. Maybe in Germany, because even if they are Communists they are still Germans. But this is France, Berger. Iron discipline is not in our nature. Steely courage sometimes, yes. Muddling through usually, yes. But discipline? You ought to attend a few of our party meetings, then you'll see how little discipline we've got. You Gaullists probably do better. But my boys will be there when the invasion comes, if they have anything to fight with."

"Thanks for the information. I'll forward your request to London, and if they say yes I'll come and approve your drop zones," said Manners. He liked this man.

"Will you come and help my people with the training or should we request extra?"

"Training is what we are here to do. But London will decide. My time is getting very stretched, but there's also an American with us." Manners suddenly saw the opportunity to kill two birds with one stone. Marat's men needed training, and it would be a good idea to keep McPhee and François apart for a time.

"An American? My boys will like that."

"Wait till you see him. He insists on wearing his American uniform and he looks like a Red Indian. It's a strange haircut they wear."

"Even better—an American Red." Marat laughed. "Perhaps you'll join me in a final drink to the revolution? Or if that offends you, let's just drink to victory."

"We have a long ride ahead of us," said Berger. "But thanks." He turned to go.

"Wait," said Marat, and turned to rap on the window again. "If Mercedes doesn't get my signal, you'll be shot as you leave."

"Mercedes?" said Berger levelly, waiting by the door. "One of your Spaniards?"

"The revolution knows no frontiers, my friend."

"That's one of the things I don't like about Hitler. He knows no frontiers either," Berger retorted, and walked out of the door without looking back as Manners shook Marat's hand.

"The Dunlop tire factory at Montluçon," said Marat, keeping hold of his hand. "Your RAF bombers got it last September. I hear it will be in production again next month. One kilo of plastique in the right place and we can knock it out again before it starts. Will you help?"

"Montluçon—that's some distance."

"I can get you anywhere by rail. We have ways, hiding places."

"How do we stay in touch?"

"Through Berger. Otherwise, he'll never trust you again. But if you must arrange something fast, go to the Café de la Place in Périgueux, just behind the cathedral. You saw Mercedes, standing guard outside? She's the waitress. Good luck, Englishman—and here." Marat handed him the book he had been reading. "I know about secret work. One part acute terror, nine parts total boredom. You might enjoy a good book."

The acute terror came quickly, when the demolition of the points at the shunting station of St-Felix went badly wrong. Young Oudinot, on his first mission, lit the fuse at the wrong place; the charge blew up in his face and took his head with it and the Milice post opened up with a machine gun. Two more men went down. Manners took a bullet through the heel of his boot as he came out from cover to help little Christophe get away from the killing ground of the railway lines, and then used his only handkerchief to make a tourniquet above the lad's shattered elbow. There was no sole left on his boot but he felt no pain as he bundled Christophe over the cinders and then through the brambles and onto the hill above the village. His own charges went off, giving some cover as the Milice carried on firing bursts so long that they must be close to melting the barrel. They had cut the phone lines before moving in to place the charges, but the Germans would have a patrol here before dawn, and the rendezvous point was on the other side of the village. He had to get across, with Christophe.

He was limping now, his foot a mass of pain and Christophe an almost dead weight, as he ducked into the shelter of the churchyard and nerved himself to cross the main street. It was dark and silent, the locals knowing too well not to stir with all the firing, but he felt a thousand pairs of eyes watching him, and imagined Milice gun barrels trained on the pavement. This would never do. He slung Christophe's good arm around his shoulder, and they hopped and tripped across, and up the side street by the shuttered bakery, and down to the stretch of waste ground near the old garage.

"Laval," he whispered urgently. "Laval."

"*Putain,*" replied François coolly, as if they were meeting on some Parisian boulevard. Heaven bless the man but he had got a van, a battered Renault with solid tires that stank of fish as they bundled Christophe into the back where another man lay groaning and clutching his stomach, blood on his chin.

The Renault refused to start. François swore as he worked the starting handle and Manners cocked his Sten and kept watch. François tried again, and with a noise as loud as the Milice guns, the engine coughed into a rough beat. Manners limped to the passenger door, which refused to open. He slid back the window and found the handle inside.

"The Germans like their fish fresh," said François, settling behind the wheel and lighting a cigarette. "So the fishmonger gets a petrol ration. What's wrong with your foot?"

"I can walk on it," said Manners, and passed out.

He woke to the furious sound of barking, and clutched his Sten and looked groggily around for the tracking hounds and Germans that must be hunting him. But he was still in the van, the engine off, a darkened farmhouse looming close, and this monstrous din of dogs.

"It's a kennel," said François. "They raise and train guard dogs for the Milice. It's the best cover I know."

A man came to the door in a nightshirt and carpet slippers,

exchanged a few words with François, and ducked back into the house. He and his wife then appeared in old raincoats. Manners fell out of the van, gasping with the flash of pain as his foot hit the ground. Then he hauled himself up and helped carry the two wounded into the barn beyond the line of kennels. They settled them on straw, and he fell again. François looked at his foot and pursed his lips. The farmer gave Manners some eau-de-vie that tasted of pears and he slept, his Sten gun still clutched fiercely to his chest. When he woke, Sybille was bathing his foot with a rag that came away sodden with blood.

"It's very badly bruised, but the cuts are all superficial," she said briskly, dressed as a nurse in a white jacket that buttoned to her long neck. It was tight around her breasts, and he blushed as she watched him stare at her. "You walked a long way barefoot on rough ground. Christophe said you carried him."

"I didn't feel much," he lied. He looked down at his foot. Where the blood had been washed away, it was blue-black with the bruising.

"Perhaps the bullet stunned the nerves. I don't know much about bullet wounds. The shock of it must have twisted your knee. It's badly swollen, but not too serious. Keep on pouring cold water onto that bandage I've strapped around it. I want to keep it damp and cool. I'm treating you as if you were a horse, and I'm good with horses' knees. You won't walk for a week or so. Now brace yourself, this is going to hurt." She dabbed iodine on the sole of his foot and he bit his lip against the unbearable sting.

"Jesus," he breathed, tears leaking from his eyes as the pain dulled into a steady throb. "I could get interested in this medicine on humans," she said casually. "The hardest part of being a vet is the way animals react so badly to pain, even when you're trying to help them. People like you seem able to manage it better.

"It's as well you're here," she went on. "The Milice are very keen on their guard dogs. I can come and go here as I wish, so it's the nearest thing we have to a hospital. And thanks to the last parachute drop, I

201

finally have some medical supplies. You must have been persuasive when you radioed London to send them."

"How are the others?"

"We buried Maxim this evening. I can't do much about stomach wounds. And I'm about to amputate Christophe's arm at the elbow. I'll have to do it here. You'll have to help with the ether. Look." She showed him the wire frame, shaped like a cup, and the gauze that fitted over it, and then showed him the tiny pipette with the rubber bulb that looked as if it had once been used for eyedrops. "I'll give him the initial dose to knock him out, and then you must put two drops onto the gauze every twenty seconds, and make sure he keeps breathing. If he stops, take the mask off his face. Let him take two or three good breaths, and then put the mask on with another two drops. Understand?"

"I understand. Does Christophe know you're going to take his arm off?"

"Yes, but we've got him drunk. And that's not the worst. You left two men dead at St-Felix. They identified Valerien, and the Gestapo went to his parents' home with the Milice, and shot his father and his uncle. They left the corpses in the square at le Buisson and made the whole town file past the bodies. They can't identify Oudinot because he didn't have a head, but they took five hostages to Périgueux. All of them children. They say they'll send them to the camps in Germany unless the English *capitaine* gives himself up."

There was nothing he could say, and they stared wordlessly at each other for a long moment. Her hair was pinned up again, with loose tendrils spilling down. She dropped her eyes, and began to bandage his foot. She swallowed, and he understood the effort she was making to speak lightly. "When I've finished this, you can give me one of your English cigarettes, and then it will be time for Christophe."

"Have you ever done an amputation before?"

"Not on a human being. But I read the textbook. The principles seem the same."

She came back every day, and was cool and brisk with Manners, except when she was helping him learn to use the crutch. He had been embarrassed at having to be held up by the farmer when he wanted to go outside to piss and crap. Sybille had brought him an old chair that lacked a seat. She placed a chamber pot beneath it, and he practiced until he could hold the chamber pot in one hand and grip the crutch in the other as he lurched his way out to the dung heap without spilling a drop. It seemed a great achievement, and he was disappointed when Sybille treated it as a matter of course. But she was motherly with young Christophe, holding his one remaining hand and telling him how proud the girls would be to walk out with a hero of the Resistance. After the war.

"And the *capitaine* will come back from England in his luxurious automobile and take you and your ladylove to the finest restaurant in Périgord, and he will tell her how brave you were," she said, smoothing the boy's hair.

"I'll have to get into training first," said Manners jovially. "The way Christophe drinks, I'll be under the table before I can tell her he saved me from the ambush. With my bad foot, I'd never have got away without Christophe helping me. It must be all that eau-de-vie he drinks. Never seen anybody who could hold his drink like Christophe."

When the boy slept, she told him that the fishmonger had been shot after the Milice reported his van had been used in the escape, and his eyes surprised him by filling with silent tears for a man he had never known.

"It's all part of the madness," she said, and smoothed his cheek, as if for the first time he had aroused that tenderness she displayed to Christophe. His tears kept flowing. "We just have to survive it. We will survive it. There will be restaurants after the war, and you will take Christophe to a glorious, drunken dinner."

"And I will buy you lingerie in Paris," he said, forcing a smile. "From Lanvin."

"Now I know you're getting better," she laughed, and left him. When she came back the next day, she brought him a collection of Mallarmé's poems, dressed his foot quickly, and said she had to leave. He felt desolated.

"I'm sorry, but you come way behind a pregnant horse in my priorities just now," she said, ruffling his greasy hair, and then wiping her hand in a matter-of-fact way on her smock.

When she left, he took the scrap of soap, limped out to the yard, stripped and bathed himself from head to foot under the pump. He came back with a basin full of water, and washed Christophe's hair as well. Then he took his Rolls razor from the small tin case that had been with him since Palestine, stropped it to sharpness, and shaved Christophe and himself.

François came later the same day, with cigarettes and a collection of De Maupassant's short stories, and a bottle of cognac that he claimed had been liberated from a German canteen. There had been another parachute drop, and Marat had provided them with information about an ammunition train that they had derailed. They did not talk about the fishmonger, nor about the German reprisals. The war was going very well without him, said François, and when he left, he took Christophe with him, to shelter on a cousin's farm.

Sybille did not come for two days, and when she did she was angry with him. "You have been trying to walk on this foot," she accused him. "The cuts have opened again."

"Not walking," he lied. "I was using the crutch and I fell."

"You're a fool," she said coldly, reaching for the iodine. "To think that you can fool your doctor."

"That's just it," he gasped through the pain. "I don't think of you as my doctor."

"Because to you I'm just a vet," she flared.

"Because you're a woman." He leaned back and closed his eyes, relishing the warm touch of her hand on his foot. He felt her hands stop their work. "Because you are beautiful and I want to be in your house watching you cook and listening to Jean Sablon on your gramophone." There was a long silence, and she continued changing his dressing.

"You just say that because you enjoy my omelets and my music. You like to relax in my little fantasy world of the time before the war," she said, her tone too forced to be light.

"No. I want it in the time after the war," he said tiredly, despairing of ever reaching that deep melancholy within her. "Before the war, you belonged to someone else. I want you to belong to me. In the war, after the war, I don't care. I want to belong to you."

He opened his eyes and stared at her, and reached out to take her hand, not knowing if she would leave or dismiss him with a joke. Instead, her mouth worked as if she were about to cry but she left her hand in his. Suddenly he knew, and he felt a great tenderness as the conviction gripped him, that there had been no other men since her husband. And the private sanctuary of her room and her gramophone, which she had shared with him, was already a privilege.

"Seize life, Sybille, while we have it," he said, knowing as he said it that this was what he believed in most of all.

"You are a fool of an Englishman. It isn't that at all," she said softly. "I am feeling very, very shy."

"So am I," he said. "Like a very foolish young boy."

She put her hand to his mouth to silence him, gazing at him with a kind of fascination as if he had told her an extraordinary secret. Her hand moved to his cheek, became a caress, and she leaned down to kiss his lips. The kiss lingered and he stroked her hair, feeling the soft mass of it. She sat up briefly, and her breasts thrust forward against her white coat as she put her hands to her head to loosen some pins and the hair tumbled down. He stroked her breasts through the cloth; she shook her head to send her hair dancing loose about her face, and her face softened into a very secret smile and she helped him undo the buttons.

"Not before the war, and not after the war," she said finally as they lay, spent and entwined, sharing one of the English cigarettes François had left him. "Just now. That's all there is. Just a little time for us."

CHAPTER 13

Time: The Present

The director of the Lascaux cave was waiting to greet them. He seemed to have been waiting some time. Awed by the eminence of his visitor, he had a fresh haircut and wore an obviously new shirt and tie. Alongside him stood half a dozen members of the staff, some of them from the duplicate cave for the tourists that lay farther along the hillside. There were guides and a gardener, an electrician and a woman who ran the refreshment kiosk. Malrand solemnly shook each of them by the hand, and Clothilde kissed cheeks with the guides. The director gave them each white coats, new hard hats, and plastic overshoes.

"Much of the damage was done not just by the breath of the visitors, as you sometimes hear, but from the microorganisms carried in on their shoes," the director explained. He bent obsequiously to tie his President's overshoes, and rose to hand him a small face mask. Lydia, who had begun to presume this was almost a customary postprandial treat for Malrand's guests, suddenly realized the director had never met his President before. This was a rare occasion. She felt honored, but inquisitive as ever.

"But were not the microorganisms similar to those already here?" Lydia asked.

"They have changed. Benzene, fertilizers—the very air we breathe is infused with our own modernity. We must protect the cave against it. The first problem we suffered was the green disease, a kind of plant growth that was probably helped by the warmth of the lighting system in the damp air. The second problem was the white disease, the tendency of the calcite crystals to grow in such conditions, helped by the carbon dioxide breathed out by more than a million visitors." It had the sound of a prepared speech, Lydia thought. He's probably said it a hundred times. "Remember that the cave had been sealed in its pristine environment for seventeen thousand years, until a tree fell in a storm in September 1940, and young Marcel Ravidat took his dog for a walk. The dog fell down the hole left by the tree, and Marcel went down to rescue it. He came back with some school friends, and they explored the cave and found the paintings. They told their teacher, a Monsieur Léon Laval, and he contacted the greatest living expert on prehistoric art, the Abbé Henri Breuil, who came almost at once and stayed to marvel."

He unlocked an iron door and led them into a dark tunnel, lit only by a dim blue light, which gave way to a chamber with smoothed walls, and then a flight of steps downward. It smelled quite dry, and not in the least musty. He opened another door, and guided them into pitch darkness. Lydia, recalling her visit to the copy of the cave and telling herself to expect a rather less impressive sight of slightly faded paintings, despite the undeniable thrill of the original, braced herself for a mild disappointment.

Then the director threw a switch, and a long, deep chamber, perhaps fifty yards long and ten yards wide, flooded with a cold, bright halogen light. Lydia heard the others gasp, and Manners cry out and protectively clutch her arm, as a great herd seemed almost to leap upon them.

Bulls, she thought. Giants from another age. The great bulls of Lascaux, on each side of her, rising. No, towering into the ceiling, and given depth and mass by the other beasts around them. She saw horses and great deer with monstrous antlers, and then what seemed almost a unicorn. My God, she thought, all sense of fear gone, her instant reaction of alarm replaced by a sense of enchanted wonder, the bulls are dancing.

Manners released her arm and stepped two paces forward, and began to spin slowly, taking in the great painted arc of roof above their heads, the beasts before them and behind, spinning and moving as if he were dancing too. His arms stretched out dreamily, his trunk swayed, his glowing face seemed at sublime peace. And realizing that she had suppressed this thought too long, Lydia knew that she wanted to bed this man.

She sensed her own feet follow unbidden, unable to stay still, unable to focus upon any one image as the animals seemed to swirl and lumber around her. She heard Manners laugh with pure joy, and her own delight surged too. She could not be silent and laughed exultantly in turn as she stepped forward. Manners, his face beaming at her, took her hand, raised it high, and twirled her as if on a dance floor. She heard Clothilde join the laughter, and Malrand start to clap his hands together, half-mockery, half-salute.

And then the darkness fell once more as the director turned off the lamps. An utter blackness, freezing her, chilling her, holding her in place as the sense of the still-looming bulls began to invade her joy. A spark, as rude as lightning, and then a tiny glow, like a feeble candle, was in the director's hand. He moved forward, taking the dim light to a great black bull with a speckled face, two horses seeming to race beneath it, and another red horse with a black mane running at its shoulder.

"This is one of the lamps they used," came the director's voice, soft and low, almost sepulchral. "It is made of stone, a small bowl hollowed out to hold tallow and a juniper wick. It reaches but one image at a time, one beast at a time, each taking its place in this pantheon of pre-history."

A complete silence fell as they all stood immobile in place, Lydia and Manners still joined by their raised hands, frozen in minuet. The director flicked on a small but very powerful torch, and played it deliberately from beast to beast, picking out faces that became distinct personalities. A big black bull to the right, its horns raised as if in challenge. Two to her left seemed to face each other almost genially, one almost jaunty with the cock of its forward legs, the other placidly bovine, looking almost surprised.

"When I first saw it by the light of a small electric torch, I thought they would devour me," said Malrand. "Then I looked at their faces, and they seemed almost friendly."

"When I first saw this, I wanted to dance too, dance and sing," Clothilde said. "This is a joyous place, solemn but filled with delights. The whiteness of the chalk makes it so light, even with a feeble candle. Even in total darkness, you know that it but waits for the smallest glow of light. This is how churches should be. If they were, perhaps I might attend them."

"Perhaps that is why Abbé Breuil called it the Sistine Chapel of pre-historic man," said Malrand. "Their God might not have borne much resemblance to our own, but their sense of worship seems very close to us. A little happier, perhaps, more at ease with the life around them. I think I understand your teacher, Clothilde, your Leroi-Gourhan, who felt it was all a balance between the male and female principle. This is a sensual place. There is sexuality here."

"There is movement, too, Monsieur le Président," said the director, shifting his torch to the right. "See the great black bull. Is he guarding or is he challenging, about to charge? But look where he points." The torch flicked to an opening at the end of the cave, an opening half-blocked by more paintings. He led them toward it.

"This great room is the Hall of the Bulls. Now we are entering the Axial Gallery. There is a turn to the right and a descent. Wait while I turn on the light." The director brushed past them, heading for the passage. As he passed, he handed the small stone lamp to Lydia. "You see the grooves and patterns scored into the handle of the lamp, mademoiselle? There are many such signs cut into the rock here. They may have been a kind of signature of individual artists, saying this is my lamp, this is my stretch of wall. We don't know."

He turned on the halogen lamps again, and behind them the whole chamber exploded into view once more, a great tumble of life.

"I made an official visit to Africa," said Malrand. "They took me to one of the game reserves at dawn, to a guest house in the trees that overlooked a water hole. It was like this, all animals jostling together. Perhaps that is how it was then, a great tumult of life."

"I spent months as a student pursuing a theory I had," said Clothilde. "I had been struck by the way this chamber reminded me of those maps the ancient Greeks made of the night sky, tracing the shapes of hunters and bears and beasts from star to star. I tried to make the beasts of the chamber fit the various models of the night sky over Périgord seventeen thousand years ago. Each time I seemed to be on the brink of success in one section, another frustrated me. But I still have that feeling of being beneath a vast vault of stars."

"A tumult of life, you said, Monsieur le Président—but also of death," intoned the director. "Look here, where we turn into the Axial Gallery—the falling horse. We are sure that it is falling, rather than simply being painted at this angle, when we look at the ears, the way they suggest the horse is tumbling backward. Perhaps this represents one of the ways they hunted, driving beasts over a cliff to fall to their deaths. And then here there is battle. See these two ibex, poised to hurl their horns against each other."

"What is that grid sign between them? asked Lydia. "Almost like a window with bars."

"Who knows, mademoiselle? There is much here we cannot comprehend. Perhaps the mark of an artist, perhaps some hieroglyph that had meaning to them, if not to us. Perhaps the indication of some kind of fence. They may not have domesticated their animals, as farming communities were to do ten thousand and more years in the future. But they may have used some kind of fence in their hunts."

One red beast, with a black face and neck that seemed slightly too small and even delicate for its bulk, caught Lydia's attention. Bull or cow? She could not tell. It carried light and slender horns, sinuous yet lethal as rapiers, and its expression looked for a moment mean and angry, and then just bewildered.

"This beast is extraordinary. It has character and expression—almost like a portrait," she exclaimed.

"I am so glad you said that," said Clothilde. "That is my theory, that these were not just generic animals, a standard bull or horse, but individual representations. I have this wild hope—that hardly anyone shares— that one day we might find a portrait of a person. There are some rough caricatures of human faces that have been found at La Marche, but I have this feeling that artists such as these not only could have produced recognizable human faces, but would almost have been impelled to do so."

"Madame is known for the daring of her imagination," said the director.

"I'm full of wild theories, you mean," laughed Clothilde.

"Your President respects your intuition, and shares your hopes," said Malrand.

"Then my President will want to find the money to finance my research project to discover new caves," retorted Clothilde. "With echo sounders and access to satellite mapping and help from the Air Force, we could identify caves all across this region. There may be more caves like Lascaux, perhaps even finer. Perhaps we could find portraits of the first French people. The Ministry of Culture supports it, but the project always dies in the Council of Ministers. If you were to adopt it as the *Projet Malrand* . . .

"No politics, please, madame. I am taking a day off from affairs of state and budget battles," said Malrand lightly.

"But you are the only man in power who loves this art as I do, the only man who could make the difference," she protested.

"Madame, enough," he snapped, in a tone so harsh and abrupt that Clothilde bowed her head and Lydia and Manners stared at the suddenly furious President. "I am not here to be badgered. You tried in the car and now you try again here. Just leave me in peace, if you please."

"These horses," Lydia exclaimed, by trying to smooth over the sudden row. "They look like the horses of ancient Chinese pottery, the same coloring and proportions."

"We call them the Chinese horses," said the director quickly, desperate to have his moment with the President unspoiled. "The parallels are striking—and horses are by far the most common animals here, four times more common than the cattle or the deer. But from the bones we found, they did not eat them. Reindeer was their main diet, and yet reindeer are very rare in the cave—there is only one, among some six hundred paintings and fifteen hundred engravings. And it is not even clear that it is meant to be a reindeer. That is why we doubt that there was a hunting ritual here, picturing the beasts they intended to hunt. Some scholars think that this painting was a work of the winter, when there was little else to do in the long nights. But they did not live in the caves, and from the tent sites we have found, there are signs that they were migrants, traveling with the reindeer herds. Allowing for the lack of domesticated animals and agriculture, they lived a little like the Evenk tribes of Siberia, a little like the Indians of North America."

"Perhaps we should move on to the Nave," said the director. "Back down this Axial Gallery, and through the narrow passage to your left. You now will see treasures that are unique. These parts of the cave have not been copied for the tourist exhibit. These can be seen only here, in the place where they were made. You will see on the ceiling above a mass of horses engraved into the rock. And now farther, into what we call the Nave. To your left, the famous panel of the black cow. And look beneath its rear feet, the checkerboards of black and red and yellow squares. Another mystery."

Lydia could feel Clothilde fuming behind her, and reached back to squeeze her hand in solidarity. Dismayed that the joyful mood that gripped their small party in the Hall of the Bulls should now have become icy, she wondered why Malrand had reacted so furiously. He was probably sick and tired of people constantly asking him for favors. But there had been a distinctly personal note in his curt silencing of Clothilde, almost as if the two of them had been involved at some time in the past. Hmm, there was a thought. But surely a presidential mistress, even if the affair were long in the past, would know better than to appeal to him in public? No, Malrand said she had tried the same gambit in the car. Perhaps that was Clothilde's point, to get some kind of public commitment.

"Behind us is my own favorite," said Malrand, his voice normal, his mood apparently equable again. "Am I right, Monsieur le Directeur, that we now see the swimming stags?"

"Indeed so, Monsieur le Président. A great work, its scale matched by its ambition." The five stags' heads stretched almost the full remaining length of the cavern, twelve or fifteen feet. Their antlers were far less ornate than those in the Hall of the Bulls, but somehow more real, emerging from a darker outcropping of rock that seemed to represent a river. Each stag's head was cocked at a different angle, giving movement and continuity almost like a strip cartoon.

"How far does this cavern stretch back?" asked Manners.

"The Nave behind you goes on, ever narrower, and then dropping sharply, for some fifty meters, into a small chamber we call the Hall of the Cats, but they are very hard to see and it is not easy to reach. Down this way, we drop into what we call the pits, and then down a steep drop of stones into a kind of well, probably scooped out by swirling waters from the times when this was the course of an underground stream. It goes on another twenty meters or so, through a gap too narrow for any-one but a devoted cave explorer. But if we are careful here as we descend, we come to something quite unique."

He played his light into a small gallery, picking out to their right the unfinished drawing of a horse; he swiveled the torch to the left, to the outline of a beast like a rhinoceros. Then he brought the light back toward them, and Manners reacted as if he had been punched.

"My God, it's a killing!"

"More than that, a combat," said Malrand. "Which leaves both par-ticipants dead."

A crude drawing of a man, almost a stick figure, lay on the ground, arms outstretched. His head had either been very crudely drawn, or had been given a long, birdlike beak. His penis was erect, and in the shape of a spike. Below him lay a stick with a bird perched on one end. Tow-ering over the fallen men was a great bison, some four feet long, its horns aiming down to gore at its victim. But a stick, perhaps a spear, was in the doomed beast's belly, and its entrails spilled in great loops on the ground.

"There are many theories about this, but only some elements I think we can be sure of," said the director. "That stick with the bird on top seems to me to be a decoy. A hunter could lie in wait in a pit with that stick poking above it. I have seen some local people hunt small birds this way. Possibly the fallen man is wearing a bird mask for the same reason. Some people call him the shaman, or magician, since we know that bird and animal masks are worn during rituals by the shamans of many Native American and Siberian tribes. And then there is another stick on the ground, with a diagonal line running from it. I think that is a spear thrower, a stick onto which a spear was placed, and which greatly increased the force and range of the spear's flight. Beyond that, I cannot usefully speculate."

"You certainly have Leroi-Gourhan's male principle there," said Malrand. "But then men do sometimes experience that phenomenon of erection in violent death."

"Do you have any personal theories about this drawing?" Lydia asked. "Not a scholar's hypothesis, but your own view."

"I think it is more than the simple portrayal of the tragic end of a hunt, mademoiselle," he said. "He may well be a shaman, but certainly I think there is ritual and magic involved, beyond the prosaic explanation of the bird as a hunter's decoy. It is the only image of violence in the whole cave, and it is a double violence, depicting the death of the shaman and the death of the beast, as if one somehow caused the other. Given the love and celebration of life that we see elsewhere in the cave, to me it does not truly fit."

"There's the portrait of early man you wanted, Clothilde," said Manners. "Killing and being killed. An artistic and philosophical statement on human nature."

"But incomplete," replied Clothilde, amiably. "There is more to humankind than that—as we see and as we know from the rest of the cave. If these artists wanted to depict our dark side, then they have overwhelmed it with images of our better nature. So if they are showing man killed and killing, I choose to believe that they have also made art which shows human beings doing better things."

"There is room for many faiths in this cave, Clothilde," said Malrand pensively. He had called her Clothilde at last, noted Lydia. "And yours is a noble one. I like to think that you are right."

Malrand left in his car alone, driven by Lespinasse, and with the escort of security men. His farewells had been charming, his parting kisses to Lydia's cheeks lingering almost as long as her flood of excitement when he whispered, "You can be assured that the art tax is dead."

"I wish I could stay longer, but I must be in Paris tonight," he called as he left for the military airport where his jet waited to whisk him back. Lespinasse exchanged a hearty handshake with Manners. And Lydia was almost convinced she had heard Clothilde whisper "Sorry, François," as he had kissed her farewell.

"Anything after this would be an anticlimax," said Manners as they clambered into the remaining limousine for the ride back to Malrand's house.

"I remember the first time I saw it, I felt the same. I still do, a little. It keeps its magic, Lascaux," said Clothilde. "Let me apologize for imposing that scene on you. I thought it was worth a try, while Malrand was under the spell, but I handled it badly. Let me make amends. Come home with me and I'll cook us all a meal."

"I'd love to, Clothilde. I'm full of questions," he said, and turned to Lydia. "O.K. with you?" She nodded. She didn't feel like being alone with Manners just yet. Perhaps that flood of lust for him had just been the effect of the cave. She liked him a great deal, but she had never been comfortable with holiday flirtations.

"I wonder when he will announce the new reward?" she asked.

"Very soon, I imagine. No point in delaying. But I suppose he'll have to talk to the police and culture ministers, probably the finance people."

"Ah no, my dear Major. Malrand does not work like that. In France, the presidency has its own funds, to be used at the President's discretion. He will not tell the culture ministry, since the minister would try to steal the credit. He will find some moment when he needs a useful distraction and make the announcement. It should bring results very fast, I imagine."

"Well, that looks like the end of our adventure, Lydia."

"Why on earth so? The painting may be recovered, which would be a good thing. But that still leaves the mystery of where it's from, let alone how your father got hold of it. And it looks as if Clothilde's cave-hunting project is not getting the presidential seal of approval, so we might as well continue our inquiries among the old Resistance types."

"I have some names for you, and some information," said Clothilde. "Not very exciting, but one friend of my father—my real father, that is—said he knew of two caves where guns were stored. The big one at Rouffignac, which goes back for miles, and Bara-Bahau. Rouffignac is a possibility. It has been fully explored, but by speleologists, not by modern experts. It's a small painting, and it's possible that some great scar on the wall was not noticed."

"But the lines continue beyond the edge of the rock, and in the background is that clear white calcite," Lydia objected. "The lines would have been noticed."

"I know, it's just a faint possibility. Bara-Bahau is out. It's too well known, and not much calcite there. I feel sure that Horst was on the right track when he talked of a cave that lay waiting to be discovered, like Lascaux in 1940, and somehow the painting came out and then the cave was sealed again."

"So your idea of the echo-sounding project would probably be a sure-fire way of finding it again," said Manners thoughtfully. "Odd that Malrand seemed to be set against it."

"I think he was set against the idea of being bullied into a commitment, rather than the idea itself," said Lydia.

"It's curious," said Clothilde. "The project seemed guaranteed of success when I first proposed it, long before we heard of your new rock. The Air Force was quite happy, saying it could fit into its training schedule. The Ministry of Culture was in favor, and we had a university and a research institute eager to help. But then it got squashed somewhere in the hierarchy, and I was given different explanations why. The culture officials said they thought it was the finance ministry. The research people said they thought it was political, the Prime Minister's office muttering that too many funds were being steered to Malrand's Péri gord. And one of Malrand's people told me it was because they thought that in a year or so we could get half the project financed by Brussels, from the European fund."

"There couldn't be any—well—sinister reason for someone trying to block it, could there?" mused Manners, almost to himself. "Somebody who may have a good reason to make sure the undiscovered cave remained unfound."

"What do you mean?" said Clothilde, glancing meaningfully from Manners to the impervious security man who was driving them. Almost imperceptibly, she shook her head warningly.

"Oh, nothing. Just a fancy," he said lightly. "Your scientific search is a good idea, and good ideas have a way of getting carried out. The European fund will probably come through from Brussels. I'm sure it will happen someday, Clothilde, and after a hundred and seventy centuries another few years won't hurt.

"I'm still awed by that place," he went on. "It opened my eyes rather. I don't know much about art, just sort of assumed there were these high points, like the ancient Greeks and the medieval cathedrals, and then Michelangelo and Leonardo at the Renaissance, and then Van Gogh and Cézanne. Just a few high points. Now I know that I've seen another, from a time long before I thought there was any civilization at all." The conversation had now been steered to safer ground. Lydia noticed it was deftly done.

"Time to add a second postcard," he went on, drawing his wallet from inside his jacket. He opened it and withdrew a small and much-worn postcard of a Vermeer. Lydia recognized it at once, the *Girl with the Pearl Earring*, a winsome portrait of deep charm.

"I was in Appeldorn, one of the Dutch military bases, on a NATO course and we took a weekend off to go to Amsterdam. They had this

Vermeer exhibition. Just by chance, since I had nothing better to do that morning, I went along, and fell in love with this girl. Carried this with me ever since. In Northern Ireland sometimes, when it was really bad, I'd take her out and look at her and feel better."

"Why not a photo of your children?" asked Lydia.

"Your own children are the kind of distraction that can get you killed—the last thing you want to think about at times like that," he said grimly. "Believe me."

"So which souvenir image do you want from Lascaux?" Clothilde asked. "The falling horse, the two bison, the great bull?"

"No, I think I'd take the swimming deer, except that now I've seen Lascaux, I already know the one I want." He pulled out one of Lydia's Polaroids of the small bull he had brought to her the day they met. "All the others from Lascaux go together, and I don't want to select just one. I would feel happier just with this one that was mine, at least for a while, even if we never see it again."

When they got back into their own cars at Malrand's place, Clothilde steered Lydia into her own car and told Manners to follow. As her little convertible roared up Malrand's drive, Lydia realized nervously that she was in for a woman-to-woman chat. Never a prospect she much relished, she felt at a disadvantage. Despite her liking for the woman, Clothilde was formidable, and Lydia was not ready to question herself about her feelings toward Manners, let alone face an inquisition.

"You aren't sleeping with him yet, are you?" Clothilde began.

"I was thinking of a similar question about you and Malrand."

"We had a very pleasant spring and summer a long time ago, when I had just got my doctorate and just before he went into politics."

"Wasn't he married then?"

"Yes, she was one of those Parisian literary ladies. Preferred to stay in St-Germain. We had the Périgord to ourselves. But you're changing the subject. You're falling for the handsome major, no?"

"Falling in love? I don't think so. Attracted, certainly. Interested, yes. He's an entertaining companion, but quite a private one. There are lots of depths to him, parts I haven't been allowed anywhere near. I don't mean the military stuff. More the way his mind works. That question he raised in the car, about whether somebody might have been blocking your project deliberately. I didn't think his mind worked that way."

"Suspicious, you mean, or intuitive?"

"Both. He presents himself as a simple soldier, very straightforward, everything on the surface. Then suddenly you see a hint of something much deeper. Looking back at how he maneuvered me into coming to Périgord with him, I think I first saw it then."

"Some of his depths are charming. Like his little Vermeer girl. Any woman would feel challenged by that, to replace that work of oil with an image of herself next to his heart. But it is very flattering that he went to such trouble to get you here, no? And if you want to satisfy your curiosity, there's only one way."

"Take him to bed, you mean?"

"Why not? At the worst, you'd have fun. He moves like a capable lover. Did you see him start to dance in the cave?"

"That was the moment I was most attracted to him. It seemed so natural, like the real him, wide open to joy."

"You'll never know until you try him out," said Clothilde. "I bought one of those silly souvenir ashtrays when I was a young girl, which carried an old saying on the base—'Men are like melons, you have to squeeze a thousand before you find a really good one.' My mother was very shocked."

They drove through the town to Clothilde's surprisingly modern house on a hill overlooking a great bend of the river. They parked, and

Clothilde led them through a narrow front door into a long, wide room filled with light from the sliding glass door that overlooked her terrace and the river. At the terrace table, a man was sitting and smoking, a bottle of still sealed champagne and a bunch of roses beside him.

"Horst," cried Clothilde. "What a lovely surprise."

CHAPTER 14

The Vézère Valley, 15,000 B.C.

The new Keeper of the Deer, who still thought of himself as plain Deer, felt considerably confused. The ceremony had been brief and almost casual, the Keeper of the Bulls gabbling through his words of praise and welcome into brotherhood, while his sponsor, the Keeper of the Horses, fumed silently at his side. His treasured possession, the lamp of the Keeper of the Bison, had been taken from him at the village and then brusquely returned to him in the cave. The other Keepers had lit his way to the rear passage, stumbling around the stepped bend, and praised his bison and his swimming deer. The Keeper of the

Bulls had then lit his lamp with his own, and stomped back to the cave entrance where the apprentices waited, awed by their guess at whatever mysteries had been vouchsafed to their former fellow. Deer chose the youngest of them, called Dry Leaf from the time of his birth, and the one who had helped him finish the coloring of the bison, to be his pupil. He would rather have chosen Moon—and he now thought of her as simply "Moon"—not for what she meant to him but simply for her talent. The other Keepers had embraced him, and the Keeper of the Bulls had managed barely to touch him during his cursory contact. And that had been all.

Without knowing exactly what to expect, he had expected more. Perhaps a ritual introduction to the beasts of the cave, or a token contribution to the work of each of the other Keepers, or a common sacrifice at the entrance fire. But no, not even a feast. This had been a routine business at the close of a routine day, and Deer felt diminished by it. Dry Leaf was looking up at him with stars in his eyes, finally believing that he too one day might ascend to the splendid rank of Keeper. Deer could not let his disappointment show before the lad, and so gave him firm instructions on the colors he would need for the morrow, and sent him scampering off down the hill, looking younger than Deer thought he had every been.

"Come eat at my fire this night," said the Keeper of the Horses, and took him closely by the arm to lead him downhill, saying nothing, but making a ceremony of it.

At his fire, all the Keeper's kin were gathered, standing to welcome them. Sons and daughters and baby grandchildren, even his woman's brothers. This was a full assembly, as if for a funeral or—his hopes leaped—a betrothal. Moon darted to the water skin hanging on its tripod and thrust two handful of moss into the water that had been warmed by hot stones. She withdrew them, dripping, and handed one to her father and the other to Deer, her eyes downcast.

"Welcome to this hearth, Keeper of the Deer," she said, her voice not quite even. They sluiced off the dust of the day. Deer sniffed the air and looked down at the roasting meat on the spit above the fire. Moon bent and gave the spit a quarter turn, and then took some wild herbs from a beveled stone and sprinkled them onto the glistening surface. He smiled in pleasure at the girl's concentration on her task.

The Keeper's woman handed a wooden bowl to her husband and another to him, and made her own welcome. Deer sipped at the fermented honey, sweet and yet sour at the same time, and burning a little in his throat. He had never drunk it before, but had helped the old man reel into his furs after taking too much of this drink with his cronies.

As they drank, he saw a small parade of torches coming toward them. The Keeper of the Ibex, the Keeper of the Bear, with their wives and apprentices. Each woman bore a wooden bowl, and they kneeled to him in turn, laying the offerings of berries, nuts, and sweet pine kernels at his feet. As if from nowhere, Dry Leaf was standing proudly at his elbow, and in his hand was the old man's lamp, fresh-filled and lit, making the boy's face lively with the dancing lights of the flame. Someone must have told the lad what to do. He felt both glad and angry that the Keeper of the Bulls had not come, comprehending that this made it a private festivity in the absence of any official one.

"Welcome to the brotherhood, Keeper of the Deer," said each of his colleagues in turn. And each took a bowl of the fermented honey and bowed to him as they sipped. Then there were gifts. From the Keeper of the Horses, a tunic of reindeer hide, the sleeves sewn to the shoulders with thongs. From the dazzling smile Moon gave him as he admired the work, he felt sure that she had made it. For him. He slipped it over his head, but then was stuck. He had never put on a garment with sleeves before. Laughing, the Keeper's woman helped him into it and tied the thong at his neck. It came down almost to his knees, and they all smiled at the pleasure he took in it.

From the Keeper of the Ibex came a fine flint ax. The thongs that bound it to the haft were cunningly seated, and plaited all the way down the handle to give a secure grip. He weighed it in his hand, feeling the easy balance. "Try it; try it," called the giver. He took a log from the pile waiting for the fire, and with four brisk strokes sharpened the blunt end into a pointed stake. He marveled at its sharp efficiency and bowed his thanks. From the Keeper of the Bears came a fine skin sack, with woven loops so that he could sling it from his shoulders and wear it on his back. He slipped it on, and felt a weight within. Inside was a woven belt, with a small pouch attached, with flint and firestone and tinder inside. His thanks were heartfelt as he put the belt around his waist, feeling the comforting weight of the pouch, his pouch, on his thigh. He had never owned such things. He had never really owned anything. He felt rich and treasured.

"I thank you, honored colleagues, for this welcome," he said, surprised that he was not stammering in his pleasure and surprise.

Suddenly, a torch flickered on the rim of the gathering, and the Keeper of the Bulls came in quickly to join them, his sister behind him with an infant whimpering in her arms.

"Forgive me, brothers. A man without a woman is not master of his time when a babe frets."

"The child is ailing," said his sister, and the other women crowded around in concern, leaving just the men around Deer and the Keeper of the Bulls. Deer noted how swiftly the focus had moved from him to the late arrival.

The Keeper of the Bulls bowed to Deer. "Salute and welcome to our new brother."

He had brought a bowl of new berries and laid them casually at Deer's feet. Then from his own belt, he took a long flint knife, a finely wrought stone of green whose blade was as curved and even as a laurel leaf, its handle wrapped in strips of shrunken rawhide. The thongs tailed off into a long loop that slung around the wearer's neck. He came up to Deer and took his arm. Staring fixedly into Deer's eyes, he ran the edge of the sharp blade lightly over the youth's forearm. He lifted the blade to his lips and blew away the scraps of hair the keen knife had shaved from the skin.

"Use it well, brother," he said, without a trace of a smile. He took the loop from around his own neck, slipped it over Deer's, and gave him the knife. It was a princely gift. The Keeper of the Bulls leaned forward and embraced Deer, who felt the power of the man, before he stood back and thanked him in deep sincerity. Perhaps he had misjudged this man, this rival for Moon. The bonds of the Keeper's brotherhood had proved sacred to him as well. He slipped the knife into his belt, noting how its narrowing between blade and handle made it fit snugly.

The woman of the Keeper of the Horses left the knot of women around the fretting babe and led Deer to the broad log before her fire and bade him sit. The other Keepers settled alongside him, and Moon took a long, green knife of flint and a smooth brown stick that had been sharpened to a point as two of her brothers lifted the long spit from the fire. Holding the meat firmly with the stick, Moon began slicing the steaming, aromatic flesh. The first and honored slice she placed on a warmed stone and brought to Deer. Her head seemed to be down-turned, but her eyes laughed with delight at him from under her lashes as he bowed and thanked her. This time he did stammer.

"You'll be ready for the time of mating," chortled the Keeper of the Bear at his side. "Looks as if someone has already chosen you."

"Is the feast always given to a new Keeper? Was this how it was in your time?" he asked, skirting the topic of Moon, although his eyes followed her as she served the other Keepers.

"My time was a long time ago. We had just started the work in the cave then. My father made a feast for me," he said. "But you have no father, so the Keeper of the Horses said the brotherhood should attend you."

"You attend me just this evening and in matters of the cave, or at all times? Forgive me, but I know not the customs."

"Why, at all times. At the hunt, at times of sacrifice, at times of betrothal, and even in time of war, the Keepers stand together. Our hearths are always open to our brother Keepers. We are bound like kin

227

to take one another's part, just as the hunters and the flint men do. We mourn one another's deaths and celebrate one another's births."

"And if this rule be broken, if one Keeper should stand against another?"

"That happens not. We have our council where all matters are discussed until we are resolved and of one mind. Yes, there are arguments, but finally we come to agreement. That is the way of the brotherhood. You saw this evening how it is sacred to us all."

The next morning, Deer took his place in the line of young men who gathered before the cave. The other Keepers stood behind the sacrifice fire, and once again the Keeper of the Bulls had donned his eagle's headdress and placed the bull's skull behind the fire. Beside the fire stood the leaders of the hunters, the fishers, the flint men, and the woodmen. Each bore his sign of office, the bow and the barbed fish spear, the great flint ax and the smooth and blackened club, whose head was carved into the shape of a bird with a sharp, pecking beak. Two boys held the young reindeer that had been saved from the slaughter at the cliff. Its front and rear feet were hobbled with thongs, but its eyes rolled and it kept trying to duck its head down between its own shoulders.

One youth from each clan had qualified for manhood at the great hunt, and they stepped forward in turn as their clan leader called them. Each stripped off his garment, and each was given the ceremonial weapon of his clan, except for Deer. The Keeper of the Bulls took from the edge of the fire the bowl of red clay and the stick whose end had been flattened and shredded into the form of a brush and handed them to Deer. No women were allowed to witness this rite.

"Mark it well for your fellow youths. Lead them this day to the common kill that will bind you all as men," chanted the Keeper of the Bulls.

Deer advanced on the terrified reindeer, which froze immobile. He painted one red circle around its eye, and another low down on its neck where the shoulders met, and another on each side where the ribs parted and rose to the soft flesh of the belly. The two boys scurried away. Deer went around to the rear of the trembling beast, leaned his chest on its rump and wrapped his arms around its haunches, clutching it to him to keep it still. A trickle of its urine splashed his feet. The lad from the fishers stood to one side, his fish spear aimed at the red circle on the reindeer's side. The young hunter stood on the other side, a little to the rear, so his arrow would penetrate deep into its vitals. The one with the flint ax stood by its shoulder, his weapon raised high to cleave down to the bones where the neck rose from the shoulders. And the young woodman stood at the beast's head, the pecking beak on the club's head pointing forward.

The fire flared as the Keeper of the Bulls tossed dried tinder into the flames, and called, "As one for your common manhood—kill."

The arrow flew, the fish spear thrust, the great ax fell, and the pecking beak slammed deep into the rolling eye, and Deer felt a great spasm of power tense the haunches as the young reindeer died and its front legs collapsed. Deer unclasped his hands, let the rump sink to the ground, and taking up his bowl of red clay moved to the great cleft at its neck to add the steaming fresh blood to the clay. He stirred it thoroughly, and then went first to the fisher, to paint the sign of the fish on the lad's heaving chest. Then to the flint man to paint the mark of the ax. Then to the hunter, to paint the curved, taut bow. Finally to the woodman, to paint the sign of the club with its bird's beak.

Then Deer raised his arms and stood stock-still as each of the other four in turn drew a mark on his chest, a long downward stripe from between his nipples to his belly, and then a fan of thinner strokes that rose to his shoulders. he looked down at his chest. It looked a little, just enough, like the brush he had used to daub the targets on the reindeer and then to daub them. They were bound now in common manhood. There was but one final part of the ceremony.

Dry Leaf emerged from the mass of boys with his lamp, and waited for the other Keepers to light their lamps at the sacrifice fire, and then came to stand beside Deer, his small hand cupped protectively around the charcoal wick. The Keepers led the way, and then Deer with his bowl of bloody clay, and then two by two, the blooded new men followed, each accompanied by his clan leader.

The Keeper of the Bulls led them into the main chamber of the cave, and stood beside the great black bull he had painted. Each of the other Keepers stood beside one of his own beasts.

"That you will have the courage of the bull," began the Keeper of the Bulls, his voice seeming to come eerily from his eagle's beak in the dim light of the lamps.

"That you will have the power of the bear," intoned the Keeper of the Bears.

"That you will be surefooted as the ibex," echoed the Keeper of the Ibex.

"That you will have the grace of horses," chanted their Keeper.

"That you will have the speed of the deer," intoned Deer.

Now Deer alone led the other four youths who had joined him in manhood deep into the next chamber of the cave. This was an act for the five of them alone, the mark of their own generation. The choice of place and sign was theirs. Deer, conscious of the time of mating that lay ahead, led them with his weak and flickering lamp to a female beast, a black cow of leaping grace. There was just room for the five of them to stand abreast.

"Here," he said, laying his hand on a stretch of white chalk beside the cow's muzzle, and handing the bowl and brush to each of the others in turn. Each of the four drew a long, vertical line, almost parallel to the next. The woodman, clumsy with the unaccustomed brush, allowed a small vein in the rock to jerk his stroke, and left a slight angle in his line. No matter. Deer drew a half line alongside it to make his own mark, not quite knowing why, but feeling that the pattern was more pleasing. Then he drew a horizontal line that joined the tops of the strokes, and met the cow's mouth, and turned and looked at his fellows, their faces solemn in the dim light.

"That bonds us as one on this day of manhood," he said.

Then he drew another horizontal line to join them at bottom, using the two outermost vertical lines to make a square. "That is the sign of the square, drawn in the blood of our kill, that shows that our friendship of this day can never be broken," he said, and with his thumb drew a small square on each of the other's foreheads. He handed the bowl to the woodman and said, "Paint one side of the square on my forehead." Each of the others in turn drew another side of the square, the hunter's tongue pursed at the corner of the lips as he concentrated to make the last corner meet.

Without another word, Deer led the other four out of the narrow gallery and into the main cave where the clan leaders and the Keepers stood waiting. They marched past them and out to the sacrifice fire, where they placed the bowl with its remains of bloodied clay on the embers and then added the brush. They stood and watched them smoke, catch fire, and burn, as the older men emerged from the cave and began to skin and joint the sacrificed reindeer, and set up spits of green wood to roast the meat.

"It is done," said the hunter. "We are men now."

"Aye," said the woodman. "We will have women tonight."

As the sun began sinking and glinting red on the river, the women came singing up the hill, the three maidens leading them with flowers in their hair. The young widows had sewn feathers into the seams of their tunics and their children danced in excitement beside them. The married men took torches, lit them in the fire, and then shuffled into two long lines, making a wide passage that led to the fire, jesting with their women as the young girls, eyes downcast, approached.

Again the Keeper of the Bulls dominated the ceremony, standing in his eagle's mask by the great horned skull, flanked by the chief hunter with his bow and the chief woodman with his beaked club. Each of them had a clan daughter to be betrothed this day. Standing in line with his four fellows, Deer caught his breath as Moon came forward with the other two maidens to lay flowers before the feet of the young men. Heads down, they backed away, and the two long lines of men began the wedding chant, stamping their feet in steady rhythm as the young widows came with flowers in their turn.

Five newly made young men, and three maidens. Two men who had lost their women in childbirth, and five widows. One of them would go back to a lonely bed this night, waiting for another year.

The chief hunter and chief woodman began lengthening the fire, poking the embers while other men brought dry wood to feed the new flames until the fire was as long as three spear lengths. The oldest woman of the village, not a tooth left in her head, limped up to the bull's skull and poured a bowl of milk, freshly taken from the breasts of nursing mothers, between its horns, to ensure that all the matings would be fruitful.

The two men who had lost their women stepped forward to the fire, one hunter and one fisherman. The hunter laid a fresh-killed rabbit at his feet, and his bow beside it. The fisherman laid a fat pike on the stone before him, and rested the shaft of his fishing spear beside it. The oldest woman went down to the group of waiting widows, and clearly by some arrangement the women had made among themselves, took two of them, one by each hand, and led them with their children to the waiting men. One hand still clasped to the old woman, each of the widows stretched out her other hand to one of the men. Each took it, and then each couple ran to the long line of fire and leaped, hand in hand, across the flames. It was done.

The old woman went back to the three remaining widows, and led them in line to the five new-made men. One had a babe at her breast, and another had toddlers clinging to her skirts. For a man who wanted sons, the certainty of fertility was important. The third widow was the fairest of all them all, but had no children with her. Deer remembered the body of her husband, the bold young hunter, being brought back to the village.

From his side, the young woodman with the mark of the beaked club still on his chest, was the first to step forward and offer his hand to the girl with the babe in her arms. She took him, and they ran to leap the fire. Then the young fisherman stepped forward and offered his hand to the childless widow. She turned her face aside to the fire, toward the bull and the immobile man in his eagle's mask. She had refused the fisherman. Blushing deep red in the thin light of dusk, the young man shrugged and offered his hand to the woman with the toddlers. She took him, and the old woman gathered the children to her as the new couple ran down to jump the fire.

Three young men remaining, three maidens. And the fair, proud widow. Deer's eyes were fixed on Moon, across the open space before the long fire, and hers on him.

The three fathers of the maidens stepped from their place among the men, and their mothers came forth from their place among the women, and each stood by their daughter.

The old woman came for the first group, led by a sturdy flint man with thick, scarred hands, and brought them to the men. Again, there had been an arrangement, this time within the clan. The flint folk often stuck together. The young flint man with the ax sign now smeared on his chest stepped forward and offered a grinning girl his hand. She took it, and her father clasped their two hands in both of his, and released them to run hand in hand to leap the fire.

Deer was trembling now as the old woman limped back to their small knot of waiting parents and maidens. She took the fisherman by the hand, and led him and his woman and his daughter toward the men. Deer's eyes were fixed on the Keeper of the Horses, his arm affectionate on Moon's shoulder. Her face was white, her body immobile.

The fisherman's daughter came to stand before Deer and the young hunter, the only two men remaining. She was fair-haired, with a round and cheerful face and plump hands, and her eyes darting excitedly from one young man to the other. Her breasts strained against the skin of her tunic and the flowers in her hair were blue. Deer closed his eyes and begged that she find favor in the eyes of the hunter. He opened them and glanced at his last neighbor, his stomach churning and not daring to breathe, and saw the lad's face alight with joy as the girl beamed devotedly at him and they each stretched out a hand at the same moment to the other. They had arranged this already, Deer thought, and a great wave of relief swept through him and he wished them well as they trotted, hand in hand and eye fixed upon loving eye, to leap the fire.

And now there was nobody and nothing in his thoughts save Moon. No fire, no lines of chanting, stamping men, no knots of women with their raucous laughs as each couple ran off, no sound of children nor crackle of flames. Not even the childless widow, standing proud and lonely where she had been rooted since she refused the young fisherman.

There was nothing but Moon, walking toward him, her head up and her eyes alight for him. His vision cleared, and he saw her mother smiling fondly at him, and the Keeper of the Horses looking proud and pleased, and there were bright tears in Moon's eyes and his own filled and the old woman cackled as she felt their young excitement. She was his. He was a man and a Keeper and Moon was his. Deer's hand came up unbidden, and Moon's lifted to grasp it, and then came a great shout of "Hold!" and the Keeper of the Bulls strode toward them.

The childless widow turned a pace toward the commanding figure with the eagle's head. He was not alone. His friend the chief hunter strode at one shoulder, and the chief woodman, with his great beaked club over his shoulder, at the other.

"Hold," the Keeper of the Bulls repeated. And as he stopped, the chanting of the men died away, and a great hush fell. They stood in tension, the Keeper of the Bulls and his two attendants, equidistant from the childless widow and the Keeper of the Horses and his woman and daughter. They formed a triangle from which Deer felt suddenly excluded.

"You have forgotten, old woman, that one womanless man remains," said the Keeper. "And a womanless man takes precedence over a new-made youth."

The childless widow, her face light with anticipation, clutched one hand to her breast, and gazed fixedly at the imposing man. This was why she had refused the fisherman, Deer understood. There was an arrangement here, he told himself, clamping down on the knot of dread that gripped his belly.

Moon looked in horror at the eagle's head and at the beaked club that rose beside it. They seemed to blur and merge together, man and club, beak and beak, each as cruel and imperious as the other. Her throat blocked, she tore her eyes away to Deer, and then to her father.

The old woman broke the moment, shuffling to the childless widow and taking her hand, and bringing her to stand between Deer and the Keeper of the Bulls. For the young woman, it was as if Deer had never existed. Her entire being was in her eyes and they were fixed upon the Keeper of the Bulls. Her hand kept twitching, as if rising to take him of its own accord.

Turning to the Keeper, as if all this was now settled, the old woman led the widow toward him. He ignored her, and the great beak pointed steadily at Moon.

Then he moved, two brisk paces and without waiting for the old woman or for her father or for anything but his own implacable resolve, he reached out and seized her wrist, and hauled Moon with him toward the fire.

"No," shrieked Moon, jerking and trying to free her hand as she was pulled half off her feet, and dragged to the fire by this birdman.

"No," shrieked the childless widow, clawing at her cheeks.

"No," cried Moon's mother, her hands at her mouth in shock.

"No," cried Deer, advancing to free Moon until the chief hunter stepped into his path, his eyes cold and his bow drawn, an arrow pointing at his chest.

"No," shouted the Keeper of the Horses. "This has not my consent." The chief woodman grinned and held out his beaked club to block the path.

"No," cried Moon, a firmer voice now, and she gathered her feet beneath her, ceased to resist. Then as the big man drew her close she darted her head down to sink her teeth deep into the muscled forearm of the Keeper of the Bulls. Her head moved like a fox worrying at a rabbit, and bright blood spurted and the man's grip relaxed on her wrist as he doubled over in pain, the headdress tumbling from him. And she darted under his reaching hand and ran, swifter than a deer, sprinting away from the stunned, immobile villagers to leap the bull's skull and vanish into the darkness beyond the fire.

CHAPTER 15

Périgord, 1944

As the spring days lengthened, Manners found himself experiencing moments of pure happiness, even beyond the snatched hours with Sybille. They came when he was alone, usually when he was cycling to a training session or meeting or just going to reconnoiter a likely ambush site, and they were always associated with a sense that he had been magically transported into a time of peace. This was not Sybille's melancholy fantasy, he knew, but his own. It was composed of English folk songs rather than the *chansons* of Paris boulevards, of flat and bitter beer rather than rough wine, of Cheddar rather than goat cheese. He had never felt more English than during this time in France.

Still, the illusion of a peaceful English countryside was as captivating as it was plausible in these quiet forest track ways and along grassy country lanes where lambs staggered to their feet and peasants sowed seed by hand now that there was no fuel for tractors. He was sleeping warm and dry in a *borie,* one of the circular stone huts with a thick slate roof that the shepherds and woodsmen had dotted through the remote countryside. Food was sufficient, if not plentiful, and the streams were no longer forbiddingly cold and his clothes were dry. Even in the old farmhouses on an evening, as he gave lectures on the art of organizing arms drops and the correct way to fold up the fallen parachutes, the placid faces of the old peasants over their pipes and glasses of *pineau* took him back to that distant time before the war. He loved the way the farmers' wives would always blush and throw their aprons over their grinning faces as he warned them against saving the parachute silk to make lingerie as the Germans were known for checking under women's skirts.

Above all, his forged papers were good. London had equipped him with an identity card that showed him born in Quebec of French parents, who had returned to Brittany in 1937. That would account for his accent. And they had given him a *certificat d'exception* to excuse him from military service on grounds of bleeding ulcers. Sybille had come up with the work papers, listing him as a vet's assistant in training, which gave him the perfect excuse to be roaming the countryside on the rare occasions when he was stopped by the SOL, the *Service d'Ordre Légionnaire,* the volunteer police that Vichy had formed.

But he knew it was an illusion of peace, even though the only Germans he had yet seen were those he had shot from afar or blown up as they rode the sandbagged trolley at the front of the train. The Milice he had seen too often for comfort and the paramilitary GMR; the *Groupes Mobiles de Reserve* staged irregular and nervous sweeps in lorry convoys along the roads that paralleled the railways. They had ambushed one, and fled from another when Malrand's captured Spandau had run out of ammunition. McPhee had destroyed two of the precious radio direction-finding trucks and damaged another in an ambush outside St-

Cyprien. Manners had arranged five successful parachute drops, and Berger's band had now swollen to forty men, and had spawned a separate group of twenty led by Frisé, which was based in the forest near Bergerac. All of Frisé's men, and most of Berger's, had learned simple demolition, and Marat's men had been given London's approval for some arms.

There were six Bren guns, twenty-seven Sten guns, thirty-six rifles, and forty Mills grenades in the standard drop of twelve containers, along with some twenty thousand rounds of ammunition. Marat had been promised a third of the drop, but there had been a nasty moment when François had shouted a warning and the two of them had guarded the containers with their own Sten guns to ensure that Marat's men did not take more than their share.

McPhee had resolved the standoff, putting his own gun down, opening a container, and pulling out one gun at a time. He laid them down in separate piles and chanted, "One for you and one for me." He made a childish game of it, and got the men grinning, although Manners saw he was careful to leave the ammo unpacked. Then McPhee walked across to Marat to drape a fresh new Sten gun, slick with oil, over the man's shoulder. Marat had taken to his American "Red," and his men were delighted to have a real *Yanqui* to themselves. Communists seemed to like Americans, while assuming that all the British were capitalists and agents of the Bank of England. He was the first of these mythical transatlantic allies they had ever seen, and they were charmed by his insistence on wearing his uniform and his astonishing haircut. Manners had heard they would go to extraordinary lengths to find McPhee new razor blades to keep his scalp trimmed.

But the mission was being fulfilled. The railways, telegraph, and telephone links were in a constant state of disruption. For a three-day period, McPhee's and Marat's men had blown all the rail lines into Périgueux, and the next week Manners had done the same to Bergerac. London and Hilaire were both pleased with them, but Manners was waiting for the inevitable German counterattack, the coming of the Brehmer Division of which Marat had warned him. They had begun to arrive in Périgueux and Bergerac, or at least the heavy units. There was a battalion of armored cars, mostly the half-track SPW troop carriers with mortars and machine guns, and some of the eight-wheeled *Panzerspahwagen* with the 20mm cannon that he remembered from the desert. He had yet to see them, but had heard that each of the Brehmer Division units carried a big arrogant B painted on the sides of their vehicles. There was a company of combat engineers, and another of the *Feldgendarmerie* military police, and roadblocks and armored patrols were now constant hazards. But General Brehmer was still waiting for his four battalions of infantry before starting offensive operations.

As soon as he heard from Marat that they were on their way by train, Manners planned to shift his base deeper into the hills and move the attacks toward the rail network that spread out from Brive. Berger had agreed to go to ground, while Frisé would head west to his family in the vineyards of Pomerol, and start blowing rail junctions nearer Bordeaux. The golden rule of the mission was to hit where the enemy was most dispersed, to disappear when they concentrated, and to keep training, training, and training the young recruits who were now flooding to the Resistance.

Which left him the problem of Soleil, one of the least disciplined but most active of the Resistance leaders. Nominally a Communist, but dismissed by Marat as an unreliable thug and black marketeer, Soleil ruled the district around the old fortified hilltop town of Belvès. By persuasion or by menace, almost the entire countryside had been recruited to his effort. Farmers hid his trucks and fuel supplies, fed and housed his men, and kept their anguish to themselves when the *Groupes Mobiles* convoys darted in to burn a barn or farmhouse in a reprisal raid after one of Soleil's ambushes. He was too dedicated to raiding banks and tobacco stores for Manners's comfort. But he had succeeded in intimidating the semitrained contingent of old men of the German 95th security regiment who now stayed huddled in their barracks in Sarlat, catching malaria from the fetid swamp on which the town was built. Malrand always claimed that one of his first postwar missions would be to drain the swamp and eradicate the mosquitoes.

Manners had never much thought about after the war. He had schooled himself to avoid any thought of such an improbably distant future, in the superstitious hope that by assuming that he would not survive the conflict, he might have a better chance of doing so. But Malrand talked of the future constantly in the shelter at night, the need for a revitalized France that would nationalize the big industries and defeat communism and modernize the country under the benign leadership of de Gaulle. He seemed to assume that Britain and France would fulfill that plan of a union that Churchill had briefly floated in the darkest days of the French collapse in 1940, with all the smaller countries dutifully following along.

What he called "Bismarck's disaster" of a united Germany must be broken up into the smaller provinces of Bavaria, Prussia, Saxony and Hanover, and Rhineland, which could after a suitable period of probation take their place in the Anglo-French system of a united Europe. Only then, he claimed, could Europe stand proudly with the otherwise dominant Americans and Russians. Only then could Europe recover from what he called its suicide of the 1914–18 war. Pipe dreams, thought Manners, but let him ramble on. Nobody in England was going to see France as an equal after the collapse of 1940, whatever pinpricks the Resistance might deliver to recover some of France's trampled honor as the British and American armies mounted the great invasion.

Manners stopped short of the top of the ridge, leaned his bike against a pile of logs, and moved stealthily forward to look down the road ahead. He always checked when he was carrying something that was certain to get him arrested. He had a haversack full of a dozen

Mills bombs and their fuses, an offering for Soleil, and some spare magazines for his Sten. It seemed quiet enough, with a long stretch of woodland and then only a small parkland of open ground before the château where Soleil had asked to meet. He looked back down the hill, walked into the middle of the road, and waved his arms to summon François. They always kept a hundred yards apart, to give the second man the chance to escape a trap.

"It looks quiet."

"I don't trust that little Marseilles *maquereau* one inch," said François.

Manners grinned. The word meant mackerel, slang for pimp. "I've heard a lot of bad things about Soleil, but that's a new one."

"It might even be true," laughed François. "But he looks like a *maquereau*, with his pencil mustache and gangster talk. I find that even more offensive than his half-baked ideas about Marxism. He steals arms from other groups. Sometimes I think the only sensible thing the Communists did was to condemn him to death. Pity they rescinded it. This war makes for some unsavory bedfellows."

"Well, he kills Germans. That's what counts. Let's go on."

It was surreal, a comic variant of his occasional delusions of peace, thought Manners, as he sat in the place of honor beside Soleil and looked at the impeccably handwritten menu for their banquet, with a small sun to symbolize the Soleil network drawn at its top. They were to start with *tourain*, the local garlic soup, and then foie gras followed by fresh trout, *confit de canard*, some Cantal cheese, and three different wines, all of them prewar. The champagne he was now sipping was a Dom Perignon '33. He had never eaten a feast like this in peacetime, let alone in war. The long baronial table stretched a full ten meters before him, the old wood glowing in the candlelight, and each place set with the requisite number of knives and forks. He toyed with one. Solid silver. The glasses were heavy old lead crystal, and a butler stood attentively at Soleil's elbow, waiting for the Resistance chief's approval of the Puligny-Montrachet.

"Excellent, excellent, my dear Chamberlain," laughed Soleil. It amused Soleil and his men to dub the servants with English names. Inevitably, they used the handful of politicians' names they knew. The joke was wearing thin, though not for the thirty members of Soleil's group. And the local farmers and shopkeepers who had been required to attend dropped their embarrassment to join in the laughs.

Manners learned that the owner of the château had been a prisoner of war in Germany since the surrender. His wife stayed in Paris. So how did Soleil come to have use of it?

"Easy, I just turned up yesterday, told the butler and housekeeper that I wanted to stage a classic dinner, just like prewar, and left two of my men to ensure there would be no surprises. These châteaux always have lots of food tucked away, and the cellars are stocked with wine. And I am sure the owner would be only too proud to entertain the fighters for freedom. Is that not true, lads?" he roared, slugging the wine in a toast to the table, as the butler directed two elderly maids in black dresses and white aprons to serve the soup.

Just as well the maids were not young and pretty, with this bunch, Manners thought. It felt like a pirate feast. In front of Soleil's plate, two of Manners's Mills bombs lay wickedly on their sides, the fuses already in. A Sten gun lay beneath his chair, and he had a revolver strapped to his leather belt. Slim and dapper, and looking about twenty-one, he reminded Manners of the young RAF fighter pilots and the dashing, romantic air they cultivated. His nails, Manners noticed, had been manicured, and he was smoking Sieg cigarettes, the German Army brand. Across the table, François sat stone-faced, just the merest quiver of an eyelid as he saw Manners looking at him. He had not said a word since they had sat down.

"Are you another one who's going to try to have me killed?" Soleil asked him. "I'm losing count of the people after me. The Germans, the Milice, the Communists, that aristocratic SOE agent of yours, Edgar. They all decide Soleil is too uncomfortable and try to have me bumped off. I warn you, it doesn't work."

"You haven't tried to steal any of my guns yet, Soleil," Manners said, joking to cover his surprise. "I've heard the stories about you, but as long as you keep killing Germans you're too useful to me alive."

"So why doesn't SOE send me any parachutages? I want more guns, hundreds of guns. I'll have a thousand men by July," Soleil boasted.

"You can't keep a thousand men round here, let alone feed them. And a thousand men would need twenty parachute drops just for the guns. We can't do it, Soleil. We have other groups to help, our own sabotage operations," said Manners. "I'll ask London to lay on as many drops as they can, but you'll have to find the sites and landing grounds. And I'll have to know where your men will be, what targets they are going for, and when the operations will be."

"Targets, Englishman? The targets are every bloody German for miles around, and those Milice pigs. I'll take care of the targets. You just get me the guns."

"We have been through this often before," interrupted Marat, his round spectacles glinting in the candlelight. "We cannot afford independent actions without central direction. We have a command structure, and the party insists that you are part of it, Soleil."

"You can stuff your party up your arse," belched Soleil. "Where was your command structure when I was killing Milice from here to Villefranche? Passing a death sentence on me, that's what your command structure tried to do."

He splashed some red wine into the *tourain* that remained in his soup bowl, brought the bowl to his mouth with both hands, and slurped it down. Manners noticed that the wine was a Léoville '38.

"We call that *faire chabrol*, finishing the soup the way the peasants do it. Try it, Englishman!" He pulled out his pistol, and hammered the butt on the table. "Hey, boys," he shouted. "I'm teaching Winston Churchill's man to *faire chabrol*. When we've killed all the Boches, we'll go over to London and teach Churchill himself, eh?"

"We're going to Spain first," shouted a swarthy-looking desperado in a heavy Spanish accent. "First we settle Hitler, then we settle Franco. We'll *faire chabrol* with Franco's blood."

Manners had heard a lot of this. Many of the Maquis were Spaniards who had fled from Franco's victory, most of them Communists, and somehow were quite convinced that Churchill and Roosevelt would turn their armies south across the Pyrenees as soon as the war in Europe was over. Manners did not have the heart to disabuse them. Just by refusing to let German troops through Spain to take Gibraltar, Franco had earned himself the gratitude of the Allies.

The Spaniard lumbered to his feet, and with a great cry of *"Arriba España,"* came around to Malrand's place and lifted him into a powerful embrace. "I salute you, Malrand, for flying with us and fighting with us. We will feast in Madrid, by the steps of Franco's gallows."

Malrand patted the big Spaniard on the back, pushed him back to his place, and sat to attack his foie gras. "Let's be thankful the Germans didn't take all of this," he laughed, and toasted the Spanish refugees across the table. Then he turned and began talking quietly to the man at his right, a neatly dressed older Frenchman with the look of a lawyer, out of place among these burly men with their thick hands.

"I'll forgive that Malrand a lot, because of what he did in Spain," said Marat.

"What about the work he's doing now for France?" asked Manners.

"Oh, that is to be expected. He's a patriotic French aristocrat, with interests to protect. This summer, with the invasion, you'll see the entire gentry of France join the Resistance and claim to have been in the underground all along. By the time your Montgomery gets his tanks to Paris, you will find an entire nation of forty million brave resisters, with a few token scapegoats like Pétain and Laval to be put on trial as collaborators. They will be France's alibi, as we all conveniently forget that in 1940, we had forty million collaborators who were happy to settle for Pétain and a quiet life. My own party went along for a while, because of that damned Nazi-Soviet pact. I'm French enough to admire de Gaulle for standing up in 1940. And Malrand. He picked his side early, I'll give Malrand that. But to fight for France is in his blood, in his character. Fighting for Spain was not. That's what makes him an interesting man, and possibly a dangerous one."

"He's dangerous to Germans, that's for certain. You should have seen him with the Spandau." The maids stood at their shoulders to serve the trout. Automatically, Manners turned his shoulder to make way for the woman, and noticed that Marat did not. He just continued smoking his pipe, staring quizzically at the Englishman, forcing the maid to wait.

"Some of the boys tell me Malrand's a good teacher and a good leader. Almost as good as you, they say."

"He's better than me," said Manners. "He gets that automatic respect that's the mark of a natural officer."

"That's a question of his class, and there'll be no more of that kind of respect when this war's over. We'll respect men like you and McPhee, professionals who know what they're doing, and know it is their duty to pass it on to others."

"There won't be much room for people like me after the war. Anyway, I don't think I'll survive it. I'm a professional soldier, Even if I survive this mission, and whatever I have to do in Germany, after Hitler's finished they'll send me to Burma to fight the Japanese."

"They'll probably ask you take Indochina back for France."

"I do what I'm told, Marat."

"So do I, Englishman, but in a different army, for a different cause." He put down his pipe, sipped his wine, and devoured his fish in four great bites. He washed the last mouthful down with wine, and lit his pipe again.

"By the way, I'm enjoying the book you lent me," said Manners. "Thank you."

"I have another history you might want to read after the Michelet, as soon as McPhee has finished it. He's reading it closely, on those few occasions when Mercedes has finished with him. Or him with her. My boys all like our Red Indian, but she likes him most of all." Marat laughed dismissively. "And don't let the name of the author put you off the book. It was written by Karl Marx, but it's about French history, how our Revolutions turn into dictatorships."

"Sometimes I wonder whether Stalin didn't do the same thing to the Soviet revolution," said Manners, grinning at the thought of McPhee and the fierce little Spanish girl. But he was struck by Marat's criticism of the Nazi-Soviet pact, wondering just how unorthodox a Communist he might be.

"Three or four years ago, I might have agreed with you. The war has changed that. The entire Soviet people are involved now. This is their war, and the place will never be the same. Stalin has understood that. He's a realist."

"Stalin?" shouted Soleil in his ear. "The Englishman wants to make a toast to Stalin." He rapped on the table with his gun again. Manners raised his glass with a grin. "Stalin, and the great Russian war effort," he said.

"That's enough drink for you," Soleil said, shoving the priceless crystal glass roughly down on the table. "When we finish this meal, you're giving your lesson. On the Sten gun."

"What, here at the table? It's already gone midnight."

"So what. Don't you know there's a war on?" laughed Soleil. "We might as well enjoy it. Here. I was only teasing you. Have some more wine. But you are going to give the lesson. I promised the boys."

So it proved. His tongue thick with wine, and swaying just a little on his feet, Manners found himself pushed to his feet at the end of the meal. Soleil's own Sten was thrust into his hand, and the pistol butt hammered for silence. He might as well do this right.

"The Sten gun," he began. "Named after its inventors. Shepherd and Turpin, of the Royal Small Arms Factory at Enfield. It may not be the best submachine gun ever made, but it's the cheapest and the easiest to make and maintain and so it is the most useful for the kind of fighting you have to do. We have made over four million of them so far in this war. It's the most popular submachine gun in the world. Just over seven hundred fifty millimeters long, weighs under three kilograms, made of cheap and easy metal stampings. So easy that the Danish Resistance have been making their own copies in underground workshops.

"It holds thirty two nine-millimeter rounds, and fires them at a rate of five hundred fifty rounds a minute. Work it out. You have about four seconds of constant firing. Never fire that long. Short bursts. Rat-a-tat-tat is the sound you want to hear. Any more than that and the muzzle starts to climb to the left. And you can't carry that much ammunition.

"It will kill at two hundred meters, even more. But you'll never hit anything at that range except by accident. The sights are fixed at one hundred meters, and you can't change them. A hundred meters is maximum effective range. Five meters is best. The closer the better. But remember, if you don't hit your German, you'll scare the shit out of him. Nobody, I mean nobody, remains standing when a submachine gun is being fired. They jump for cover because there's a lot of lead flying in a very short space of time.

"If you want to make them keep their heads down even longer, here's a useful trick. Take a wet cloth or towel, and wrap it round the Sten's barrel. Pull the trigger, and it sounds just like a heavy machine gun. Only don't keep firing too long or it overheats. But for the first shots of an ambush, or if you want to discourage a pursuit, I recommend the wet towel trick.

"The worst problem is that the Sten can jam, so only load thirty rounds. Never the full thirty-two. If it jams, clear the bolt, like this." He tugged it back, the hard metallic sound cruelly efficient in the rapt silence in the great room. "If it still jams, hit the butt on the floor and then clear the bolt twice. If it still jams, throw it at the Germans. And you then have my permission to run." He got the expected laugh.

"Now, throw me another Sten and a big handkerchief." Malrand, grinning because he knew what Manners was about to do, took one of the big damask napkins from the table, and came around to tie it into a blindfold across Manners's eyes.

"The most useful thing about the Sten is its ease of maintenance. It likes being greased and oiled and taken care of, but it will forgive you if you're too busy fighting." He laid the two Sten guns side by side, thumping them clumsily onto the table because of the blindfold. "Right, who has a watch with a secondhand?" Somebody shouted out that he did. "Tell me when to start, and then time me," he said.

"*Trois—deux—allez-y,*" came the cry. And despite the blindfold, Manners's hands moved almost too fast to see. One Sten, slip the magazine, release the bolt, withdraw, flick the sear, and release the spring. Lay them down, one by one. The next Sten, the same procedure. "Finished," he shouted.

"Nine seconds," came an awed voice.

"Right. Soleil, mix up the parts from the two guns so I don't know which part comes from which gun." He heard the clatter, smelled the garlic mixed with Soleil's cologne.

"Good. Now time me again." And still blindfolded, he reassembled the two guns. The spring, the sear, the bolt, the magazine. Safety on. Do it again. Lovely old Sten. Doesn't matter which part comes from which gun, they all fit together just fine. "Finished."

"Twelve seconds."

He whipped off the blindfold. "Now, Soleil, which gun is yours and which is mine? You can't tell. But take one of those two apart and put it back together. We're not timing now. But Soleil will show you how easy it is. Who's the youngest here?"

A dozen voices cried that Little Pierrot was the one, just sixteen. He came up and easily put the second gun back together.

"Who's the oldest?" called Manners, stripping it down again. The elderly lawyer-type who had been speaking to Malrand rose hesitantly. "I have never handled a gun, monsieur, not in my life."

"All the better—you'll show them how easy it is." Most of these men would be accustomed to firearms from childhood, shotguns and rook rifles, military service. The lawyer handled the parts gingerly, had trouble with the spring, but finally handed the reassembled Sten to Manners with a proud glint in his eyes. "Well done, monsieur."

"Right, how many rounds do you load in the magazine?"

"Thirty," they all shouted.

"What's your best range?"

"Five meters."

"What do you do if it jams?"

"Release the bolt. Bang it on the floor."

"And if that doesn't work?"

"Throw it at the Germans." They all roared, laughing now, delighted with themselves and the gun and with him.

"Enough. We'll shoot some in the morning." He turned, clapped Soleil on the back, and headed off to sleep in the barn, the sounds of continued revelry building behind him. He had barely got to the hall when Marat caught him.

"That was a very impressive performance," he said. "It had to be."

"Why?" Manners asked bluntly. He was tired and drunk and did not want any more verbal jousting that night.

"It's what I came here tonight to tell you. Brehmer's infantry battalions are due to arrive at Limoges tomorrow night. Three battalions of Russian renegades, Vlasov's men. And one battalion of Georgians, who have been transferred from fighting Tito in Yugoslavia. They are hard and terrible men who know they are lost if Hitler is defeated."

"What do you mean, Vlasov's men?"

"He used to be a general in the Red Army, a good one. But when he was captured in one of the big encirclements, he turned his coat and joined the Nazis, and went round the POW camps recruiting more. Most of them probably joined up for the promise of a square meal. They claim to be fighting for a non-Communist Russia, but they're renegades now. Doomed men. Traitors."

"Limoges tomorrow night," mused Manners. "Then they have to move them to Périgueux and Bergerac, get them into barracks, food and sleep. That's another day. Refit them, issue ammo, re-caliber their guns at the range, and a couple of lectures on tactics, communications, rules of engagement. Russian troops will need German liaison officers, and then some French speakers. The staff work for that will take some sorting out. Another day, and then at least one day familiarization with the country. Right, thanks, Marat. We have four days, minimum. Maybe five. Are they using road transport or local trains to move them to Périgueux?"

"Three local trains have been assigned. They are to be available from dawn, two days from now. But the armored train that escorted them here will stay for that. It's too risky to ambush an armored train."

"If we are to try anything at all, we have to hit them before they're ready. Malrand has more ammo for the Spandau. We're well off for supplies." He was thinking aloud. Take the plastic out of the Gammon bombs, and he could probably take out one pillar of a viaduct. No—the armored cars would watch the viaducts and the obvious bridges and cuttings. These men have fought partisans. Maybe this was too big a target. The priority was to have the Maquis trained and ready for the invasion, not to lose their strength and morale fighting superior fire-power too soon.

"Perhaps we should duck this one and disperse, start up again else-where," Manners said.

"They'll torture peasants till they find the arms dumps, round up the parents of the boys who have run to the Maquis. If we leave now without a fight, the people will never trust us again," said Marat. "I thought you might radio for an air raid on the rail station."

"Bomber Command doesn't do that kind of favor. And anyway a night raid would flatten half of Limoges, kill too many civilians. Remember the way the American bombers hit Bergerac when they were trying to get the airfield. No, we'd do better to hit them early, and then disperse. Can your railway men get me to Périgueux and up that track to Limoges tomorrow? And can you get a message to McPhee and his boys to stand by?"

"We can use one of the trolleys if we have to, claim a signal repair. I can reach McPhee."

"Right, wake me in good time. And send Malrand to me in the barn. We have to talk about this."

"Malrand will be busy," he said with a wry grin. "Mercedes came here with me."

"I thought he hated Communists."

"She's a woman, that's different. And she's a Spaniard. They love him, Englishman."

"I thought you said she was with McPhee?"

"She is, when he's around. But tonight he isn't, and Mercedes has been at war since Franco launched his coup eight years ago. She lives for the day, and she likes men."

"I suppose it's that free love idea that you Communists believe in," said Manners, suddenly worried by the implications for the mission of a woman coming between McPhee and François.

"Mercedes hates fascists because she spent three days being raped by Franco's Moorish troops when she was barely out of puberty," said

Marat. "She has not had much time for your bourgeois conventions of fidelity ever since. And loving her like my own daughter, I can't say I blame her. We've been fighting a different kind of war for a long time, while your friend McPhee was playing at being a novelist in Paris, and while *you* were playing polo."

CHAPTER 16

Time: The Present

Horst pulled a manila file from a fat briefcase that stood by his knee, and tossed it with casual pride onto the table beside the champagne and the roses.

"I am honored to meet you, Major Manners. Your father is the unsung hero of this fruit of my researches. This is the war diary of the *Kampfgruppe Brehmer*, a specialist anti-Resistance unit, stationed in the Dordogne during April and May of 1944. It comes fresh from the *Kriegsarchiv*, the German military archives, where it seems I was the first visiting scholar ever to bother to study it. It was filed under the unit records for *HeeresgruppeOst*, the section that dealt with the Eastern Front, where the Brehmer Division was formed. By chance, I came across a reference to it in the Order of Battle for Army Group G, the command for southern France. So I put in a trace request and the librarians found it for me. And I think it points to the area where our lost cave may be rediscovered."

He bent forward to offer his hand to Manners, while Clothilde tried to embrace him on both cheeks, and Lydia hovered, her hand half-outstretched. Manners opened the file.

"You read German, and German script, my dear Major?"

"I can make a stab at it. NATO courses, you know," said Manners vaguely, skimming through the sheaf of photocopied pages and stopping at a passage where the margin had been lined in red ink.

"There are several references to Resistance actions," said Horst. "The first one came even as they were first deploying by train, just outside the village of la Farde, about fifteen kilometers north of Périgueux, just after the track crossed the small river Beauronne. The usual reprisals were inflicted, and the unit intelligence report claimed that they were a Communist band led by an American Red Indian and a mysterious Englishman—that would seem to point to your father, Captain Manners. There is a cross-reference to Gestapo records, which have not survived for this region in the archives. But I think that means the information was obtained by torture."

"Two dead, four wounded, one truck destroyed and one armored car damaged. Not much of an ambush," said Manners, skimming the casualty report.

"That was because the Brehmer Division had not yet taken formally under command some battalions of auxiliary troops, Russian refugees. They report only their own casualties from the armored car unit. There's an appendix on the auxiliary casualties—forty-two dead and over a hundred wounded. It was quite an ambush, and the Red Indians, as the Brehmer Division called them, then became the unit's top priority. The unit intelligence officer was a Hauptmann Karl-Heinz Geissler, a former panzer officer who had been badly wounded in the Kursk salient in the summer of 1943, and after convalescence, was transferred to antipartisan duties. That's where he joined Brehmer. He was obviously a clever man and kept good records. He was killed in the Battle of the Bulge.

"The really interesting reference comes on the sweep operation the Brehmer unit staged after Geissler brought some brains to bear on the problem. He backtracked over all the most recent guerrilla actions and arrested and interrogated a large number of villagers from le Buisson, where there had been a demolition of the railroads and a couple of associated ambushes. They found three villagers with relatives who had joined the local Maquis. Geissler, using the routine developed on the Eastern Front, systematically arrested all the other family members, starting with those who lived on farms, on the assumption that they would be providing food to the Resistance. One from each family was shot in front of the others, and the survivors were then questioned in the usual vicious way. As a result, one arms dump and a Maquis camp were found on the plateau of Audrix, near a well-known cave called the Gouffre de Proumeyssac."

"I know it well," said Clothilde. "But it's a tourist cave with stalagmites and stalactites—no art at all."

"But this arms dump was found in another cave, which the intelligence report says was marked on no known maps. It goes on: 'The arms cache was booby-trapped, but surveillance reported no subsequent guerrilla action in this district.'" Horst looked up. "That's one place to start looking. There are a couple more. First, apparently there are catacombs under Belvès that link it to some older caves."

"No, I know them quite well," said Clothilde. "They grew mushrooms there. Well searched, and no cave art."

"O.K., what about Rouffignac? Geissler says the Red Indians put up 'a fierce resistance' when they sent a column to search the cave there. They found a base camp, some food supplies, but no arms dump. Geissler had the cave searched, and kept a couple of companies there for a week, just looking."

"We've thought of Rouffignac. We'll look again, but it has been well searched."

"All right. I saved the best for last. You know Perony's famous site at la Ferrassie, where he found the burials?"

"Yes, I know it well. I worked on Delporte's subsequent dig there in 1973, when we found the skeleton of the two-year-old. But that's not a cave, it's an overhang. And it was Mousterian period, maybe as much as fifteen thousand years before Lascaux."

"In the hills above it in May 1944, on a flat plateau near a small village called Cumont, the Brehmer Division managed to interrupt a parachute drop. They captured a couple of farm carts and the parachutes and some containers and a lot of British guns, and under interrogation, one of the captured carters said he knew they were taking the guns to a secret place near la Ferrassie. An Englishman was in charge of the operation. That's it. He died under interrogation. They searched high and low but found nothing."

"I know of no caves around there," said Clothilde. "None at all."

"The carter was not a local. He was a railway man from Normandy called Marcel Devriez who was working in Périgueux and the Milice records listed him as a suspected Communist. Under interrogation, he said he was only driving the cart because the farmer who was supposed to drive it was shot when the Germans opened up, and he was trying to get it away. He was unmarried and had no surviving family in the region. The Gestapo raided his home address in Périgueux, and found it empty. But they did find a lot of anti-Nazi propaganda in both French and Spanish.

"From the Resistance records in Bordeaux, I traced Devriez. He's on the Périgueux war memorial for 1944, and was listed in Bordeaux as a member of the FTP, the *Francs-Tireurs et Partisans*, who were mainly Communists. He was in a group run by a shadowy man called Marat, who was one of the aides to the famous Colonel Georges of the Limousin, and very definitely a Communist. Marat disappeared in the summer of 1944, according to the few available FTP records, possibly killed in the attempts to attack the SS Das Reich Division."

"Surely all those bodies were recovered and identified," said Manners. "That's how the names got on the war memorials."

"Not Marat's body, along with eight more of his men, and possibly some more who are simply listed as 'Spanish comrades.' Marat was last seen in Brive on the eighth of June, trying to persuade the Gaullists and other Resistance groups to join the general uprising on the day after the British and Americans landed at Normandy. He was turned down flat. The Resistance, which took its orders from London, had been told very firmly to get involved in no such foolhardy adventures. The FTP archives assume that Marat and his men were among those killed in the fighting in Tulle, or in the German reprisals. A lot of buildings were burned down, with bodies inside, and that seems the most likely explanation why they were never found. The Limoges command of the FTP was one of those that sent out in May 1944 the order to launch the national insurrection as soon as the Allies came ashore on D-Day, whenever that would be. Limoges was Marat's base. The order probably came from him, or he felt bound by it. Anyway, despite all the pleas from London and from the Gaullists, the FTP went ahead with this mad plan to seize control of the district, starting with Tulle and Brive. Tulle alone proved too much for them, and the German garrison held out until some panzer reinforcements came from the Das Reich division. They smashed their way through the FTP guerrillas, and starting hanging the prisoners.

"That's it." Horst sat down again, looking drawn. Clothilde came and sat down beside him, and put her hand on his.

"That's brilliant, Horst," said Lydia, making herself busy with the roses, looking for vases. "You look shattered, you poor man. But really very well done. It just shows what a professional scholar, a true researcher, can do." Roses in one hand, she thrust the unopened champagne bottle at Manners. "Here, make yourself useful."

"This has been very difficult for me. I had not done this kind of research before, and I am sickened by what I found," Horst said to Clothilde. "I knew, you see, what had happened here in theory. But I didn't really know until I started going through those war journals and intelligence reports. All in clipped, official language."

"I know what you mean, my dear fellow," said Manners. "I've written some of those things myself. Terrible language, trying to be as flat as possible while writing about terrible things. Like writing back letters to the wives and mothers of men who have been killed under your command. Grim stuff." He went into the kitchen, and with the skill of an old campaigner immediately found the cupboard where Clothilde kept her glasses, and came back and started to pour. "Tell me, Horst, did you come across the name of Malrand in your researches?"

"Just that formal report that Lydia gave me in Bordeaux. Nothing in the FTP or German military archives. but quite a lot about his brother, Berger. I've read his memoirs, of course, about getting captured and then being imprisoned in Toulouse."

"What about a chap called Soleil, code name for a Resistance leader in Belvès, real name René Coustellier or another fellow called Lespinasse?"

"Soleil, yes there is a lot about him in the Geissler reports, when they staged a big raid on Belvès. Soleil got away. And Lespinasse was the name of one of the families from le Buisson who were interrogated because a son or nephew had run off and joined the Resistance. Their farm was burned and some family members deported. It's all in the file."

Horst fell silent and remained so throughout the meal, but he drank a great deal, and smoked Clothilde's cigarettes between courses. They told him about their day with Malrand, the new reward offer, and his rejection of Clothilde's proposal for a scientific search for new caves. Each time, he only grunted. The wine they had so enjoyed buying went down without comment or pleasure. Manners, still poring over the research file Horst had brought, didn't even get a reaction when he detailed the connection between Malrand and his father. The three of them kept up a lame conversation, trying without success to bring Horst into it. Finally, pushing aside his cheese, Horst asked for brandy, lit another cigarette, and reached for Clothilde's hand.

"One more thing in those files," he said. "I wasn't going to tell you, but you'll find it anyway when you read it. Another name I came across in Geissler's intelligence reports. It was Alfonse Daunier, your father. He was listed as the only source Geissler had inside the Resistance. He was the one who gave Geissler the parachute drop."

He poured out another glass of brandy and pushed it toward Clothilde. She took it without a word, her eyes fixed on his, her face suddenly bloodless.

"It wasn't what you think," Horst went on slowly. "He wasn't a collaborator. It was your mother. She was pregnant and Geissler brought pressure through her. He had her arrested, threatened her with a concentration camp, and then released her. He called it 'the usual measures.' Your father fed them information through her, to save her. And to save you, I suppose."

"Does it say how he died?" she asked flatly.

"No, the Brehmer Division was transferred in late May. Geissler's final report said he had handed on her file, as a source, to the Gestapo." He gripped her hand, tightly. "It needn't be true, Clothilde. Intelligence officers make up sources all the time, just to have something to tell their superiors."

"So it's a lie, what they put on the war memorial—'fusillé par les Allemands'—shot by the Germans. The Resistance records are a lie."

"No, they're not. He was killed at Terrasson when the Das Reich division stormed through to open the road to the railhead at Périgueux. The Resistance records are clear, the date, and the place. The body was found, Clothilde. You know that. Your father was shot by German troops, trying to fight them. The war memorial is true."

"It's just the rest that is a lie, then," she shot back. She poured herself another brandy, and pushed the bottle over to Lydia. "Whatever am I going to say to my mother?"

Lydia decided to announce that she was giving up and going back to London when they all met the next morning at Clothilde's museum at Les Eyzies. Clothilde had drunk her way down the bottle until her head sagged, and Lydia had thrown the two men out and bedded down on the couch, after putting Clothilde to bed and washing up the dishes. She had woken early, made coffee, and felt her spirits steadily droop as the watched the morning mist hang dully over the river. The sky was gray and it looked like rain. She took the small photograph of Manners's rock from her bag and looked at it reproachfully. What a mess it had caused. She roamed through Clothilde's bookshelves, pulling out Leroi-Gourhan on Lascaux, and a monograph by Clothilde on bone tools and their uses. Desultorily, she glanced through the pictures, read Clothilde's conclusion while barely comprehending a word of it, and then turned to a picture book for children about life in the Neolithic age. That was more her level, she told herself glumly.

Even after her shower, there seemed little point in her staying. Malrand's big new reward would probably get the rock back. Horst was far better at the archive research than she would ever be. Manners was clearly more interested in Horst's damned old archives than he was in her. And the whole project had become thoroughly depressing. She didn't even feel so interested in Manners anymore, she told herself, as her hangover thumped steadily behind her eyes. Still, she was a lot better off than Clothilde, who looked like death when she rose, gulped the coffee Lydia had made, and disappeared into the bath for nearly an hour. She emerged, drank more coffee, lit a cigarette, and came out to the terrace to put her arms around Lydia and hug her tightly.

"Thanks for staying. I'm very glad you did." Smelling marvelous, Clothilde was dressed with her usual dash. She looked as if she had made a miraculous recovery. Lydia wished she could.

"This is the kind of day when I ought to go to Paris and buy myself a new pair of shoes," Clothilde said. "You look as though you could use the same therapy."

"I'm not sure why I'm still here," said Lydia. "The whole thing has become very upsetting. For you, for Horst, and I'm feeling wretched. I think I'll go back to London."

"And leave your handsome major to me?" laughed Clothilde. "Don't be silly. These things that happened in the war happened to other people, not to us. They lived in an impossible time and had to do impossible things. We live in a time of possibilities. There are things we can do, people we can interview now we know so much more. There are geological maps we can look at, places to be searched on the ground. We can find this cave, Lydia, and teach Malrand a lesson."

"Where on earth do you get your confidence?"

"From you. Last night was a disaster for me, and you rolled up your sleeves, took care of me, cleaned the place up, and fed me coffee this morning. You were confronted with a problem and you tackled it. Thank you. And while you had to wait for me, you carry on research-ing." She gestured at the open books.

"Now we have another problem to tackle, finding that cave. I'm not going to let you go back, Lydia. Your friendship is one of the good things to have come from this whole drama that has been launched upon us. We have all been conscripted into this, and we have to see it through."

She went into the kitchen, made toast and boiled two eggs, and forced Lydia to eat. They went out to the car, and Clothilde put the hood down, handed Lydia a headscarf and tied another around her own ginger curls, and raced off down the narrow back road to Les Eyzies. They had climbed the long stairs to the old château tucked into the rock ledges above the town, the building site of the new museum busy below them, and found Horst and Manners already there, poking amiably around the exhibit of tools made from reindeer bones and antlers.

"Did you know that I'd have to kill thirty reindeer to make you a necklace like this?" Manners said to Lydia by way of greeting. "Worth every terrified moment. You do look a treat, both of you. Poor old Horst and I had to nurse our hangovers with lots of coffee and croissants. You two look as if you're fresh from the beauty parlor. Don't know how you do it, but I'm very glad you do."

Horst did indeed look grim, but Manners's cheerful babble got them across the embarrassments of the previous evening, and a determined Clothilde marched them into her office and started spreading very large-scale maps across her desk. Her office was small and neat, with a spectacular view across the river, but she quickly bustled them into action.

"That's the map for Cumont and la Ferrassie, where the parachute drop took place. And that's the geological survey map of the same district. Major, find some drawing pins and stick them up on that corkboard on the wall. Horst, you know the geology. See what you find, and then you and the major can go and tramp the ground. He's a soldier. If anyone can identify the kind of place his father would have picked to hide guns, he can. I suggest we meet back here just before the museum closes at five, have a drink, and compare notes."

"What are you two going to do?" asked Horst.

"Well, we can't go surveying the ground dressed like this. If you find anything worth a closer look, we'll dress for it tomorrow. Today, Lydia and I have some old Resistance men to interview. Or we may decide we need to shop for a new pair of shoes."

"In which case," smiled Lydia, "We'll call you from Paris to put off our drinks."

The first two men they called on were also on the list that Manners had been given by Morillon back in Bordeaux. The railway man from le Buisson was called Étienne Faugère, and his memory was sometimes precise, sometimes vague. He lived with his married daughter, who made them coffee as they sat in the neat little garden to talk. He remembered Malrand, and a trade union organizer called Marat, and remembered being beaten up by Russian soldiers in German uniform while a French Milice tough he had been at school with asked him question after question.

"I shot him the day the Allies landed," the old man said proudly. "The local police decided it was time to change sides, arrested the local Milice types, and brought them to the square beside the cinema. There wasn't much of a trial. But I told what he had done to me, and the chief of police gave me his revolver, so I went up and spat in his face and shot him in the head. He was crying. I had to shoot him twice. Your mum was there in the crowd, Clothilde, with all the women. Some of them came up and kicked the body. He'd been a devil with the women, that one, particularly the ones whose husbands were off in Germany. Then we went off to Tulle, and spent two days shooting Germans till they sent the tanks against us. I got away, but a lot didn't."

"Is that where Marat was killed?" Clothilde asked.

"Marat? He wasn't at Tulle. I saw him at Brive, just before we all went up to Tulle. All the commandants had this meeting at the monastery of St-Antoine, trying to decide what to do, who would go to Tulle. There was a big row between our lot in the FTP and the Gaullists who said they had orders from London not to go. But Marat stayed behind, with those Spaniards of his. No, I got to see most of the lads at Tulle because they had me taking round ammunition, what little we had. I was a strong young lad in those days. Marat wasn't there. I'd have known."

"Do you remember meeting an English officer or an American?"

"I heard about the American. We called him the Red Indian

265

because he had one of those funny haircuts. I never met him. I saw the Englishman one night, when they'd blown up the junction at le Buisson. I heard all these explosions and gunfire and went to the window and saw him getting away. I told the Germans that, when they beat me up. I had to tell them something. I couldn't tell them about Marat and the way we got him all around the place on the trains. We had this tool chest on the trains below the coal. We never used it because we always rigged up hooks so the tools we needed were in easy reach. Two meters long but very narrow. We hid him in there. I couldn't tell them that."

They thanked him and left, and took the road for Audrix, to the next name on the list. Albert Escarmant had been one of the youngest of Berger's group, the son of a farmer who had started by helping with the parachute drops. Now he ran the farm with his sons, who took the milk and butter and yogurt they made down to the local markets. Clothilde said she always bought from them, and knew the old man well. As they pulled into the muddy farmyard, Clothilde grinned at Lydia and said, "Remember those new shoes we talked about? Well, these aren't new, but they are different." And she pulled two sets of rubber boots, one very old and one quite new, from behind her seat, and handed Lydia the new ones.

Old Albert remembered the English officer, le Capitaine Manners, and the crazy American, and Berger and his brother, whom he called "young François." He remembered the night the Germans had roared into the parachute drop at Cumont, their guns blazing.

"We wanted to scatter, but *le capitaine* wouldn't let us," he recalled. "He got us down into cover and firing back, and then ran among us, getting some to go round and take the Germans in the flank, and some more to try and help him creep up on the armored car with a Gammon bomb. It was one of those big ones with eight wheels. He didn't get it, but he got us enough time for young François to get most of the guns away. Young François got me to cut the dead horses loose so we could get the carts. I finished up pushing mine and it was a nightmare. I had to jam a bough into the wheels to stop it running out of control. But the Germans didn't get it."

"Where did you take the guns, Albert?"

"I took mine down that track that goes past la Farge, and then down the hill to that dip just before you come to the ruined old windmill on the road that goes over to Rouffignac. That was the rendezvous point. We always had a rendezvous prepared. Then Berger sent me back up the hill to help with the horses, but it was all over by then and I was on my own. So I went the other way, across the ridge toward Limeuil, and swam the river to get back to the old camp we had by the Gouffre. The Germans had found that one, but I knew a place to hide before I tried to get back to the lads."

"Do you know where they took the guns that night?"

"No, there was a big argument about it, young François and that Commie bloke Marat, shouting at each other in whispers when I got that cart down to the dip. Marat wanted to take the guns and divide them among his Spaniards and scatter to get away from the Germans. I call them Germans, but they were Russians mostly, Russians and some other lot, swarthy blokes. Anyway, young François wasn't having that, and Berger was trying to sort it out when he sent me back up the hill. It was daft. I could hear that big twenty-millimeter cannon going back up beyond la Farge, and there were these two arguing like fishwives."

"What I remember next was the big explosion, as I was going back up the hill. One of the carts we had to abandon was full of ammo. *Le capitaine* crawled up to it, took the pin out of a Mills bomb, and stuck it between two of the cases, so when the Germans came to move it, the lever snapped back and the whole cart blew. There were bullets cooking off all over the place. That was when it ended. *Le capitaine* told me about it later. We had a laugh about it the last time I saw him, when he came over for old Lespinasse's funeral."

"Where did young François want to take the guns? Did he know a place?"

"Oh, he had places everywhere, that one. He knew everybody, all the farmers and their sons, and most of the daughters too, knowing young François. I suppose he knew old Dumonteil, up on the ridge. The Germans deported him, and burned the farm. But we'd never have got the carts up there. Young François must have had somewhere else nearby, some little cave or hollow. He knew it all like the back of his hand, because of his hunting. He was a great one for hunting as a boy. Still is, come to that. You can have all these political crises up in Paris, and he'll still come down here and take a day or two hunting the *bécasse* with me. The best hunting in the world, he calls it, the fastest, most cunning bird of them all. Even round here, he can still show me little corners that I don't know, where he says we might get lucky, and sure enough, there's a *bécasse*."

"Maybe the guns were just abandoned that night, with all the fighting and the argument," Clothilde pressed.

"Oh no, we'd never do that. And anyway, I know we got some of the stuff that night because *le capitaine* had promised us some of those new wonder drugs, sulfa drugs they called them, for our medical supplies. And I know we got that because they used it on me when I got shot later on at Terrasson, when that Das Reich division came through. About a week or ten days later, it must have been. I remember it very well. It was a powder, and they sprinkled it on my shoulder where the bullet had gone through. Strapped me up with a bandage, and told me I was as good as new. I wasn't, mind, but young François said since it was my left shoulder, and that didn't stop me firing a gun. I was young then, and healed fast, and it was all so exciting that you couldn't stop. That's where your dad was killed, Terrasson."

"Where did young François get the sulfa powder from? Where had he kept it?"

"He gave some of us a medical kit to carry with us. I remember Lespinasse had one, because he had to use it at Terrasson. Young François was using that Citroën car by then, the one he'd pinched from the Milice in le Buisson. The old *traction-avant* with the running boards. It was a lovely car, that. He'd pile five or six of us in, guns and all, ammo in the trunk, and those medical kits he made up, and off we'd go. The mobile reserve, he called it. That was a joke, because the real Mobile Reserve was the Vichy one. Real bastards, they were. He always made sure we had some medicinal brandy in the back of the Citroën, brandy and cigarettes. He couldn't do without his cigarettes, young François. That's how we got to Terrasson, in that Citroën. We had to make a detour round Rouffignac, because the Germans had burned it."

"Was the English *capitaine* with you at Terrasson?" asked Lydia.

"I don't know, mademoiselle, I don't remember seeing him. He didn't come in the Citroën. He used one of the trucks we got from the Falange, a nasty bunch of North Africans. Sort of police, based in Périgueux, led by a real bastard called Villeplana, used to be a professional football player. We ambushed them and got one of their trucks. *Le capitaine* was off a lot around that time, attacking all the German petrol dumps so the Das Reich couldn't refuel. He took us in the mobile reserve along on one attack on the big fuel bunkers they kept at the Roumanières airbase. That was just before Terrasson. He might have come along with us after that to Terrasson, but I don't remember. Sorry. It was all a long time ago.

"Do you want me to show you the place where we hid, the camp the Germans found?" he went on. "It's just down the track and through the woods, near the old entrance to the Gouffre, the one where they had the horse with the long rope that would let people standing in this giant bucket down into the cave . I think the people at the Gouffre are using it again, if you pay extra. No horse now, of course. An electric winch."

He took them around to the barn, where a muddy Land Rover was parked. They drove down the road toward le Bugue for half a mile before turning off on a rutted farm track, and then into the woods along a track that Lydia could not begin to discern. The big car heaved and jolted, splashing through a thick stretch of bog, before Albert began climbing again. He swung the wheel sharply to avoid a big oak tree and parked below a sudden outcrop of smooth limestone.

"This was it," he said. "You see the *borie* over there." He pointed to a low, circular stone hut, little more than a ruin now, its roof gone and saplings growing through it. "That's where *le capitaine* slept, him and young François, and where they kept the ammo. Then we had the cave." He plunged forward to the rocks, shouted to Clothilde to bring the torch, and began pushing through a tangle of bushes. Lydia looked with dismay at her clothes, saw Clothilde smile and shrug, and they followed the old man in.

With the torch, they could see it was more overhang than cave, no deeper than five meters, but about thirty meters long with a low roof and dry, gritty floor. The inner walls were smooth, and there were no gaps, only some curious scars in the rock. Clothilde moved forward intently, to see if they were ancient engravings, and Albert said, "That's the German cannon." Then he steered the torch to one side, where the cave wall and floor had been charred black. "Flamethrower," he said. "They didn't get us. We'd left by then. One of Berger's rules. Never too long in the same place." He stood in silence for a while, remembering.

"Were there any other caves you used, Albert?" Clothilde asked, gently. "I'm looking for one where there may have been some of the old cave paintings."

"The big one at Rouffignac, of course, the one where they have the train. We used that a bit. And a couple of the ones near Les Eyzies, but only for the odd night because they were so well known. The Germans just had to use a tourist map and they'd had found us. We slept in Combarelles once, but never stored anything there. Young François took us to a couple near la Micoque, on the way up to Rouffignac, but they were like this, more overhangs really. I never saw any paintings."

"Could you find them again?"

"Oh yes, I think I could, But you ought to ask young François. You and he were very close once," he said kindly.

"He's a busy man, Albert."

"Sure, I'll take you. But you'll find no paintings."

"I might find a midden, one of their old rubbish tips and latrines. You can find out a lot from latrines, Albert. Like what they ate, and what kind of tools they used. You can measure the pollen and tell what the weather was like."

"Ice Age, wasn't it?"

"Not all the time. The time I'm mostly interested in, when they were doing the cave paintings at Lascaux, it was pretty much the same climate as now, a thousand-year-long warm period between the cold spells. They had trees and brambles just like these." She led the way back to the car, chatting about the tools they made from reindeer antlers until they reached the farm. He insisted on giving her a box of eggs and a bottle of his homemade *pineau*, and waved them off, calling, "See you at the market, and give my best to your mum."

Manners's face was brick red from his day in the sun, and Horst looked exhausted, when they found them on the terrace of the Cro-Magnon Hotel. They were drinking pastis, and nibbling olives, and Horst ordered them some drinks while Manners described the search pattern they had followed on the large-scale map. Clothilde leaned over the map and told them Albert's story, of the flight down the track with the cart, and the row in the hollow by the road, and the booby-trap Manners's father had set with the grenade.

"We also found out that Marat was not at Tulle, nor were his Spaniards," said Lydia. "Wherever he was killed, it wasn't there. And he had a big row with Malrand on the night of the German attack on the parachute site, about who was to get the guns and where to take them."

Manners flipped open Horst's research file. "Here we are. The night of May twentieth, acting on information received, a company of *Frei-*

williger—that's the Russians, they called them volunteers—and a squadron of armored cars broke up a parachute drop at Cumont, killed four Maquis, and captured the weapons. Casualties described as 'light,' except for one container that blew up. They brought in another company the next day to set up roadblocks, and two more to search the district. Nothing more found. Arrests, interrogations, three farms burned as reprisals. Hang on, there's a cross-reference."

Horst took the file, and thumbed through to the back, where stapled sheafs of photocopies were neatly labeled with differently colored tabs. "They set up a special unit, called the *Höhlegruppe*, the cavern team, for attacks on caves. They were equipped with Panzerfausts—that's like your bazookas—and flamethrowers. They brought the *Höhlegruppe* in for the search, so they must have thought they were looking for a cave. A *Leutnant* Voss commanded it, and he reported no action that day." He looked across the table at Clothilde. "The first thing I did was to check every cave Voss mentions. There's not one that isn't listed or marked on your maps."

"There's an easy solution to this, surely," said Lydia. "We just ask Malrand. He must know what happened to the guns that night. But if he knows, then whatever cave it was won't have any paintings. Malrand would have said."

A long silence fell. "I wonder if he would," said Manners. "He certainly hasn't been much help on Clothilde's project."

"Remember what I said to you in Bordeaux, Lydia," Horst added. "Malrand is a politician. He doesn't want a scandal about his wartime partner stealing a cave painting. He just wants it back and put on display, with no questions asked. We have our own various reasons for wanting to find the cave whence it comes, but I don't see that he does. And look at Clothilde—we already know that delving back into this wartime history is like lifting a stone—you never know what grief will come crawling out."

"This business about Marat is very curious," said Manners. "He has a row about guns with Malrand, who hated Communists anyway. Then he disappears."

"Not quite disappeared," said Clothilde. "He was seen again after May twentieth. He was seen almost three weeks later, at Brive, just after D-Day in Normandy, trying to get the Gaullists and the rest of the Resistance groups to join this Communist uprising. Where he did not turn up was at the battle in Tulle, where you would expect him to have been, on the eighth and ninth of June."

"Where was Malrand then?" asked Lydia.

"Trying to slow down a small army. Say a thousand tanks and twenty-five thousand men. The Das Reich division was one of the SS units, which were twice as big and far better equipped than the usual panzer divisions. After D-Day it was moving north from Toulouse to join the fighting in Normandy, and fighting Resistance ambushes all the way," said Manners.

"But where exactly? Was he at that meeting in Brive of all the Resistance groups, the one where Marat was seen? And where was your father, Manners? Was he there too?"

"We know Malrand was at Terrasson," said Clothilde. "Albert told us that. But he had a Citroën, he could get around fast."

Horst checked his sheaf of archives. "June eleventh, Terrasson was cleared by units of the SS Das Reich division fighting their way along the road to Périgord, which they reached the next day. It was a busy time. That was the same day the Germans burned the village of Mouleydier, after Soleil's group held the bridge across the Dordogne and beat off repeated attacks. There was another battle at an armored train that day, just outside Périgueux. The whole region was erupting."

"The poor devils assumed that the Allies were about to send in an airborne division to liberate them," said Manners. "They didn't know they had two months more to wait before the Germans finally pulled out. Still, they did the job London wanted, delaying the Das Reich division."

"We're missing the point here," said Lydia. "The chap who finished up with the rock was your father, not Malrand. So it is your father who is our connection to this unknown cave. It's his movements we ought to be following. If we can."

"Oh, quite," said Manners. "But it's interesting you used the word following. Horst and I rather got the impression we were being followed today, both here in Les Eyzies and then when we went tramping around la Ferrassie looking for a cave. More than just an impression, in fact, because I saw him twice, each time in a different car, and once he was wearing a beret to disguise his bald pate. What's funny is that Malrand is supposed to be in Paris, and this chap told us that he always traveled with him. But I'll take my oath that it was that presidential security man, Lespinasse, whose father was in the same group as Malrand and my pa."

"More than that," said Lydia. "Old Lespinasse was at the battle in Terrasson with Malrand on June eleventh, and drove around with Malrand in some special team he had."

"So of the four key people who might know where this cave was, Marat and Lespinasse and my father are all dead. Which leaves Malrand, who doesn't seem to want to find it," mused Manners. "Curiouser and curiouser."

CHAPTER 17

The Vézère Valley, 15,000 B.C.

H e finally found her in the one impossible place, a chosen refuge he could never have foreseen. Deer had searched late into the night as the wind rose steadily, along the fringe of the woods and down along the riverbank, calling her name. Three times, he turned back to the village, to the glowing fire of her mother's hearth where her parents sat feeding the flames with fresh wood, vainly waiting for Moon to reappear. Each time he looked at them in silent hope, and each time they shook their heads before he set out again. The last time, the wind gusting hard now and bringing the first lash of driven rain, he had gone to his lonely tent, surprised to find Dry Leaf lying asleep in the old man's buffalo robe. He collected his gifts, his new bag, and his lamp and ax and knife, and filled the bag with smoked meat. He put fresh tinder in the pouch, slung an old water skin over his shoulder, and felt ready for whatever the new day might bring. Lightning crackled in the sky, and the rumble of deep anger came from the heavens. There was cause enough for anger this night.

He only had this one night to find her. The chief hunter had seen to the bleeding arm of the Keeper of the Bulls, wrapping it with moss and bark and thongs, and promising to pick up the girl's trail when the sun rose. The rest of the village was dark as he moved through it. The childless widow had sobbed herself to sleep. The hearth of the Keeper of the Bull's sister seemed to simmer in angry silence. From tents here and there, he heard the laughter and whispers and warm cries of the newlyweds, and tried not to think of what he had lost.

Finally, less because he thought he might find her than because of the comfort its familiar feel and smell might bring him, he headed past the rain-dampened ashes of the long fire and into the cave. From long habit, he had lit his lamp on an ember pulled deep from the buried heart of the fire, and the dim gleam of his own lamp made him slow to realize that there was another glow, far back in the cave. His heart jumped. Of course she would be here! But no, perhaps the Keeper of the Bulls had come, to take new strength from his own beasts. Deer put his hand to the hilt of his knife, slipped the thong around his neck, and crept forward, past the ghostly bulls and down past the bend where the tumbling horse fell forever, and then down again toward the well where there was always water.

Moon was shrunk far back but defiant in the small cavern, a rock clutched fiercely in her hand, a smear of the Keeper's blood still on her cheek. Her face eased as she saw him and then brightened. But she held the rock close, and he took his hand from his knife and squatted. Beside her were a small bowl of the dark earth and a thick stick of charcoal.

"I will not go back. Not to him," she said.

"I know," he said softly. "I have a bag full of food and tools. I have come to take you with me."

"The hunters will follow us and bring us back."

"I think I know a way they cannot follow," he said. "I will never let them take you to him to be his woman."

"They may take me, but he cannot have me. He is doomed," she said.

"The hunter put the moss on his wound. It is not likely that he will die from a bite."

"No. The Great Mother has come to my aid. She directed me here, and put the darkness into my head. When I woke, she had left me with the knowledge of what I must do. I have doomed him. Look," she said, pointing at the wall behind Deer's shoulder.

He turned, and then started back, stunned and frightened, and awed by the evidence of a power in Moon he had never suspected. This was woman's magic, mysterious and chilling, and his hand moved instinctively to cup his groin. He needed no explanation to understand that what Moon had said must be true. The Keeper of the Bulls was doomed, condemned by the destructive power of his own art.

That was surely him, stretched dead on the ground in his eagle headdress, his arms outstretched and his maleness as cruel as it was assertive, the shape of a bull's horn. Beside him lay the symbol of the power he had usurped, the beaked club that had guarded him as he had dragged Moon away to rape and subjugation against all custom and her own father's will. And two more horns were poised to gore him as he lay, by a beast itself doomed from the spear in its guts and the entrails spilling on the ground.

"It began in my head as a bull, but there is a reason I know not why it had to become a bison."

"It is the last of the bison," he explained, the meaning clear and terrible to him. "The old man is dead, who was their Keeper. He was the last of the old cave, as the cave and the art and the fellowship of the Keepers used to be before this cruel madness came upon the Keeper of the Bulls. The Keeper of the Bulls was destroying the cave as it had been, the old way dying with a spear in its belly but not yet dead, and strong enough still to kill the evil."

"What it means," he said slowly, as much to himself as to her, "is that the cave itself is doomed."

He took his lamp and peered closer at the terrible painting Moon had made, studying the way she had painted the bison.

"It is in his style," he said, marveling. "The beard on the chest of the beast and the tuck of its head and the curl of the horns. It could be his work. The spirit of the old Keeper has guided your hand this night."

"Then he worked with the Great Mother to lead me. I felt her presence and fulfilled her will."

His lamp guttered and he felt the currents of the air as the wind searched for them, even this deep in the cave.

"We must go from here and travel through the storm. It will protect us from pursuit."

"The Great Mother sent the storm to aid us," she said, in simple confidence.

He stretched out his hand toward her, and she smiled as she took it. "I wanted to take your hand earlier this night. I take it now. I take you now."

Hand in hand, they climbed from the low gallery and down the long chamber of the bulls, looming suddenly around them as the lightning flared nearby, fierce enough to send its brilliance into the dark cave. They paused at the entrance, rocking a little in the gusting wind as the thunder rolled awesomely above them. And although the long fire had long been quenched, they ran to it and leaped across its sodden ashes and stopped and turned to laugh into one another's faces. For the first time, he took her in his arms and held her, his brow against hers, the rain spilling down their faces.

"Moon," he said. "My Moon," and as she nestled against him, the lightning exploded around them and they heard a sharp crack that was louder than the voice of the thunder, and a strange, sharp smell filled their air. Moon shrank into his embrace as they turned to the pillar of fire that rose high above the cave. A great tree on the mountain that seemed still to crackle with the power of the lightning jerked in its place as it split and then toppled, bringing a gathering escort of rocks and stones as it tumbled slowly and then with increasing speed down the slope. Like a great spear, it seemed to plunge into the ground and quiver as it came to rest before the entrance of the cave, and then the avalanche of earth and rocks poured after it. The cave was sealed.

"The Great Mother has done this," breathed Moon, as Deer stared in disbelief through the driving rain at the tumbling rock fall. He remembered thinking as he saw her frightening drawing that the cave itself must be doomed. The shock of the village, of all the people of the valley, would be terrible. And so would their vengeance. They must get far, far from here.

Shaking himself, he led them down through the fringe of the woods to the river, where Deer rolled a fallen log into the water. He placed his sack upon his head, and the two of them pushed the log deep into the middle of the current where their feet no longer touched the riverbed, and floated fast downstream, leaving no trial for hunters to follow, as the great storm rolled furiously overhead.

Deer knew they had gone farther than he had ever traveled before. The river ran faster than a running man and it had been night when they first entered. And now the rain had finally stopped and the sun was rising high into the sky. Moon had straddled the log just after dawn, her teeth chattering and desperately needing to be out of the water. The first time he had tried to join her, he almost tipped her into the river.

But then as the sun broke through the thinning clouds they came to some shallows where the water was less than waist-deep. After guiding it through and keeping the log pointed straight downstream, he was able to stretch out and feel the sun on his back while his straddling legs kept the log from spinning. They had seen spirals of smoke from sheltered fires not long after dawn, where the river had curled in series of long bends and there were caves and ledges in sheer cliffs. Then the river ran wide and more slowly, and there were the familiar conical tents on a broad stretch of sand. He had seen them from afar, so he and Moon had slipped from the log into the water, keeping their heads on the side away from the tents, and there had been no cries of greeting or alarm. There had been no sign of people since then, but many of the storm. Uprooted trees floated with them, some with small animals in their branches. There were others toppled on the banks and the river was brown and full.

It was on another of the long bends that he saw the rolling hills coming close to the bank, and a narrowing where the river raced and a vast tangle of fallen trees seemed to stretch from one side to the other. Once there was a rending sound and perhaps a dozen trees broke away and began rushing downstream at great speed and the water seemed to race toward the spot as if to chase them. He knew enough of the log's ways to know they could not survive such a rushing of the water and he slipped off and start kicking desperately to steer it toward the shore. His efforts made little difference, and with fear rising like blood to his head he felt the log gather pace. They were saved by the tree that had floated alongside them throughout the morning. It seemed to hit something, and pivoted in the water to slam into the tangle on one side of the gap. Their log went with it, and ground deeply into the dam, spilling them both off, but able to haul themselves from bough to bough and into the shallows where they collapsed on their knees and arms, coughing the water from their lungs and shivering from shock and the river's cold.

As their breathing eased, they clambered onto the bank. Sodden but safe, he saw that they were on the side of the river where he had seen the narrow valley, and they made their way along the bank to the point where a smaller stream joined the great river. Automatically, he stopped to pick feathers from the brush, slipping them into his sack. He would need arrows. They followed the small stream between two gentle hills and came into a flatter valley of grassland and thin trees. Moon stopped him with a gentle hand on his arm, and pointed to the bank of thorny brush loaded thickly with berries. As they ate, the sun warm on his face, he looked around with growing confidence. It was the kind of land where he would expect to find reindeer, and there would be fish in the stream. He saw nut trees, and a rabbit darted down one of a series of holes in the bank. He had some thongs in his sack that could make traps. They could live here, if they could find shelter.

He had seen no sign of people and no smell of man, no ashes from old fires or bones or signs of fish traps along the bank, and no tents here nor the wooden frames his people erected to dry hides. None of the trees or saplings that he had seen bore the mark of the flint ax. He edged up to the higher ground, in the direction of the setting sun. The trees thinned further there, and he should be able to see both sides of the ridge. It was a low plateau, rising slowly, and as he breasted it cautiously he saw a small herd of reindeer cropping unconcernedly below. The wind was toward him, and with a bow he would have fresh meat. It would take him half a day to make one, and sufficient arrows.

He trotted down the slope toward Moon, still walking up the rising valley to where a rocky outcrop emerged above the trees. He caught his breath with pleasure as he watched the grace with which she moved, seeming to slip from tree to tree. He looked back. Nothing. He caught up with her as she came to the base of the rock cliff, where the sun shone full on a grassy bank and into the shallow recess beneath the overhanging rock. That would keep them dry from rain, and he heard the trickle of water. There was no dung beneath the rock, no sign of bear or even foxes. He put down his pack, took out the pouch, and set his tinder to dry. Deep in the crevice beneath the overhang, wind-blown twigs and dried leaves would provide him more. He looked carefully for signs of earlier fires. None. He followed the sound of the water and found a small spring trickling from the side of the rock, a scatter of stones around it. One by one, he carried four of them back to the overhang and set them in a loose square to make a hearth, while Moon refilled the water skin.

"Here?" he asked her. She nodded. Here. Swiftly they gathered fallen wood, still damp from the storm, but they stacked it along the back of the overhang where the sun and air would dry it. He took the thongs from his sack, cut them into lengths for his traps, and they strolled together to the warren where he had seen the rabbits. She left him setting traps, and came back with his sack full of young cob nuts, and they strolled back to the rock, a soft shyness growing between them, with the sun still warm and strong in their faces.

When they reached the overhang, she stood unmoving for a long moment, her eyes unseeing on the rock. And then, saying quietly, "This is still damp," she lifted her tunic over her head and laid it casually on the hearthstones. As he gazed down the long slim length of her back to the perfect flaring curve of her hips, she turned her head slowly and looked over her shoulder at his rapt face. He could not read the flashing look in her eyes, but he moved in a daze toward her, his eyes dreamy but his heart pounding, and stretched out his arms to embrace her. Fast as a fish, she turned into his chest and buried her face in his neck.

"Yours is still damp too," she murmured, and untied his belt and lifted his tunic and they drew it off together. Then she lifted the knife thong from his neck, and there was only the magical smoothness of her against him and he sank to his knees to run his face against the firm high breasts, and feel his lips drawn to the perfect rosebuds that tipped them. She sank down to join him, and her arms were very strong around him and the fresh young grass rippled warmly around them in the gentle breeze.

It was the next day that they found the cave. They had risen from the grass as the sun began to fall, and made a fire. Deer left her feeding it with the sun-dried wood, and went to look at his traps. He brought back a plump rabbit, and Moon took his knife to skin it and they roasted it on a spit. He kept stretching out his hand to touch her, unable to bear this separation of their flesh, and while they ate she entwined her legs with his and leaned against him, feeding him choice morsels until the hunger of their bellies was appeased and another, fiercer hunger took its place.

When he woke at dawn, the dear, soft length of her against him, he began thinking of all the things he must do. She must have skins to keep her warm, skins to lie on, skins to sling on tripods of sticks that could hold water and be warmed by hot stones. That meant more skins to make the rawhide thongs. And then she must have a tent, which meant more skins and more thongs again. And skins meant reindeer. He must make a bow this day, with the short length of thong that remained to him after making the traps. Arrows he could harden in the fire, but he must find flint and perfect his clumsy skill to make scrapers for her to clean the skins. She would need a knife to cut her food, sharp-pointed awls that could make holes in the skins that she could then sew together with a needle made from reindeer bone. He was thinking of all the tools that he had taken for granted and left far behind in the village, and did not notice her awaken until her hand slipped softly around his neck and pulled him to her.

There were two more rabbits in the traps, and he blew the fire back into life as she skinned them. She began to roast the meat as he went to the stand of saplings by the spring, bending and flexing them to find one sturdy enough to make his bow. His thong was short and his arrows without flintheads, so the bow must be the stronger. His ax cut it down and trimmed it, and then he cut down two more long ones, using creeper to tie their ends together. He leaned them against the rock. The meat they did not eat could hang up there, safe enough from foxes. There was a pine beyond the spring, and he scraped off the resin with his knife, and back at the fire transferred it to one of the hearthstones to soften.

"I would climb the other ridge today, and see what is to be seen there before exploring to the end of this valley," he said. "Our valley."

"We must look for flint," she said, rising to sling the uneaten rabbit on the poles. "I need a knife and scrapers." Then she took his ax and cut herself a long, stout sapling, trimming to a rough point.

He sat by the fire to shape the ends of his bow and carve the notches for his string as she fed him. He stood to test it, drawing it almost to his shoulder. Now the arrows. He cut four of the straightest saplings, pointed their ends, and showed her how to harden them in the fire, using spit to stop them burning. Then he sliced the thin grooves into their ends for the feathers he had collected, coated the quills with the soft pine resin and slid them home. As he finished, he saw that she was hardening the point of the spear she had made for herself.

His new bow over his shoulder, and Moon on his arm with her spear over her shoulder, they set off down the slope to the stream. It ran fast and babbled, almost wide enough to jump. He paused on the bank, looking to the stillness under the trees for the ripples that would tell where the fish lay. The stream narrowed just below them, and there were stones enough to build a loose dam to trap them, and willows to weave into a light fence that he could use to trap the fish as he splashed them downstream to the dam. More willows could make a loose basket and Moon could then scoop out the trapped fish. Then he saw the reddened clay by the rocks, and the darker earth that would flow when it was burned, and he felt the promise of color that lay trapped within them and he felt a yearning to be at his work again. And then he heard her call lightly to him, and he turned to see her rushing to the stream, her eyes intent as she gathered her legs for a great leap that took her almost across the stream to fall just a little short, and land, splashing and laughing, in the water.

He waded across, picked up her fallen spear and held her, her face and hair wet as they had been in the storm and on the river, in what seemed now to be another and barely remembered life. Gently he moved his face toward her, and licked the beads of water from her eyebrows, from her cheeks, and then from her lips. They opened and he felt her warm tongue on his own lips, her hands on him, and they fell to the warm bank and into each other again, into a world so perfectly new and theirs that he was sure no one before them had ever known it before.

"I can weave baskets from the willows to catch fish," she said much later. And he squeezed her proudly, feeling happier than he had ever been, and they rose and began their climb up the shoulder of the hill to the ridge. Carefully skirting the skyline and taking cover in some shrubs, he looked across and saw the great river glinting to his left. The great tangled dam of trees was half gone, the river running placidly, and no other movement to be seen save for the darting of the birds. She squeezed his hand in relief. Each of them had been thinking privately about the danger of pursuit.

They turned along the ridgeline to their right, aiming for the head of their valley through knots of trees and sudden hollows, welling springs that rose and bubbled and disappeared back into the earth. They crossed another rabbit warren on a warm and sun-baked slope, which took them up to a rolling plateau from which they looked down across the stream to see the rock outcrop where they had made their camp. Gray and bare but rounded, with no jagged peaks, the rock continued on the far side of the valley before rising toward them. They followed the gentle rise of the plateau, walking easily on the soft grassland, until they reached a soft crest and saw range after range of hills rolling away from them dappled with trees and the distant movement of game. None seemed near, but he saw a scattering of reindeer dung and moved forward to probe the dropping. They were still warm inside. The beasts were close. Not sure enough of his own skills to track them, he took his bow from his shoulder and an arrow from his sack and began trotting with his face into the wind, into a thin screen of low and stunted trees. The winds could be fierce up here.

They scented the deer before they saw them, one stag to their left and three does with their young grazing the shrubs ahead. Moon froze. He crept forward, notching his bow, and thinking he would have time for but one shot. Unless he hit one of the young, and the doe stayed. He had known since he made the arrows that they would not be strong enough for a kill, even if he were sure enough of his skill to aim for the heart. He would have to try for a belly shot, and the long running chase until the beast died.

The stag's head rose in suspicion but scented nothing and saw no movement. It bent again to the soft grass. Deer's breathing felt very loud in his ears as he found space in the undergrowth to stand and draw the bow. The doe was perhaps twenty paces away, her young one a still target as it muzzled at her belly. He sighted and released the string, hearing the sharp sigh of the arrow's flight and the stag's warning bark as the beasts turned and fled, leaving the young one frozen in shock, its mother's milk still wet on its face and his arrow high and deep in its belly, just below its back. The rear legs collapsed, and it began bleating, its shoulders moving in jerks as it tried to turn to follow its mother. She halted and turned, and took a hesitant pace back. Behind her, the stag bellowed. She froze and then moved forward again, to come and lick at her infant. Deer's second arrow took her in the throat, and as she turned and fled, Deer began to chase. But the stag turned back toward him and pawed at the ground. Suddenly Moon was with him, giving a great shout at the stag, her spear pointed grimly ahead of her. The stag stopped, glaring. Moon shouted again, stamped her foot, and advanced a pace. The stag turned and fled after his wounded doe, and Moon was ahead of Deer as they followed the blood trail.

They came back dragging the gutted bodies of the deer and her fawn on two frames that Deer had cut with his ax. Two long saplings lashed together at one end with creeper, and then a crossbar lashed to the other ends to make a long, thin triangle. Another crossbar and then the two frames were complete for the long haul back down the valley. The rocks above their camp would be too steep, and Deer wanted to avoid the long route by which they had come. So they tried to find a path down the head of the valley, but brush and sudden cliffs and gullies forced them farther and farther off their route.

Finally they came to a group of rocks with a short drop to a stretch of grassland below that led to the stream. Deer sent Moon down the rock and taking the weight of the straddled legs of the first frame, pushed its apex down toward her, rested the width of the frame on the lip of rock, and then scrambled down to join her. They lifted the rest of the frame down, and he scrambled back up for the second, heavier frame that carried the doe. It was then that he saw the dark mouth of the cave between the rocks, as tall as he and perhaps twice as wide. First, they brought down the second frame, and then Deer threw a stone into the cave and listened to hear if he had disturbed any creature within. Silence. He took Moon's spear and stepped into a short tunnel, dry underfoot and rising gently. He waited for his eyes to grow accustomed to the darkness after the sunlight outside and crept forward.

Beyond the tunnel, the cave widened and the roof rose and he was in a chamber that seemed almost light from the whiteness of the chalk that formed the walls. He reached out to touch it, as smooth as the walls of the cave he had known so well, a canvas that cried out for his skill. Feeling with his feet, he felt no dung, no signs of habitation, and there was a cool blandness in the air of the place that suggested no living creature had lived here.

He called for Moon to join him, and she came, her arms and face wet from where she had been rinsing the dried blood from her limbs in the stream that ran down the rocks. Her eyes grew big with wonder as she entered the broad cavern, and she said, "We hardly need your lamp."

They explored farther, and found another much lower tunnel at the rear of the cave, where the chalk walls gave way to a browner stone. They heard the trickle of water ahead, sounding muffled as if by an echo, and he had a sense of great space but now there was too little light to see and the ground began sloping steeply under his creeping foot so he turned back. It was then that he saw, below the chalky walls, the glint of smooth, almost polished stone. He bent and tugged, and a fist-sized chunk of flint came away in his hand. There were more stones along the base of the wall, and as he went to the tunnel to show Moon, the light made the flint in his hand almost green.

She had left the cave and was studying the site, the rocks behind them, the running stream and the stretch of meadow that reached down to the stream below. They could see the rock where their camp lay, but the place where they had slept was fringed by trees. They could see far down the valley to the bend beyond which lay the great river.

"This is a good place," she said, and took his hand. He showed her the flint, and she nodded, as if such bounty was always meant to be. He left her building a fire, and he went down across the stream and through the trees to their old camp, to bring the rabbit from its cache and carefully brush away all signs of their earlier fire. But he spent a long moment looking at the grass where they had first lain together, at the sheltering overhang under which they had slept. There was another rabbit in his trap, and he came back to her burdened and then moved at the fittingness of it, his woman skinning the deer they had caught by their fire, the shelter of the cave behind her, and the promise of walls for his craft.

CHAPTER 18

Périgord, May 1944

The ambush site was not perfect, but it was the best Manners could do. They were far enough from a road or track to delay any counterattack from the armored cars. And McPhee was stationed at the only possible approach route with ten men, three Bren guns, and enough Gammon grenades to fashion a mine that could blow the wheels or tracks from any vehicle that tried to use it. Manners had left him checking the rag stoppings in the Molotov cocktails.

The cutting was old and shallow, and ended in a curve that ran alongside a stand of old timber. Some of the oaks were fifty feet high, and the woodmen had sawn their trunks more than half through, supported the gaps with wedges, and pushed mud into the fresh scars in the trees to disguise them. Lacking water, they had all pissed into the earth to make the mud. Manners had rigged belts of plastique around each trunk. Once the armored train had passed, he intended to blow the trees to prevent it from coming back to bring its guns into the fight. He had placed another camouflaged charge at the entrance to the cutting, to prevent the target train from reversing out of danger. The escape routes were planned, the ammunition was checked, the Mills grenades had their fuses in place. And on the far side of the cutting, Malrand's Spandau was well dug in and carefully camouflaged. Manners had walked the cutting twice, his foot sore but just about healed, to check if the ambush could be seen.

He was more than nervous. This was the most ambitious operation they had tried. Sixty men and four trucks hidden in the woods, two of them on loan from Soleil. If this went wrong, it would undo almost all that his team had achieved since they landed, and cripple the Resistance in this part of France. But it was worth the risk, and not just because of the importance of the target. This was an operation that had Berger's Gaullists working hand in hand with Marat's Communists of the FTP. Getting those two to put aside their differences and work together was a crucial part of his mission. And crippling the Brehmer Division before it became operational made military sense. He bit down the thought that the reprisals against the local civilians would be savage. If half of what Marat said about the Brehmer troops was true, they'd be burning and killing their way across Périgord whether he fought them or not.

And when the armored train came into view at last, he understood just how viciously the Brehmer Division intended to fight this war. The first thing he saw, being pushed along in front of the locomotive, was a flatcar loaded with French civilians. God, they had children there, too, with machine guns trained on them! No Frenchman would be able to detonate a mine under the front of that train. Thank the Lord his plan didn't call for that.

The armored train passed slowly, that dreadful flatcar, then the locomotive, the coal tender, and the steel boxes with loopholes on each side. Then the sandbagged flatcar with the twin 37mm antiaircraft cannons, and another steel box. Then the gap, and the second locomotive came into the head of the cutting, one of the familiar local trains with a long line of passenger carriages, the usual sandbagged machine gun posts at front and rear.

The timing would be crucial now. The armored train began to take the bend, picking up speed as it left the cutting, the antiaircraft guns about to disappear around the curve when he fired the detonator. The five explosions came almost as one, a long, deafening ripple, and the great oaks jerked and began to lean. Oh, Christ, that first one was falling to the side where it would block the others. No, the second one swayed slowly, ponderously into it and gathering speed they both crashed down the slope and onto the antiaircraft gun and the last armored carriage of the locomotive. There was the deep, clanging sound of a great bell being rung, and as the dust rose he saw a great heaving barrier of wood and boughs and leaves that were still whipping back and forth. And the Spandau began ripping at the thin wooden sides of the passenger cars on the second train.

The noise was deafening as the Bren and and Sten guns joined in from his side of the cutting, and Manners watched the sparks rising frantically from the locked wheels of the second train as it tried to brake. But with slow, inevitable grace, it ground on, thrusting the sandbagged flatcar before it into the tangle of fallen trees. Soldiers jumped and scrambled from doors and windows as the flatcar upended and twisted to one side and the locomotive plunged like a blind bull into the crushed ruin of what had been the last carriage of the armored train.

The shriek of escaping steam almost drowned out the sounds of firing and Manners saw rather than heard the flashes of grenades being tossed down onto the train as its carriages seemed to bounce and then sag their way off the tracks. But the Germans were fighting back, the machine gun post at the rear of the train spraying the ridge of the cutting through the great spray of sand and dust that showed Malrand's Spandau was trying to suppress their fire. More grenades dropped, and Manner's saw one of Marat's men beside him tumbled back with his jaw torn away by a bullet, the moistened towel around his Sten suddenly soaking bright with blood.

Manners ducked beneath the skyline and darted along to the trench where Lespinasse and three of Berger's men were waiting to ambush any flank attack that might come from the troops who had been in the front of the armored train. The fools, they were out of the trench and over by the tree stumps, craning their necks to see the damage. He pushed them angrily back into position behind the Bren. He had to be sure this flank was secure.

Back to what was now a firefight, and it was getting time to leave. Earth was kicking up constantly from the edge of the cutting as the Germans began to reorganize, and there was too much dust to see where the third train might be. He looked around desperately for his detonator boxes. The ground that had come to seem so familiar in the hours of waiting was now unrecognizable after the disappearance of those landmark trees. He clenched his eyes shut and concentrated. The tree stumps were there, so he had been here. He edged to his right and looked again. He was on the lip of the little hollow where he had waited. The boxes were less than a yard from his hand. He scurried down and pressed the handle on the second detonator to fire the charge that would blow the tracks behind the ambush, half expecting a failure. Any stray bullet or excited boot could have cut the wire. But no, a crashing explosion that even his ringing ears could hear.

He took the whistle from his pocket and began blowing long, regular blasts, the signal to disengage. No firing from Lespinasse's team on the right. No sounds of battle from McPhee's post back at the track half a mile behind him. Still blowing his whistle, he bent to the crumpled man with the shattered jaw whose hand clutched at his throat, trying vainly to stop the pumping jets of blood from his artery as he stared in dying desperation at the English captain. Manners turned away and trudged along the line, blowing his whistle and telling his men to pull back and disperse. He could count on Malrand's Spandau to hold off any counterattack from the third train. He could always count on François.

Sybille's gramophone served the useful purpose of blanketing the sound of the radio, when he listened to the personal messages that were read over the French service of the BBC. And at six-thirty one evening, as he strained to hear over the sound of Maurice Chevalier's "Valentine" from the parlor, Manner's heard the alert message. *"La fée a un beau sourire."* The fairy has a lovely smile. He smiled and forced himself to listen to the mystifying remainder about the panda being a bear and the camel being hairy and the carrots being ready to cook, and then leaped in the air, turned off the radio, and spun Sybille into a brief, twirling dance.

"The invasion. It's coming," he said, beaming at her and kissing her boisterously. "That's our alert."

"What? Tonight?" she gasped, squeezed too tightly in his arms.

"A week, ten days. But it's coming. They're on their way." He threw his head back and closed his eyes, hardly aware of her stiffening.

"If they are on their way, then so will you be," she said quietly, not looking at him. Her eyes were shadowed with tiredness. Up half the night at Boridot's farm for a dying sow, and then out again to St-Alvere tending two boys with stomach wounds who had been shot when the Germans raided a training camp. She looked as if she had not slept for days.

"I suppose I should thank you," she said, almost angrily. "I am out of my hibernation, out of my little sheltered space where I could tell myself there was no war, no Germans, no great drama sweeping us all away into causes and passions. You pulled me back to this anguish we call living, living for the moment."

"Berger pulled you back, Sybille. I only met you when the war had already pulled you back to life," he said in a tone so reasonable that he knew it was a mistake as soon as he spoke. Her eyes blazed and she pulled back her hand as if to slap him, then her shoulders slumped and she seemed to soften, turning the threatened blow into a nervous plucking at his arm, and then lifted her hand to stroke his cheek.

"Soon you will go," she said dully, and came into his arms.

"But then will come the Liberation, and I'll be back," he said. He looked at the room, the heavy furniture and faded carpet, a little Godin stove that glowed almost red in winter, the chaise longue where they had made urgent love when François brought him back from the kennels. The scent of lavender was familiar to him now, mixed with the antiseptic from her surgery. And he wondered whether he would see it all with the same fond eyes after the war.

"Another soldier promised me that he would come back," she said against his chest. "In this very room. I don't want to lose a second man. I have given enough to this war already."

"It's almost over, Sybille. The invasion is coming. The war will be over by Christmas."

"They said that in 1939. And they said it in 1914. They always say it and it's never true. Your invasion could be thrown back, or frozen in four more years of trench warfare."

"That's why I have to go now. Down here in Périgord, all over France, people like us listened to the radio tonight and are getting ready to make sure the invasion doesn't fail. The more Germans we fight here, the fewer there will be on the beaches."

Dry-eyed and unsmiling, she took him up the stairs to her bed and took off her clothes as if she were undressing for a bath. He watched her fold them carefully and lay them on a chair. And then with more determination than passion, she took him to her, and for once her eyes remained closed throughout. With so little response from her, he felt wooden and almost mechanical, his flesh urgent and pumping but his mind remote and concerned. He slowed and kissed her neck, her cheek, her closed eyelids.

"I cannot leave you like this, Sybille, but I cannot stay," he murmured.

"Don't go," she said, her arms tightening around him, and she began to move beneath him, her hips rising gently to press him in a rhythm that she controlled. It was slow and insistent, like the rocking of a boat in the tug of the tide, and it surprised him with her strength. A part of his mind was still detached, observing, as she seemed to make love to him and to pleasure herself by an act of pure will. Her urgency released a great wave of tenderness in him that swept him almost peacefully away, until his breathing slowed again and the room came back into focus and he saw that her face was wet with tears.

"I'll come back, Sybille," he said. "I'll always come back. This is my home now, with you." With a final, lingering kiss, he rose and dressed and was washing his face at the kitchen sink when the soft rapping came at the back door.

It was Lespinasse, looking grim and frightened. "There's bad trouble at Terrasson," he said. "Young François has a car."

This was a strange new period for Resistance work, both safer and more dangerous at the same time. The Germans and the Vichy forces had both started concentrating their troops in order to mount big sweeps and searches to attack the growing numbers of Maquis bands. But it meant they had withdrawn posts from the smaller towns, and there were hardly any small patrols, so it was safer for the Resistance to move around and to steal and requisition cars and trucks. The gendarmes who remained at their small local posts were siding, more or less openly, with the Resistance. So Manners, who had started on foot and then progressed to a bicycle, was now accustomed to racing around the countryside by car. If they did meet the enemy by accident, it probably spelled disaster because the Germans now traveled in big and well-armed columns. And there were no more soft targets on the rail networks.

"It's that bastard Marat with those guns you let him have," François spat, when Manners joined him on the road above the cemetery. "He took his men into Terrasson last night, probably with the agreement of the gendarmes. He blew down their door, took their pistols and rifles, robbed the post office, and then shot the local legion chief and some woman they accused of informing."

"So?" said Manners. "This must be the ninth or tenth time he's pulled something like this. That's the FTP strategy. What's the fuss? And did you hear the message from London, the alert?"

"Yes, I heard about the invasion. I'll believe it when I see it. But I'm angry because Marat told the townspeople that he was acting on your orders, and the English *capitaine* and the Gaullists had guaranteed that there would be no reprisals. Terrasson is supposed to be under your and my personal protection."

"Will they believe that?"

"They believe the fact that McPhee was with him. Everybody in Périgord knows about the Red Indian from America. McPhee is the living proof that Marat is obeying our orders, and McPhee is fool enough not to stop him. And they'll believe the fact that he didn't shoot the gendarmes. Don't you see what Marat is trying to do, the trap he is laying for us? He tells the people that he's acting under our orders and that we will protect them, and then we fail, and what's left of the town turns Communist because they'll never trust us again. This is what I warned you he would do all along. It's the Communist way," François said urgently.

"And another thing. That alert message, the fairy's beautiful smile. There was no confirmation of that from our Bureau Central, nothing from General Koenig in the Gaullist broadcast. Whatever alert signal is coming from London is from you and the Americans—not from Free France."

"I have to follow orders, François. You know that. I've had the *Plan Vert* signal, which means an all-out attack on the rail network. I'm sorry about Terrasson but there's nothing I can do."

"I have friends in Terrasson. So do you—people who've fed you when their own kids were hungry."

"The sooner the invasion succeeds, the sooner they'll eat. You know that."

François stared at him fiercely. "So we don't lay an ambush on the Terrasson road?"

"What with? Bren guns and Gammon bombs, against the panzers and the artillery they'll send out from Périgueux? As soon as they hear our bullets tapping on their frontal armor they'll hit us with howitzers and mortars. We'd be wiped out."

"So we let the bastards get away with it, haul our friends back to the Gestapo dungeons?"

"François, we carry on doing our job, which is keeping as many Germans as we can tied up down here for as long as we can. And if we have to stage suicide attacks, it will be for a better target than a reprisal column on Terrasson." He knew François well enough to understand that the only way to get him off this track was to focus his quick intelligence onto something else.

"SS Das Reich, you mean."

"That's what *Plan Vert* means to me. We blow the rails so the Das Reich can't use them. But then we have to stop an entire armored division coming up from the south by road. That's why we still need Marat and his boys. I don't care if they are Communists or Martians. We'll need every man and every gun in Périgord because we can only hope to slow the Das Reich down with cannon fodder. We can't destroy the tanks, so we have to use every bridge and every village, every bend in the road to lay ambushes on their infantry and their trucks. If we can't stop the tanks, we can shoot up their fuel trucks. It's the only thing we can do. If you have a better idea, François, then for God's sake tell me."

"Even with bazookas, it's a suicide mission," said François. "And we haven't even got bazookas."

The parachute drops were becoming routine, and despite the reprisals the Maquis morale was sky-high after the success of the ambush. But Manners told himself not to get overconfident as he carefully approached the rendezvous point by the water tower at Cumont. He felt edgy, that visceral knot of warning that he had learned in the desert never to ignore. The moon was rising, and Berger was already waiting. François had the laundry truck waiting at a farm in the valley. It amused him to use petrol the Germans had allocated to get their uniforms picked up and cleaned.

"I could only get one tractor. A couple of farm carts and trolleys," said Berger. "It should be enough. The fires are ready. Here." He passed to Manners the inevitable flask of brandy, although the nights were warm now.

"We're starting to lose some men, you know. They're leaving the *Armée Secrète* and joining the FTP. The Communists are saying the Allies will never invade and the Red Army is doing all the fighting."

"We've lost nobody. We get more all the time."

"Not in our group, no. But in Périgueux and Brive and Bergerac, it's all FTP. They even claim Soleil is one of theirs. Round here, it's different. We have the reputation, after that attack on the Brehmer Division. But Marat has been claiming the credit for his own group, with you and the American. The way Marat tells it, we might not even have been there. Our lads know better, but all those new recruits coming into the Maquis, they want to join the FTP Commies and have a crack at the Boches."

"It's all the same to me, Berger," said Manners. "FTP or *Armée Secrète* or even Soleil's lot. You know London's policy. We don't care who gets the recruits as long as they get results."

"You've seen this?" Berger handed him a small, single-sheet newspaper. "Marat has a printing press somewhere that's turning this out. He calls it '*Audace*,' and to read it you'd think only the Reds were doing any fighting. He says the Germans call this region 'Little Russia.' Can you get me a printing press by parachute?"

Somewhere far off, an engine backfired in the night. Too far to worry about. And Berger was experienced. He'd have sentries on the approach roads. Manners checked his watch. Any time now. Moonlight and scudding clouds, the scent of fresh horse dung mixed with Berger's cigarette. He was taking another swig of brandy when he heard footsteps coming, and a whispered "Laval." It was young Daunier, with someone behind him.

"Good evening, comrades." It was Marat.

"What in the devil's name are you doing here?" said Berger grimly. "And you, Daunier, back to your post."

"Come for my share. We can't leave my lads defenseless," Marat said. "I've got enough to make two more battalions of *franc-tireurs*, but I need arms. Come, *Capitaine*, you're a reasonable man. Tell this Gaullist we're supposed to be allies."

"We are allies," said Manners tiredly. "But how did you learn about tonight's drop? I'm more worried about security than the guns."

"Some of your men are not so greedy as Berger here. At least they understand we're on the same side."

"You two sort it out between you. I'm going to check the sentries and the fires. The plane will be here anytime now." Manners shouldered his Sten, checked the spare magazines in his pouches, and left them to it, angry at the endless politicking. He wondered if it would be the same in an England under occupation, different organizations for the conservatives and the socialists, and another lot for the liberals. And probably some more for different football clubs and county cricket teams. But there'd be no parachute drops for a British resistance, not with Canada and the U.S.A. so far away. They wouldn't even be able to communicate by radio. Unless there were submarines offshore . . .

The sound of aircraft engines stopped his wandering thoughts. Close enough. He lit the first signal fire, saw the next ones ignite, and as the roar of the bomber on its first reconnaissance run drowned out everything else, he waited for the plane to make its turn into the wind and for the parachutes to start spilling down. There was always a marker assigned to each container, and Berger had them posted downwind, where the parachutes invariably dropped. As the first one tumbled from the belly of the lumbering Halifax, whipping as the canopy opened, he began kicking the loose earth over his fire. They always made him nervous, these telltale beacons. A good even drop, holding steady as the plane's momentum died, they began to drift downwind, one after the other. The markers were running, and he heard the engine of the tractor cough as it began to lumber down toward the containers . . .

That was no tractor! Even before the thudding of the cannon began he knew the German armored cars had caught them. Running instinctively toward two of his men who seemed frozen in surprise he pushed them down and got them firing. They just needed telling what to do. There was only one German cannon firing so far, and no flashes of gunfire from infantry. The cars had raced in too fast for their support troops. Crouching and running toward the village he ran, literally, into Albert. He knew horses.

"Get the carts loaded and get those guns down to young François. Cut the horses loose if they're shot and push the buggers. Get the others moving. We can still get those guns. I'll take care of the armored car."

Firing short bursts from his Sten as he ran, as much to identify himself to his men as for any good it might do, he sprinted and rolled to his left, where a Bren was firing in steady, controlled bursts. That was

Lespinasse, a trained man who'd been in the Alpine troops. He wouldn't need telling to cover the withdrawal. He was changing barrels when Manners flung himself beside him, and shouted, "Covering fire—I'll go in from the left."

"Here—you'll need this." Lespinasse took a Gammon bomb from the haversack at his side. Manners clutched it to his chest, tried to control his breathing, counted to five as Lespinasse shifted position and locked in a new magazine, and began his sprint as the Bren opened up again, sounding puny against the bark of the cannon. Still no German infantry, the fools. They'd sprung the trap too soon.

The armored car was moving cautiously out of the village, one of its crew squatting on the rear deck, braced against the curling stanchion that held the aerial, and firing a Schmeisser in random bursts at the gaps between the houses. Two small fires still burned where some of the boys had tried using Molotovs. The Gammon was awkward to throw, four pounds of plastic wrapped in tarpaulin and attached to an impact fuse. He sprayed the back of the car with his Sten, saw the crew man fall, set his gun down, and took the Gammon in the palm of his hand. Think cricket, he told himself, a long throw to the wicket keeper to stop that third run. It doesn't have to hit the stumps; it's a big target. He threw it hard but even as it left his hand he knew it was falling short. He picked up his gun and ran out of the village, fumbling for a new magazine as the German infantry turned up, and the first crump of mortar shells began falling between him and the drop zone.

There were two sounds from the desert war that he'd never forget. There was the whip-crack of the high-velocity 88 cannon, which came with the instant relief that if you could hear it, your tank had not been hit. But you had no more than five seconds to get under cover before the next round. The other sound was the mortars. The Sobbing Sisters were the worst, six-barreled beasts that moaned eerily as they fell. They could demolish a platoon or even a tank squadron if they caught the men outside the tanks and in laager. But any mortar was bad, a close-range mobile artillery that every German infantry company seemed to carry with it as a matter of course. And they got them firing so fast. Just as soon as the machine guns made you take cover, the mortars blew you out of it. It was like being sniped with high explosive.

He reached the trees, running wide to avoid the mortars. German machine guns were firing steadily, but from a long distance. Another armored car had joined the first, and was firing steadily as crew members milled about forming into a line. He saw the glint of a towing hawser in the moonlight. His Gammon must have hit a wheel. The mortars were increasing their range, stalking their way across the field, and he saw the old tractor wrecked and burning. Then he saw movement, a jolting, jerking movement and an appalling noise of pain. An old farm horse, its haunches on the ground, was trying to haul itself away from the madness by its two front legs, its neigh a scream as the weight of the cart kept it flailing uselessly. The cart must be loaded.

He told himself it was the horse that made him do it, running out from his cover toward the cart, and firing a short burst into the poor beast's pitching head. But he'd already thought it through. The cart had to be still for what he wanted to do. There was no possibility of saving the guns; they had to be destroyed. He took the first Mills bomb from his pouch. No, there was a better way. He removed the pin, keeping tight hold of the lever, and felt into the back of the cart. He jammed the grenade between two of the parachuted containers. He managed to push the second bomb between a container and the cart's side.

Then he turned and half-fled, half-fell down the slope into the woods, his gun held high before his face to protect him from the branches, until he slammed into a tree and seemed to bounce dazedly off it down the hillside. Tumbling and disoriented, when he finally came to rest his mouth was full of blood and he had lost his gun. He groped vainly in the dark until the mortar shells seemed to be hunting at random down the slope toward him, and he was nearer to panic than he had been since he came to France. The sickening sense of defeat and disaster unmanned him. He had no idea where he was, where his men were, how many were left nor where the rendezvous point might be. And the Germans were not finished yet. He heard himself sobbing as he scrambled like an animal to get away from the still-searching mortars, wondering how many men they'd lost, and which of them was the informer.

When his boots felt the crunch of the road, Manners began to come back to his senses. He took out his knife and made two diagonal slashes into the bark of the nearest sapling to mark the spot. Then he stepped forward out of the tree cover, and into the faint lightness of the stars. Just enough light to see the blazes he had made in the tree. The moon was down, but there was the blessed, familiar Plow, with its two stars of the blade pointing forever north to Polaris. His sense of direction came back. The slope had brought him down to the Rouffignac road, which wound its way uphill all the way to the ridge above Savignac. Knowing he'd be safer in the hills than taking the road down to the river valley, he moved to the soft verge and began to trudge uphill. He paused every few moments to listen for the inevitable German patrols that would soon be sweeping this and all the other roads around the drop zone.

The mortaring had stopped, but odd shots still thumped faintly in the distance, and then came one bigger, rippling explosion followed by an endless crackling of gunfire. He began to move again when it stopped, but had gone no more than five yards when a whispered "Laval" came from behind him.

"*Putain,*" he replied automatically. And stood still, his arms by his sides.

"*Capitaine?*" It was Lespinasse, his whisper urgent. Thank God the lad had made it.

"This way, *Capitaine.*" His arm was grabbed and he was pulled off the road and felt the loom of rock, the movements of other people. "Were you hit?"

"No, no, I'm O.K. Just stunned by a fall."

Berger and François were suddenly at his side, putting a flask to his mouth. He gagged, the spirit stinging on his torn lip. He tasted blood and brandy, and then the stars seemed to swirl and he blacked out. When he came to, he was sitting on the ground. He pulled himself to his knees. Then, gingerly, he stood up.

"Where are the guns?" he asked.

"Here. We saved two carts," said François. "Six containers. The lads did well."

"Here? Right by the road? They'll be sending patrols any minute."

"The carts are empty. Little Jeannot has gone for a couple of horses. The containers are under cover. It's the best we can do."

"Is anybody at the rendezvous point in case of stragglers?"

"That was Lespinasse. That's where he found you. He's gone back."

"How many of us here?"

"Just six," said Berger. "Us three, Florien and Pierrot. And Lespinasse, when he gets back. Albert has gone back up to the plateau to look around. Marat was here with Carlos but they thought they'd better try for le Bugue when the mortars hit the truck."

"Six? We had nearly thirty at the drop zone."

"Most of them scattered. There wasn't much of a pursuit after you got the armored car, except for the mortars. Then the cart blew up. Lespinasse said that was your doing."

"What's your plan?"

"Wait for Jeannot and the horses, then he and Florien take the empty carts back to the farm at dawn. The rest of us go up this gully and over the ridge toward Rhode. Then we scatter, lie up for the day, and head for Rouffignac. We'll come back for the containers with a truck when the Germans move on."

Manners looked around, trying to get a sense of the place. He felt smooth rock to one side, and open ground on the other. He paced the distance to the road. Five meters to a thin fringe of saplings and bushes. Jesus, this wouldn't do. He followed the line of the rock, under a steep overhang, and his boot hit one of the containers.

"We can't leave these here. It's too near the road. We'd come back to find an ambush or a booby trap."

"There's nowhere else, not without transport and we dare not use the road. And we can't get them up the gully. And besides, the sign makes it so obvious the Germans probably won't give it a second glance."

"What bloody sign?"

"La Ferrassie. The big sign for the national monument," said François. "It's an old caveman burial site or something. There was a big archaeological dig here, back at the start of the century."

"I may have something better. Get Lespinasse back here on the double." Manners considered. Only six men, and each container weighed well over a hundred fifty pounds. Three men to each container. Three trips. It could be done. He went across to the first cart. The long leather straps they used to lift the containers were still there. That made it easier.

It had been the bloody mortars that had done it, the first thing he ever had to thank them for. Plunging down onto the slope to explode in the trees and blast lethal wood and metal splinters everywhere. Except this one had landed at the base of an old tree and blown a crater that sent the tree toppling sideways down the slope, levering out a great chunk of earth with its wrenched roots. It was the tangle of roots that had stopped Manners's plunge down the slope, and as he tried to get to his feet the earth had given way beneath him and he had slid down farther. That was where he discovered that he had lost his gun, had begun groping with his hands and found the smooth rock on both sides and then curving to meet above his head. The air had been cool and dry, the ground smooth and gently sloping uphill, but almost level underfoot as he crept in farther, his outstretched hand following the line of the rock. Turning, he looked back to see the slightly fainter darkness of the night through the hole. The roots of the fallen tree made a kind of natural ladder that he was able to scramble up, back to the open air.

He had turned back into the cave, thinking that the tree must have grown at the very entrance, its roots distorted and forced to the downhill side of the slope by the rock. With all its roots on one side, the tree had been too precariously embedded to resist the force of the mortar blast. He went further into the cave, down what seemed to be a tunnel, high enough for him to walk without bending, and not quite two arms-widths wide. The tunnel went for about ten meters, still sloping gently uphill, and then widened again. It was pitch black and utterly quiet. Safe, he had said to himself. Safe. And slumped down to wait the night out.

It was duty that called him back to himself. Or at least that part of it which was composed of guilt. Even as he thought of safety, he thought of his men, wounded and frightened and scurrying through the night with Germans on their heels. His men weren't safe. And every code he had lived by, every lesson he had learned in eight years as an officer and nearly five years of war, warned that he had no right being safe when his men were in danger and demoralized without him. Alone in the blackness, he confronted himself and rolled to his feet, stretched his hand out to the rock and directed his feet firmly downhill through the tunnel to the tangled roots that made it so easy to climb back into his duty and his war.

"Here's Lespinasse," said François, his voice wary and uncertain.

"Right, Lespinasse. Any other men turn up? No? Very well. Take me back to the spot where you first saw me. The exact spot, mind you. And then we creep slowly downhill, looking at every single tree for two knife slashes I made. Understand? François, Berger, you get those containers loaded into a cart. That will make it easier. When we come back, I'll lead you to the best hiding place in France. Then we go and look for our wounded."

He followed Lespinasse back down the road, the trudge farther than he had thought. Afraid of speaking, Lespinasse clutched him and pointed to himself and the spot where he had been waiting. Then he led Manners to the place he had first seen him. Manners nodded, stayed on the same southerly side of the road and began walking slowly, scrutinizing each tree. Ten meters, twenty, fifty, a hundred. His eyes were seeing spots with strain when Lespinasse tapped his shoulder. Manners looked back. There were his blazes on the tree. He had missed them. He slapped Lespinasse on the back and told him to stay right there.

Into the trees and up the slope, as straight as he could, trying to remember how far it had been. It would be the very devil to haul those containers up here. But they had men enough and straps, and necessity to spur them. He felt supremely confident that he would find it again, as if repeated bouts of terror at the hands of German mortars was finally being repaid by this one that had resolved to serve his purpose. Again, the fallen tree came to his aid, as he had been sure it would, and he blundered into the thin leaves and branches of its toppled crown. He skirted it, following the trunk until he came to the giant clod of earth and the knotted roots, and there was his hole.

Back down to Lespinasse, telling him to stay exactly there, moving not one inch. He strode with increasing vigor back up the road to la Ferrassie, turned in at the bloody silly sign, and found them loading the fifth container onto the cart. He helped them with the sixth. Six men, it was easy.

"Follow me," he said. No further explanation seemed necessary. He picked up one of the shafts, put his weight into it, and felt it start to move as the others joined him. "François, get a bough to brake the wheels," he said over his shoulder, and led them out onto the road, sublimely convinced that there would be no patrols to interrupt them.

It took them until almost dawn, heaving those heavy containers up the hill, the leather straps knifing into their shoulders as their hands groped for trees and branches and even spiked brambles as they fought to stay upright and maneuver the damn things through the undergrowth. The others cursed and groaned and sobbed with effort but never complained, carried along by the sheer assurance of his will. It seemed an inevitable part of the way his luck had turned that just as they laid the last container beside the tangle of roots, they heard the plod of horses' hooves and there was Little Jeannot, in perfect time to take the empty cart back to the barn.

He went down first with François. The others took the straps from their aching shoulders and spat on their hands to take the straps in a firm grip and ease the containers down the sloping ramp of earth as if they were so many coffins being lowered gently into a grave. Pierrot and Florien came down to help them haul the containers up the tunnel. As the sky lightened and the first birds began to sing, Manners looked at the last container and stared for the first time at the stenciled markings on its side.

"Load D," he breathed, as if in the presence of a miracle. Load D, the rarest and most marvelous of gifts. Load D, with its four bazookas and twenty-four rockets for each one. And 154 pounds of plastic explosive, 8 Bren guns, 10,000 rounds of ammo, and 234 field dressings with medical kit. He had six containers, which meant half a load. It was still a miracle. He opened the first container, took out the medical kit, and went off to look for his wounded.

CHAPTER 19

Time: The Present

Clothilde's parents lived in what at first seemed to be a small house when they parked by the river and climbed up the narrow street of Limeuil. But the gate opened onto a broad and sunny courtyard where an old man sat reading *Sud-Ouest* and the sound of a radio and clattering pots came from a large kitchen. An elderly but still handsome woman came out beaming and wiping her floury hands on an apron as Clothilde kissed her stepfather. Lydia braced herself for a difficult encounter, but Clothilde had insisted that she come along. "If only to drive the car when I start crying," Clothilde had said.

"I never knew there was so much money in what you do," said Clothilde's mother, when they were settled around the courtyard table with drinks and a plate of olives. "A million francs reward, they said on the radio, for one of those rock paintings of yours. Some announcement by the President."

Lydia pulled out the photograph from her bag and showed it to them while Clothilde explained. Then she worked out the currency conversion. A million francs was about $130,000. Heavens!

"I looked up those things you wanted about the Resistance," said her stepfather. He looked like a scholar, with wispy hair and clear blue eyes that twinkled over his reading glasses. "Not much about caves being used, except for Bara-Bahau and Rouffignac, and you know about them. But there's a fair bit about these tensions with the Communists." He opened a fat book at a page he had marked.

"This is Guy Penaud's *Histoire de la Résistance en Périgord*, and he cites the *Armée Secrète* report on the Communists' refusal to join the attack on Bergerac on June seventh: 'The Communists of Bergerac would not move, and when several days later they were asked to return the weapons entrusted to them, they refused to give them up. I believe this defection was the result of an order from the Party, received at the last minute. The Communists, it cannot be doubted, sought to build an army under their own control . . .' Blah-blah-blah . . . There's quite a lot like that, of the Communists refusing orders, stealing arms and keeping them for their own purposes," the old man went on. "There was one called Marat, who was a particular offender, according to the *Armée Secrète*. Your father was attached to one of the units he ran out of Périgueux."

Clothilde leaned forward at the mention of her father, swallowed hard, and was about to speak when Lydia quickly broke in: "We're trying to find out what exactly happened to Marat. He seemed to disappear."

"Fate unknown. Old Lespinasse told me before he died that he'd seen Marat killed somewhere in the confused fighting between Brive and Périgueux. He couldn't remember where. But there was quite a battle at Terrasson, where the Germans had all the men lined up in the main square and were going to shoot them. The mayor managed to distract the German commander with a bottle of wine. Sturmbannführer Kreuz, the German's name was. And it turned out it was his wedding anniversary, so he let the men go to try and put out the fires instead. But in Mussidan, after the Germans fought their way into the town, they just lined up all the men against the walls and shot them down, forty and fifty at a time."

"The Germans claimed later that they were acting in retaliation for some atrocities against them, but they always said that. They said it about Oradour, after one of the commanders was captured and shot by the Maquis." He turned to Lydia. "You know about Oradour, mademoiselle?"

"Was that where the SS forced all the women and children into the church and then set fire to it?" Lydia said.

"Yes, Sturmbannführer Otto Dickman's First Battalion of the Der Führer Panzergrenadier regiment of the SS Das Reich division. They deliberately burned alive over four hundred women and children. When they tried to escape through the vestiary door, the Germans poured in machine gun fire and grenades. I suppose those who died that way were the fortunate ones. June 10, 1944.

"At their trial for war crimes, after the surrender, some of the SS men said they were told that a high German official had been captured and was to be burned at Oradour. Others said they made a mistake, they were supposed to be taking reprisals against another Oradour some distance away, where the Communist FTP had been shooting German prisoners. Others claimed that were angry because they had seen German corpses desecrated. Castrated. They said anything that they thought might save their lives."

"Could any of it have been true?" asked Clothilde.

Her stepfather shrugged. "It was war, and guerrilla war at that. The SS had no qualms about gunning down women and children, not just in Oradour, but near here, at Carsac, Rouffillac, Gabaudet. No doubt some of the Maquis were not prepared to take prisoners in such circumstances. And there were some units — like Marat's Spaniards — that were known for being haters. One of Marat's men was captured at the ambush of a train, and the Germans fed him into the locomotive's furnace. They were not inclined to be merciful after that. Old Lespinasse told me that Marat had a reputation for shooting Germans in the stomach and knees, and leaving them to die slowly."

"And you say that was the unit my father was in?" asked Clothilde quietly.

"No, not the Spaniards. They had all come from the war in Spain, where Marat had also served. Marat was a kind of commissar, a political rather than military chief, and there were several FTP bands under his orders. Marat even had some escaped Russian prisoners of war serving under him. He was supposed to have learned to speak Russian in Moscow. Your father was in a group led by Hercule, around Terrasson."

Clothilde looked at her mother. "There's some new information come up about my father, which is very worrying," she said. Her mother sat very still, then looked across at her husband. Lydia held her breath.

"What do you mean?" her mother asked, her hand straying to her throat. "What information?"

"A German war diary from the Brehmer Division. It mentions my father as a *collabo* — a collaborator with the Germans."

"You mean about his being forced to give information to stop your mother being hauled off to a concentration camp?" said the old man, gently. His wife bent at the waist and gave a hard, dry sob, as if about to retch. He reached across and put his hand on her shoulder. "Your mother told me about it the night I asked her to marry me. I told her it showed how much he loved her. I'd have done the same, Clothilde. I'd do the same for your mother now. The evil was the Germans, using a pregnant woman in that way. Using love in that way. They were beasts, Clothilde. Unspeakable beasts. Remember Oradour. Your mother and father did what they must to save your life, Clothilde."

Her mother sat up and looked at Clothilde, stricken, as Clothilde put the palms of her hands flat against her face and her eyes. Lydia felt incapable of movement, but this awful tableau had to be broken. She reached over and rested her hand on the back of Clothilde's neck, and the Frenchwoman put her hands down and reached her arms out to her mother. Lydia quietly let herself out of the courtyard and leaned against the gray stone wall, looking down the sloping street to the grassy bank with its picnickers and pizza stall and the confluence of the two rivers beyond it. The meeting of the Dordogne and the Vézère, as lovely a place as any in France, and the valleys that said more about the ancient history and glorious achievement of humankind than any other spot on earth. And just as much about the evil that humans could wreak upon each other. Those older humans had been more civilized than those of this century, Lydia thought. But perhaps only because they left so little trace of anything but their achievements. It took a different kind of civilization to leave records of its wickedness.

"So in the end, they were saved by love," Lydia told Manners after dinner that evening. "Clothilde's stepfather was right. The Germans had used and abused the love of Clothilde's parents for their wicked ends. And that dear, wise man, her stepfather, showed us all this evening that love was the only redemption. The love Clothilde's parents had for her. The love he had for Clothilde's mother, even after she told him of what she had been forced to do. And finally, the love of Clothilde for her mother."

"So in the end, love does conquer all," said Manners pensively. They were dining alone at a simple restaurant that overlooked the Vézère. "It's a very moving story, Lydia, and you tell it marvelously well. I feel almost as though I had been there, but in a way I'm glad I wasn't. Clothilde seems such a formidable woman, it must have been a shock to see her in such a raw moment."

"It's not something that we often see, in peacetime." She gestured vaguely at the river, the placid calm of it all. "It's a shock to learn what happened here, in these picturesque villages, within living memory."

"It was a shock in Northern Ireland, to see all that hatred taking place in streets that had Woolworth's and Barclays Banks and familiar British cars," he said. "It was that kind of furniture, the streetscapes, the advertisements, the sound of the BBC, that made you think you were at home when you weren't. Horror amid the familiar and normal things is the worst horror of all."

He paused and filled her glass. "And I must confess that there were times, when I was called out to see what had happened to one of my patrols in Ulster that had been blown up by a land mine, or saw one of my men shot down by a sniper in Bosnia when he was trying to keep the peace, when I felt that blind, terrible fury that probably consumed the Germans here. It needed all my training, all the codes of decency and discipline that a professional army tries to live by, to stop myself from reacting like a beast, like some SS thug."

Lydia looked at him solemnly, feeling that she had just been privileged to hear a very rare and private confession, and she admired him for it. This was not a man who would ever want to admit that his self-discipline had ever come close to bending. It was not something she would ever care to admit herself. Normally, their reticence was something she liked in the English, and she felt touched that he had chosen to break it with her. She nodded in sympathy.

"As often as not, that barbarism is what they're trying to provoke you into doing.

Vengeance is self-defeating." He learned back and took a photocopy from his jacket pocket. "Let me tell you what I mean."

"Listen to this. It's from Horst's research file, a message from the commander of the Das Reich division, General Heinz Lammerding, to his commander at 58th Corps. He sent it from quite near here on June tenth, the day he had initially been expected by the British and Americans to arrive with his tanks in Normandy. I'll translate it as I go. 'The region Souillac-Figeac-Limoges and Clermont-Ferrand is in the control of tenacious and well-armed bands, totally in the hands of terrorists. German outposts and garrisons are cut off and in many cases besieged, often reduced to a single company of effectives, and French government forces have been totally paralyzed by the terrorists. The paralysis of the German positions is absolutely scandalous. Without a brutal and determined repression, the situation in this region will become a threat whose scale has not yet been comprehended. A new Communist state is being born here, a state that governs without opposition and that coordinates its attacks. The task of eliminating this danger must be transferred to locally based divisions. In their fifth year of war, the armored divisions are too good for that.' General Lammerding sent that message just a few hours before his men burned Oradour."

"He certainly delivered his brutal and determined repression. And he actually said that his armored divisions were too good for such a job?" Lydia inquired. "Good God."

"Yes, he did. And he was right. It wasn't their business to go round chasing guerrillas or burning women and children in churches. Their job was to get to Normandy and throw the Allies back into the sea. So here you have an experienced general, knowing what he should do, and then through anger or vengeance or sheer frustration, he fails to do it. General Lammerding wastes time and energy. His tanks don't leave Périgueux until June fifteenth, eight days after he was first ordered to Normandy. Some of his units don't get there until June thirtieth. One of the best military formations in Europe arrives piecemeal, and is thrown into the battle in dribs and drabs, patching a hole here, filling a gap there, instead of being used to punch a single armored fist into the invasion forces. It was a military disaster for the Germans."

"And thus it was a military victory for the Resistance of the Dordogne," said Lydia.

"Yes. Although won at monstrous cost."

"It's odd," said Lydia, as the bill came and Manners paid. "We came here expecting to concentrate on the history of seventeen thousand years ago, and we have been caught up, consumed I suppose, by what happened just a few decades ago. And it's all connected. The one leads to the other. This same river where men died stopping German tanks was the same river where ancient artists drank and fished. They even used the same caves."

"And we still have our own cave to find," said Manners. "Come on, I'll walk you along this lovely riverbank as the sun sets." She looked at him thoughtfully. She'd enjoy a walk, but there was something in his tone that alerted her. Twilight, riverbank, romantic setting. Brace yourself, my girl, she told herself. I do believe the man is girding himself to make a move.

"You're determined to go on?" Lydia asked, taking his arm as they strolled down the steps by the bridge and onto an embankment that ran along the river's edge. "You don't want to give up now Malrand has advertised his reward."

"No, not even with his security man snooping round to keep an eye on us. I want to finish this. How about you?"

"There was a moment when I wanted to go back to London, when I thought it was all too depressing," she said frankly, enjoying the easy way their steps fell into rhythm. "But then seeing Clothilde with her mother this evening—I suppose I realized that matters must be resolved. It doesn't do to duck them."

"I'm glad you're going to stay," he said, squeezing her arm and placing his hand on hers. "Most of the fun would go out of this without you, Lydia."

"Fun?" she said, startled. Where on earth did he think this conversation was going?

"I haven't enjoyed the company of a woman so much as far back as I can remember," he said soberly. His voice sounded almost gruff.

Aha, thought Lydia, biting back a smile. The tongue-tied but decent

Englishman is finally building up with grim fortitude to what seems to him to be a romantic declaration. She could feel his tension under her arm. He was looking firmly, even sternly ahead to the bend in the river. Should she help him, tease him, or remain silent? She couldn't resist the tease and said lightly, "You seemed to spend most of your day enjoying the company of Horst."

"Oh, he's all right," said Manners. "I wish it had been you, though." He stopped, turned, and put his hands on her shoulders. "You are witty and interesting and lively, which are all qualities I prize highly. And I think you are kind. You were marvelous in looking after Clothilde."

She felt her lips quiver as the smile began to break through. Would this man ever get to the point?

"You are marvelous altogether," he said. Not quite stammering, Lydia noted. She had better stop this cool, detached observation of his—what would the appropriate military term be?—his deployment. She didn't want to frighten the poor man off, and she hoped that she was looking suitably encouraging. Or at least not forbidding.

"You're also very beautiful," he said, and kissed her, hesitantly at first, as if he were out of practice, and then with growing enthusiasm.

Well, about time, thought Lydia, and kissed him back. She enjoyed the feel of his arms about her, and the bulk of his chest. She felt his hands come up to her face to cup her cheeks and he kissed her again, lingeringly. Mmmm, she said, or perhaps she only thought it. His beard was a little rough, but not abrasive, and his hair short enough for her hand to feel the smooth skin of his neck as her arms rose up his strong, broad back and he kissed her again warmly. She pressed against him, feeling agreeably conscious of her breasts. This, she thought, amid the gathering dusk, was decidedly pleasant, kissing in public like a teenager, and not caring who saw. He was a handsome and interesting man, and she did indeed feel rather beautiful and distinctly romantic. And she was content for this pleasure to continue to its logical conclusion. More than content, she thought. Distinctly eager.

"Manners," she said as he broke off and beamed down at her with a rather endearing foolishness on his face. "Dear Manners. Don't you think it's time you took me to bed?"

Clothilde came onto the hotel terrace, looked at Lydia stretching contentedly like a cat in the sun, and glanced at Manners eating his morning croissant. Sipping her coffee, Lydia felt Clothilde's amused gaze, and stared innocently back. Clothilde gave a distinct wink, sat down to join them, and said, "I was telephoned at home by the London Embassy late last night. They had a message that the ransom is accepted. Your father's cave painting is being returned later today."

"Jolly good," said Manners. "I've had a message as well, from Malrand. It was dropped off at the hotel here first thing this morning."

Clothilde looked pointedly at her watch. "First thing? It's nearly eleven." Manners blushed, and Lydia smiled quietly. "Mine came before eight A.M. A cocktail at his house tomorrow evening at six," Clothilde went on. "Mine had a small note added—not to let our German friend know about it."

"Very well. It will give us a chance to ask him why his security chap has been sniffing round in our footsteps. And to see if he's prepared to tell us about Marat and the hiding of the guns," said Manners. "Do you have any plans today, Clothilde? Lydia and I rather thought of looking round la Ferrassie again, trying the far side of the road toward Cumont."

"I have some museum work I must do, and a meeting with architects about the new building. But I'm rather more intrigued by Malrand asking us to see him again," said Clothilde. "In the meantime, I had a call from my stepfather about the parachute drop at Cumont, the one the Germans ambushed. He did an oral history project with the children at his school, getting them to interview all their relatives about their memories of the Resistance. He used some of it in his book. Something was jogging his mind, so he went back to the papers they had written, and pulled out two. I went to get them, had them photocopied, and here they are. They are very vague, but they might be significant. My mother sends you her warm regards, Lydia, and says she appreciated your delicacy yesterday."

Lydia covered her embarrassment by reaching for the papers. She felt a touch of relief. She enjoyed bedtime romps, but chose them with such care and infrequency that she had never got accustomed to sharing breakfasts the next morning. Conversation the morning after so often seemed so forced and fraught with forbidding amounts of meaning that the occasion cried out for the distraction of a newspaper. In the bedroom when they woke, Manners had solved that problem in the most satisfying way. But now over coffee, and feeling a little shy about her own emotions for the man and nervously hopeful that this affair would last, she was glad of the prospect of some work.

The photocopies were of the small *cahiers*—notebooks—of graphed paper that French schoolchildren use, in the neat round handwriting that used to be standard. It was the handwriting that Clothilde still used, neat and legible. They took one sheaf each. Lydia's was from a girl called Margueritte Perusin, and she began to read.

My brother Jeannot was sixteen years old when I was born, and he was the member of my family who fought with the Resistance even though he was very young. He helped with the parachute drops that came from England and America. Because our family has a farm, Jeannot was very good with horses. My mother says that Jeannot was away all night at one parachute drop near Cumont just before the invasion at Normandy when the German soldiers came to shoot the Resistance fighters and the horses they used. The Germans were very cruel. Jeannot came back home in the middle of the night to take our horses so that he and his friends could move the carts and take the English guns away. Jeannot went to la Ferrassie, but there was only one cart and it was empty because the guns had been hidden in a cave by the Englishman who was called *"capitaine."* Jeannot was frightened of the Englishman who was very fierce. Jeannot took the carts away to hide them, my mother said. My father said that he was very cross with Jeannot when he came back because he was frightened we would lose the horses. But Jeannot had boasted that the work was very important to the war. They now had special guns that could shoot at the German tanks, and when the invasion came Jeannot went off to fight the tanks. Jeannot said the Englishman had taught him how to fight tanks, and how to fight Germans. They had to be as cruel as the Germans to make them angry so they would not think clearly and charge into ambushes. My mother said Jeannot cried once when he came back because of the bad things he had done to some Germans to make them angry. Jeannot stayed away all that summer and autumn, and came back on leave in a French uniform and went back to join General Leclerc's Free French Army. He was wounded in 1945 in the fighting at Strasbourg, and then stayed in the Army after the war and was killed in Vietnam. He sent me a paper fan from Saigon. I only saw him when he came home on leaves and never knew why my mother and father still call him Little Jeannot, because he was very big and very nice to me. My mother cried when we learned that he had been killed at Hanoi. Jeannot was very brave and fought and died for France and we have his medal at home.

She passed Margueritte's essay across the table to Manners and picked up the one he had read before she realized that he was staring intently at her. Or was it lovingly? Staring as if he were fascinated. So he should be, the dear man.

"You have astounding powers of concentration," he said.

"Do I, darling?"

His eyebrows lifted. "That's a lovely word when you use it to me. I hate it normally. It sounds like actresses and old-fashioned drawing room plays."

"I'm very particular about the D word," she said, putting her hand on his. "I didn't plan to use it. I suppose it slipped out because I meant it."

"I'm feeling ridiculously happy," he smiled. "Tired and spent and full of energy and capable of anything."

"Anything?" she laughed. "Oh good. It was a delicious night, Manners. Or do I mean a lubricious one? Anyway, I'm looking forward to another, and another. But in the meantime, we have work to do. Order us some more coffee and read this sad story about Little Jeannot."

Young Claude Mourresac had written:

My uncle Pierrot was in the *Chasseurs Alpins* before the war, and fought the Italians when they invaded in 1940. He was not made a prisoner of war in Germany and he joined the Resistance of the *Armée Secrète* very early, even before the Germans occupied the Périgord. He was in the *Groupe Berger* and blew up trains with plastique explosive that an Englishman showed him how to use, and an American whose hair only grew in the middle of his head. They called him the Red Indian. The Englishman had a special razor called a Rolls-Royce that kept itself always sharp. This made my uncle very jealous because there were never any razor blades. The only time he saw the Englishman really angry was when the Red Indian stole his razor to cut his hair. They lived in caves and in the woods because the Germans wanted to kill them for blowing up trains. There were some Russians fighting for the Germans, which my father, Pierrot's brother, could not understand because the Russians were supposed to be fighting the Germans in Russia. There were also some North Africans fighting for the Germans, who burned the farm next to ours, although it was our farm that was supplying most of the food to Pierrot's group. We kept extra chickens and pigs in the woods that were not counted by the men from the Préfecture who came to count all our fields and livestock and tell us how much food we had to provide each week. The Resistance got their guns by parachute from London, and had special radios to talk to the pilots of the planes and to London. My father was allowed to hear the radio one night when General de Gaulle said it was time for all Frenchmen to rise and fight the Germans. My father built a windmill to get electricity to listen to the radio, but the wind was either too weak or too strong and one night it blew down. My father had been helping with the parachute drops, even though our farm would have been burned had the Germans known. There was one night when the Germans attacked a parachute drop and killed several Resistance men, but my uncle and the Englishman and the famous writer François Malrand got the guns away and hid them in a cave. Later some Communists tried to steal the guns, and my uncle told my father that the Communists were not true Frenchmen and he would have to fight them after he won the war against the Germans. My uncle was killed in the month after the invasion when the Germans sent tanks to recapture the liberated Périgord. He died for France and we are very proud of him and will never forget him.

Lydia read it again, and drank her coffee. So the Englishman and Malrand got the guns away and hid them in a cave. And Communists tried to steal the guns. What a drama must lie behind those simple words. So there was a cave, and from the tale of Little Jeannot the cave was near la Ferrassie.

"Well, that settles it," she said, rising. "Let's go to la Ferrassie. The cave is obviously near there."

"This is awful," said Manners, tapping Margueritte's essay on the table. "I don't like the sound of these bad things he says my father made them do to provoke the Germans. And this business about the Communists trying to steal the guns at the cave sounds ominous." His brow was furrowed and his eyes were throughtful, but he rose decisively from his chair and Lydia watched, both sobered and fascinated, as this man she had just slept with visibly set his jaw and girded himself for action. It was alien, she thought, but distinctly exciting.

They parked the Jaguar at la Ferrassie, on a small clearing off the Rouffignac road, where a green metal grill protected the earth beneath a large overhang of smooth rock, and Manners took a small collapsible spade from the trunk of the car. There was not much to see. The archaeologists' diggings had been filled in, the ancient skeletons moved. Even to Lydia, it was a good site. There was a spring with fresh water, shelter from the elements, and a pleasant stretch of grass in front of the shelter.

"It would drip a lot in the rain. And no protection from your enemies, but I've slept in worse," said Manners. "Horst and I explored this gully behind the shelter pretty thoroughly. We went all the way up to the top of the rock, and then cast around on the other side, trying to keep to a grid pattern so we missed nothing. We concentrated on the bits Horst said looked promising for caves from the geological survey, but we didn't find much. There wasn't much time for more than a cursory look at the far side of the road, so I suggest we start off by finding that cart track Albert used to get down from Cumont. I marked it on the map, and it looks as if it has been paved since the war."

They left the car and set off up a winding, narrow road, whose center was crumbling with thrusting vegetation, and climbed steadily through thick woods to a plateau with a magnificent view over fold after fold of ridges. They strolled along a dirt track and into a field that stretched away to a small village dominated by a circular water tower. Cumont. This would have been the dropping zone. And if Albert got away down the track they had just climbed, the Germans had presumably come from the opposite direction. This was hopeless, thought Lydia, breaking off to admire a restored farm with a handsome pigeon tower, swimming pool, and the distant sounds of tennis balls being hit. A Mercedes with German license plates was parked in the driveway. Germans, here. How far away the war must already be, she thought, unless you had reason to relive it. The sheer amount of ground was far bigger than it had seemed on the map. Cumont seemed a long way off.

"Now we know Albert got down to the rendezvous point, and there was no cave there, so it can't be that way," said Manners. "And since the Germans came from over there we can rule out that direction. And we know from Little Jeannot that the cart was empty when he brought the horses to la Ferrassie, so they must have unloaded it down there. So what we have to find is the other way down to the road. Through those woods."

He took her hand, and strode off along the track that led toward the Mercedes, and helped her over a gate into a wide meadow. Lydia was glad she was wearing slacks and training shoes, however unflattering. Manners had some battered green Wellingtons with his trousers tucked into their tops. The sound of tennis balls faded as they dropped down the slope, Manners with map and compass in hand. A formidable wood loomed ahead, and he marched them into it, stopping to check his bearing. Under the shade of the woods, the ground was soft, almost boggy.

"Oh good," said Manners. "It looks like we've found a stream. That's the obvious way down, and our best starting point."

They pressed on downhill, arms up to protect their faces from twigs and branches, stepping carefully over patches of brambles and around coppices, and came to a brief stretch of rock, and then a sudden drop. The trees below them had grown high enough to block their forward view. Manners checked his compass and edged to his left. The way down seemed easier here and the trees thinner. They scrambled down a dry gully beside a low rock outcrop, and saw farther to their left a patch of green, thick and almost lawnlike, dotted with wildflowers, and tucked neatly between the cliff and the trees. A stream gurgled down the rocks beyond it. A lovely spot for a picnic, thought Lydia, if it only had a view, and picked her way through the undergrowth toward it. One old tree leaned at what seemed an impossible angle, although its branches looked healthy enough.

"Never seen more solid-looking rock. Not even a hint of a cave," said Manners, taking a bottle of mineral water from his pack and passing it to her. She drank, sat down on the grass, and began undoing her shoelaces. He looked on, amused.

"Barefoot in the grass. One of life's great pleasures," she said, tucking socks into shoes and putting them behind her. She rose and felt the delicious coolness under her feet, the tickle of grass between her toes. She was feeling distinctly sensual. Was Manners one for making love in the open air? "Come on, Manners, try it." He laughed and complied, and capered a little for her, spinning around with his hands outstretched in the sun, looking at the rock, the stream, the trees.

"A glorious spot you found, Lydia," he called. "The most private place in Périgord." He looked across to where she now lay outstretched in the sun, her eyes closed. He bent and gathered a small handful of wildflowers, purple and yellow, and went across to kneel and present them to her.

"For the lady of the glade," he said, and bent to kiss her. Her arm came around his neck, slipping inside his shirt to caress his chest, and then unbuttoning his shirt. He slipped it off, stretched out beside her, and ran his hand along the length of her from shoulder to knee, and then back up to linger on her throat and cheek. Her eyes remained closed, her lips slightly parted, her hair loose around her cheeks. So very beautiful, he thought. Very slowly, and with all the time in the world, he undressed her, pausing to lay a yellow wildflower here, a dash of purple there, kissing each spot where the flowers glowed against her skin. Fair against the green, and as lush as the grass, she was the loveliest sight he had ever seen, and he told her so, slipping off the rest of his clothes and joining her in this perfect Eden.

CHAPTER 20

The Vézère Valley, 15,000 B.C.

Deer began with a thick stump of charcoal that he had ground against a stone to a smooth point and traced the first outline of the stag's head, remembering the way it had pawed the ground and defied him. The first beast they had fought, on the flesh of whose doe and fawn they had lived as the skins dried on the wooden frame he had made. It was the first to be depicted. And he bore its name. That was fitting, and it had been a brave and noble beast. The antlers had been bent toward him, the neck bunched with muscle and the shoulders tensed to charge. He closed his eyes and summoned the image again, to reproduce it on the virgin white wall that stretched before him. The body had been not quite straight toward him, the neck bent. The fawn had been down on its hindquarters and the doe's head raised to the sky by the shock of his arrow.

"This is not complete without you and your spear and stamping foot," he said to Moon, who stood beside him with the two hollowed stones in which he had showed her how to mix the earthen colors. He smiled fondly, admiring her as she stood now and as she had challenged the stag. "But I can never draw the sound of your shout."

She dipped a finger into the red earth, addressed herself to the wall, and drew the first outline of his straightened back, his arm bent to the bow, his head slightly forward in concentration. She took more paint for his braced legs and the curve of his buttocks. In her mind, the thrust of his loins did not look right. Surely the line had been straight from his head down his back to his rear foot.

"Take up the bow again," she said, and studied him as he modeled the action for her. This time she had it right and she dipped her finger again for the curve of his chest. She wanted this first image of him to be simple, just one silhouette of Deer the archer in plain color. It should not detract from the threat of the stag poised to charge, but balance it and show the story. She took the sharpened stick as he had shown her, to trace the thinner line of the bow.

"Now you draw the fawn, down on its rump, its forelegs floundering," said Deer. She looked worriedly at him. She had not expected this, still touched by the mystique of the beasts and the old rule that only men should draw them.

"Come," he said, taking her hand. "You remember." And he led her out of the cave to the stream, where they had spent the morning sketching designs in the smoothed mud with thin twigs. Her last drawing, of the infant deer, was still just visible, where the lips of mud had not quite closed over the grooves.

"You see how you made the curve of its haunch here, and then used the same curve again for the tilt of its neck to its mother?" he said, pointing with his finger. "That was so good, that is what you must remember." He led her back into the cave and stood close behind her as she took up the charcoal and began to draw.

He began to color the stag, that rough but silky texture of the reddish fur, and the whitish yellow at its muzzle and belly. He used moss for the thicker color and dry grass for the thinner wash. The chalk here was even smoother than that at the great cave, and he saw that the dried grass could be used to trail off his colors into thin lines, almost like the grass itself. He closed his eyes again for the image. Yes, the grass. The way the earth had been kicked up by the pawing hoof of the stag, which had sent the grass stirring. He remembered that, and now saw that it was the parted grass and not the hoof itself that had given him the impression of movement and power. Why did they never paint the grass on which the beasts ran? Why did they never do anything but the same images again and again? He bent down to brush his dried grass lightly against the wall by the hoof of his stag, and lifted it quickly away. Almost right. He touched the dried grass to the wall again, and let his hand move a little as he lifted it. Yes, there were the thin wisps, parting before the power of that hoof. He stood back; a little awed by his own boldness. But that was what he had seen.

And this was his cave, his and Moon's, where the old rules did not apply. Of course Moon must use her gift here in their cave, and he had found joy in showing her the skills he had learned, a joy that went beyond the wondrous pleasure of her. To watch her talent flower with the new skills of color and brush and charcoal that he had showed her was a happiness that was almost as sharp as the joy he found in her body. And if that old law against women was so plainly foolish, then what was the sense of the rest? There was no need of the ritual of the Keepers, limiting him to one beast, to an endless repetition of form. No law ruled here that said he must paint only beasts and not the land on which they stood, the trees and grass where they grazed, the rivers where they drank, the shape of the hills he had seen rolling away into the distance.

Suddenly the vision came to him, that the deer and horses and bulls and bears that he itched to paint could take their part in a greater whole. Beasts in their settings, bears in their rocks, deer in their copses, horses in their herds moving delicately and with some secret protocol down to the river to drink.

Exultant, he crossed to the other wall, and sketched a high line of rolling hill, tumbling into the outcrop of rock where he and Moon had sheltered that first night. And then imagination leaped beyond the constraints of memory and he drew the mouth of a cave that had not been there, and the shape of a bear, lumbering slowly after its long winter sleep, emerging to sniff the air. Then a tree, he thought, a high tall line to balance the bear's bulk. But trees meant green, and how was he to find the color of green in the earths and clays? An image darted into his mind of children playing by the river, sliding down a long steep slope of grass that tumbled them into a pool, and the smears of green it left on their bodies. There was green in grass. How to obtain it, to make it into a color for the wall? He bent to the floor and picked up a small pebble of chalk, too hard to crumble in his hands. He left the cave, and at the stream, took one of the flat hearthstones and a rounded stone, wrapped the pebble in a handful of fresh grass and then dipped it all in the stream. He withdrew it, dripping, and slowly crushed the chalk into dust, rolling his stone until the whiteness of the chalk had taken on the greenness of the grass. It was a duller green than the grass had been, but it would serve. He sat back on his haunches and looked at the trees above him. They were not a single, simple green, but richer with other shades, flashes of yellow and gleams of white from the reflected sky. As he scraped his new color onto a small, flat stone to take it back into the cave, a part of his mind was already asking what he would do for the blue of the sky, and thinking of the colors in the wildflowers and how they would mix with his chalk.

He had left her early, after the first morning drink from the stream, to search his traps for rabbits, and to use the new thongs they had sliced from the cured hides. Moon wanted the old, supple thongs to sew their winter cloaks of rabbit fur. She had already woven a basket and soon they would fish. And they would have to start to smoke meat for the winter, which meant more reindeer skins to build the smoking tent. He begrudged each moment he spent away from the cave, away from Moon, with whom he felt a fellowship far closer than anything he had known among the Keepers and apprentices. She took his ideas and gave them back to him in different garb, and offered her own plans for the great wall of their cave that spurred his mind into new directions.

It had taken its full shape now, just as he had dreamed. The vast stretch of hillside and grassland covered the whole wall, with its sleepy bear and grazing deer, its horses bending to drink at a riverbank fringed with reeds, its great black bull standing guard over a docile cow, and the ibex perched on the rocky outcrop. This was the world as they knew it, as a cradle and a backdrop for life and movement. It was what they saw, and what they had labored so joyously to depict. There were reeds and trees, the spots of color from the wildflowers, the ripples in the water that spoke of fish, and an evening sky of dusted reds and violets. They had been Moon's idea, when the blue of the sky had defeated him, the flimsy petals of the purple flowers failing to bring him the color he needed. And her idea was better, he thought. It gave a sense of time, of a day ending, a fleeting moment caught.

Along the passageway into the cave were the smaller sketches they had made, the bull that he had done first to be sure of the proportions, and then her delicate deer and the two horses, one at rest and one prancing. They made a fitting entrance into the great space of the cave beyond, with its large landscape on one side, and on the other, the tableau of him and Moon confronting the stag and doe and fawn. The far end of the cave remained blankly white, and he had not yet seriously applied his thoughts to its possibilities. He had been musing about it the previous evening after they ate, wondering about trying to recapture the moment of the great hunt, the tumbling reindeer, and the boys riding the beasts in their hunger to be men. There was something in it that inspired him, but to recapture what he had seen, rather than what he had felt, would be untrue to his own eye. What he had seen, mostly, was dust, and if he felt that he lived by a single law in the glorious voyage of discovery and exploration that he and Moon were making, it was to be true to what they saw.

And what he had seen was Moon at the stream bank, sitting cross-legged and sketching in the clay, looking up at him from moment to moment, but not to catch his eye nor to smile at him, but with a steady concentration. She was sketching him again, as she had done the first time he had become aware of her talent. He had noted that she was making tiny, carefully chosen lines in the clay, rather than her usual long and fluid strokes. Curious, he had begun to rise to look at her work, but almost sharply she had told him to remain where he was. So he had been content with watching her until she stopped and studied the clay, and then finally looked at him, smoothed out her work, and came laughing into his arms.

And now, as he hung the rabbits on their frame and removed his sack and laid his flint ax in its place by the cave entrance while waiting for his eyes to grow accustomed to the darker interior, he was aware of Moon standing by that far, untouched wall. He became aware, too, of some large, round design taking shape upon it. He swallowed the instant rush of anger and affront, that she had embarked upon the work without the discussion and agreement that had become their custom. He had not asked her about the first line he had drawn on the rolling hill of what became their wall, he recalled. This cave was her work as much as his and he knew the ever-rising level of her skill and the trueness of her eye. In truth, he had nothing left to teach her. He closed his eyes and sat in silence, waiting for them to adjust and to see her work as she was seeing it, and smiling as he thought of her. Weaving, hunting, painting, loving, splashing in the water and tending the fire, skinning the game and sewing the hides into panels for their smoke tent. As brave as a man and as capable, and mistress of all the things that women did. He heard her footsteps approaching, and began to blink.

"No," she said firmly. "Don't open your eyes, not yet. Come, let me guide you." She helped him to his feet and led him down the passage and into the cave. She took him three, then four paces inside until he thought he must be standing almost in the center, with the great land-scape to his left and the tableau of him and Moon and the stag to his right. She stopped him with a hand to his chest, and then came and stood behind him and covered his eyes with her hands.

"Open them now," she said, and withdrew her hands, resting them lightly on his cheeks, and he saw himself for the first time. It was him, just his face and shoulders, as he had glimpsed them in the stillness of a pool of water. His hair, thick and curling over his brow and on his shoulders, his shape. He raised his hand to his own jaw, his mouth, his nose, his cheekbones and found her hand there and pressed it.

"I never thought . . ." he said, his mouth too dry to speak, his thoughts too confused, his reactions tumbling over each other from shock to fear to admiration. He took a deep breath. "I never thought this could be done. I never knew or dreamed."

He stepped forward, breaking the spell that bound him to her, and discovered himself. The painting of him as seen by Moon. He had not known that his eyes were that color of brown with those flecks of green, that his lips were so red, or his nose that shape. He raised his hand to his cheekbone, feeling the sharpness that she had conveyed to the rock. He felt his own jaw, his fingers searching for that groove she had placed in his chin, the corner of his mouth for that half-smile she had given him, his neck for the slim length of it.

The painting was huge, so much larger than his own head that he felt dwarfed by it. His face was the scale of his chest and stomach, bigger than the stag or the bear or even the great bull in their landscape. He was a giant, but he looked kind. He had a face, but this was more than flesh and bone and eyes. It was a character, a mood, and a person who thought and saw and spoke. This was not just the head of a man, but him, Deer, as seen and re-created by the woman he loved.

He stepped closer still, to see how those faint lines on each side of his nose had been lightly drawn in charcoal. Then he noted how she had given the depth to his nose by the lighter patch of color on one side, and used a tiny fleck of red in the corner of his eye. And he saw that she had used his trick of the dried grass to catch the texture of his hair.

He began moving backward, his eyes fixed on the portrait of himself, farther and farther until his back touched the corner of the cave where it opened into the passageway. Now he could see how right she had been to give the head this great size. Balanced by their other work on either side of him, the scale of the portrait was precise and fitting. It dominated the cave without overwhelming it. It put man in his proper place in this universe they had made between them, apart from the beasts and landscape that he shared with them, apart and different, something distinct. A person, a single person, with thought and character and a look that made each human creature unique.

"This makes you the real Keeper of the Deer," he said, trying to find words to express his awe at her achievement. "Of this Deer. Me." He had not noticed her move, but suddenly she was beside him, her hand on his arm.

"Then you are Keeper of the Moon," she said, and slipped her arm around his waist, resting her head on his shoulder. She felt his body trembling.

"This is the most wonderful work I have ever seen," he said. "I cannot wait to try this new thing, to paint you. How could we never have done this, thought of this, before now? This changes everything I thought I knew about our work."

334

He turned and looked at her with wonder, his eyes scanning her face, his hand reaching up to touch her hair. Amid his awe, amid his love for this woman, which was filling him and swelling his chest, he was looking with a painter's eye at the planes of her face, thinking how to catch the forms and colors.

"That is why I left that great space to the side," she said. "I knew, or I hoped, that you would want to paint me."

"But you have left more space on each side," he said.

"Yes, for there will be children," she said, smiling and putting his hand on her belly. "I have been thinking of painting your face for a long time. It was taking place in my head, and then last night I started making the sketches when I was sure that we will have a son to look at his father's likeness on the wall."

"Or a daughter to look at her mother's," he said, his delight huge as he hugged her to him. "I cannot wait to start painting you, young mother."

"Not just yet," she said, loosening the thongs at her shoulder to let her tunic fall to the floor, and slipping her hand to his thigh. "There's time for everything."

He knew not what it was that woke her, but he felt her hand tighten on his shoulder and sat up, reaching for his ax, and thrusting her back into the passageway toward the cave. She moved clumsily, the babe heavy in her belly, but scooped up her spear and his pack as she scrambled into shelter. He saw nothing but the night stars and the trees rocking gently in the autumn wind, but he felt the presence of others nearby in the night just as surely as he felt the loom of the rock behind him. He groped for his bow and quiver of arrows, biting his lip in anger at himself at the scraping sound his bow made as he caught it on the passage wall.

Moon was safe behind him, her spear ready. He had his bow, his ax, and his knife. He could hold this passage against any beast, and most men, unless they had the patience to starve them out. He and Moon had rehearsed their defenses. There were water skins and smoked meats in the cave, and rocks with which to build a wall that could block the passage and give him cover to shoot. He craned his ears and heard a whispering outside. Men. Then he heard nothing, but saw a glow as they stirred the embers of his fire into life and settled around it to wait until dawn. They could be strangers who had caught sight of their fire and would move on. But strangers would not be out at night, and if they were, they would call out and seek the hospitality of the hearth. The dread began to build with the realization that somehow, finally, the Keeper of the Bulls had caught up with them. Moon came and held him tightly. He took off his knife, slipping the thong around her neck, and they waited.

"Daughter—Little Moon." It was the voice of her father, the Keeper of the Horses.

"Father." Her reply was instinctive. Angry with herself for breaking silence she called out, "Why are you here. What do you want?"

He showed himself, standing alone at the cave mouth, his arms stretched out a little from his body to show that his hands were empty.

"I mean you no harm," he called, and walked up the passage toward them.

"Far enough, old friend," said Deer, as the Keeper reached the low wall of stones. The older man's eyes darted to the sketches on the passage walls as the dawn outside strengthened into day. "How many are outside with you?"

"Many," he said. "The Keepers, the hunters, the leaders of the woodsmen and flint and fishermen. And your mother, Moon."

"So many?" she said.

"We have lost our cave. We have lost everything that made us."

"There are other caves," said Deer, an arrow notched in his bow. He kept looking at the empty passage behind Moon's father. "The storm took your cave, not me. Not us."

"The storm came in anger at what you did. That is what the Keepers have decided. You must come back and make everything as it was."

"You would give me to the Keeper of the Bulls?" spat Moon. "He would not want a woman heavy with Deer's child. And you would not want a daughter who would be a Keeper and paint with your fellowship."

"You are having a child?" he said gently. "My grandchild."

"Look beside you, Father," said Moon. "The bison and the bear are your daughter's work."

They saw that he had aged as he peered at the paintings in the passage.

"How did you find us?" asked Deer.

"After you left, the chief hunter saw that a log had gone and guessed you went down the great river. He followed you, but found no track, until by chance he found people at the great rock who had seen you pass. He went on searching, and coming back, searching farther each time. Then he found a place where there had been a barrage of trees, and began scouting, thinking that is where you would have stopped. He saw your fire, watched you, and came back to summon the rest of us. It has been a long journey, the longest of my life."

"We will not come back," said Deer.

"Then I fear the others will seek to kill you," said Moon's father. "They are frightened and angry. They want life to be as it was."

There was an impatient shout from the cave mouth. Moon's father turned and called for them to stay back. A head appeared, the chief hunter, and then darted back. Deer smelled smoke, and knew that his fire had been moved to the cave mouth and they were using branches to fan the smoke into the passage. They could be smoked out. He had not thought of that. The Keeper of the Horses began to cough.

"You had better go, Father," said Moon.

"No, little one. I would hold you again, and see your work."

Deer considered, remembering the kindness of this man, and his love of painting, and then stepped back, inviting him in. "As Moon's father, as my friend and teacher, you are welcome here," he said formally. He crouched behind his puny wall. The smoke was less here.

Inside the cave, the smoke was still thin enough for the old man to see the great landscape and then he stood stock-still as he caught sight of the two great portraits on the end wall.

Deer and Little Moon, side by side, human but on the scale of a great bull, and he tottered as if he might faint.

"What have you done?" he demanded of his daughter, his eyes daring in bafflement from the flesh and blood woman before him and Deer's giant image of her on the wall. His voice was appalled. "This is wrong . . ." he said weakly, and then muttered, as if to himself, "but it is wonderfully wrought."

"Deer painted me," said Moon. "I painted him."

"You? Did this?" he whispered. The smoke was hanging heavily in the cave, and Deer's eyes were watering. Another angry shout came from outside, and then an arrow flashed out of the smoke and snapped on a rock of Deer's low wall. He moved to his left, so that the rock would cover his body when he drew his bow. Another arrow came, higher this time, and bounced off the side of the passage to clatter inside the cave. He glanced back. Moon and her father, their arms around each other, were huddling against the side wall.

Suddenly, the passageway darkened, and he drew his bow and shot into the smoke. A cry of pain. Then a pause, and then it darkened again, and he shot twice to no effect, seeing a black bulk bearing down on him with spears on each side, and realized that they had taken their skins and stretched them over a wooden frame as a shield. He dropped the bow, took his ax in his right hand and Moon's spear in his left, and waited.

They were as blind as he, but he was closer to his target, and as the spear points came above his wall his ax flashed down onto each of them, and he jabbed the spear down low beneath the shield to hit the unprotected legs. A foot crashed down on his spear and tore it from his hand. The leather shield was charging into him, and he scythed his ax as he went down, feeling it jar as it hit rock. And then there were men all over him, lashing his arms and legs with thongs, and they dragged him down the passage by his hair into the fierce sunlight and the clean air. He gasped in pain as they hauled him over the coals of the fire and then propped him against the rock.

A shadow of a man stood before him, a man who had once been big and strong, but whose flesh now hung in folds over wasted muscles. Where the bones jutted from the skin, there were weeping sores, and the hands were stiffened claws. Only the eyes were fierce and strong beneath the eagle's headdress. The Keeper of the Bulls was a dying man, just as Moon's sketch had foretold, and in his hand was the great club with the beaked head.

Two young men brought Moon out of the cave, firmly but gently enough, and her father limped after them. Deer knew them both, his brothers of the ceremony that had made them men. Around him were faces he had known since his childhood, Keepers and hunters, and Moon's mother hurrying to embrace her daughter, her eyes wide in surprise at the bulge of the child.

"I will not come back," said Deer, and spat blood and what felt like a tooth from his mouth, repeating himself to say it more clearly.

"No more will I," shouted Moon.

"You have bewitched us with evil," said the Keeper of the Bulls, his voice eerily familiar. "You have destroyed our cave and put the sickness upon me. Our hunters find no game and the fish escape our nets and the children cry with hunger. All this you have done."

"We destroyed nothing," cried Deer. "You brought evil upon the people. You with your pride and ambition. You brought the new worship. You tried to fool the fates with your false omens of eagles. You set yourself up as lord of the skull, lord of the skies. You put on the head of a beast. You are the evildoer. You destroyed the old customs. You tried to take Moon against her father's consent. You brought down the sickness upon yourself, the rocks upon the cave, the anger upon the people. It was your madness that we fled."

"What you destroyed, we made," called Moon, in a strange high voice, chanting the words, her head held high and her eyes looking far away across the trees and into the morning sky. "What you broke down in lust and anger, we built up in love.

"What you destroyed, we made," she repeated. "Show them, my father. Show them what had been done under the hand of the Great Mother."

And the Keeper of the Horses led them one by one into the passage and into the marvel of the cave, and as Moon continued staring far into the sky, Deer watched their awed and frightened faces as they emerged. The Keeper of the Bears was stiff with shock, or was it outrage? The Keeper of the Ibex gazed keenly at Deer, and called to him, "All your work?" And Deer shook his head and said that Moon had shared in it. The Keepers huddled in silence. The young hunters looked uncertainly at Moon. None of them, clearly, knew what to do. The anger and violence of the storming of the cave had passed. Deer's attack upon the Keeper of the Bulls had sobered them. Moon's stance and bearing in her pregnancy and chanting as if the Great Mother were speaking through her had awed them.

"Untie me," said Deer to the young hunter beside him, and without thinking, the man bent and began to loosen the thongs.

The last to enter the cave, and the last to leave it, was the husk of the man he knew as the Keeper of the Bulls. As the old man emerged, he leaned weakly against the rock, even the feathers around his beak seeming to droop. Then he gathered himself as if he felt challenged by the new uncertain mood of the vengeful band he had brought here. With a visible effort, his back straightened and he marched across to where Deer lay trying to free himself, and pushed the young hunter aside.

"Evil," he cried in a voice that echoed like thunder. "Evil that would bewitch your souls, evil that would dry up the rivers and empty the plains and destroy us all."

He turned as if to confront Moon, but it was a movement that brought the great beaked club high and gave it a whirling force and with a great shout he slammed it down onto Deer's helpless head.

Moon screamed once as he advanced upon her, the rest all stunned and immobile, and only this still powerful man with the head of an eagle and the great beaked club that dripped blood and loomed high above his shoulder seemed capable of movement.

"Evil," he cried again, and took the last fateful step, the club whirling down. But Moon had broken the spell, darted forward beneath the blow, and came close to his chest as if to embrace him. Faster than the falling club, she slid to one side with Deer's flint knife still in her hand. And the Keeper of the Bulls sagged slowly to his knees as his entrails gushed out from the great slash in his belly and slopped to the ground before him. The eagle's head bent to look at the steaming, bloodied loops, and then lifted to look at Moon as she spun on her heel to slam her foot into the side of his beaked head and send him toppling into the mess that had leaked from his guts. She leaned down and brutally wrenched the eagle mask from the Keeper's head, and threw it onto the fire. A gush of fresh blood surged from his mouth, and his body stiffened, and then shuddered into death.

She walked slowly across to Deer and studied the crushed and lifeless head, as intently as she had studied him for her sketches, placed both hands on her swollen belly as if to embrace her unborn child, and closed her eyes. The only sound was the crackling of the fire, as its smoke and the stench of burning feathers drifted across the stretch of grass where all stood immobile around the two dead men.

"The evil is gone," she chanted, her voice thick with grief. She gasped for breath, gathering herself, her jaw working as she fought within herself for control. Her eyes opened but gazed far above the silent people, looking even beyond the weak morning sun and the new day it brought.

"The evil is gone," she repeated. "But it has marked us all, divided us all, cost us all. The evil has changed us utterly."

The smoke drifted and the fresh blood steamed in the morning.

"It has broken the brotherhood of the Keepers, broken the bond of man and wife, broken the bond that tied us to the cave." Her voice was rhythmic, but softer now, almost lulling.

"Bonds can be forged anew. And the evil has been defeated by life." Her voice sank yet further, a deeper timbre, almost the low tones of a man. Blood trickled down her trailing hand, gathered into a thick and tear-shaped drop that trembled on the end of her finger and glinted in the sun before it gathered itself and fell.

"The evil has been defeated by life," she said again, a tone of wonder in her voice, and her thoughts drifted back to that night when she had first bitten blood from the evil man . . . no, from the Keeper who had himself been captured by evil. She felt the new life suddenly kick in her belly. And she smiled, remembering the warm, lulling touch of the Great Mother, who had come to comfort her in the cave that night before Deer had come for her. It was the Great Mother who had granted her the magic that had finally doomed the Keeper of the Bulls. The Great Mother had given her a man and taken him, given her an enemy and the strength to defeat him. And given her Deer's child. There was a balance. It seemed very clear to her now.

Her upturned face looked down, and it seemed to her frozen audience that she was aware of them for the first time. She paused, scanning their faces. Her father, her mother, the men who had known her since she was an infant. They needed something from her, she understood, a forgiveness for their part in this horror.

"Deer lives in me and in our work in our cave, and in the beasts we honor in our painting and in the lives of us, our people. Life after life, generation after generation, the people, the beasts, and the land," she said simply, the words coming unbidden. "We flow like the river, and always past the same place. We will be here forever. My child. Deer's child. Your own young."

She stopped, spent, and staggered a little. But the spell she had cast upon them was not quite broken. They hung still on her words. Beyond her forgiveness, beyond her acceptance, they needed yet more from her. A guidance, a direction. She understood that they needed to be told what to do, to be released from this thrall she held upon them. And she knew that she too needed release from that same thrall, and in a last gift from the Great Mother it came to her that her power over them lay in that image of her that had stunned their spirits when they first saw the portraits in the cave. It was not the blood sacrifice that had awed them, but those giant images of her and Deer. It was a greatness she did not need, a weight she could not bear. There might be other men, but there would be no other Deer, and no other portrait. A magic lay there that was beyond her will to comprehend. She knew only that it must not be repeated. And the people still needed her direction.

"Father, I will come back with you," she said. "But take Deer within the cave, so that he may gaze on my image in death, and then take wood and earth and stones and seal the cave. Our work here is done."

CHAPTER 21

Périgord, June 1944

Manners had never seen so many *Tricolores*, so much red, white, and blue suddenly dancing from every bridge and truck and half the windows in every town they passed. He was riding in a police truck, driven by a gendarme driver who would probably still have tried to arrest him a month earlier, and would have shot him on sight a couple of months before that. Now he was helping load explosives. Manners's stocks of plastique had been used to blow the rail tracks on both sides of the bridges across the Dordogne. The crossings at Mauzac and Trémolat, le Buisson and St-Cyprien, Beynac and Mareil and St-Denis were all sealed, and at each one he had left volunteers cheerfully lighting great fires to heat the straight rails so they could be twisted into knots around trees. The Germans would have to carry trainloads of their own rails with them if they were to use these routes. Still no time to rest. Every quarry had some authorized stocks of industrial dynamite kept under lock and key at gendarme and Milice stations, and the truck had made the rounds of every one. He had nearly half a ton, and the Vézère bridges had still to be blown at le Bugue and Manaurie.

"Another roadblock," muttered the driver. Manners resigned himself to more cheering at the sight of his British uniform, more waving of Sten guns and old Lebel rifles, more salutes from old men holding themselves ramrod-straight. But the roadblock stayed closed, and the guns stayed leveled at him. There was a large red flag flying alongside the *Tricolore*, and "Stalingrad" had been chalked on the stone-filled farm cart that blocked the road. His gendarme driver looked frightened. Manners opened the door and stepped onto the running board as a short, thin man with pale knees beneath his shorts walked to the truck and demanded, "What are you carrying?"

"Explosives, for the rails across the Vézère."

"We need them," said the man, and the pistol held loosely by his side was suddenly pointing at Manners. "These explosives are requisitioned in the name of the people," he shouted, for the benefit of the curious faces on the defenders' side of the roadblock. "You'll get a requisition paper, properly signed by me. Out."

"You can't requisition from me. I'm a British officer and I'm fighting on your side," said Manners reasonably. "And there's an SS armored division coming this way from Toulouse unless I blow those rails."

The man fired a single shot into the air. "Out, I said."

"*Capitaine, capitaine,*" came a loud, delighted voice. "Welcome to liberated France." It was the big Spaniard from Soleil's château, and he came across to kiss Manners heartily on both cheeks, pushing the thin man casually out of the way. "Comrades, this man is the master of the Sten gun. He builds them blindfolded," he called. "Clear the road for the brave *capitaine*." And he put his own massive shoulders to the farm cart and swiveled it aside for Manners's truck to pass. "Good luck," he called, and gave the truck a cheerful clenched-fist salute.

"Full of bloody Reds, this place," said the police driver as he accelerated away, his hand trembling as he lit a cigarette. Manners grinned at him in relief and carried on trying to work out how much dynamite he would need to do the work of a plastique charge. When he got to le Bugue, not far from the site of his first ambush, he had to go through the town and past Sybille's house to get to the station. Half a dozen cheering youngsters waving French flags jumped aboard and hung improbably onto the back as he lurched along the rails to the river. A French flag had been hanging from her upstairs window, but her door was closed and there were shutters over the surgery window and he pushed the thought of her bedroom into the back of his mind.

He tried three sticks of dynamite, which was enough to blow the rails and sleepers out of their beds, but not enough for the damage he wanted. So he tried two charges of ten sticks, and blew an impressive crater in the rail bed. Feeling pleased with himself, he repeated the blasts at the farther end of the bridge and added ten more sticks for luck, as a cheerful and swelling crowd gathered to watch. A middle-aged woman came running down from a small hamlet of honey-colored stone, carrying a dusty bottle, and handed it shyly to his driver.

"Have you come by parachute?" asked a small boy.

Manners grinned at him. "Flew in by special plane," he said. He got the driver to push them all back to somewhere near safety as he lit the fuses and sprinted for cover. He almost didn't make it, the blast stunning him just after he landed in the ditch, and a thick rain of small stones from the rail bed pattered onto his back. He limped back to the truck, feeling the worse for wear, when the small boy darted up to him and asked, "Where's the rest of you?"

"Coming," he said. "Coming soon," and the crowd cheered and

started shouting "Winston Churchill," and breaking into the "Marseillaise" when he waved wearily to them and tried to explain that they should throw the rails into the river.

But as the truck jerked away, he thought it was a very good question. There was something frighteningly premature about this local mood of liberation, with the Allied armies still coming ashore on the beaches four hundred miles to the north. And there were an awful lot of German troops between them and Manners, and an entire armored division heading straight for him and all those flimsy roadblocks and kids with their French flags and Churchill V-signs. And for Sybille. When they got to le Buisson, and saw the dead Milice men in the square and a fat man with his trousers around his ankles hanging grotesquely from a lamppost, he felt even more worried.

"Cheer up," said the driver and broke off half the ham sandwich that someone had given him at le Bugue. The bottle was between his knees. "Have something to eat. This eau-de-vie is the real thing. And there's lots of dynamite left."

"I know, but too many road bridges," said Manners, chewing appreciatively. "Take the road along the river to Siorac and then Souillac. I want to know what chance we have of stopping the bastards now they can't come by train."

He had four bazookas back in the cave, the only weapons he had with a chance of slowing the German armor. Something like two hundred tanks and self-propelled guns that were almost as good. Being SS, they'd probably be equipped with Mark V Panther tanks, which were a generation ahead of anything he had faced in the desert. A bazooka wouldn't even dent the frontal armor of a Mark V. All he could hope to do was slow them, force them to stop and deploy, organize standard attacks with artillery and infantry. He might delay them for a few hours if he was lucky. Twenty thousand men, and over two thousand vehicles. They would have to disperse against air attack. At fifty yards between vehicles, which was the minimum the British Army decreed for armored units, the Das Reich division would cover fifty miles of road. They would use at least two roads, probably three if they could. Still ten to fifteen miles of vehicles on each road, a big traffic jam if it had to stop and bring forward heavy weapons. They would put a reconnaissance battalion in the lead, with motorbikes and armored cars and a company or two of Panzergrenadier infantry with mortars. Maybe a couple of self-propelled guns if they were expecting trouble. Could he let the reconnaissance battalion pass, and then ambush the soft-skinned vehicles behind? No, that would have to be a simple hit and run, and he needed sustained fire if he were going to force them to halt and deploy. He would have to try and stop them head-on.

They were coming from Montauban, just north of Toulouse. They would have to come through Cahors and Figeac, and then their route to Normandy would be through Brive or Périgueux. The question was, where would they cross the rivers? They were the only choke points he had. His map showed fifteen bridges across the Dordogne, and he had just four bazookas. He had to work out which road they would take and use the remaining dynamite to demolish the main bridge, and then ambush their alternative crossings. It was hopeless, and probably lethal for any of the Maquis who manned the ambushes with him. But he had to try.

There was only one glimmer of a chance. If his pinpricks were relentless and frequent enough, if the great armored beast were stung so hard and so often, it might just forget about its charge to Normandy and stop long enough to lash out at all the little hornets that were tormenting it. It was not what he would do, and not what any professional soldier would do. Normandy was the crucial battlefield for an armored division, not the soft belly of the Périgord. But the SS were not always coldly professional soldiers. They were political soldiers, driven by their mad creed. They might just be provoked into the stupidity of reprisals. With quickening excitement, he realized that they could even be driven into losing the one thing they did not have: time.

God help him, but he might be able to slow them by offering the helpless targets of the French civilians he was supposedly here to help. To do his best, he had to make the SS do their worst. So, take no prisoners. Butcher their wounded. Desecrate their corpses and leave them on the bridges. Hang them from trees over the road. Madden the Germans with rage. Nobody had given him such orders, and nobody in his army ever would. Nor would they ever forgive an officer who broke the code by doing so. But a cold dread spread through him as he realized that this was the battle he had been sent here to fight. He reached for the bottle of eau-de-vie and looked for places where he might commit atrocities and for men ruthless enough to help him. He had to find Marat.

The fog of war, Clausewitz had called it, and an utter density of uncertainty, ignorance, and impotence had closed around Manners. He had never felt so helpless. The Germans had moved far faster than he had thought possible, and he had been forced by accident and disaster into virtual immobility. And finally now that he had found them, he had neither men nor arms nor plan, not anything at all with which to meet them. Far less stop them.

The little village of Cressensac had grown up around the junction where the main *route nationale* from the bridge across the river Dordogne at Souillac to the south was joined by the road from the medieval hillside shrine of Rocamadour, and then the combined road went north to Brive. There was a church, two hotels, and two cafés all lined up along the main street.

"Not a bad place for an ambush," said McPhee. "If they had a tank trap, an antitank gun to command that long road, and a swarm of bazooka gunners in the houses."

"Well, we haven't. We're just observers," Manners replied, as the apparently sleepy town erupted in a long burst of machine gun fire. A column of soft-topped trucks, motorbikes, and staff cars had suddenly appeared coming at speed over the slight rise in the road beyond the town. The day was clear and the visibility perfect. They could see the kicks of earth in the ground where the bullets hit. There was a moment of shock as time slowed, and Manners was reminded, not of the static quality of toy soldiers but of the clockwork train set he had been given as a boy. A tiny and artificial landscape in stillness save for the whirling movement of the train. Then a truck and staff car collided and German soldiers in camouflage smocks rather than the usual field-gray scrambled out.

"Are these Krauts insane?" marveled McPhee. "No patrols out ahead. No armor up front. Rommel would have knocked every officer back to private if any of his units had ever been so stupid. Maybe the French have a chance."

There was chaos on the road, as trucks reversed, swung to the side, stalled, and just remained blocking the road as their drivers jumped for cover. Now the French machine gunner had a target, dozens of targets, and rifles and Stens opened up.

"Oh, Christ, if we had a mortar platoon," said McPhee. Or even the bazookas, thought Manners. Then they could have done the bastards some damage. He looked at the ground to left and right. Some cover, and there were other roads coming into Cressensac. This would not take the Germans long. A standard flank move, covering fire, and that would be the end of this small firefight. Time to go. He nudged McPhee, turned, and prepared to take the long straight road back to Brive, but could not resist a last look at the brave, doomed Frenchmen who had taken on an armored division.

Even as they watched, they heard the growl of a big engine and the clatter of metal treads chewing up tarmac as a Mark IV accelerated over the rise like a maddened bull. Its short-barreled 75mm gun fired into the houses on either side of the village as it simply knocked aside the clutter of trucks and drove on. A half-track loomed quickly behind it, and then another, which stopped at the brow and began the fast punching of its cannon. An antitank gun appeared beside it and opened fire. There went the church tower and the hotel, and then the lead tank stopped and turned at the end of the village and began pumping shells into houses. A sudden flower of fire flashed on the road, well short of the tank. Somebody must have tried throwing a Molotov. Tiny figures began running from the backs of the houses toward the trees, and then went skidding as the machine guns started hunting them. It had taken less than twenty minutes, and there was only one other roadblock before Brive, just as flimsy and ill armed as this one. It was 4 P.M., and the Germans would be in Brive within the hour, where half the Resistance leadership of the region was going to be rounded up and arrested unless he could warn them in time. That would simply put the cap on his twenty-four wasted hours of disaster. He and McPhee jumped into the Citroën and raced away.

It had begun the previous evening at Siorac, a town where the local butcher with the nickname "Le Bolshevik" ran the Resistance. There had been a flimsy roadblock, with only Sten guns to hold it. But they directed him to the station where he found a railway man who knew Marat, and the old lady who ran the *Postes et Télégraphes* began calling every other switchboard she could reach. Marat had been at Limoges. He was expected at Périgueux, at Brive, at Bergerac. Manners left messages at each place, and sent more by the railway men's network, for a meeting at Brive the next morning. He went back to his truck and his driver had gone, the empty bottle still propped on the seat. Dismayed, he looked in the back. Empty. The dynamite had gone. He tapped the petrol tank. Just as empty. He had no transport, no explosives, no allies, and no communications. He found the genial Bolshevik in the church, where his men were taking weapons from their hiding place in the roof, and traded his empty truck for an ancient motorbike and an extra can of the oil and petrol mixture it needed.

It took him two hours to reach the Hôtel Jardel as night fell, by the bridge over the Dordogne that led north. Trees had been felled across the road every few hundred yards, but there were no guns to cover them so the armored bulldozers of the German combat engineers would simply push them out of the way. They slowed him a lot worse than they would the Germans. The small village of Grolejac lay just down the road, and there was not a roadblock to be seen. There was, however, a *Tricolore*, so he warned the two men he found in the bar, who looked at him with bleary-eyed lack of interest, as if an angry British officer was a common event. And as he took the road over the bridge and north to Brive, he had the first puncture. He rode until the tire shredded, and continued on the metal wheel, every bone in his body feeling as if were being slowly, methodically broken, and then the wheel seized. He continued on foot in the pitch dark and was nearly run over by a truckful of FTP men coming from Sarlat. He persuaded them to take him back to the town, where they left him at a small command post and raced back toward the river to reinforce Grolejac. He found a man he had taught how to run parachute drops, and at 3 A.M. was sleeping in the back of a commandeered car and being driven to Brive. Then they ran out of petrol, but his escort thought it unreasonable to wake the famous English *capitaine* who was obviously so exhausted. They woke him shortly after dawn with a fresh omelet, and a glass of wine, and the news that a horse had been sent from the nearest farm to find some petrol. He was too tired to weep.

Manners finally reached Brive just after midday, too late for the meeting he had called with Marat. The town was prematurely celebrating its liberation, despite the desultory sniping at the Germans besieged in their command post at the Hôtel Bordeaux. More time lost. He finally tracked Marat down at the monastery of St-Antoine, where an angry meeting was under way and a couple of hundred well-armed Resistance fighters lounged outside, some of them drinking, some striking poses for the local girls. Marat's Spaniards were grilling sausages around a pair of trucks with "Madrid" chalked on one tailgate, "Teruel" on the other. Manner's face widened into a smile as he saw McPhee among them.

"What's going on?" Manners asked, shaking him warmly by the hand and steering him away from the truck to talk in private.

"The commanders are all inside, arguing about who's in charge and what they should do," shrugged the American. "The Gaullists want to fight for the river crossings. The Communists want to reinforce the attack on Tulle, where a full German garrison is supposed to be on the point of surrender. The rest want to hold Brive as a fortress."

"A fortress? The damn fools—it's not even a sandcastle. What do you think?"

"Well, since they have left me cooling my heels for the past couple of hours, I've worked out three answers to that question. The military one is the easiest. They haven't got the heavy weapons to hold the bridges, and somehow I don't see these guys making a Stalingrad out of Brive," said McPhee. "That leaves Tulle. It doesn't make a lot of difference. We aren't going to stop an armored division.

"Then there is the political answer. Our dear François, who is one smart guy, is trying to manipulate the Communists into holding Tulle and Brive because he thinks the Germans will kill them more efficiently than he ever could. François has worked this out, but the other Gaullist chiefs don't understand it yet, and François dares not tell them—at least not in public. Fighting for Tulle and Brive will wipe out the Reds in this part of France, and leave it open for the Gaullists. I'm sitting here wondering how to get that lesson into Marat's thick head. And that brings me to the third answer, also political, which is that the French aren't listening to us foreigners anymore. They won't even let you in the door."

The armed guards on the door were respectful but firm. They had orders to admit nobody. Manners suddenly realized, and he supposed he should take a certain pride in it, that his job was virtually done. This was now a French battle, being fought and run by Frenchmen. Finally one of them understood his urgency and went in. After a few minutes, he came out with François, who was wearing a British Army battledress with a *Tricolore* on his sleeve, a Cross of Lorraine on his chest, and the rampant eagle on his shoulder that gave him the rank of colonel. Manners raised an eyebrow and grinned. "Congratulations on the promotion."

"This will go on for some time," said François blandly. "Marat is making a speech."

"You haven't got much time. There's not a roadblock worthy of the name here and the river. The panzers could be here tonight."

"We are assured the panzers are taking the road to Tulle, to relieve their garrison."

"Assured by whom?"

"It's the one thing on which the Communists and we agree. We've both had reports from our men at Figeac."

"Well, get me a car and an escort and I'll drive down to Souillac and come back within the hour with an eyewitness report because I think they'll be coming up this road too."

"Wouldn't you do better to drive back to the cave and get the bazookas?"

"Not until we know where best to use them. I don't think you're going to stop them at Brive, but the rails are all blown north of here. I think they're going to have to head for Périgueux and go north by rail from there. When we know, we throw everything we have at them. But we have to know where the hell they are, and right now we don't."

"Agreed." François waved across to an elderly police sergeant and told him to give the *capitaine* some transport, and went back inside. The sergeant looked baffled, so Manners looked inside a sleek black Citroën *traction-avant,* and saw that the key was in the ignition. He climbed in.

"You can't take that. It belongs to Colonel Malrand," shouted the outraged sergeant, as Manners fired the engine and turned the car with a squeal of tires. He braked to a halt beside McPhee, leaned across to open the door, and yelled at the American to jump in.

Thus they had got to Cressensac, and had seen the tanks and armored cars coming straight up the road that the Germans were supposed not to be taking. They had raced back to the monastery, the horn blaring nonstop, and this time François was already outside and waiting. Manners forced himself to climb out sedately and walked up to the gate. Never show panic before the men. Then he gave François a crisp salute.

"They've just come through Cressensac, destroying it on the way. McPhee and I saw it happen. It's certainly the Das Reich. They had Mark IV tanks, self-propelled guns, and half-tracks full of panzergrenadiers in camouflage smocks. They were right behind us, and there's one roadblock at Noailles that won't last ten minutes. If you don't end this meeting now and get dispersed within the next twenty minutes, they'll round up the lot of you. And that's the end of the Resistance for this part of France."

"Come with me," said François, and they went into the monastery where he told the story all over again. By the time he came out and jostled his way through some Spaniards to climb into Marat's car, they could hear the German artillery. The escaped Russian prisoner of war who had appointed himself Marat's bodyguard thrust a Schmeisser into Manner's neck.

"*Spokoyno,*" Marat growled. The Schmeisser was lowered.

"You want to come to Tulle?" asked Marat, amused. Manners put his hand on the gear lever to stop it moving, and urgently made his case. Tulle might stop the armored column heading its way. There was nothing to slow the one coming through Brive. Except Marat the ruthless and his Spanish haters.

"The English gentleman wants me to hang some German prisoners at the side of the road and slice their balls off for their friends to find them?" said Marat levelly. "It sounds as if you have learned something about war, here in France."

"I leave the details to you. The only way to slow the Germans now is to get them so furious they start burning and killing here."

"So in the absence of English guns, we have to slow them with French blood."

Manners said nothing. He had nothing more to say. He began to climb out of the car and look for François. Then he heard a car door slam behind him as Marat emerged, and saw the Communist's spectacles glint as he walked to the back of the truck where his men sat, armed to the teeth.

"I want some German prisoners and some rope," he rapped. "And a blunt knife. From now on, we're fighting this war Spanish style."

There was a truck parked at la Ferrassie when the fast black Citroën that François had commandeered drew to a halt on the road from le Bugue. In the headlamps, it was empty and deserted.

"Ours?" inquired François, as Lespinasse cocked his Sten gun. Manners shook his head as he saw "Madrid" scrawled on the tailgate. "Marat's Spaniards."

The three of them toiled up the hill to the cave, guided by the sound of work and curses, and found Marat and McPhee standing by the uprooted tree while one man labored to widen the hole and more were at work inside.

"How thoughtful of you to bring an electric torch," said Marat amiably. "Our hurricane lamp ran out of paraffin." He raised his voice. "Igor? *Gdye ty?*"

"*Vot ya, tovarishch,*" came the reply from the Russian behind them. He must have been watching them from the moment their car drew up and followed them up the hill. Manners recalled the Schmeisser.

A head emerged from behind the uprooted tree. It was Florien, one of the lads who had helped them put the bazookas into the cave. He must have guided Marat here. Manners sighed inwardly at the complications of French politics.

"We have come to take the bazookas to Terrasson," said Manners.

"It's a joint action of the *Armée Secrète* and your FTP comrades to try and hold the road to Périgueux. We might as well go together."

"I regret that my orders do not mention Terrasson," said Marat. "I am not throwing away my men's lives on foolish gestures against tanks."

"And no doubt your orders tell you to keep the bazookas as souvenirs," mocked François. "They'll come in useful after the war."

"Hey, calm down," said McPhee. "We're taking them to Périgueux, to blast our way into the Gestapo building in the Credit Lyonnais, and some others to hit the Hôtel Normandie at Bergerac. It's my idea, the only artillery we've got to take out their HQs. The battle of the Das Reich division is over, you guys. We lost it. They roll on. We stay, and take out the garrisons they leave behind."

"That is not what the joint command has agreed," said François calmly. "Those orders bind you as well as me, McPhee."

"Orders have to change when the situation changes. That's what we're trained for. To use our initiative," said McPhee.

"This is getting us nowhere," said Manners equably. "Let's be sensible about this. You say you need a bazooka to hit German headquarters. Fine. Take two, and half the rockets. And let us have the other two for Terrasson."

A long pause.

"Sounds good to me," said McPhee.

Malrand shrugged. Marat nodded and waved his Russian across to join them. Igor shouldered his Schmeisser and headed down into the cave.

"And you won't believe what's in there," said McPhee, turning to follow him. "Not guns, I'm talking about. It's an art gallery down there."

François fired his Sten, two short bursts, one that toppled the Russian into the pit and the other that cut down Marat. Lespinasse, not needing an order, fired a long burst into the jumble behind the tree roots, and stunned with shock, Manners saw the American crumple. Then François tossed a grenade.

Manners dove to the ground at his side, expecting the grenade to ignite the rockets, or more gunfire from the Spaniards in the cave. There was no cover. He hugged the ground, his hands over his head and the grenade went off with a muffled crump. Then silence. One more short burst from a Sten. Then silence.

"You weren't much use," said François.

Manners rolled over and looked at him. He was standing over the body of Marat, his gun still aimed down. Lespinasse changed magazines.

"You're insane," Manners said, and scrambled to his feet to look for McPhee. His torch still glowed on the ground. He picked it up and looked at the carnage. Marat was dead, the back of his head shot away. That must have been the last burst he heard.

McPhee and the Russian were tangled in the tree roots, both dead. And below them was a mass of tree limbs, shredded by the grenade. Manners plodded dully across to McPhee's body, his mind a jumble of horror at an accident and suspicion of deliberate murder, at the hatreds of French politics, and the Spanish girl and human jealousy. The American lay on his back, his head drooping into the hole that led to the cave. Blood had spread across his face and over his shaved scalp. Sickened, he turned to François, his voice thick and tired, but he had to ask. "Was this politics or Mercedes?"

"Don't be a fool. This had nothing to do with women. Lespinasse, help the *capitaine* clear that mess away," said François, as calmly as if he were ordering dinner. "We need those bazookas."

Manners hauled McPhee's body clear of the tree limbs. The burst had caught him across the top of his chest and throat and the American's head dangled. The Russian had been shot in the back, and Lespinasse helped pull him aside. François took the torch, and shone it down into the cave mouth. Lespinasse hauled on an arm, and it was Florien. Manners helped pull the body clear.

"Our little traitor," said François.

The two Spaniards beneath Florien were jammed in the cave entrance. Lespinasse went down but couldn't tug them free.

"Try pushing them down into the cave," said François.

His back against the big taproot of the tree, Lespinasse began pushing with his feet, grunting with effort. Manners coughed with the stink of cordite, and then turned aside and retched. Down in the cave something gave, and Lespinasse called something cheerful as the tangle cleared. He crawled into the passage, and then shouted back, "It's O.K. There's room to stand here."

"Let's get our rockets," said François. Manners just looked at him, still incapable of speech.

"I'm sorry about McPhee," said François, as he clambered down into the cave. Then he stopped and added, "He just got caught in Lespinasse's burst. It was an accident of war, Jacques. I liked McPhee, you know that."

Wearily, Manners picked his way down the tree roots and into the passage he remembered. Lespinasse was dragging the dead Spaniards into the big cave, and François's torch picked out the parachute containers, the latches still open as Manners had left them. Then the torch lifted at something on the wall, and François said, "What the devil . . . ?"

It was a bear on the passage wall, a big and prowling black bear. The torch moved on to a brown horse with a black mane, one of its legs disappearing into a fresh bullet scar on the rock. Manners moved forward to look more closely and something crunched heavily beneath his feet. It was a slab of rock, sliced off the wall. He kicked it out of the way, nearly losing his balance as his feet slid on wet blood.

François had gone on into the main cave, and the torch picked out a big stag, its antlers down, and its feet churning up turf as it pawed the ground ready to charge. A doe with an arrow in her throat stood beside it, and below that, a pathetic fawn collapsed on its rump, with the silhouettes of two human figures behind. One was drawing a bow. The other, female, crouched, holding a spear.

"Another Lascaux," said François, and turned the torch to the far wall. "This is better than Rouffignac, better than Font-de-Gaume. It's better than anything I have ever seen."

A great landscape unfolded before them in the dimness of the torch. It was recognizably this same countryside of Périgord, the smooth, curving rock of the cliffs, that swirl of river and line of trees, that wide evening sky with the pinks of sunset, but a landscape that teemed with long-gone life. A bear was emerging from a cave, a great bull with flaring horns stood beside his cow, and a herd of short and sturdy horses, almost like Shetland ponies, were moving to drink.

"It's marvelous," breathed Manners, lost in the painting. The gunfight might never have been. This was another world, an innocence, and a lost perfection. To think that this had been waiting on the walls around him when he first stumbled upon this hiding place for his weapons.

"I do not believe this," said François, as he moved the torch yet again, and a huge face leaped at him from the rock. A handsome youth, half-smiling and with lively eyes, a slim face and firm jaw and long, curling hair. Then the woman appeared, lovely in that combination of shyness and assurance that had first attracted Manners to Sybille. He thought, I could fall in love with her. I have already.

"Our ancestors," said François. *"Les premiers Français."*

"You could be right, sir. He looks a bit like you," said Lespinasse. So he did, that sharp intelligence with the fine features and slightly dreamy eyes.

"Right," snapped François, bringing them back to reality, and suddenly Manners could smell again the cordite and the blood in the air. The spell had broken. "Let's get the guns out."

He and François linked their belts together to haul the containers along the passageway. François climbed up, propping the torch in the tree roots, and with Manners and Lespinasse heaving and François hauling, they managed to wrestle them up and out, to roll onto the wide stretch of grass.

"You two stay down," said François. "And I'll push the bodies down to you, one by one. We'll have to leave them in the cave. If the Communists and Spaniards didn't kill us in retaliation, the Americans would." Manners felt almost grateful to him, for putting the nightmares of retribution into words.

Little Florien, the Russian, Marat, and finally McPhee, flopping down headfirst. Lespinasse took the shoulders and Manners took the feet, and half dragged them down along the passageway and laid them, side by side, in the center of that splendid tomb that had already disappeared again into darkness. As they crawled back out, Lespinasse in the lead, Manners knocked into the slab of rock he had pushed aside earlier, and in the torch glow, he saw the shape of a bull on the whiteness of the chalk. He picked it up to study it more closely, and found it not as heavy as he had thought. It seemed the natural thing to take it with him.

François had rigged the small charges of plastique while they were laying out the bodies. One beside the tree root, another in the rocks on the shelf above. That seemed oddly fitting. The place had been opened by a German mortar. British explosives could seal it again. They manhandled the containers down to the road and into the truck. Then they went back for their guns, and to light the fuses. After the explosions, they checked that the place was sealed. And then they went back down through the trees, Manners slithering clumsily with his rock in his hand. Lespinasse and François took the Citroën, and Manners drove the truck. In Le Bugue, he stopped in the square where the old men played *boules*, and let himself in the back gate into Sybille's yard. The place was dark, the door locked, and her bicycle was gone. He slipped his slab of rock behind the rabbit hutch and left. Then he climbed into the truck and drove woodenly on toward Terrasson and a last, despairing effort to stop an armored division, his mind locked in an ancient landscape and his heart yearning simultaneously for Sybille and for a girl who had been dead for thousands of years.

CHAPTER 22

Time: The Present

Everything about Malrand's house was the same, except that Lespinasse was waiting for them inside, looking grim and formidable beside the big fireplace, and there had been different security men outside. The big security man nodded cool recognition at Manners as Malrand came forward to kiss Clothilde and Lydia, and shake Manners's hand.

"There is champagne, of course, but I need something stiffer," said the President. He was dressed in stout shoes and old corduroys and a worn leather jacket, and they made him look his age. "Major, perhaps you'll join me in a scotch?"

"I hear from Lespinasse that you came close to your goal when you were stumbling round la Ferrassie," Malrand went on. "There is a lost cave, of course, where your father's painting came from, and I suppose it's time for the secret to come out. And time for the dead to be properly buried. I'm far too old to campaign for this job again, and I'd rather the truth came out than find your British government dropping all sorts of ponderous hints about unfortunate repercussions."

"My government?" said Manners. "What does my government have to do with this?"

Malrand gave a cold smile. "I have been in this business too long to believe in coincidences, my dear Major. Your father had his own reasons to keep silence, but I always assumed that his death would open Pandora's box. The disappearance of the painting and the consequent publicity simply confirmed my fears. If you didn't steal your own painting, then I am sure you are well connected with the department of British Intelligence that did. I presume you found something in your father's papers, a memoir, something that told you how this mess began. Something that a President of France would want very much to keep secret and that your British Intelligence would use to put pressure on me."

"I'm not attached to any Intelligence department," snapped Manners. "And although I still don't understand why you want to keep the cave secret I suspect that you organized the theft of that rock as part of your own cover-up."

"My cover-up!" snorted Malrand. "If only French Intelligence were so efficient." He turned away with a shrug. "You don't understand much about politics if you think a politician would ever entrust that kind of secret to his Intelligence agencies."

Lydia felt her head turning from one man to the other as if she were watching a tennis match. A cough came from the fireplace. Lespinasse had broken silence.

"Not Intelligence, Monsieur le Président. Us. Your security team. Trying to forestall potential embarrassment. Saw no need to trouble you with it." Lespinasse chewed on his mustache. "In fact, we had a bit of help, just between us, from our British colleagues. Just a favor between professional colleagues, you might say. We understand these political things that are best kept quiet."

Lydia gaped in astonishment. She had never felt more American in her life. What an arrogant, overbearing, dreadful kind of system these damned Europeans operated. They lived by the cover-up and the conspiracy. And all this useless hunt and Clothilde's tragedy and her embarrassment and the barefaced theft from her auction house had all stemmed from their secret little ways of doing favors for each other and their feudal masters. Gathering her rage, she braced herself to tell them what she thought of the lot of them when she heard a funny, creaking sound.

It was Malrand, and he was laughing. Laughing so hard that he could hardly catch his breath. He bent over, one hand groping for the support of a chair, the other for a handkerchief. Lydia turned to glare at Manners, but even as she looked his face twitched into a grin, and his shoulders started to shake as the laughter infected him.

"I'd be very surprised if the British government knew anything about it," Lespinasse added with a big wink at her and smiling broadly. He was going to say more but his shoulders heaved as a great gust of laughter began to shake his big frame. Speechless with outrage, Lydia suddenly heard a fit of giggles from Clothilde, who grinned at her, looked at the helplessly guffawing men. and then threw up her hands in mock despair at the whole ridiculous world of men and began to belly laugh in her turn. Lydia felt her own mouth beginning to pull and her throat constrict and her tummy shake as the infection caught her as well. Dammit, she thought as she heard herself laughing helplessly, what instinct is it about us humans that won't let us keep a straight face when everyone around us is chortling like idiots?

"Oh, my sainted aunt," heaved Manners. "What a glorious mess!" And collapsed into guffaws again.

"Governments don't know a thing about it," wheezed Malrand, weakly. "We never do, you know." And that set him off again.

"You're a pair of dreadful crooks," chortled Clothilde, red-faced, her hair in disarray, but squinting at Malrand and Lespinasse with definite affection.

"You're all bloody intolerable," groaned Lydia, holding her stomach.

A door opened and a nervous maid peeped in, her eyes bulging as she took in the scene of mass hysteria. That set them off again, but a little more feebly, and Malrand wiped his eyes and stood up straight and got himself back under control.

"God," he said. "Haven't laughed like that in years. There's no medicine like it." Lydia found it impossible to gaze at them with anything other than a warm, benevolent grin on her face, and a particularly warm glow when she looked at Manners. What a splendid, genuine laugh he had.

"And what do you plan to do with the reward money, Lespinasse?" Malrand asked, still beaming in pure delight.

"Not collect it, Monsieur le Président. The painting has already been delivered to the Embassy, so it's in French hands." That set him off again, and a softer, but still sympathetic detonation from everyone else.

"And now it's time for that drink," said Malrand. "Damn the scotch, I need champagne. Lespinasse, pull yourself together, you old crook, and open the bottle."

They clinked their glasses, still grinning warmly at one another. Malrand turned to Manners. "Was there anything in your father's papers?"

"No. All I found was an old photograph of a handsome woman in the back of the case where he kept the rock. The name 'Sybille' was scrawled on the back."

"Sybille," said Malrand, drawing the name out. "Our doctor. A vet, in fact. They had an affair, I recall. A lovely woman. I envied your father. She looked after him when he got wounded in the foot, you know. I suppose that's when it began. She was killed at Terrasson, while helping the wounded."

"Did you know about the house?" Lespinasse interjected, turning to Manners.

"What house?"

"Her house, and the vet's surgery. Sybille's. She left it to your father in her will. She had no children, no other relatives."

"That's how he was able to take the rock back to England," said Malrand. "He put it there on the night he found it, and then when he came back after the war, he took it back in his car. I never objected. He'd fought for it, in a way. He certainly had a right to it."

"I had no idea," Manners stammered, a faraway look in his eye as he began to absorb the depth of the things he had never known about his father. Lydia's heart went out to him.

"He gave the house and the surgery back to the town and the commune, asking that they be kept as free housing for a vet, in her memory," Lespinasse said. "Every time he came back here, he'd go over there and just stand in the rooms for a while. After my father's funeral, I took him over there. When he came out again, he was humming some old Charles Trenet tune and there were tears on his cheeks. She meant a lot to him."

"To dear Sybille, a French heroine," said Malrand, raising his glass. "*Morte pour la France.*"

"She was killed at Terrasson you said, in the last fight against the Das Reich division?" pressed Lydia. There were things she wanted clearing up.

Malrand nodded. "A lot of people were killed at Terrasson."

"But not this man Marat."

"No, Marat died at the cave during an argument over some British guns. They were ours, and he tried to steal them for the Communist Party, probably to be used in some future attempt to seize power. There was a shootout and Marat was killed, along with a Russian who was with him, a couple of Spanish Communists, and tragically the American officer who was with us, McPhee."

Lydia felt her mouth fall literally open. Clothilde sat down with a thump. Malrand simply sipped reflectively at his champagne and lit a cigarette.

"That's the great secret. I didn't want the cave open because it's still a grave. And when those bodies come out, the scandal would have ended my career."

"Your father and I survived, along with Lespinasse's father," he went on, breathing out a long plume of smoke. "That's why he's here. Quite a family reunion. Anyway, first I think I ought to give you this. Your father wrote it, and entrusted it to me. I wrote a similar account, and gave it to him. My version was sent back to me after his death by his lawyer, in a sealed envelope bearing the instructions that it should be sent to me in the event of his death. Here is his. He wrote it in this very room."

He went to the desk, opened a drawer and handed Manners a slim brown envelope with a blob of red sealing wax on the flap. Manners ripped it open, and began reading aloud:

To whom it may concern:

This statement describes events which I witnessed at the cave at la Ferrassie, outside Le Bugue, on the night of June 9–10, 1944, as a captain in the British Army attached to the Special Operations Executive and working with the French Resistance. Along with Colonel Malrand of the Free French forces, and Captain James McPhee of the United States Army, we had gone to the cave to recover a cache of arms which we had stored there after German forces interrupted a parachute drop at Cumont nearby. I found the cave by chance, after German mortar fire knocked down a tree and opened the entrance.

The guns were being appropriated by a leader of the FTP Resistance organization known as Marat, a devout Communist who had fought in Spain. Marat was accompanied by a Russian agent and two Spanish Communists. Determined to appropriate the guns, they attacked us, and in the subsequent shooting, Lieutenant McPhee was killed along with a French Resistance fighter attached to Colonel Malrand's unit known to me only as Florien. Marat and his team were all killed. We left the bodies in the cave, sealed it with explosives, and took the weapons to Terrasson, where they were used in the attempt to deny the road to the SS Das Reich division. The cave was found to contain a number of remarkable wall paintings, probably many thousands of years old. In view of the highly charged political situation at that time in the war, Colonel Malrand and I took the view that it would be irresponsible to the Allied war effort to publicize the murder of an American officer by Communist militants, including a Russian agent, in their attempt to steal weapons. We took this decision on our own responsibility, and now make this written statement to affirm our joint wish that the existence of the cave and its remarkable paintings, along with the tragic events of that night, should be made publicly known after our deaths.

Signed, John Philip Manners
Witnessed, François Malrand
Hervé Lespinasse

Manners then unfolded the second sheet of paper from his father's letter, a rough sketch map of the cave's location, showing Cumont, la Ferrassie, and the track between them.

"I believe we must have come very close to it," he said, handing the map to Lydia with a smile.

"Tell me about the paintings," said Clothilde.

"I imagine you'll see them soon enough," said Malrand. "But you will be gratified to learn that your theory is right. La Marche cave is not the only place where prehistoric man left images of human faces. It contains portraits, one of a man, the other of a woman. They are extraordinary. I have never been able to forget them. There is also a landscape, with animals depicted among trees and rocks and a sky, which I found very beautiful."

"I suppose I can understand why the two of you decided to keep the cave and the shootings a secret during the war when the Russians were still our allies," said Lydia. "But why afterward, during the cold war?"

"Politics, I'm afraid. I had embarked on a political career, and with French Communists getting twenty percent of the vote, I would not have had much future as a Gaullist who had shot some. And then there was the complication of the dead American. And for your father, my dear Major, a career in the British Army would not have been helped by getting involved in that kind of French political mess. It was not very brave, but I still think it was wise. We decided to let sleeping dogs lie. It was what you Americans call a cover-up."

"And now?" said Clothilde.

"I'm not sure," said Malrand. "I think I'll leave it up to you. You can open the cave, publicize the paintings, revolutionize all our theories about art and prehistoric man, and provoke an interesting political drama, perhaps even a crisis here in France. The newspapers and the opposition will have a wonderful time. And I suppose it will increase the value of my memoirs."

"What do you want to happen?" Lydia asked him. She felt somehow that there was something missing from the story, something on which she could not put her finger, but that did not ring true. Malrand seemed too comfortable with all this, like someone retiring tactically to a reliable second line of defense after the first one had broken. At the same time, if he were getting away with something, she didn't really mind. She had developed a soft spot for the old boy.

"I have been thinking about that for a long time," said Malrand. "I want two things, and the first is that we should all now climb into the car, and I will take you to the cave site. Then I'll tell you the second."

This time they all piled into a single limousine. Lespinasse drove, Manners sat beside him, and Malrand had somehow managed to place himself in the back with a woman on either side. He looked very pleased with himself. They parked at la Ferrassie, and Malrand led the way, Lespinasse coming after with a large picnic basket from the trunk of the car. It was a brisk climb, but the old man seemed infused with energy and set an urgent pace. Finally they came out, as Lydia had suspected from the sketch map, on the same green sward where she and Manners had disported themselves so delightfully the previous day. She caught his eye and tried one of Clothilde's winks. He blushed. Good.

"Here we are," said Malrand. "I come here from time to time. It's a lovely spot. The first time was with your two fathers, in September of 1944, after they had liberated Toulouse and got me out of prison. We collected all the cartridge cases, and tidied up the mound of rocks, over there behind that leaning tree."

Lespinasse opened the picnic basket, and took out a small silver tray, some flutes, and a bottle of champagne. The cork popped noisily, and he poured five glasses. One for himself, Lydia noted, approvingly.

"Was that the tree that was blown aside by the German mortar?" asked Manners, strolling across to it, as Lespinasse served the champagne.

"Yes, and still alive. I suppose the taproot gets water." The tree seemed to emerge from a large, grass-covered mound. There was no sign of fissure in the rock.

"Well, a toast to your dear father, and may he rest in peace, along with yours, Lespinasse," said Malrand, sipping and surveying the grass, the trees, the sky, as if it were simply marvelous to be alive on such a day.

"You were going to tell us the second thing you wanted, François," said Lydia, her curiosity too insistent to be silent.

"Yes, I was," he said slowly. "I spent a lot of time dreading that this tale would come out, and now it has, I'm not sure it will be so bad after all. And above all, I think I want to look at the portraits of our ancestors, that first Frenchwoman and Frenchman, those first children of Périgord, once again before I die."

He strolled over to the grassy mound and rested his hand against the leaning tree.

"I particularly want to see her again, the woman of the cave. I have carried a great *tendresse* for that woman since 1944. So did my English friend, your father. And the older he got, as we sat up late at night and talked about it all, the more he seemed to confuse her with his Sybille. Or the more they seemed to come together in his mind. And you can appease an old man's vanity by confirming or refuting something that has nagged me for over fifty years. Something your father said, Lespinasse, about the portrait of the man looking rather like me. I'd feel very honored if it were true."

He raised his glass in salute to the mound. "To them, our ancestors, whoever they were," he said, and drank.

Author's Note

This is a work of fiction, which seeks to remain faithful to the little that is known of Neolithic culture some seventeen thousand years ago and to the far better known history of the Resistance of the Périgord region of France in 1944. The connections between the two go far beyond the simple coincidence of geography. The Resistance frequently took advantage of caves in which to sleep, shelter and store weapons, caves that in some cases had been inhabited almost continuously for thirty millennia. In the course of researching this book, I learned that "Berger," the Resistance name of the celebrated writer and future Gaullist minister André Malraux, boasted during a visit to the cave of Lascaux in 1969 that he had stored weapons there, even leaning his bazookas against the famous sketch of the eviscerated bison and the slain man with the head of a bird. Like many of Malraux's reminiscences, this seems to have been rather too cavalier with the truth.

André Malraux and the late President François Mitterand, whose complicated politics included a period of apparent adherence to the Vichy regime before he joined the Resistance, are the joint inspirations for my fictional character François Malrand. André Malraux, who wrote ambitious and grandiose novels of love and revolution and fought in Spain in the 1930s, was a Resistance leader in Périgord along with his brothers. The fictional country home of President Malrand is based on the Château de la Vitrolle, near Le Bugue, which during the Liberation was briefly the secret HQ of Malraux and the British and U.S. officers on his team. Malraux was wounded and captured by the Germans, imprisoned in Toulouse, and released when the city was liberated by a Maquis force that had been organized, armed, and led by a British agent of SOE, the Special Operations Executive known as *Hilaire*. His real name was George Starr, and he indeed became a deputy mayor of a French commune, ran the Wheelwright network, and is deservedly honored here. One of the most petty acts in General de Gaulle's career was to expel Starr from France in September 1944, apparently for no better reason than affront at the central role an Englishman had played in the Liberation of a large part of France.

Three other real figures from the Périgord Resistance have blended their way into the characters of François Malrand and Captain Jack Manners. One is the former playboy aristocrat Baron Philippe de Gunzbourg, code names *Edgar* and *Philibert*, an SOE agent who cycled some fifteen thousand miles around southwestern France organizing parachute drops and sabotage operations. The second is Commandant Jack, code name *Nestor*, whose real name was Jacques Poirier. Although French, he was widely taken for an English officer, and most of the arms with which the Resistance tried to slow the movements of the SS Das Reich division were supplied through him. The third is George Hiller, who attended the original banquet in the château organized by the redoubtable Soleil, René Coustellier, which concluded some time after midnight with a lecture on the Sten gun. Soleil was indeed at different times sentenced to death by the Communist

Franc-Tireurs Partisans and by the *Armée Secrète*, and remains a controversial figure in the Périgord to this day, although his charismatic leadership and courage, like his heroic defense of Mouleydier, are beyond question.

The factional rivalries and thefts of arms among Communist, Gaullist, and other wings of the Resistance are a matter of historical fact, as is the meeting and the arguments at the monastery of St-Antoine on the outskirts of Brive on June 8, 1944. Despite the honorable intentions of most of the rank and file, who thought they were all fighting the same battle, it proved desperately difficult to rally Communists and Gaullists under a common command. The report on the role of the Communists in Bergerac that is cited in the text is a historical document, authored by Maurice Loupias, code name *Bergeret*, who was the regional commander of the *Armée Secrète*. Preparations for a Communist seizure of power as the Germans departed were forestalled by the return from Moscow of the exiled French Communist leader Maurice Thorez, who was under orders from Stalin to squash any disruption in France while it remained the crucial logistic base of the Western front against Nazi Germany.

The dreadful march of the second SS armored division, Das Reich, in June 1944, from Toulouse in southern France to the Normandy invasion front, is a central element of this novel and every effort has been made to describe it correctly. All German orders and reports cited in the book, including the one by the Das Reich commander, General Heinz Lammerding, are genuine. Its strength and units and composition, its route through the Périgord, the insurrection in Tulle, the brief battle of Cressensac, the tragedy of Terrasson, and the appalling atrocity of Oradour were all very much as described here. There is no historical evidence for my fictional suggestion that in the absence of heavy weapons, Resistance leaders were prepared to provoke the Germans into reprisals in order to delay them. During their postwar trial for the Oradour massacre, German veterans claimed that they had been angered by reports of the killing and abuse of their captured comrades. They carried little credibility. But it remains a startling and unprofessional dereliction of military duty that the German Army allowed one of its premier armored divisions to spend time hunting down the Maquis when it was desperately needed to fight the invasion in Normandy. M. R. D. Foot, in his magisterial official history, *SOE in France,* concludes: "The extra fortnight's delay imposed on what should have been a three-day journey may well have been of decisive importance for the successful securing of the Normandy bridgehead."

Details of rationing under Vichy, the organization of Vichy security forces (including the notorious North African unit), the location of German Headquarters, and the texts of BBC messages are as accurate as current research can make them. The Centre Jean Moulin in Bordeaux is an imposing and helpful library and a memorial to the Resistance. I am indebted to André Roulland's *La Vie en Périgord sous l'Occupation,* to Jacques Lagrange's *1944 en Dordogne,* to the memoirs of René Coustellier in *Le Groupe Soleil,* and to Guy Penaud's magnificent *Histoire de la Résistance en Périgord.* I also sought within the limits of fiction to base my accounts of sabotage and military operations on reality. Readers of George Millar's *Maquis,* one of the outstanding books to emerge from the Resistance, will recognize my debt to him. I must also cite my reliance on Max Hastings's *Das Reich,* an admirable work of research and reconstruction.

I was introduced to the Périgord by my friends of three decades Gabrielle Merchez and Michael Mills, whose kindness and welcome kept bringing me back. My friend Jean-Henri Picot, son of the renowned *Compagnon de la Résistance* Paul Picot, opened for me his family archive and recounted his boyhood reminiscences of being able to eat eggs and chicken daily in the Périgord countryside in 1942–44. Other friends and neighbors in the Périgord were generous with their dinner tables, their time, and their memories. I have borrowed some of their names, some of their personalities, and tried to recapture some of their warmth in this novel. Jean-Louis and Kati Perusin introduced me to the songs of Charles Trenet. And I am indebted to Jo and Collette da Cunha, and their invaluable personal library. It was Jo who first acquainted me with the local *pineau*, which he makes himself, and whose charms ensured that this book took rather longer to write than expected.

Anyone who has seen the extraordinary paintings of the Lascaux caves has probably asked themselves why artists of such genius limited themselves to the paintings of horses, bulls, deer, ibex, and bear, and did not seek to depict their landscapes and settings, or indeed themselves. Art and humanity are so closely entwined that the urge to portrait, whether in the statues of ancient Greece or in the paintings of the Renaissance, seems to be a logical and even inevitable part of the artistic process. But there are prehistoric images of the human form, in statuettes and in the caricatures of faces engraved at a Marche, near Poitiers. The lifestyle I ascribe to the people who created Lascaux, which seems to have borne great similarity to that of the North American Indians and Siberian tribes like the Evenk, is based on the fractional achaeological and anthropological evidence. The work and theories of l'Abbé Breuil and of André Leroi-Gourhan, allowing for fictional embellishment, are much as I describe. Without their efforts, we would know far, far less than we do, and M. Leroi-Gourhan, and Arlette Leroi-Gourhan, and Brigitte and Gilles Dellux have been, along with Ann Sieveking's *The Cave Artists* and the museum at Les Eyzies, my constant guides.

Finally, there is nothing outlandish about my suggestion that there remain undiscovered caves that could contain artistic riches to rival Lascaux. Two or three new caves are discovered, or rediscovered, in southwestern France each year. In 1994, cave explorers in the Ardeche region of France discovered what is now known as the Chauvet cave, containing over four hundred paintings and engravings that are at least thirty thousand years old. And in the year 2000, another magnificent cave gallery of engravings dating from a similar period was discovered at Cussac, near le Buisson, within strolling distance from the house at which this novel was being written. The Cussac cave, some 900 yards long, also contains some silhouettes of women, and erotic designs. Who knows what might emerge next in this cradle of humanity that the people of Périgord call the *Vallée de l'Homme?* It remains the small, enchanting part of Europe that has known the longest continuous human habitation. And anyone who knows its climate, its geography, its food, its people and their generous welcome will understand why after over thirty thousand years it is still going strong. And as the English learned in the fifteenth century, the Germans in the twentieth, and successive governments based in Paris have always known, the people of Périgord have an admirably tenacious disinclination to be run by anybody but themselves. It has been a privilege to get to know them, and to admire the courage of people who tried to stop a panzer division with nothing more than guns, grenades, and petrol bombs. As M. R. D. Foot has suggested, they may have decided the outcome of the D-Day invasion and thus of World War II. And as far as we know, their ancestors at Lascaux were the first to assert the extraordinary creative potential of humankind.

Martin Walker
Périgord, 2000